The Fate of Champions

a novel by
DAMON J COURTNEY

Novels by Damon J Courtney

THE DRAGON BOND TRILOGY

Baptism of Blood and Fire
The Burden of Faith
The Fate of Champions

damon@damonjcourtney.com
www.DamonJCourtney.com

For Violet.
You complete our own little trilogy.

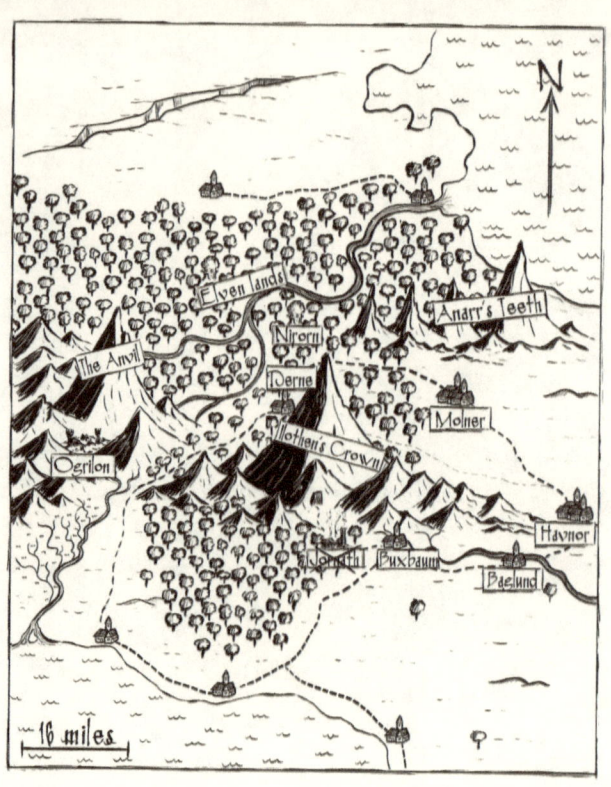

THE FATE OF CHAMPIONS

PRELUDE

"THESE ARE SOME of the finest dragonmage trainees on Gondril today," Master Cythyil said.

He motioned to the group in front of him. The man beside him folded his arms and nodded as they watched the boys go through their spell practice. Cythyil looked on with approval as each cast their spell perfectly. He waited a few moments longer so that the man could see how good they all really were.

He was not disappointed.

The man watched with approval. He looked to his servant beside him who nodded solemnly.

"Of course, these are the third years and very near to hatching their eggs," Cythyil said. "Your son would begin at age twelve like those boys and girls over there, but I can promise he will be casting his first spell within weeks."

That pleased the merchant well enough. He walked past the older boys to observe the younger ones practicing their motions on the other side of the yard. With a few flicks of her wrist, one girl finished her spell and created a small ball of light in her hand. She held it for the three men watching to see, looking into her master's eyes most of all.

"Very good, Denara," Cythyil said. "Denara is my new prize pupil. She only started here two weeks ago, and already she has surpassed the other boys in her class."

The merchant nodded.

"How is it they can cast such spells with no magic to call from? I thought they needed dragons to draw magical power."

"Most trainees have some magic of their own," Cythyil said. "That is why they are chosen by their village or parent to train. They have already shown some aptitude or some well of magic within themselves."

"And if my son has no such *well*?"

"I doubt that your son has *no* magic," Cythyil said, "else you would not have chosen this path for him. It matters little either way."

Cythyil reached out a finger and lifted the amulet Denara wore around her neck. He held it up to dangle on its chain before the two men. Then he held up his own, a golden sun encircling a blue gemstone.

"These amulets give the children enough of a magical well to cast from until their own can mature and their dragon is hatched. Once their dragon is bonded, the amulet is no longer needed."

"Because the dragons give them limitless power?"

"Not limitless, but immense, yes."

The men nodded, and the merchant waved his arm to continue the tour. Cythyil gave Denara a pat on the shoulder and turned toward the large manor house, not looking back to see if the men were following. They passed the older students again, and he gave them a stern look when he saw them beginning to flick simple, annoying spells at each other.

"This way," he said, "I'll show you the library."

Cythyil touched the sun amulet at his chest and drew the magic held within into his waiting hand. He gave a wave, and the door in front of him swung open at their approach. It was a simple parlor trick any first year could perform, but it never hurt to give a little show for the parents. This merchant had come looking for a school for his third son, and Cythyil was not above a little theatrics to ease his mind that *his* was the right choice.

"Where is your dragon?" the man asked coming up behind him.

Cythyil involuntarily winced but hoped the man had not seen it beneath his robes.

"I lost my dragon many, many years ago."

"Oh. I assumed that since you trained dragonmages you must be one yourself."

"I was once," Cythyil said. "The best masters are the ones who no longer have a dragon."

The man snorted, and his servant chuckled beside him.

"Of course you would say that."

"No, it's true," Cythyil said evenly. "Without a dragon I have no further place in the world of mages. Though I live above Baglund, I no longer have means to protect it. That is no longer my job. Instead, it falls to me to train the best dragonmages I can to send out into Gondril to protect her."

The man shook his head and motioned for Cythyil to move on, which he did, though with his shoulders and head a little higher. The double doors to the library stood open wide. He stepped aside to allow the two men to stand fully in its grandeur. Cythyil's library was one of his biggest achievements and greatest pleasures, and it was grand even by a rich merchant's standards.

The men were sufficiently impressed, he noted with pride. The stacks of books stretched from the floor to the second-story ceiling high above. Each one lined with tomes and manuals he'd collected throughout his life. Aside from training new mages, collecting rare and wonderful works had been his life's work since losing his dragon so many years ago.

"Quite a collection," the man said, admiring the books. "What are they doing?"

He pointed to the students sitting at the long table that extended the length of the room.

"Studying," Cythyil said.

"How can they learn magic sitting in chairs?"

"The casting of spells is very precise," Cythyil said with a bristle. "The students must first learn the proper motions before weaving the magic. If the movements are not correct, the spell could have unintended effects."

"And my son will spend his time reading *books*?"

"A good deal of his time, yes," Cythyil said, spinning to face the man.

"My son already has a tutor," the man said. "I pay a fair coin to teach him to read and write, I want *you* to teach him to cast spells and find him a dragon."

"That all comes in time," Cythyil said, pulling himself up to try and match the man's height, but it was no use. "I have trained many young mages, sir, and I can assure you that this is the best method. Your son will have to work just as hard as everyone else, but I can promise you that he will leave my school a *proper* mage."

The merchant looked to his servant who only shrugged.

"Carry on," the man said. "I want to see the dragons."

"Oh, there are no dragons here today," Cythyil said.

"No dragons at a dragonmage school?"

"Why would there be? Once a mage bonds his or her dragon, they go off into the world. They definitely do not want to stay here with *me*."

Cythyil laughed, and the men chuckled politely.

"Then show me the dragon eggs," the man said.

"Of course," Cythyil said.

He led them through the library. He walked slowly to admire his own books and give the men time to do the same, but they no longer seemed interested. Exiting the other door and back into the long hallway running the length of the house, he followed it to the large, wooden door at the far end. Pulling it open, he braced himself for the wave of heat that always followed. It blasted from the doorway like a dragon's fiery breath and made him catch his own. The two men behind him didn't seem bothered by it.

"The incubation chamber is kept quite warm for the eggs," Cythyil explained.

The merchant nodded and waved his arm for Cythyil to lead on. The stone staircase went down several stories, lit only by dancing, magical flames of light that rested in tiny nooks along the wall. There were no handholds, and Cythyil reminded the men several times to watch their steps. The deeper they went, the hotter it got, until Cythyil felt tiny beads of sweat on his forehead.

When they finally reached the bottom, the stairs ended in a floor of sand. Cythyil slid his light shoes off to enjoy the feeling between his toes. The men behind him did not follow suit, he noted.

"Just around the corner," Cythyil said, leading on.

As they rounded a bend, a cavern opened up in front of them. It wasn't high, just tall enough for a man to walk without stooping. But the cave was not what impressed visitors. Cythyil always liked to save this for the last stop on his tour because of what it contained.

Dragon eggs.

Eight of them at the moment, all in various stages of incubation. Though it was impossible to tell just by looking at them how far along they were. It didn't matter. The men behind him seemed appropriately stunned.

"We have eight right now," Cythyil said. "Three copper, three bronze, one brass, and a silver."

A look passed between the men that Cythyil couldn't interpret, but he only smiled as they both walked past him to get closer. The merchant walked to the first egg, a bronze gleaming like the metal in the magical firelight that illuminated the whole chamber. The man reached out and ran a hand over the outside of the smooth, flawless shell while his servant stood back a few steps and watched.

"A bronze," Cythyil said, in case they couldn't tell. "One of the older boys'. Should be ready to hatch in just a few months. Though sadly, its mother was killed."

"Killed?" the man asked.

"By the dragon-hunting wizard," Cythyil said as though the man should know exactly why.

"Is that what they're calling him these days?"

"He tried to hunt dragon mothers to extinction and killed the beloved Eldest Ferin."

"Yes, that was a terrible thing," the man said. "Good thing someone killed *him*."

Cythyil eyed the man and gave a cautious nod of agreement. Why was this man so callous about the death of the dragon mothers? Cythyil had to remind himself that some people outside of his world did not care about its goings on as much as he did. The man was a merchant and probably cared for nothing more than his coin. He had told Cythyil from the beginning that he wanted to train his son so that he could protect his holdings.

The man ran his hand over the egg once more and then looked around the rest of the cave.

"If I send my son to your school, when will he receive his dragon?"

"Well, assuming we can find him an egg after his first year, he should receive his dragon after his fifteenth birthday."

"What do you mean *assuming* you can find him one? Isn't that what I'm paying for?"

"Dragon eggs are not for sale at any price," Cythyil said. "You are paying me to *train* your son, nothing more. We will do our best to find a dragon mother willing to give us an egg."

"And what of this ban on dragonmages business?"

"That is… unfortunate," Cythyil said. "The new Eldest has made it law that no eggs shall be given to dragonmages."

"Then how do you plan to get my son an egg?"

"Truthfully, I don't know that I can. The dragonmage conclave is trying to work with the new Eldest to lift his decree. Until then, I can only train your son and hope that we receive an egg from somewhere."

"I could buy him one," the man said. "I know a man who has promised he can get me a dark dragon egg for a price."

"No!" Cythyil shouted. "I do not train dark mages, sir, and you would do well to avoid such dealings. It will only lead your son down a terrible road."

"But you can't promise my son an egg. What else am

I to do?"

"I cannot promise him one, no, but I will do everything I can. There have been some dragon mothers willing to donate eggs anonymously since the ban was put in place. That silver egg there was donated anonymously a month ago."

"Anonymously? Is that how it's done now?"

"I'm afraid it's the only way."

"And what if you're caught by this *Eldest*? What would he do to you and your little school if he found out you were stealing dragon eggs?"

Cythyil opened his mouth to speak but only sputtered.

"We have not stolen anything!" he said. "Except for the silver, these eggs have all been here at least a year or more. Long before the new Eldest came along and made his *foolish* law."

"Foolish?" the man said, his voice rising. "You think it is foolish for a leader to protect the children of his people?"

Both men had spun to face Cythyil now. He backed away from them slowly.

"We have bonded dragonmages for more than a thousand years," he said. "The new Eldest is making a mistake by destroying that bond between man and dragon."

The merchant laughed, followed by his servant.

"I don't think my school is right for your son," Cythyil said, turning back for the stairs.

"Don't run," the man said coolly behind him.

Cythyil stopped in his tracks.

"You must have known I would come," the man said.

Cythyil kept his back to the men, trying hard to

formulate a plan of escape. But he already knew it was no use.

"Who gave you the silver egg?" the man asked.

"I told you… it was donated anonymously."

"I do not believe for a moment that you don't know *exactly* where that egg came from."

"It was brought in a wagon and left at my doorstep."

"Oh, how quaint," the man said. "Was it in a little basket with a blanket as well? Did they pin a note to it and ask you to care for it?"

Cythyil stood trembling, trying hard to find something to say.

"Why are you doing this?" he managed.

"Because I am the Eldest," the man said, "I make the laws for all of Gondril, and it is no one's duty but my own."

"Your laws are over dragons. You do not speak for mankind."

"There are none higher than dragons in the eyes of the gods, so yes, I *do* speak for all of Gondril, little man."

"The conclave is not just going to sit by and let this happen."

"Your conclave means nothing to me. I am protecting the children of my kind. Now, tell me who gave you the egg, and I will take it and go. Or, you can refuse, and we can do this the *fun* way."

"I don't know where the egg came from."

A hand dropped onto Cythyil's shoulder, and he felt his knees go weak.

"I don't believe you," the man said, leaning to whisper in his ear.

Cythyil jerked his shoulder away and spun on the man.

"Believe what you will, Kalustroth, it makes no difference to me."

"You *dare* speak the name of the Eldest," the servant said, suddenly stepping forward.

"It's fine, Vaylin," the man said. "Call me Kalus. Kalustroth is so formal. Not even my mother calls me that, though she *has* been dead for five-hundred years, so I suppose she doesn't call anyone anything."

Cythyil stared hard at the man he feared he might one day see. Though he never expected him in human form. Kalustroth'ul'Grallitharr, the Eldest of all dragons on Gondril, had come.

Cythyil knew he shouldn't have accepted the egg. But there were no eggs for his students. With Kalus's law forbidding new dragonmages, there seemed no other way. His students had worked so hard for so many years, they didn't deserve to be turned away now.

"Why not come in your true form?" Cythyil asked. "Why this game of a merchant father?"

"Well, it's more fun, isn't it? Watching you squirm like this makes the whole thing *far* more interesting to me. Also, your children up there can't start running before I get to them."

"Please, they had nothing to do with this!"

Kalus shook his head with a smile as he strode over to the silver dragon egg resting comfortably in the little nest Cythyil had built for it. Kalus reached his hand out and brushed it over the shimmering, silver surface of the egg with a gentle touch.

"You steal my children, and you want mercy?"

"They are but children themselves," Cythyil said. "Do not punish them for what I have done."

"You humans are so arrogant," Kalus said.

The world slowed as Kalus shook his head again. Cythyil knew in that moment that nothing he said mattered. Kalus turned to smile at him and then moved to brush some sand from the egg.

Then, in one sharp motion, he slammed his fist into its pristine surface. It hit with a loud crack. Dragon eggs are made of hard stuff. But a dragon's hand, even in human form, was harder.

The egg shattered as Kalus's hand went right through it without pause. A hole gaped in the shell, oozing with the precious life inside. When he pulled his hand back, Kalus grabbed at the edges of the hole and yanked, widening it further. Cythyil tried to move, but he could only stand and watch as the egg's innards spilled out. What would one day have become a beautiful, silver dragon, washed over the sands and was gone.

"You…" Cythyil struggled for words, but he trembled, both in fear and rage. "This is how you treat your children?"

Kalus looked over his shoulder with a casual eye and brought his hand to his mouth. To Cythyil's continued and growing horror, Kalus brought his human fingers to his lips and licked the goo from them.

"Honestly, no," he said. "I usually prefer to poach them first."

Cythyil looked at the other man, Vaylin Kalus had called him, but he stood perfectly at attention watching the whole thing. He betrayed no emotion whatsoever.

"You would stand there and let him do this?" Cythyil asked, daring the man to look at him.

"I am the Eldest," Kalus said. "I make the laws for my people. You humans would do well to remember it."

"You're a monster. And a murderer."

"I did this little dragon a favor. Better to die here, now, than to be born a slave."

"The bond between man and dragon was never slavery. It is brotherhood."

"Oh, I don't really care," Kalus said. "Vaylin, go back upstairs and kill all of the children. Make it painful if you can."

"You can't!" Cythyil shouted.

"And be slow about it. Let them run a bit to give them a sporting chance. But, you know, not *too much* of a sporting chance."

"Yes, Eldest."

The man nodded and headed for the stairs. Cythyil reached a hand out to try and stop him, to do something, *anything*. But the man just shoved past him without a word.

"You cannot do this," Cythyil whispered. "This is murder. Of innocent children."

"Oh, I plan to murder more than just children," Kalus said.

He raised his hands, and Cythyil heard a spell on his lips.

CHAPTER ONE

LEAVING

"YOU CAN'T GO," Rinn said as Elody passed him for the hundredth time.

"I have to," she said without pausing.

He stepped out of her way. Rinn stood on the stairs in his aunt's house trying to talk some sense into his sister, but she was hearing none of it. She wouldn't even meet his eyes. She just walked past him from room to room gathering her things.

"You don't even know where you're going," Rinn said.

"West. I'm going West."

"What does that *mean*?" he yelled.

"I don't know, but that's where Jalthrax says we have to go."

"He's a dragon, El! And he doesn't even speak!"

"I know enough to know that that's where he says he's being pulled, so that's where we have to go."

"This is stupid. This is completely stupid."

"I can't just sit around here in this house all day waiting for something to happen to me," she said. "Jalthrax has been telling me to go West for weeks now, and I can't just ignore him."

"No, you just ignore me."

That made her stop. Elody turned and put her arms around her brother, and he pulled her close to him.

"It's dangerous," he whispered.

"I know," she said. "But I have to go."

"Then let me come with you."

"Your place is here. You've only been training for a few months now, and Aunt Jelena would never let you go. You need to stay and learn."

Rinn opened his mouth to say something, but she put a finger to his lips.

"I'll be fine," she said. "I have a silver dragon with me, who's going to stop me?"

"A baby silver dragon," Rinn said.

"He's not such a baby anymore."

"But you don't even know where you're going."

"I have a direction. That's all I need right now."

With the matter settled, at least for her, Elody went back into her room and continued packing the rest of her things. Rinn tried to think of something else to say, but nothing would come. He finally gave up and went downstairs to find some support, but he had a pretty good idea he would get none from his aunt.

"She can't go," Rinn said as he came into the kitchen where his aunt was.

"She's a grown woman, Rinn. It's not your place to tell grown women where to go."

"Then whose is it?"

His aunt laughed, something she had done more freely of late, but it was still not something he was used to.

"No one but ourselves, Rinn. Are you ready to go?"

"There's been talk of bandits on the road. I should go

with her."

"No, you should not. This is her journey to take. You are already on one. One that you cannot abandon simply because you choose to."

"It's not like I'll never come back."

"No. I told you when you began training with me that this was a commitment you could not break. Becoming a wizard is not something you can just decide to do whenever you feel like it."

Rinn hung his head and sighed.

"She just turned sixteen not even a week ago," he said. "She's too young."

"And what were you doing at sixteen?"

Rinn thought for a moment, and a grin spread across his face.

"Exactly," Jelena said. "Getting into trouble no doubt."

"This is different," he said.

"She'll be all right, Rinn. She has Jalthrax. Your sister is tougher than you give her credit for."

"But ever since we lost Dad, I've been the one to protect her."

"Is that so? Seems to me you've spent more time drinking than watching over your sister."

"I haven't been out in months."

"No, but neither were you paying attention when your sister was playing at magics she could not control. I'm not accusing you, Rinn, I am simply reminding you that your sister can take care of herself."

Rinn started to say something else but instead just nodded.

"Now," she said, "are you ready to go? I have a patient to visit, and I could use your help."

"You don't need my help, you're just trying to drag me out of here."

"I'm an old woman, I need you to carry my bags."

"I've seen you cast that levitation spell a hundred times now, you don't need me to carry your bags."

"Do I need to remind you again of our agreement?"

"Do as you say, when you say it, how you say it."

"Oh, good, then I don't need to remind you. Now get up."

"Can I at least say goodbye?"

Elody tromped down the stairs a second later carrying a large pack on her back.

"Here's your chance," Jelena said.

"Aunt Jelena, do you have some food I can take?" Elody asked.

Jelena smiled and picked up a small pouch from the table.

"I made this for you," she said.

"This won't even be enough to get me to Derne," Elody said.

"I think you'll find there will always be something inside when you need it," she said with a wink.

"Oh," Elody said. "Right."

Elody threw her arms around the older woman in a big hug, and Rinn could see the tears at the corners of his aunt's eyes.

"Sixteen years old," Jelena said. "I remember when your mother turned sixteen. We had quite the celebration that night. Not something nearly so exciting as an adventure though."

"I wouldn't call it much of an adventure," Elody said. "We don't even know where we're going."

"Well, that's what makes it an adventure then."

Jelena smiled and pulled her close again.

"You be careful," she said with a sniffle. "Don't let Jalthrax lead you off a cliff."

"He's not that brave," Elody said with a chuckle.

"Yes, but *he* can fly," Jelena said.

They parted, and their aunt held her shoulders a moment longer before spinning her around and pushing her toward Rinn. He wanted to reach out and hold her. His little sister, only not so little anymore. She had turned sixteen less than a week ago, but it felt to Rinn like she was still that five-year-old girl who was always stealing his wooden sword.

She put her arms around him, and Rinn felt his chest tighten. In his heart, he had thought he would convince her not to go. In his heart, he never thought he would be standing here saying goodbye. Yet here they were. It all felt too real. He wanted to tell her one more time not to go, but he knew that her mind was set.

"You always were stubborner than a mule," he said, and he heard her laugh through her tears.

"I learned it from the best," she said.

She pulled back to look at him, and they both just stared, silently, for what seemed like minutes.

"I love you," she said.

"I love you too," he said, his voice hoarse.

He couldn't resist one last hug, and she was happy to let him. With a final squeeze, he felt her pull away and turn for the door.

"Be careful," he said, trying to steady his voice.

"I will," she said.

With the click of a latch, his sister was gone.

***

Rinn ran to catch up to his aunt. Though she was quite a

bit older than him, and constantly claimed to be much feebler, it always seemed like *he* was the one struggling to keep up. Of course, carrying her immense bag of trinkets and tools didn't make his going any easier.

"Why do you always carry this bag?" he shouted to her back.

"One never knows what one might need."

He jogged a few more steps and finally reached her side.

"I thought this was a simple potion that you already made."

He looked back over his shoulder at the road behind him. The road out of town.

"It is, but do you always know when you walk out the door what you will face? You never know who or what you might run into."

Rinn shifted the bag to his other shoulder and immediately felt the pain as it sagged under the weight.

"You should really clean this thing out."

"You should learn to carry it more lightly."

"What does that mean?"

"Well, you've seen me carry it a dozen times at least, and I don't struggle the way you do. And I'm an old woman."

"Yes, but you're a wizard."

His aunt gave him a sharp look and then looked around to see if anyone had heard him.

"Sorry," he said. "I just mean that you have magic."

"And you have none?"

"Not like you."

"Try."

He looked at her as she stopped and turned back for him.

"I taught you the spell," she said. "It's a very simple one. Try it."

"I… I don't think I'm ready."

Though the streets weren't crowded on this side of town, she moved closer so that their conversation would not be overheard by others.

"You have been studying that book for almost a month now," she said. "Try."

Rinn sighed and put the bag down. His aunt didn't know it, but he *had* tried. He'd tried a dozen times to make minor spells work, but he had met with only minimal success. He thought he had made a pencil roll off his desk from across the room once, but it could have just been the wind. The spells were too hard.

Being a wizard was nothing like the magic he had learned to cast as a dragonmage. Even if his time as a true dragonmage was brief. He had studied for years, but when he failed to bond with his dragon, that magic was closed to him forever. He still held in him a small well of power, and he knew how to draw it out and cast with it, but it would never be the kind of power he should have had. The kind of power he would have had if he'd bonded with his dragon.

"I can't do it," he said softly. "I've tried, and I just can't do it. I can't get the words right. I can't memorize all of those words and motions."

She moved closer and put her hand on his shoulder.

"Did you not memorize the same kinds of motions when you trained as a dragonmage?"

"Yes, but that's different. It's the words that make it hard. I can't say them right. I don't know how wizards do it."

His aunt gave him another stern look.

"I would warn you again about using that word. Ours is not a profession to be standing in the street talking about as though you and I are humble bakers."

"I'm sorry."

"Being what we are is not easy, Rinn. If it were, everyone could learn to do it. The language of magic is spoken by the dragons of old. It is the language spoken by the gods themselves. It cannot be learned in a day. For some, it cannot be learned in a lifetime."

But his aunt had learned. From what he had witnessed, she had learned *a lot* in her lifetime. Rinn had seen Jelena's true power even before he knew what she was. She played the part of the humble old witch woman, but he knew the truth. She might be one of the most powerful wizards on Gondril for all he knew.

And he was her failing student.

She was saying something, but he wasn't listening. He couldn't stop thinking about Elody. Rinn scratched his head and unconsciously looked over his shoulder again. His aunt squeezed his shoulder, and he turned back to see her smiling.

"She'll be fine, Rinn."

"What if she needs me?"

"I'm not trying to be hurtful when I say that she doesn't need you. Your sister can take care of herself just fine."

"I know," he said softly.

"It doesn't mean she doesn't want you."

"But we've always been together. Dad wanted me to protect her."

"Your father asked you to protect a little girl who needed her big brother. She's a grown woman now with a dragon by her side, and you are a grown man whose time to find his place in the world has long passed."

He started to say something else but only nodded instead.

"Now, we still have work to do today before we can get back to your training. Are you going to carry that heavy bag the whole way by yourself, or do you want some help?"

"You want to carry it?"

"I offered you some help, I didn't offer to carry it. What good is an assistant if I can't make you do the mule's work? Do you know that your grandfather made me go and fetch four buckets of water?"

"Every single day, yes."

"And why do you think he did that?"

"The same reason you make me carry this bag. To torture you."

Jelena laughed, and Rinn couldn't help smiling. She laughed a lot more lately. More than he had ever seen her do in all the years his family lived in Jornath. Aunt Jelena would come and visit every High Harvest, but she was never much fun to be around. Truthfully, Rinn used to always avoid her.

"There may be some truth to that," she said with a wink, "but no. He did it because one bucket would have been too easy. Two buckets would have only taken me one trip. Four buckets took me four trips because my arms got tired."

"Did you put four buckets of water in this bag?"

"No," she said, laughing again.

The twinkle in her eye reminded him of his mother. She looked so much like her sister. He found he liked making her laugh for that reason.

"Then what was the purpose of sending you to get

four buckets?"

"After weeks of doing it, I was so determined to never carry those buckets again that I studied that featherweight spell until I could cast it perfectly. My father knew it, too. He was standing there with the biggest smile on his face the day I came home carrying all four buckets at once. Two in each hand, as though they weighed nothing at all."

Rinn looked to the bag resting on the ground beside him, and his shoulders slumped. Just the thought of picking it up again made his back ache.

"What if I mess it up?"

"Then you'll try again."

That was always her answer. Rinn sighed and lifted his hands. He had memorized the featherweight spell just as his aunt had told him, had been telling him for weeks. In his mind, he knew it forwards and backwards. He could actually hear the words, like a song, in his head when he recalled it. His fingers itched to follow the motions, to weave the magic he would create with his words in the old tongue.

"Right here?" he asked, looking around.

"If you're quiet enough, people will just think you're talking to yourself. Which is a good skill to learn on its own. The movements are small and simple."

Rinn sucked in a deep breath and glared down at that bag. His enemy. His nemesis. That bag would be the death of him, he knew it. He balled up his fists and was about to kick it. And then, just like that, he saw what his aunt had been telling him. He was determined not to let that bag defeat him. The bag would *not* win. Rinn threw his shoulders back and recalled the words of his spell.

The movements were simple. A quick flick of his

wrist, and a few words, and the bag would become as light as the air itself. When he had trained as a dragonmage, this spell would have taken him no more than an hour to learn. He would have pulled the magic from his amulet, or from himself, and had the motions down in no time.

But being a wizard was different. Everything was in the words, in the song his aunt called it. If he didn't get the words right, if he didn't say them exactly, the power he conjured could be wrong. Even dangerous. His aunt had warned him so many times in the beginning about not casting until he could speak the words perfectly. Doom and fire could rain down upon them all if he got it wrong.

So he almost never tried. He would speak the words one by one when he was studying, and he memorized them just like she had been teaching him, but once he had the whole spell, he was too nervous to cast it. Too nervous to try.

"Try," she said again. "It's only a few words, there is no harm."

Rinn lifted his hands and held them low at his waist. Though the movements were slight, he didn't want to alert anyone walking by to what he was doing. Casting spells without a dragon nearby was a sure way to get you labeled as a wizard. Which was not a good thing to be. If it hadn't already been a bad word for the last thousand years, it was definitely one now after what the wizard Velanon had done only a few months ago.

With a simple thought, and a very powerful artifact, the elf had murdered the eldest dragon on Gondril. A dragon loved by the people, who protected the people. And with her death, he gave Gondril the new Eldest. A cruel dragon, by all the tales, who had now made it against dragon law to give eggs to anyone. The word *wizard* was once again a word that might get you killed.

Rinn realized his aunt was staring at him and waiting for him. With a last look down, he shook his hands out and steadied himself.

"Okay," he said, "here I go."

His aunt smiled and waited. Rinn recalled the words of the spell, the words that would summon the magic to his hands that he would then weave to his bidding. He rolled them around on his tongue several times, trying hard to get the feel for them before he actually spoke them. He could feel his aunt watching him, waiting. It felt like the whole world was watching him.

Rinn said the words.

There were only three words to the whole spell, but they felt like marbles in his mouth as he spoke them. He could feel each one falling clumsily from his fat tongue. But then he felt something new. Something familiar yet altogether different. His hands tingled, and he brought them up to stare at them. He could see his aunt smile out of the corner of his eye.

"You've got it," she said. "Now get rid of it."

With a confidence he had not felt in all the months he had been training as a wizard, Rinn gave his hand a swish and a flick and watched as tiny sprinkles of magical energy floated down over the bag at his feet. He knew he got it right. He knew it. Rinn's hand didn't hesitate when it went for the bag. Using nothing more than a single finger, he lifted it and held it high for his aunt to see.

"I did it," he said, staring at the bag.

"I knew you could," she said with a grin. "Now, come

on. We have a sick goat that needs a potion."

She pulled a small vial from her belt and waggled it in the air.

"Tomorrow," she said, "we can take the rocks out of the bag!"

She spun on her heels and was walking away before Rinn even heard what she had said. He cocked his head at the bag now dangling lightly from his finger and pulled it close to him. Unbuckling the two straps that held it closed, he opened it and peered inside.

The bag was full of rocks.

He could hear his aunt laughing an entire block away as he ran to catch up.

CHAPTER TWO

STARTING OUT AGAIN

"GIDDAP!" ELODY SHOUTED.

She snapped the reins for added effect, but it only made things worse. The donkey in front of her little cart refused to budge. She waited a minute to see if he would move.

"We have to go," she said.

The donkey remained frozen, refusing to even look at her. This was going about as well as she hoped. Elody huffed and snapped the reins again.

"You're the one who says we have to do this. I wasn't the one pulling you to go."

The donkey turned to look at her and snorted. The blast hit her in the face, and her arm instinctively shot up to block the expected burst of cold air. Only it wasn't cold. It was warm, and a bit fetid.

"Hah!" she said. "You can't blow anything but stench at me as a donkey."

The donkey's tail twitched and lifted.

"Don't you dare, Thrax."

The donkey huffed again, sending a warm, fetid stench wafting up. By now they were causing something of a jam up in the road. Other carts, driven by much more cooperative beasts, were forced to go around them as they blocked one full side of the trail. A few drivers looked to stop, but a sour glance from Elody made them keep going.

"This is how we have to do it," she said.

The other drivers were staring at her now, most just rolling their eyes at the crazy girl talking to her donkey.

"Can we at least pull off the road so people will stop staring? Drawing more attention to ourselves is what we're trying to avoid."

The cart lurched forward so suddenly that Elody had to grab the seat to keep from pitching over into the back. She held on as the donkey pulled off to one side of the road and came to a stop.

And there they sat.

"I will remind you again that this was your idea."

Snort.

"What do you want me to do?"

The donkey looked up and nodded his head at a lone man riding by on horseback. Elody frowned. They'd been over this already.

"You can't change yourself into something bigger yet, and you'd look silly as a small horse. You're the right size for a donkey, so that's what we've got. The day you can change yourself into a horse, we'll do that, but for now we're sticking with donkey."

Jalthrax huffed.

"Is it the cart? Do you want to leave the cart, and I'll walk the whole way? It's bound to be a long journey, but I'll walk if you want me to."

She started to climb down when the cart jerked forward again. But she was ready for it this time. The only thing more stubborn than a dragon might be a dragon in the magical guise of a donkey, but Elody knew that appealing to his nobler side would make Jalthrax move. He wasn't going to let her walk the whole way.

Elody settled back onto the buckboard and let the reins dangle in her hand. She didn't need to tell him where to go. He may have looked like a donkey, but Jalthrax was quite capable of doing things on his own. He glanced over his shoulder every few minutes to look at her. Who knew donkeys could express such displeasure with a simple look.

"Stop looking at me like that," she said. "This whole trip is your idea, I'm just trying to keep us safe. It's not a good time to be a dragonmage right now, and having a dragon is usually the first clue."

Jalthrax looked back at her and snorted, the air hitting her in the face again. It was his favorite form of argument, but it held considerably less weight without the freezing dragon breath that usually accompanied it. Elody had more to say, but she let it drop. He was ignoring her anyway.

As much as his changing into other forms unnerved her, Elody was glad for it in that moment. In the nine months since Jalthrax's birth, the world of Gondril had become a dangerous place for dragons. Considered by some, mostly themselves, to be the most powerful race in the realm, no creature was invulnerable. And some dragons had become the hunted. Most by their own kind.

Word had spread quickly of the demise of the wizard Velanon. Like all dragonmages, Elody had rejoiced at hearing of his death. For almost a year the wizard had slaughtered the beloved dragon mothers of Gondril.

Without them, there would be no dragonmages, which was what Velanon had sought to do. The dragonmage conclave, indeed all dragonmages, rejoiced at learning the wizard had been killed.

But only for a moment.

With news of Velanon's death also came the decree from the new Eldest. There would be no more dragonmages. Any dragons caught giving eggs away to the mages would be hunted and killed. With a single decree, the Eldest, a gold dragon called Kalus, had ended a thousand-year bond between dragons and mankind. And now dragons hunted and killed other dragons.

It was not a safe time to be a dragon.

Elody absentmindedly snapped the reins, which earned her another snort from Jalthrax.

"Sorry," she said. "Old habit."

She dropped the reins and let them hang on her foot so she wouldn't do it again. Treating Jalthrax like another farm animal was definitely not going to make him anymore pleasant about the whole situation. He really didn't like being a donkey, but Elody had seen no other way. They went back and forth for days before she made the final decision and put a stop to the argument.

As if that was enough. But she didn't have a better idea. Jalthrax had only recently learned to change his form, an ability of all silver dragons, but he was very limited in it. It had taken a few weeks, but he had learned to change himself into anything that was roughly his shape and size. Everything else was beyond his current skills.

After a while it seemed Jalthrax had resigned himself to his fate and stopped looking back to glower at her. He stopped lurching suddenly to make the cart jerk and throw her off balance, and they eventually settled into a rhythm. Elody let her mind wander as a cool breeze blew through the trees. It felt good in the summer heat. The journey to Derne would take several days, with stops, but if the weather held, it would be a pleasant one.

Elody reached into the little pack her aunt had given her and was surprised to find an apple and some cheese. Other than that, the pack was empty. Hardly enough food for a journey. She took the apple and cheese and then closed the flap. Opening it again, she found two small rolls and some nuts.

Aunt Jelena.

Elody shook her head and smiled. With something to snack on, Elody leaned back and enjoyed the journey. Hours went by with nothing but the clip-clopping of Jalthrax's donkey hooves. Elody savored every breath and closed her eyes as they bounced along, listening to the calming sounds of the forest. A snort and a blast of air woke her from her revery. She opened her eyes, ready to yell but stopped when she saw a man ahead on the road. He waved at her to stop.

Elody didn't know what to do. Rinn had warned her about bandits on the road. What if this man was one? Then she remembered who she was and who her traveling companion was.

"Easy, Thrax," she said when she saw his muscles tighten.

She pulled the reins to signal Jalthrax to slow as they got nearer, but he ignored her and kept walking.

"Whoa!" she called out dramatically, adding a little sternness to her voice.

Jalthrax stopped before reaching the man, leaving him just in front of them.

"Hello there," the man called.

He tried to walk forward toward Elody and the cart, but Jalthrax pulled to the side, putting himself between them, and the man stopped.

"Nervous little fella you have there," he said.

"Just anxious to get moving," Elody said. "We have a long road ahead."

"Where are you headed?"

"To Derne."

Jalthrax snorted. Loudly.

"I hear they're still rebuilding after the goblin hordes," the man said.

"We're bringing supplies to help," Elody said.

She patted the heavy canvas covering the load behind her in the wagon. In truth it was nothing more than some straw and hay just to make it look as though she carried supplies. She thought it would make her look a little less suspicious.

"We?" the man asked.

Elody silently cursed herself.

"Donkey and me," she said trying to cover her slip.

"Could I ride with you? I'm looking for work."

Jalthrax snorted again, but Elody ignored him. She looked the man up and down trying to discern his motives. He was young, maybe a little older than Rinn. His clothes were dirty, but the rest of him looked clean. But something wasn't right about him, and Elody knew it. He seemed a little too anxious to join them. Jalthrax knew it too.

"There's not really much room," Elody said. "I'm sure someone else will be along and offer you a ride soon. This road is well traveled."

She shifted in her seat even as Jalthrax pranced back

and forth.

"I've heard travelers have been having trouble with bandits," the man said.

He took a small step forward, and Jalthrax pranced to the side a bit to intercept him.

"I've heard the same, but I think we'll be all right."

"A young girl like you, all alone, should have a man protecting her."

Elody narrowed her eyes and let the reins drop.

"I don't need anyone's protection," she said coolly. "Come on, Thrax."

Jalthrax took two steps forward, and now it was the man's turn to get in front.

"Look," he said with a disarming smile. "I need a ride, and you could use some company."

He reached a hand up for the bridle around Jalthrax's head, but he'd had enough. The donkey's dull, gray skin stretched and popped, sounding like branches breaking in a strong wind. The man backed off a step, uncertainty crossing his face. Elody just crossed her arms and waited. It took only a moment for the transformation to complete.

Where the donkey stood only a moment ago was now a glinting, gleaming silver dragon. Jalthrax spread his wings wide, stretching almost twenty feet from tip to tip, and let out a roar, a frosty, white cloud floating out from his jaws. The man scrambled back, his look of concern turning to fear. Elody had already begun weaving a spell just in case Jalthrax's show wasn't enough, but she stopped when she saw the man backing away.

Jalthrax sucked in his breath and blew out a cone of freezing ice. It flew to the side of the man, just nicking his shoulder. Not enough to cause real damage, but enough to send him running. Elody let the magic fall from her hands and watched a moment longer to see if she could see him running. Jalthrax blew another puff of ice after him.

"Well, that was certainly laying low," Elody said as she leapt from the wagon.

She moved to stand beside Jalthrax, and the two of them watched the forest for any sign of the man. She was pretty sure he wasn't coming back. Picking up the tack, she inspected it while the dragon kept watching the trees.

"You better hope you didn't break any of this," she said.

After a thorough inspection of everything, she was satisfied nothing had broken.

"Can we please get moving now?"

Jalthrax looked back at her, and she motioned to the harness and tack. He snorted, hitting her in the face with a shocking blast of cold.

"I'll be glad when you're a donkey again," she said. "Now let's get moving."

***

Rinn and Jelena walked together down the street. He was so used to trailing behind her that it took him a moment to notice it was different. His mind was on other things though.

"It's only been a few hours," Jelena said.

"What?" Rinn asked, broken from his trance.

"You're worried about her, I know, but she's only been gone a few hours. What trouble can she get into on the road to Derne?"

"I've heard bandits have been stealing along the road."

"From a dragonmage?"

Rinn smiled a little at the thought and then fell back into silence. They walked like that, side by side, for a while. Rinn wasn't even sure where they were going, so he just stayed in step with his aunt. She seemed content to let the silence hang in the air, and Rinn appreciated it.

"Are you happy?" he finally asked.

"With what?"

"I don't know. With your life?"

"Am I happy with my life?"

"Yes."

"I suppose so, yes. I lay my head on my pillow at night as content as I can be."

"Don't you ever wish you had met someone?"

She smiled just a little.

"What makes you think I never met someone?"

"You mean you have?"

"I'm not saying that, I'm just wondering what makes you think I never did."

"Well, you live alone."

"No I don't, I have you and your sister. Well, just you now."

"You know what I mean," he said.

"Yes, I know what you mean, but I don't much agree with your conclusion."

"I don't—"

"You have concluded that because I don't have someone to spend my life with that I must be unhappy. That's what your question implies"

"That's not what I meant."

"That's exactly what you meant."

"Well, I didn't mean it to sound as harsh as you just made it."

"You didn't hurt my feelings, Rinn. I'm a grown woman. My ego is not so fragile as your young one."

Rinn hung his head.

"Being what we are is lonely sometimes," she said. "I told you when we started that it would take an immense amount of focus and practice to become great."

"But what if I don't want to be great?"

"Then why do it? Why do anything if you don't wish to master it?"

"I don't know. For fun?"

"You think I'm training you for a lark? If that's what you think, then we can call this day done and stop right now."

"I just mean that you don't have to strive to be the best at everything."

"Yes," she said, "you do."

"You've said that my mother trained, but I don't think she trained to be the best."

"Don't count on it. Elara trained harder than anyone I'd ever seen, certainly harder than I did. She could have been truly powerful if she'd wanted to, perhaps one of the most powerful."

"But she didn't."

"When your mother wanted something badly enough, she let nothing get in her way. Kind of like your sister. When Elara fell in love with your father, she told me how much she wanted to be with him. How much she wanted a family. She wanted you and your sister more than she wanted her magic."

"She gave up her training to marry my dad?"

"She didn't have to, but she did. People like us don't often marry. It takes too much time to master the art. More time than can be found when you have a family, I think."

"But dragonmages marry all the time," Rinn said.

"Dragonmages don't require the same kind of discipline. They don't need to focus on growing their power. They simply gain power as their dragon gets bigger and more powerful. Dragonmages have it easy."

"If they bond."

She rested her hand on his shoulder.

"Some bonds fail as yours did," she said. "All that means is that I can give you something even greater."

"Yeah, but I still don't get a dragon."

She smiled.

"That is a downside to our kind, I admit. Dragonmages have a big dragon to protect them. We have no one watching our backs but ourselves."

"Do elven wizards marry?" Rinn asked.

"They have a lot more time in this world than we do. I can't imagine how much I would achieve if I'd been given eight hundred years. We humans have only a few short decades to master our craft. And that requires absolute focus."

"How do you keep from being lonely?"

"I have rarely felt lonely in all my years. I had my family before they all passed. I've had you and Elody here with me. I have no time to feel lonely. Too many people around that need something from me."

Rinn laughed.

"Speaking of not feeling lonely," she said as she pointed over his shoulder.

Rinn looked back and saw a woman his aunt was pointing at through the crowded street. As the press of bodies parted just enough, he saw Oryna standing there with the biggest smile on her face.

Rinn turned to ask his aunt if he could stop for a bit, but she was already walking off down the street with a little spring in her step and a tune on her lips. Rinn saw Oryna cutting through the crowd to meet him on his side of the street. They stood together for several moments, staring at each other as the throng of people flowed around them.

"I…" she started. "I haven't seen you in a while."

"I know," he said. "I've tried to come to the temple, but my aunt has been really busy, and I'm with her all the time now."

He held up the heavy bag he was holding for emphasis. The lightening spell he'd used had worn off while he and his aunt were chatting, but he didn't want to put her bag down in the muddy street.

"I've been quite busy myself," she said. "A lot has happened in the months since Molner."

Rinn nodded. They stood, just looking at each other as another minute passed.

"I'm sorry I didn't have a chance to say goodbye," she said.

"I understand."

"I did not realize they would send us so quickly."

"Where did you go?"

"A small group of us went to meet with the knighthood. When news reached us of the wizard Velanon's death, we went with a contingent of knights to the dragonmage conclave."

Rinn nodded again. He didn't know what else to do or say.

"Did you come straight back here?" she asked.

"I… I waited a week for you to come back, but Elody and I decided to travel back with Berym once we received news of the new Eldest and his new laws."

"I'm sorry I couldn't see you before I left."

"I was just glad I got to spend the week with you before you did."

She smiled and looked away.

"I was glad too."

Rinn felt like some young, lovestruck boy standing there in the street. The crowds surged and moved around them, but they just stood, looking at each other and then away.

"I knew you came back two weeks ago," he said at last.

"How did you know?"

"My aunt told me."

"How did she know?"

Rinn shrugged.

"She's a witch. She knows things."

"Why didn't you come and see me?"

"I didn't… I didn't know what to say. You left in such a hurry, I didn't know where we had left things. I didn't know if we could pick up where we left off or if it would just be awkward."

"Unlike this," she said.

Rinn tried to laugh, but she was right.

"I didn't come to see you either," she said. "For the same reason."

They both tried hard to look at anything but each other, but as hard as they tried, their eyes kept drifting back. As Rinn looked away again, he spotted someone that drew his attention away from Oryna.

"Eliath?" he said.

Oryna looked up then, following his gaze to the man riding by on horseback. He was right, it was Eliath. Rinn hadn't seen much of him since Molner. Not since Tark died in the big battle. Eliath wasn't the same after that. After the battle, he'd returned to Havnor with the rest of them, but as a broken man.

He had taken a room at the Dragon's Roost where he'd been for the last few months, though Rinn had no idea how he could afford it. Elody had tried to see him a few times, but she said he had just turned into a drunk. Falling down, stumbling over his own words. Rinn had some sympathy for him, but not much.

But what was he doing here, now, and on horseback? He looked like he was heading for the town gates, and with enough food for a trip.

"He looks better than the last time I saw him," Oryna said.

"Yes," Rinn said, "he does."

He did look better. Cleaner. Sober. Rinn wasn't sure what change had come over him, but he hoped it was permanent. Elody had spent months worrying about Eliath, and no matter how much Rinn tried to convince her to move on, she wouldn't give up on him. Rinn didn't care for him much, but a part of him was glad to see him cleaned up.

"It cannot be easy," Oryna said. "Losing his dragon like he did."

"I can't imagine so," Rinn said.

Rinn had lost a dragon once, but not like Eliath. Rinn's dragon failed to bond. Eliath had been bonded for more than a decade before he lost Tark in Molner. As much as Rinn didn't like Eliath, he understood a little of what he must be going through.

But what was he doing now?

"Where could he be going?" Rinn asked.

Oryna shrugged and reached out to take his hand. Rinn forgot all about Eliath in that touch. He turned back with a big smile he couldn't erase.

"Are you leaving again soon?" he asked.

Standing there, holding her hand like that, he couldn't help feeling nervous at her answer. The week they'd spent together in Molner after the goblin battle was the most amazing week Rinn could recall in his life. It wasn't anything like the other girls he'd been with.

A walk here, a touch of the hand there, a kiss goodbye. Perfectly innocent and sweet, and Rinn had treasured every second in his memory until now. That sweet, knowing smile on her face was quickly making this moment one of his new favorites.

"I have no plans to leave again," she said.

"Berym used to say that all the time too."

"Well, I may follow requests of the church, but more than that the Goddess has taught me to follow my own heart."

"And what does your heart tell you?"

She squeezed his hand.

"To stay right here."

Again Rinn found it hard to keep the smile from his lips.

"Lady Oryna!" someone shouted.

The moment dashed, they both looked up the street to where a man in bright, polished plate armor was making his way through the crowd. A few waves of his massive gauntlets had people stumbling to get out of his way and open a path.

"Bullus," Oryna said. "Rinn, this is Keeper Bullus. I think you may have met in Molner."

Rinn smiled and nodded. He did remember Bullus.

Keepers were the name given to the paladins of Threyl who guarded her priests and priestesses on missions. Rinn had met four separate ones that Oryna claimed as her own. Rinn didn't know how he felt about the idea. Four big, strong men around her all the time?

"My lady, you must come to the temple."

"What is it?" she asked.

"News from the conclave, Mother. I will tell you more when we are back at the temple."

"Tell me now," she said.

Rinn wanted to hear what was going on, and he made very little effort to hide the fact. Bullus glanced at him and then back to Oryna.

"My lady, the dragonmage conclave has sent word that the Eldest has declared open war on all dragonmages."

Oryna looked at Rinn, lines of worry written across her face.

"When did this happen?" she asked.

"We only just received word. The Eldest attacked a school in Baglund. He... he burned the school and murdered the teachers and children."

Oryna clapped her hand to her mouth and whispered a prayer he couldn't make out. Rinn stood in stunned silence. There was only one school for dragonmages in Baglund. Master Cythyil's school. The school where Rinn and Elody had both studied. Where Elody gained a dragon and Rinn lost one.

"Why?" Rinn managed to ask.

"The Eldest claims the master of the school was stealing eggs. That this was a punishment for enslaving dragons."

"What has the conclave said?" Oryna asked.

"That all dragonmages are to go into hiding immediately. The Eldest has sent loyal dragons across Gondril to hunt them all down."

"Goddess, no," Oryna said.

"Elody," Rinn said.

He looked up as Oryna took him by the hand.

"She's out on the road alone," he said.

"Where is she going?" Oryna asked.

"She doesn't know. West is all she said."

"The elves have offered refuge within their borders," Bullus said. "Perhaps that is where she is going."

"She doesn't know *where* she's going," Rinn said. "She doesn't know what's happened."

Rinn was having a hard time forming thoughts. Elody was on the road, alone. She didn't know what had happened. She didn't know how dangerous her life had just gotten.

"I have to find her," he said.

"But you said yourself, you don't know where she's going," Oryna said.

"She mentioned Derne. She's going there to see Berym before moving on. If I leave now, I can catch her."

Rinn looked at his aunt's bag resting on the ground and then back up to Oryna.

"Please tell my aunt that I'm sorry."

"How will you catch her?" she asked.

"I… I don't know. I have to find a horse."

"Come on," Oryna said. "Bullus will get you a horse from the temple's stables."

"Yes, my lady," Bullus said.

Oryna picked up Jelena's bag, huffing only a little as she hefted it from the ground.

"Come on," she said. "We have to move quickly if

you're to catch her."

Rinn followed them to the temple where Bullus had a horse saddled and packed with some food for a few days not long after. Rinn was off, chasing after Elody, within the hour.

He only hoped he could catch her before someone else did.

CHAPTER THREE

LIVING

GORTOGH HURRIED ABOUT his little cave, picking up what few meager possessions he still kept from his former life. A leather pouch that he pulled over his head and hung around his neck. A small, bronze ring he slipped on his gnarled finger. And a longsword, shiny and polished, he slid into a scabbard and slung over his back. Everything he owned in the world.

He left the cave with his head high and his shoulders back. Still playing the role of chieftain. His eyes rolled at himself, and he quickly slumped to his natural posture. There was no one to impress or rule here. Not in this life.

Down the mountain he went, picking his way along the craggy trail until he reached the bottom. The eyes of the forest were on him as soon as his feet touched the dirt. He could feel them all around, though he could only guess at who or what was out there.

It didn't matter.

Gortogh reached back to touch the hilt of his sword and relaxed a bit. Sometimes he needed a reminder that he had little to fear. The forest was crawling with his kin, most of whom would attack him on sight, but he wasn't worried. Not a goblin on Gondril could match him in battle. Probably not even ten of them together. Still, he preferred to avoid them if he could.

Sneaking along, he saw goblin sign everywhere. This was their part of the forest now, after all. Ever since their defeat at Molner. Gortogh felt a pang of guilt at his role in that battle, but he pushed it out of his mind.

It wasn't his fault. It was Ogrosh's fault.

Moving silently along a well-marked game trail, Gortogh ducked off to one side to check a snare he had set the day before. He had a brief moment of hope when he didn't see the snare hanging there, but it was short lived. The whole snare was gone. Either someone had stolen it, or some poor creature had broken it and run off with it around its neck.

"Praise Ogrosh," he whispered.

With deft hands used to doing the trapping work of goblin women, Gortogh set a new snare and moved on. Shuffling leaves to his left made him freeze and press against a tree. A moment later he heard voices through the fading light of day. Goblin voices. Just a patrol, no doubt. Probably heading back to camp. The goblins rarely patrolled once the sun set, and it was near dark.

Gortogh let a smile creep onto his face as he moved in behind them and followed them back to camp. He wasn't very stealthy in his movements, but neither were his kin very observant. The four patrolmen shouted something as they approached the camp, and a shout was returned. Gortogh stopped behind a tree and waited for the rest of the daylight to fade.

The bonfires of the goblin camp flared to life as the last fingers of sunlight faded through the thick trees. He could hear the chanting growing louder and louder as he approached. The goblin shamans were summoning animals for the bloody slaughter. He held back as their prayers reached a crescendo.

He knew what would come next.

Minutes passed in silence as the tribe watched and waited. They didn't have to wait long though. Ogrosh was quick with the meat, that much had always been true. Gortogh watched from a ways away as they came.

Three deer and three boar, each one enough to feed most of the tribe by itself, walked proudly among the goblins. They had no fear, such was their enamor of the goblin priests. The animals were held enthralled by the call of the shamans and made to do their bidding. They stood still, waiting.

The goblins leapt on them, knives in hand. One by one they were slit from ear to ear so that their lifeblood could drain out. The proud beasts never moved.

The goblins knew their part well. They threw up praises to Ogrosh and let the blood pour over their arms and chests. They bathed in the gushing life of the animals, all the while singing praises to the Blood God. Howls of laughter and power were sung to the heavens.

Praise Ogrosh.

The goblins wasted no time in skinning and dressing the poor creatures. Within minutes, each was tied and hung from long saplings and roasting comfortably over a fire. It didn't take long for the smell of sizzling meat to reach Gortogh. His stomach grumbled in protest of his meager breakfast and lunch. Nothing but nuts and berries. Meat hadn't been on his menu for over a week now.

Gortogh crept closer, sidling from tree to tree until he was just outside the large ring that circled the main campfire. The whole tribe had gathered around one large bonfire tonight with only enough smaller ones to cook all of the meat. Something bigger was to happen tonight. Which was why Gortogh had come.

He watched and waited for more than an hour.

The meat was carved and passed around. Gortogh heard his stomach so loudly he thought it would betray his location, but the goblins were too loud to even notice. He waited and listened. It would start soon.

Why did he come? Gortogh asked himself the same question every time. He was risking his life being so close to those who now considered him an enemy, yet he felt compelled to come. Maybe he was just lonely. Being alone in that cave for months was wearing him down.

The chattering from the goblins grew quiet. Gortogh dared a peek around the big tree he had nestled against and saw the cause. The goblin warriors to one side of the fire parted in a wide swath to let someone into their circle. Goblins fell to their knees and kissed the ground. Gortogh could hear the clacking bones long before he could see the newcomer.

Kurgh, the high shaman of the goblin tribe, entered the circle. Around his neck was draped strand upon strand of bones that swayed as he walked. What creatures the bones came from, no one could say, but they clattered against each other in an awful, clacking symphony with each step. The belt above his loincloth was made of black feathers from some large bird. They tickled those who reached out to touch Kurgh as he passed.

"Brothers," Kurgh said. "Praise Ogrosh for this feast."

"Praise Ogrosh!" the goblins shouted in unison.

Kurgh paced around the circle, each goblin lowering

his eyes to the ground as he passed. He let the silence hang in the air long enough that it made even Gortogh uncomfortable. When he finally came to a stop next to the fire, he turned and stared straight in Gortogh's direction.

Gortogh started to duck behind his tree but then steadied himself. There was no way Kurgh could see him. Goblins had no trouble seeing in the dark, but his eyes could not see through the fire and into the darkness this far. Still, Gortogh shivered as the shaman looked right through him.

In the months he had been coming to hear Kurgh speak, Gortogh had gained a new respect for the shaman. Once, before the Battle of Molner, they had a very different relationship. One in which Gortogh was the one in power, and Kurgh was nothing but a sniveling bootlick. Kurgh once bowed to him as all these goblins now bowed.

"Far away," Kurgh began. "Deep in the Twin Crest Mountains lies the city of Ogrilon. The greatest city of the greatest nation Gondril has ever known. The goblin nation."

"Praise Ogrosh!" the goblins cheered.

"So high are its walls that none could breach them," Kurgh said.

"Tell us about dragons!" one goblin shouted.

Kurgh stopped speaking and narrowed his eyes as his head whipped around to find who had interrupted him.

"Yeah, the dragons!" another said.

Kurgh's face softened into a smile.

"You wish to hear of the war between dragons and goblins?"

Shouts of agreement all around.

"Very well."

Kurgh did two more turns around the circle, looking into each goblin's eyes as he passed. He was eating up the attention. Gortogh almost laughed.

"Five thousands years ago," Kurgh said and then paused. "Five thousand years ago there was a great war. Not like the war between the humans kings, no. No, this was a time before humans walked. When Gondril was ruled by the four races of power. When goblins were the highest and most powerful of all the children of the gods."

"Praise Ogrosh!" they chanted.

Gortogh's nose crinkled in disgust. He had heard the tale a few times, and it never sat well with him.

"The dwarves and elves had been locked in a hundred-year war. But another war, between the most powerful races, was about to begin. It was Anarr who struck first... and we all know who struck last."

Laughs all around.

"Anarr, eldest of the gods, saw a chance to defeat his youngest brother and wipe his creations from the world. The goblins and ogres of Ogrosh were the greatest and most powerful civilization, and Anarr was a jealous child. He sent his dragons against the great cities of Ogrosh. Against Ogrilon itself. But the goblins could not be defeated."

At this, Gortogh scoffed. Loudly. Kurgh cocked his head in the direction of his tree. Gortogh jerked behind the trunk and cursed himself. There was a long stretch of silence. Stupid. His hand inched toward the hilt of his blade and hovered there.

"The goblins were too powerful," Kurgh continued. "Ogrosh had blessed his people with the strongest magic of all. Blood magic."

Gortogh relaxed as the story continued. After another moment, he pressed his belly to the trunk and peered around again to watch. He knew the show well enough to know the next part. Kurgh already had the dagger in his hand.

"Ogrosh gives us power in blood," Kurgh said.

The shaman pushed the bone knife into his arm, biting deeply into his flesh, and raked it across leaving a big, open gash. Dark, red blood poured from the wound and ran down his arm. The goblins nearest him scrambled to catch even a drop in their hands and taste it.

Kurgh smiled and offered his arm up to his brothers. He held his arms wide, letting the holy symbol of Ogrosh scarred into his chest show to the heavens. Blood poured down his arm and dripped from his elbow, but he made no move to bind the wound. He didn't need to.

A moment later, the wound was gone. The shaman's ugly, green skin stitched itself back together, leaving no evidence the cut was ever even there. Even though he'd seen it dozens of times, maybe hundreds, Gortogh was still left speechless by the display. Truly the shamans of Ogrosh wielded his greatest gifts.

"With blood," Kurgh said, "Ogrosh's people fought the evil dragons. Our magic was strong, as strong as the blood of the goblins who wielded it. But the dragons were stronger. The blood of goblins was not strong enough to defeat the dragons."

Some of the gathered hissed, and Gortogh chuckled again.

"But Ogrosh's magic is born of blood. The stronger the blood, the stronger the magic. The shamans soon learned that using the blood of ogres would give them even greater strength. Enough to harm the dragons and begin to turn the tide of the war. That was when the shamans captured their first dragon. That was when they used the blood of the dragons against their own kind."

"Praise Ogrosh!" the goblins cheered.

"With dragon blood at their command, the children of Anarr could not stand against Ogrosh. The shamans took the war to *them*, capturing dragons and draining them of blood to use against their own kind. Anarr fought, but his dragons could not defeat the mighty goblin armies. He could not defeat Ogrosh."

"Praise Ogrosh!"

Even though he knew the story, Gortogh began to tremble with anger. They believed every word of it. They swallowed every lie he told them. His people, Ogrosh's people, *Gortogh's* people, would believe anything it seemed.

"The shamans hunted the dragons. They would nearly destroy every dragon on Gondril before Anarr came, groveling, to Ogrosh for mercy."

The goblins laughed and cheered. Gortogh had heard enough. To his own surprise, he found himself growling and charging out from behind his tree. The goblins nearest him jumped aside, startled to find someone pushing past them.

Kurgh wasn't surprised. Not at all. He even smiled at Gortogh's approach.

"Our fearless leader," Kurgh said.

"You fill them with lies!" Gortogh shouted.

"I have spoken no lies this night."

A few goblins leapt up and drew their swords, but a wave of Kurgh's hand stopped them.

"They believe you," Gortogh said. "You are a shaman of Ogrosh, and they *believe* you."

"And they should. I speak the truth."

"You tell children's stories!"

"These are the stories of our people. Passed from shaman to shaman, from tribe to tribe, so that they live on."

"Goblins that could defeat dragons? Hunting them down? Were you there at the battle of Molner?"

Gortogh looked around into the eyes of his brothers.

"You were all there," he said. "You saw just as I did. Ten thousand goblins, nearly destroyed by *four* dragons. Do you really think that we once hunted them as he says? That *we* were the ones to be feared?"

"Ogrosh gives us power through blood," Kurgh said. "Through his blessings, we can defeat any enemy."

"And where was your blood magic in Molner, Kurgh? Where was Ogrosh then?"

"We did not have Ogrosh's blessing."

"You're a fool. I have felt Ogrosh's blessing. He is not worthy of your praise."

Kurgh's jaw tightened and his eyes narrowed.

"It was *you* who led so many to their deaths, *Mighty One*. Never forget that."

"I don't, Kurgh. I remember it every day. I remember feeling the blessing of Ogrosh on that battlefield. I remember the look in those eyes as they chanted his name and charged to their deaths. Yes, I was the one who brought us to that battle, but do not doubt that it was Ogrosh who led the charge."

"Leave!" Kurgh said.

He slashed the knife across his arm, the blood flowing instantly. It ran down to his hand where it pooled, swirling around his fingers. Gortogh stood still, his hand itching to reach for his sword, but he knew it would be his death. He could never fight so many.

"You blame Ogrosh for your own failings," Kurgh said. "It was you, and only you."

"How easy it must be to give thanks to Ogrosh for everything good while laying the blame for failure on someone else."

Gortogh looked left and then right at the stunned faces around him.

"It is time to stop pretending," he said. "Stop pretending we were once some great society. We are not powerful. Perhaps we were once, but no more. You are all just weak, sniveling *goblins*."

"Leave now!" Kurgh screamed.

"You are trash," Gortogh said. "Ogrosh's abandoned trash."

Three warriors drew their swords again, but Gortogh was already turning to leave.

"Let him go!" Kurgh said. "He deserves to live out whatever painful fate Ogrosh has designed for him."

Gortogh ran.

He ran as fast and as hard as he could to escape, though there was no one chasing him. When he was sure he was clear of the goblin camp and its patrols, he slowed down. He wanted to run as fast and as far as he could, to get away from all of them. But he had nowhere to go.

And no one but himself.

He checked another snare on the way back to his cave and found, to his delight, that a rabbit had gotten caught in it. It was lying still on the ground, but he could see its chest still breathing slowly. He quickly snapped its neck and picked it up.

Looks like he'd be getting meat for dinner after all.

"*Praise* Ogrosh," he said with a sneer.

He jogged the rest of the way back to his cave where he lit a fire and set to work skinning the rabbit. It was work he was accustomed to, and he was fast at it from all the practice. Trapping and skinning were jobs for the women of a goblin tribe. And Gortogh was usually included with the women growing up.

He'd never been strong, never been handsome or a good hunter. He was smart, but that was not a desirable trait among his people. Goblins preferred their warriors tough and stupid. The only path for Gortogh would have been to become a shaman. But somehow, even at a young age, he hated the thought of that even more.

Damn Kurgh. And *damn* Ogrosh.

Kurgh was right. He was in pain, and it was all Ogrosh's fault. As he sat there skinning that rabbit, all he could think of was the pain he'd been through. The pain he'd caused.

All for Ogrosh.

Gortogh felt his blood boil again. He ripped the pouch from around his neck and tore it open. Turning it over, a small, bronze disc fell into his waiting hand. He immediately felt its power. There was a time when he could feel nothing from the amulet, but now, as though permanently awakened by his touch, he could feel its energy. It hummed in his hand.

Gortogh held the blood of Ogrosh himself in his hand. He turned the amulet over a few times, looking at its simple surface. The symbol of Ogrosh, a fist with a drop of blood dripping from it, covered the surface. It had not been there before when he first received it, but it had been etched into the metal ever since it awakened. Beyond the symbol, it was nothing but a simple bronze circle. Something anyone could mistake for just a worthless piece of bad jewelry.

But the amulet made Gortogh all powerful to his people. It made him appear as Ogrosh made flesh. He had not worn it, had barely looked at it, since the battle of Molner. He could lie to himself all he wanted, but he knew who it was that led those thousands of goblins to their death. Gortogh curled his fingers around the amulet and squeezed with all his strength. His whole body trembled. Kurgh was right. It was all his fault.

No.

Those goblins would never have followed him if not for the amulet. They would never have gathered to his call if not for the blood of Ogrosh. And he would not have the amulet if Ogrosh did not want him to have it. If Ogrosh had not allowed it. This was all Ogrosh's doing. Gortogh leaned back against the rocky wall of the cave and sighed.

He threw the amulet against the far wall. The bronze disc clanged loudly against the stone and rang throughout the cave. But the amulet just dropped to the ground without so much as a scratch. Gortogh had made a hobby of trying to destroy the thing, but he'd learned early on that nothing could harm it. Nothing would destroy the blood of Ogrosh.

Now it was a just a cold reminder of the deaths on his head. Every time he looked at it, every time he felt its power, it reminded him of all the blood. All of his brothers and warriors killed in battle. All for Ogrosh. The amulet was the fate Kurgh spoke of. Ogrosh wanted him to suffer it for all eternity.

Gortogh walked across the cave and stared down at it. He bent to retrieve it but paused. His hand hovered over it a few seconds longer before snatching it up. He expected the same warm energy in his hand, but he was surprised to find something different. A new energy he had never felt before. The amulet pulsed in his hand. Gortogh uncurled his fingers to look at it.

What was it doing?

A tingling sensation crept through him. He threw the amulet again, hard. It clattered against the opposite wall and fell with a thump to the dirt. Still the tingling continued through him. It scared him. The energy flowed, without stopping, to every corner of his being. And then Gortogh knew what it meant.

The amulet was telling him to go west.

CHAPTER FOUR

HUNTING

BERYM CREPT LOW through the trees. With the bulk of his armor gone, he was able to remain mostly silent. Not that his target would even notice. In the months of hunting them since the battle of Molner, he'd learned that goblins are not very observant. Especially when they're weak and outnumbered. They were usually looking for a quick retreat more than a foe.

He saw his a quarry ahead. A single goblin stood sentry for the little encampment, his back to a tree. It was half asleep from what Berym could see, it wasn't even looking up, just down at its feet. Berym would have almost felt guilty killing it if he'd gotten the chance. Before he could rush from hiding, a single arrow pierced the creature's chest and stuck it fast to the tree.

Berym looked over his shoulder with annoyance, knowing full well that he wouldn't see his companion. That blasted cloak of his made sure no one would see him unless he wanted to be seen. Berym stood up a bit and crept on. With the sentry gone, the camp would probably be completely unaware of their presence now.

A few more feet, and he heard voices. The goblins

were fighting about something. There was a lot of yelling, which meant there would be very little notice of his approach. Berym stood up, stretching his back after all the crouching, and walked on. The shouting grew louder as he got nearer until he could actually see them fighting. Still they didn't notice him.

Three goblins were fighting over the mostly eaten remains of a chicken carcass. A few more were still asleep, or trying to sleep, on the ground around the small camp. It was sad to look at. All of them looked starved, their ribs poking out from beneath taut, green skin. And all they had to fight over was chicken bones with a little meat and fat left on them.

Berym wanted to just turn and walk away. These goblins wouldn't be hurting anyone, much less their village. They had stolen the chicken, but they didn't want a fight with anyone. He doubted they could fight even if they wanted to, they were so weak.

The fight between the goblins escalated. Swords were drawn and the yelling grew louder. The other goblins jumped from their beds and drew weapons as well, each one taking a side. Berym was content to just let them kill each other until an arrow burst through the chest of one of the arguing ones. Blood sprayed the other two and everyone froze. Even Berym was too stunned to move at first.

Another arrow took a second goblin through the throat before the whole scene devolved into chaos. Berym burst through the brush, leading with his sword and shield. He stabbed one through the back before it could even turn and get its weapon up. He shouldered past it and into the fray.

The goblins were in disarray.

Berym took one's head from its shoulders. The next one managed to get its sword up before an arrow went through its chest. The three who were still standing took only a second to contemplate running, but it was too late. Berym chopped through the side of one as it turned to flee. Another arrow shot one in the back. The last one managed to get away.

Berym grabbed a bedroll from the ground and wiped the blood from his blade. He was getting tired of seeing blood everywhere. It seemed his whole life had been nothing but blood sometimes.

"Three for you, five for me," a voice behind him said.

He didn't even look up as Eryninn sidled up to him.

"You let one get away," Berym said.

"*I* let one get away? I got the one there in the back as they were running. You should have run after the last one."

"I'm tired, Eryninn."

The half-elf was silent. He knew what Berym meant. They didn't need to discuss it again.

"I thought a little fun killing goblins would lift your spirits."

"This is not fun for me," Berym said. "I don't enjoy killing weak creatures who are just fighting over some food, and neither should you."

"These creatures would see you and your village starved if it meant they would eat."

"Would you not do the same in their place?"

"I would not starve a village so that I may eat."

"Not even a goblin village? Would you steal from goblins to stay alive?"

"That is different."

"It's not. You know it's not."

"Goblins are creatures of evil. They do not deserve your pity."

"Not even mercy?"

"You gave them mercy. You ended their suffering."

Berym sighed.

"I'm tired. We've been out here for more than a week, let's go home."

Eryninn scoffed. Berym didn't press. He just turned back to the east and started walking.

"Are you coming?" he called over his shoulder.

"In a bit," Eryninn said.

Berym didn't stop to ask.

***

It was hours later when Berym finally rode within sight of the village of Derne. They had been tracking the goblins farther out than he had remembered. It seemed their hunting expeditions were growing less and less needed by the week. The goblins had mostly been scared south beyond the mountains, and what few remained were nothing but ragtag groups. Nothing like the organized army that attacked Molner.

Berym smiled and waved as he rode past the fields, the sun just behind his head. Nearly time for the day to end. It was harvest time, and most of the villagers were bringing in the wheat. The goblins had trampled and burned the fields when they marched through months ago. Everyone had made it through the summer with hard work and help from neighbors, but they would not survive without the harvest.

Shouts echoed across the fields, passing from villager to villager as Berym rode on. Hands went high in the air, and Berym smiled and waved back to each and every one. A boy shot out of the fields and ran on to the village. A dozen or more of these hunting expeditions, and they still greeted him like a hero upon his return. Though he usually shared the attention with Erynnin, who was never happy to receive it.

"Berym!" someone shouted.

Berym waved to the man in the field and rode on. He could already see the crowd gathering on the western road as he approached. It was good to be home. It had only been five months since the battle of Molner, but Berym knew that's what Derne was to him now. Home. He had traveled his whole life, rarely finding a place where he belonged. But that's where he was now. He knew it the instant he saw her.

Narissa.

The smile wouldn't leave his lips. While everyone shouted and cheered for him, she held her hands over her heart and smiled. He could see the tears on her cheeks even from here, and it made him sad and so happy all at the same time. When at last he was among them, he slid from the saddle and rushed to take her in his arms. The crowd parted to let him through, some laughing or shaking their heads, but Berym didn't care.

Narissa.

Home.

He swept her off the ground in a great hug and kissed her passionately. He struggled to keep from squeezing her too hard. He missed her so much. Their lips parted, and he set her down to look at her, but it only lasted a moment. Soon the crowd was there, everyone wanting to know what had happened.

"Slow down," Father Meral said. "I'm sure Berym will tell us everything once he's had a moment to catch his breath."

Berym smiled. The older priest was always looking out for him it seemed. Berym raised his hand to quiet the crowd.

"I will tell you everything at dinner tonight."

Some grumbled, but everyone nodded.

"I promise you, there is not much to tell. And I'm thankful for that. But I will tell you everything when we all sit down to eat."

The crowd dispersed, but not before Father Meral could give Berym a firm slap on the back.

"Good to see you back in one piece," the priest said.

"If I weren't, I'd expect you to put me back together again."

The old priest laughed and then caught up with everyone else going back to the village. Though there wasn't much village left these days. Berym did notice something new.

"Is that the forge?" he asked.

He pointed at a plume of smoke drifting high into the air.

"Yes!" she said. "We got it finished while you were gone."

"That's wonderful," he said.

Berym held the reins of his horse in one hand and Narissa's hand in his other. They shuffled along behind the villagers back toward the square.

"I was beginning to worry," she said.

"We went farther out than I had expected. It might be our last hunt though."

"Do you think?"

"We followed every new track we came across, and the only thing we found was a single camp many miles from here. Truly, it seems the goblins have all but disappeared from the area."

They walked on toward the village, what little there was left of it. When the goblins marched through Derne on their way to Molner those months ago, they burned everything in their path. The villagers were safe, hidden away in a cellar of the village church, but everything else was gone. Everyone had worked together to rebuild, and they were finally making some progress it seemed.

Most of the church was still standing after the goblins left, so that was rebuilt first. Then they built a long hall across from the church that would house everyone and serve as a place for communal meals. Many still slept there at night, but the rest of the village was slowly coming back to life. When the goblins couldn't kill the people of Derne, they'd done their best to snuff out everything else. But here it was, rebuilt piece by piece.

"Do you really think this might be your last hunt?" Narissa asked.

"I hope," Berym said. "I would like nothing more than to stay right here and spend my days with you."

He squeezed her hand and moved closer in response, nudging her shoulder against his.

"They'll probably crack open a barrel of beer when they hear the news," she said.

"They should crack open *two* barrels."

She laughed, and he put his arm around her shoulder.

"Where is Eryninn?" she asked. "Staying back to avoid the crowd?"

"Still hunting, maybe."

"Did you not clear out the camp you found?"

"No, we cleared it out, but one got away. Perhaps he went after it."

"What else could he be doing?"

Berym shrugged.

"I never quite know with him."

***

Eryninn considered, briefly, going after the escaping goblin. No doubt he could track him with ease and kill him with a single shot. The creature would never even hear him coming. But something else had tickled his senses. Something in the woods. He walked around the camp, examining the remains of the goblins for anything interesting.

Nothing.

Berym was right, these goblins didn't even have enough food to eat. Most of them looked like they would have died in a few days even without their intervention. Eryninn had no pity for them. Goblins were evil creatures. Their whole existence was based on the destruction of all things good. No, Eryninn felt nothing for these creatures. He could kill a hundred more without pause.

There it was again.

That feeling in his peripheral. Like someone was watching him. He thought it might be the goblin coming back, but there was no way it could sneak up on him and get this close. There were few on Gondril who could get close to Eryninn without him knowing it. Which was enough to tell him exactly what he was feeling. Eryninn looked all around, thinking to find who was watching him, but he knew it would be as useless as them trying to sneak up on him.

So he sat down instead.

Crossing his legs and laying his bow across his lap, Eryninn sat and waited. He didn't have to wait long.

"You look like a sitting duck," a voice said.

Eryninn recognized it.

"Come out, Alranir."

"You remember me, then?"

The elf stepped out from behind a tree barely ten feet from where Eryninn sat. The elf was good, Eryninn had to admit that.

"It's not often I forget an enemy."

"I am not your enemy, son of Tarin."

"What do you want?"

"I was sent to give you a message."

Eryninn stood and slung his bow across his back.

"I don't want your message, and I don't want you following me."

Alranir laughed, a strange sound coming from him.

"We have had someone following you since Molner."

"Why?"

"Because we were ordered to."

Eryninn knew whose orders they were following.

"Your uncle wants to see you," the elf said.

"I don't care."

Eryninn turned and walked off, but he knew the elf would follow him.

"I cannot order you to come with me," Alranir said, "but you should not refuse a request of your king."

"He is not my king. You made that very clear the last time we met. I am not of your people."

"Then you should not refuse your own family."

"He is not my family, either. My father told me all about my family, and I have no desire to meet any of them."

"You know nothing of what you speak."

"My father told me enough."

Alranir slipped in front of him on the path.

"Your uncle only wants to meet you," he said.

"Half of me, you mean."

"You speak of someone you know nothing about. Have never even met."

"If he's anything like you, I know enough."

"You know even less about me."

"Your disgust for me, for what I am, was plain enough the last time we spoke. Don't try and hide it now because you found out my uncle is the king."

"This is not about what I think of you, nor what you think of your uncle. He only wants to meet you and keep you safe."

"Keep me safe from what?"

"There are things happening on Gondril that you do not know. While you are hidden away in your little village with your human friend, the world is changing right under your feet."

"Give me your message and then go," Eryninn said.

"The Eldest, Kalus, has declared a war on all dragonmages. He has placed a bounty on their heads and the head of their dragons. My people, your people, have offered asylum within our borders, but things will no doubt escalate quickly."

A war on dragonmages? The worry on Eryninn's face must have been painfully obvious.

"Yes, you should be worried," Alranir said. "This Eldest is a terrible beast, unlike any we have seen in Gondril's history. Most of the gold and silver dragons have allied against him and are safely within our realm, but this Kalus still has enough power to rip Gondril apart."

Eryninn shoved past him.

"I have to go."

"You should come with me!" the elf shouted.

"And leave the people I care about to their fate? That may be your way, but it is not mine."

Alranir jogged up beside him.

"You should accept your king's offered hand instead of slapping it away."

"Go home, Alranir. I have to find a way to warn my friends."

Chapter Five

On the Road

Elody's eyes flew open. A buzzing in her head was getting stronger and stronger, and she could no longer keep sleeping and ignore it. She was disoriented for a moment before her head started to clear and her memory returned.

Her spell.

The alarm spell she had cast on the surrounding area outside her little campsite. It was going off in her head, just as she'd cast it. It could have been laid to sound a loud, audible alarm, but at the moment she cast it, Elody had the thought that sounding an alarm wouldn't really be a great way to remain inconspicuous. So she'd opted for the silent alarm that was now magically rattling her brain.

Elody sat up in her uncomfortable bedroll and looked at Jalthrax. He couldn't hear the alarm in her head, but he didn't need it apparently. The dragon was already awake and scanning the trees. The little fire she'd made had burned down to coals, providing very little light, but the moonlight was enough to see by.

Who was it? It could be an animal, but it would have

to be a big one, which didn't give her any comfort. No, it had to be a person. Human? Goddess, not a goblin. She'd had her fill of goblins for one lifetime.

Elody rose slowly to her feet. Who could be out here this late at night? The bandit she'd run into earlier that day? Elody had made her camp far enough off the road that no one would see it, even with the small fire she'd made. But just in case, she'd cast a small spell to mask the light from the fire as well. And just before going to sleep she had set the alarm spell.

Something crackled in the trees.

Whoever it was didn't know about the alarm spell and was still moving closer. Now, at least, she had a direction. Elody reached out to Jalthrax and felt his magic flow to her instantly. She didn't need to pull much for the spell she was casting, and the hand motions were simple and quick. She finished casting and flung her hand out into the woods.

A flash and a bang went off in the trees just outside her camp.

"Ow!" she heard someone, a man, say.

Elody was running then, with Jalthrax right behind her. The spell would only stun the man for a moment, whoever he was. If it was the bandit, she decided right then that she'd feed him to Jalthrax. He was moving slightly, trying to turn over on the ground directly ahead of her. Elody ran and stood above him, Jalthrax just peering under her arm.

It wasn't the bandit. It wasn't anyone she would have expected to see.

"Eliath?" she said.

Elody couldn't believe her eyes, and actually rubbed them to make sure she was awake. She drew just a pinch of magic from Jalthrax and swirled her hand up, cupping it to her as a flame leapt to life. It provided just enough light to see that she wasn't crazy.

It was Eliath.

"Hi," he said, shielding his eyes from the flame. "You didn't have to hit me."

"You were sneaking around my camp! I thought you were a bandit!"

"Well, I could have been. Then what would you do?"

Elody pulled her shoulders up and put her free hand on her hip. Eliath tried to rise, but she was standing over him. She and Jalthrax backed off to let him up.

"What are you doing here?" she asked.

"I came to find you," he said.

"I didn't know I was lost."

"Not like that. I came to make sure you were okay."

"Why wouldn't I be okay?"

She was being too defensive, but she couldn't help it. Eliath was the last person in the world she expected to see out here. In truth, she thought she may never see him again after she left. It had been a month since they'd last spoken, and it hadn't ended well.

"I…" he started, "I just wanted to find you. To make sure you were okay."

"Well, you found me."

She spun on her heels and marched back to her camp. She threw the flame from her hand into the campfire, lighting up the rest of the camp. The magical flame didn't actually burn, it only produced light, but it was early summer. There was no need for extra heat.

Jalthrax stood next to her as they waited for Eliath. She had told the dragon to stay in his donkey form, but after much snorting and other unfortunate noises, she had relented and let him sleep in his true form. He would probably do it anyway once she was asleep.

Eliath shuffled in after them and stopped just outside the firelight. He leaned against a tree and waited with his head down.

"Why are you here, Eliath?"

"Because I needed to find you."

She waited.

"Herlin told me you came looking for me at the Roost."

"I did. He said you weren't there, but I didn't believe him."

"I wasn't there."

"I just thought you must be passed out drunk somewhere."

Eliath winced, and she felt a brief moment of regret.

"Well, I wasn't," he said.

"I just wanted to tell you goodbye. You didn't have to follow me all the way out here for that."

"Look, I wanted... I just wanted to say I'm sorry for how I acted the last time I saw you."

Elody looked down, her hand falling to Jalthrax's neck.

"You said you wanted me to leave you alone and never come back."

"I did say that," he said. "I was drunk and stupid and out of my head."

"You were very clear to me."

"I'm sorry, El. I can't... I can't explain how it's been for me since..."

"I know," she said.

"No, you don't. And I hope you never do. I couldn't bear that for you."

Elody walked over and sat down on her bedroll. It was all coming back now, and she was finding it hard to stand. Sadness and tears she'd let go of months ago when she finally let go of him. Let him sink into his drunken pit, knowing full well that he would probably never emerge. She had let Eliath go because she couldn't watch what was left of his life.

And now here he was, in front of her, apologizing. She didn't know what to think or do. He hadn't been drinking, that was obvious. Too many times since Molner she had seen him drunk, and she knew all too well what that looked like. Not that she blamed him. The thought alone of losing Jalthrax the way Eliath lost Tark would bring a quiver to her throat. She couldn't even imagine it.

She had watched Tark die right in front of her. She wasn't going to watch Eliath do the same. He told her to never come back, and she said her goodbyes to him. That was more than a month ago, and she'd cried almost every night for a week after. Now she felt all of that coming back again.

"I can't," she whispered. "I can't be there for you."

"I'm here for *you*," he said.

"The best thing you can do for me is to just go back to Havnor."

"I'm better now, El. I stopped drinking after we... after you left. Someone offered me some help, and I took it."

"I offered you help dozens of time."

"I know," he said. "I wasn't ready for help then. But now I want to help you."

How could she let him back in? Some part of her, the smaller part, was screaming for him to leave. Turn around and go back to Havnor and leave her be. But the other part wanted to believe him.

"How can you help me?" she asked.

"I want to go with you."

Elody laughed, snuffling a little.

"I don't even know where I'm going."

"Well, wherever you go, I go too."

"Why now, Eliath? Why not any of the hundreds of times before? I came to see you every day since Molner. Every day I went in to find you passed out in bed or sometimes worse."

"I remember."

"Why now?"

"Because I need to do something with my life."

"I can't be your something, Eliath."

"That's not what I meant. Someone came and helped me see how foolish I was being."

"Who?"

"A man named Selex from the conclave."

"Someone from the conclave came to see you?"

"I was surprised too."

Even when Eliath was a dragonmage, he rarely spoke with the mages of the conclave. Tark was a red dragon, which made Eliath a dark dragonmage in the eyes of the conclave. They would barely give the two of them a thought when Tark was alive, and she found it hard to believe they would come to him now that he was no longer even a dragonmage.

"Why?" she asked.

"The conclave has been paying for my living expenses ever since Molner. Something they said they do for neutered... for mages who've lost their dragon. Said they would take care of me because of Tark's bravery in the battle."

Eliath tried to speak, but nothing would come. A single tear ran down his cheek. Elody wanted to leap up and run to him, to hold him. But just as quickly as it came, he brushed the tear away, cleared his throat, and kept going.

"They've been paying for food and my room at the Roost ever since, but I didn't care. I only wanted to drink myself to death, and I was happy to do it on their coin. I wanted to die, and I didn't care who paid for it."

Now it was Elody's turn to hold back the pain again.

"I was close to doing it too," he said. "A few days after I last saw you, a man from the conclave came to see me. We talked. For hours it seemed. He told me about how he had lost his dragon many years ago, but he'd made a life for himself, and now he sat on the conclave."

Eliath walked over and sat down next to her. Jalthrax was breathing loudly where he had already fallen back asleep. The conversation wasn't stimulating enough to keep him awake it seemed.

"He said that I could still have a life as a mage. Mages like your master Cythyil were very important to the conclave even though they had no dragon."

"He wants you to teach?"

Eliath laughed.

"Can you imagine that?" he said.

"I seem to recall you being a pretty good teacher," she said.

"Well, I asked about that, and he said not at first. But there are things that I could do. The mages need any help that's offered right now."

"Then what are you doing here?"

He smiled.

"Protecting you," he said.

Elody was about to protest, loudly, when Jalthrax's head shot up and looked into the forest. She heard a crack of wood, and she and Eliath both turned at the sound. She hadn't reset her alarm spell.

A roar cut through the silence of the night as something charged.

***

Elody didn't have time to prepare a spell. Eliath's hands were already moving. Jalthrax was standing up, but before any of them could react, a man burst through the brush and into camp.

"Stop!" Elody yelled.

She grabbed Eliath's arm, breaking his concentration and costing him the spell he was casting. To one side of her, she heard Jalthrax suck a deep breath.

"No, Thrax, it's Rinn!"

Jalthrax deflated a little and then puffed a blast of cold air in Rinn's stunned face. He looked around, obviously a bit confused by the scene in front of him. His eyes went from Elody, to Eliath, and then back to Elody.

"What is going on here?" he shouted.

"What are you doing here, Rinn?" Elody asked.

"I was coming after you!"

"I thought I remembered telling you *not* to follow me."

"I wanted to make sure you were safe. I heard about the declaration of war and couldn't let you be out here alone. I didn't know you'd already arranged a traveling companion."

"Eliath is *not* my traveling compan — wait, what declaration of war?"

"The Eldest," Eliath said. "Kalus has declared open

war on all dragonmages."

Elody's mouth hung open as she turned to stare at him.

"When were you going to tell me this?"

"We had other matters to discuss first."

"Wait," Rinn said, "how did you know? I only just found out."

"I was praying at the Goddess's temple when I overheard a messenger," Eliath said.

"So you ran off after Elody?" Rinn said.

"What did you do when you found out?"

"I... ran off after Elody."

"Wait a minute," Elody said. "Tell me what's happened. You two are both talking at once, and I don't understand."

"The Eldest has declared war on dragonmages," Eliath said.

"Dragons are now ordered to kill mages and their bonded dragons on sight," Rinn said.

"He's ordered dragons to kill other dragons?" Elody asked, stunned.

"If they are bonded to a mage, or they oppose his law, yes."

Elody tried to find words, but none would come.

"When I heard the news," Eliath said, "I came riding after you."

"How did you know where she was going?" Rinn asked.

"She told Herlin before she left this morning, and he gave me the message. I wanted to protect her."

"That's my job," Rinn said.

That snapped her out of it.

"It is not the job of either of you to protect *her*," she

said. "*She* can protect *herself* just fine."

Jalthrax huffed and nodded.

"I thank you for delivering the news, now both of you go home."

Eliath and Rinn crossed their arms so fast, and at the same moment, that they could have been twins. Stubborn, petulant twin boys. Elody crossed her arms right back at them.

"I will be fine on my own," she said.

"Why won't you let me come with you?" Rinn asked.

"Oh, you want to come with me? All I hear is how you want to *protect* me."

"What is the difference?" Eliath asked.

"If you want to join me, then join me. We can work together, but I am not looking for a bodyguard."

"May I join you then?" Rinn asked.

She tried to maintain her angry pose, but the thought of having Rinn beside her again made her feel... safe. She threw her arms around him.

"I thought you'd never ask."

"May I join you as well?" Eliath asked.

That one she wasn't so sure about. Elody stepped back and looked Eliath up and down. He did look better. Cleaner, and sober. But it was hard for her to let go of the hurt he'd caused. Months and months of him yelling and crying at her in rage after drunken rage had left her heart hardened.

"I don't know," she said at last.

"Go back to Havnor," Rinn said. "You can't do anything to help."

Eliath took a deep breath and shook his hands out.

"Don't," Elody said. "If you're going to come along, I'm not going to listen to you two boys fight the whole time."

"You're letting him come?" Rinn asked, incredulous.

"I can't very well stop him from following us, so he might as well ride with us."

"We don't even know what he's doing here!"

"I told you. I was praying when the messenger came rushing in from Baglund with the news."

Elody felt her stomach drop.

"What… what news from Baglund?"

"El, I'm sorry," Rinn said, taking her by the shoulders. "They… destroyed the school."

"They who?"

"The dragons. The ones loyal to Kalus."

"What about the students? What about Master Cythyil?"

"I'm sorry, El."

Her legs went numb. Only Rinn holding onto her shoulders kept her from falling.

"When?" she whispered.

"Three days ago," Eliath said. "The news was slow from Baglund. Everyone was afraid to leave their homes."

Her teacher. Her friends. Friends she had spent years with, many ready to receive dragons of their own. All dead.

"Why?" she asked, trying to hold back the tears.

"The Eldest claimed Master Cythyil was stealing eggs from dragons," Rinn said.

Elody couldn't stand any longer. Rinn held her as she sank to the ground. How could they do this? A war against dragonmages? A war against their own kind? Like the other mages, Elody had believed that in time the new Eldest would rescind his law and find a way to make peace between dragons and mages. She never expected something like this.

Elody cleared her throat.

"What do we do now?"

"The elves have offered refuge to all mages within their borders," Rinn said.

"Well, that's on my way as far as I know."

"What do you mean?" Eliath asked.

"Jalthrax has been telling me to go west. The elves are west. That's why I was going to Derne."

"I thought you wanted to say goodbye to Berym," Rinn said.

"I do. But Eryninn is there as well, and I need his help to get through the elven lands."

"Why through them?" Eliath asked. "It sounds like we should get there and stay there until this thing is over."

Elody looked at him, wiping the tears from her cheeks.

"Do you think this will just be over some day?"

Eliath started to say something but then just shrugged.

"Kalus is not going to just let this end. He has a plan, and whatever it is, it's not going to end well for us or for Gondril."

"We don't know what will happen," Eliath said.

"He started a war," Elody said. "He killed children and unborn dragons."

"Then we go west," Rinn said. "Keep going west until we reach the elves. The faster the better."

Elody looked at Jalthrax and nodded.

West.

They would keep going west.

CHAPTER SIX

GOBLIN ATTACK

ELODY COULDN'T DECIDE whether she liked this new arrangement or not. On the one hand she wasn't alone anymore, and she now had two people to talk to. On the other hand, the two people she had to talk to didn't really like talking to each other, and each of them went to great effort to let the other one know it.

She wasn't alone though.

Not that she was ever truly alone. Jalthrax was always there with her, and he always would be. Elody hadn't truly felt alone since the day they were bonded. Even when he was far away, she felt a bit of him inside her somewhere. If something happened to him, she would know it instantly. He was always there with her.

He just wasn't much of a talker. Yet.

It would be maybe another year before Jalthrax developed the vocal chords to speak her language, and Elody could hardly wait. She had spoken to dragons many times in her life, and it thrilled her each time. And Jalthrax would always be there to talk to. Plus she didn't really care for his current method of communication, which was to blow freezing cold air in her face.

That was the only good thing about him being a donkey. Though he did seem to huff quite a bit more in this form. But he couldn't outdo the huffing from her new companions. Rinn and Eliath both rode horses beside her little wagon, one in front of the other. Several times already they had played this silent game of getting in front of the other.

Why did men always have to try and lead?

Elody clicked her tongue to speed up and received a glare from Jalthrax. He wasn't going to go any faster, and he made that very clear by slowing down. Rinn kicked his heels in and pulled in front of Eliath again, forcing him to slow down to keep from running into Rinn.

"Stop it," Elody said.

Both looked at her with wide-eyed innocence.

"Both of you," she said. "You know exactly what you're doing."

"I know the way to Derne," Rinn said. "I was just taking the lead."

"I know the way as well," Eliath said. "I have been all over Gondril, from shore to shore and back again. I know my way around quite well."

Rinn scoffed.

"*You two* are along for the ride," Elody said. "I know where I'm going just fine without either of you, so you can both behave, or I'll put you in back behind the wagon."

Rinn started to protest, but a snort from Jalthrax hit him in the face and cut him off. He pulled on the reins a little and let his horse fall back in line beside Eliath. Now they were riding side by side and glaring at each other. Maybe that wasn't such a good plan after all. It did get Jalthrax moving a little faster though. Males liked to be in front no matter the race, it seemed.

"So where are we headed?" Eliath asked.

"To Derne," Elody said, "and then I'm not sure."

"You're not sure? Then why are you going?"

"Because that's where Jalthrax says we need to go."

Eliath looked at the donkey who glared back at him. He was normally a happy dragon, easygoing and playful, but not this journey. Usually he would be flying high through the sky and hunting. Being a donkey afforded no such opportunities. Elody was beginning to dread this trip.

"West of Derne is nothing but forest and mountains," Eliath said. "How far are we going?"

"*I* am going as far as I need to go. You are going as far as Derne, and then we'll see."

Rinn chuckled.

"You too, Rinn," she said.

"Well, I'm not going home now. Aunt Jelena is going to kill me."

Elody was about to say that he should have just stayed home, but something above caught her attention. She looked up, wondering, hoping it was a bird. It wasn't a bird.

A dark shadow covered them as a dragon flew low across the treetops and then made a path that followed the road. It went right over their heads, slowing as it did, and Elody got a good look at its belly. A brass dragon. Elody felt the reins pull as Jalthrax tensed.

"Whoa," she whispered. "Take it easy, Thrax. Everyone just stay calm."

Rinn and Eliath were tense too. Elody silently hoped the dragon wouldn't come down for a closer look. They were just travelers on the road, one cart and two horses among many, but they weren't doing a good job of hiding their true feelings.

Everyone breathed a sigh of relief when the dragon picked up speed and flew along down the road. Toward Derne maybe? Elody hoped not, though she didn't think there were any dragonmages in the village. She wished, not for the first time, that she were strong enough to cast a sending spell to warn Berym. Did he even know there was a war going on? Surely the knighthood would have delivered a message by now.

"What do you think it was looking for?" Rinn asked.

"Us," Eliath said. "Well, Elody and Jalthrax anyway."

"Might have been bonded," Elody said.

"Maybe," Eliath said, "but it seems likely that a solo dragon out this far is one hunting on the Eldest's orders."

The Eldest. Kalus. The name gave Elody a shudder. Everything about the new Eldest was troubling, even before he had started this insane war against dragonmages. The laws he had made gave no room for interpretation. Kalus hated dragonmages and wanted them gone. She just never thought he would go to these extremes.

"Why is Kalus doing this?" Elody asked.

"No one knows for sure," Eliath said. "He's said to be over a thousand years old. Maybe he's lost his mind with age."

"Why would they make him Eldest?" Rinn asked.

"Because he is the oldest living gold," Elody said. "Did you study at all when you were in school?"

"Some," Rinn said. "I had other things on my mind."

Rinn and Eliath shared a little smile but then quickly went back to scowling at each other.

"When an Eldest dies," Elody quoted, "by Anarr's decree, the oldest gold dragon on Gondril becomes the new Eldest."

"Yes, but what if that gold is a loon?" Rinn said.

"I don't think there's room for interpretation where the decree of a god is concerned," Eliath said.

"He's destroying everything," Elody said softly.

"A thousand years of peace and bonding between man and dragon," Eliath said. "He may have even been alive during the wizard wars. All those deaths, on both sides."

"But that was a war against wizards," Rinn said.

He and Elody shared a sideways glance. Eliath didn't know anything about Aunt Jelena or that she was a wizard and was training Rinn. Elody knew Eliath well enough to know that it wouldn't bother him, but it still wasn't something you went around telling everyone.

"And what has happened to dragons since the wizards were wiped out?" Eliath asked.

"They've grown more powerful," Elody said.

"More than just powerful," Eliath said. "They've grown to be the most powerful creatures on Gondril."

"They always were," Rinn said.

"Yes, but the wizards had powerful, powerful magic. Magic they could pull from the very fabric of Gondril, the song I've heard it called."

Rinn chuckled. Elody had learned a bit about wizardry, but Rinn had been studying for months. No doubt he wanted to show off his knowledge and put Eliath in his place, but Elody was amazed to see him purse his lips and keep his mouth shut.

"Some wizards became very famous as dragon hunters," Eliath continued. "Even the oldest of dragons could be killed by a single wizard if he had enough magic. Now that they're all but wiped out, there is no one left to oppose the dragons."

"Is that what he's doing?" Rinn asked. "Trying to take over Gondril?"

"I don't know," Eliath said. "But it seems that way."

"But a war is going to cost lives," Elody said.

"Yes, but which side will lose the most?" Eliath asked.

Elody knew the answer. They all knew the answer.

Jalthrax stiffened and came to a stop. Rinn and Eliath rode a few steps ahead but then noticed and stopped as well.

"What is it?" Elody asked.

Jalthrax lifted his head and sniffed the air. He looked back at her, a silent question in his eyes.

"No," Elody said. "We can't risk it. That dragon just flew over minutes ago, and he might still be around."

He wanted to change into his true form. He must have caught the scent of something, but his senses weren't as keen as a donkey. Jalthrax lifted his head again and snorted before walking on.

"What is it?" Rinn asked.

"I don't know," Elody said. "He caught a whiff of something maybe?"

"Lots of people on the road," Eliath said. "Maybe that dragon stopped up ahead and is waiting for us."

Elody looked around from side to side, scanning the trees for sign of trouble. The dragon was big enough that he couldn't just hide somewhere. Brass dragons couldn't change form the way some of the dragons of light could, so she knew he couldn't be hiding in another form. But what if it was something else?

She got her answer soon enough.

Rinn and Eliath both moved in front of the wagon

and scouted ahead. They each took one side of the road and looked into the trees and bushes as they passed. Elody was so intent watching them that she didn't see the attack coming.

Jalthrax lifted his head again and then started backpedaling as something burst from both sides of the road and came at the wagon. Elody was up in a second, her training filling her mind instantly. Her hands were already moving before she even got a clear look at her attackers.

Goblins.

Lots of goblins.

Elody held the magic in her hands and weaved desperately, trying to complete a spell when she felt them around her. A quick shove, and she was falling. She yelped as she went tumbling from the wagon and hit the ground hard.

"Elody!" Rinn shouted.

She heard them coming, but the pain and fear wouldn't let her open her eyes. All around her she could hear scrambling feet. Someone kicked her in the stomach. She curled into a ball and tried to scream. Another kick hit her back. Elody cried out.

The wagon creaked and rocked beside her. She heard Jalthrax the donkey scream. Then the familiar popping and snapping sound. She wanted to cry out, to stop him, but another kick stopped her.

"Keep girl, kill rest!" she heard someone shout.

The goblins laughed. Someone grabbed her, and she felt something being wrapped around her legs. Elody dared a look and saw she was surrounded. Maybe a dozen or more goblins around her. A roar cut through the air.

Jalthrax.

He was in his true form now. His roar sounded bigger and louder than Elody had ever heard it, and it had the intended effect on the goblins.

"Stay down!" Eliath shouted from somewhere.

She heard a crackling sound followed by screams. Goblin screams. Then she heard Jalthrax suck in a large breath. Elody rolled to the side. Her legs were bound, and someone was reaching for her hands, so that was all she could do. She spun her body and rolled under the wagon with only a second to spare.

Jalthrax's frost breath blew out in a cone of icy destruction. The goblins scrambled, but they couldn't move fast enough. Elody dared a look and saw three, four, then five hit the ground, their frightened faces frozen in death.

The hands that were reaching for her, trying to pull her out, were gone then. She heard the whoosh of fire and saw flames lick the side of the wagon. Two more goblins fell. Then all she saw were feet running away.

"Elody!" Rinn shouted.

"Here," she said. "I'm under here."

Rinn and Eliath's faces appeared as they ducked down to find her. They both reached in and pulled her out. Eliath took the rope around her legs and pulled it off, freeing her.

She looked all around and saw Jalthrax near the trees ready to launch himself into the air.

"No!" she said.

He looked back at her but didn't fold his wings.

"I said no, Thrax."

Jalthrax obeyed and lowered his wings.

"Are you okay?" Eliath asked.

His hands were running over her. She winced every time he grazed her stomach and ribs. She also couldn't suppress the flutter in her heart at his touch.

"Ow," she said as he pressed on her stomach again.

"What hurts?" Rinn asked.

He stepped between the two of them, and Eliath backed away without argument.

"I don't feel anything broken," Eliath said.

Rinn checked over her again and then nodded.

"She's okay," he said.

Elody didn't agree with their assessment. There was blood on her hands where she scraped them on the ground, her chest hurt to breathe, and she felt lightheaded enough that she had to lean against the wagon to keep from falling over.

"I need to lie down," she said.

"Climb into the wagon," Eliath said. "I'll drive it while you rest."

Elody sat up to tell Jalthrax to change back into a donkey, but to her amazement, he was already shifting. It actually made her sad to watch the transformation. To see him go from such a beautiful, silver dragon to a donkey in the blink of an eye. With only a twitch of his long ears, Jalthrax backed up to the wagon and waited to be hitched.

Rinn got Jalthrax settled in while Eliath tied his horse to the back of the wagon. Elody smiled a little, which hurt, when the horse immediately snuck his head under the cloth and started eating the hay hidden beneath. The jostling of the wagon as Eliath climbed in made Elody's head throb. She was about to protest when Eliath snapped the reins, and the wagon started moving.

That made everything worse.

"Don't snap the reins at him," Elody said. "He doesn't like it."

"Sorry, habit."

Elody curled into a ball and clutched her stomach. Everything hurt. She felt lucky to be alive. Good thing the goblins wanted her alive, or she most definitely would not be.

They rode on until Elody couldn't take the pain anymore and then stopped for the night.

***

Elody heard voices. A groan escaped her lips as she rolled to her side, and the voices stopped. Her hand came to rest on something hard and cool. Jalthrax. She could feel the cold air of his breath blowing across her feet with every breath.

It took a minute to remember what happened. Her head was foggy. She remembered stopping to camp and Rinn laying out a bedroll for her. Eliath had said not to light a fire, and that was the last thing she could recall. She must have passed out after that.

When she opened her eyes, it was to deep darkness. A small amount of light shown through the trees from the moon, just enough that she could make out shapes, but that was all.

"How bad is it?"

It was Rinn.

"Not too bad. Maybe a cracked rib."

Eliath.

"Will she be okay?"

"Derne must have a church, probably a priest."

"Father Meral," Rinn said.

"She'll be in pain," Eliath said, "but I don't think there's any danger to her."

Elody wanted to sit up and join the conversation, but she willed herself to remain still and quiet. Rinn and Eliath never got along enough to speak to each other, and certainly never about her. She didn't want to break the moment. Maybe a reminder that they both cared for her would help smooth things over between them.

"I can probably find some herbs in the morning. My aunt taught me a tea we can brew for the pain."

Eliath chuckled.

"Taking up the life of a witch?"

Rinn stuttered something but then stopped.

"She's just been teaching me potions and herbs. I help her out."

"Sounds exciting."

"Well, without a dragon, I guess I have to find something else to do with my life."

Elody winced. Maybe it wasn't such a good idea for them to talk.

"You never had a dragon," Eliath said.

"No, not like you, but I still feel the loss."

"You can't imagine what this feels like."

"I don't guess I can."

Minutes passed in darkness and silence. Elody almost closed her eyes to go back to sleep.

"How did you cast that lightning bolt back there?" Rinn asked.

"The same way you cast your flaming hands spell. With my own magic."

"Yes, but I don't have enough to cast a spell that powerful."

"I have more magic than you."

"I can see that, but how?"

"I don't know. Some people have more power than

others."

"But I've been practicing drawing my own magic for years. You've only been doing it a few months, if that."

"I was a dragonmage for over sixteen years. You don't think I learned to cast my own magic in that time?"

"I thought you would have just used Tark's."

Elody winced again at the mention of Tark, and a bit of sadness crept into her heart. The silence from Eliath told her he felt the impact of hearing the name too.

"A dragonmage still has to use his own magic sometimes," Eliath said at last. "The more you use it, the bigger the well is."

"Mine has grown a little, but not as much as yours."

"Then you have only used it a little."

"My aunt is always telling me not to use it at all."

"Why?"

"Because mixing my own magic with the song can create unintended consequences."

"The song?"

Rinn was talking too much. Elody forced herself to sit up, eliciting a yelp of pain. Jalthrax woke and lifted his head, and Rinn was at her side in an instant.

"Hey there," he said. "How are you feeling?"

"Like a tribe of goblins kicked me in the stomach."

Rinn forced a laugh and helped her sit up.

"I'm going to go see if I can find some herbs to make you something for the pain."

Rinn flicked his wrist and cupped his hand where a small flame appeared.

"I'll be back as soon as I can."

He turned to Eliath.

"Can you get a small fire going?"

"It's not safe," Eliath said.

"I need something to brew the tea."

Eliath thought for a moment and nodded. Rinn went off in search of herbs, and Elody laid back down to wait. Her hand fell to Jalthrax and unconsciously stroked his neck. Within minutes, Eliath was back with wood and had a small fire going. Elody looked at him, and they both just stared for a moment. He looked down to where she was petting Jalthrax, and she removed her hand.

"Don't stop," Eliath said. "Tark loved it when I rubbed his neck."

"How could you even reach his neck? His neck was taller than I am."

Eliath chuckled.

"It wasn't easy when he got bigger, but we managed. I would lean against him and just rub against one spot. He had one scale, right at his shoulder, that was darker than the others. That was my spot."

Elody smiled, but in the low firelight she could see Eliath turn away. She wanted to reach out, to touch him, to hold him. But they had been here before, and he would only push her away again. The silence dragged on until Elody couldn't stand it.

"I'm sorry I ran away," he finally said.

"You… you did what you needed to do."

"I drank myself stupid, that's all I did."

"Then that's what you needed to do."

"It was all I knew to do. It was the only thing that could make the pain go away. When I slept, I didn't have to think about… about what I lost."

Elody stroked Jalthrax's neck again and looked down at him. He raised his head and met her eyes, and she saw his sadness as well. He couldn't speak yet, but he understood everything.

"I tried to be there for you," Elody said at last.

"I know you did."

"I came to see you every day for months."

"I know."

"I can't do that again, Eliath."

"You don't have to. I promise you."

She wanted to believe him. She had to believe that he could pull himself through the pain and be whole again. Even if she didn't see how that was possible herself. If she lost Jalthrax...

He moved to stand near her. She reached for him and felt a stabbing pain in her chest again. She winced, and he knelt down in front her, his face level with hers.

"Where does it hurt?" he asked.

She touched her chest and her stomach.

"All over here."

He reached out and touched her chest, feeling around her ribs. He was so close she could feel his breath on her, and it made her shiver.

"Are you cold?"

"No."

He pushed on her ribs, and the pain increased. She yelped.

"Sorry," he said. "Probably cracked, at least a little."

Elody didn't care. The pain was excruciating, but being so close to Eliath again, she could almost forget it all. She leaned close to him, and his head lifted to meet her eyes.

"I got it!" Rinn shouted, stumbling back into camp.

Eliath stood and shuffled back a few steps to lean against a tree.

"They weren't hard to find," Rinn said as he pushed through the brush. "I'll have something brewed up in just a few minutes."

Rinn looked at the two of them and scrunched his eyes.

"Everything all right?"

"Her rib is definitely broken," Eliath said.

"Father Meral can heal her when we reach Derne," Rinn said. "The herbs will help until we get there."

Rinn knelt down and started crushing things into a small pot he pulled from his pack.

"This should help with the pain," he said.

But Elody's pain was lessened already.

CHAPTER SEVEN

DERNE

ELODY'S LITTLE WAGON bounced into Derne late the next day, and she was quite ready to get off of it. The rest of their journey had been uneventful, but the jostling in the back of the wagon had been painful. She was ready to get out and never get back in.

Eliath sat at the front driving Jalthrax the donkey, and the picture made her smile a little every time she looked up. Rinn rode beside her and kept watch over her. She gave him a scolding look a few times, but she had to admit that his herbal tea had done a lot to ease her discomfort. Not entirely, but enough that she no longer felt like crying every time they hit a bump.

"There's nothing left," Eliath whispered.

"What?" she said.

"I've been through Derne a few times over the years, but this is not the Derne I remember."

"Berym said the goblin armies destroyed everything," Rinn said.

"He was right."

They rode on, Eliath doing his best to avoid the holes in the road. As they neared the edge of the village road, some men came from the fields as others joined them from the village. Elody sat up to get a better look. Eliath brought the wagon to a stop.

"Good day," he called.

A man stepped forward and spoke.

"If you're traveling through, the south road is not safe from here. Goblin raids have been frequent."

"Derne is our destination," Eliath said. "Though it is smaller than I remember it."

The people whispered to each other and shifted nervously.

"We have no place to stay, I'm afraid," the man said.

"We are looking for Sir Berym," Elody said. "Or our friend Eryninn."

The people moved aside as a man pushed his way up from the back. Elody recognized the chain armor and the bushy smile immediately.

"Berym!"

She scrambled off the back of the wagon, wincing in pain as she hit the ground, and hobbled over to him.

"Elody!" he cried. "Goddess, what are you doing here?"

He scooped her up in one of his big bear hugs. She laughed, but a squeeze from the older knight was more than she could bear. She cried out in pain, and he set her down and looked at her.

"Are you all right?"

"We were attacked on the road," Rinn said.

Berym looked up at him.

"And Rinn too? Well, this is a surprise!"

Rinn slid out of his saddle and shook the big knight's hand. Elody held her hand to her stomach and tried to smile. She hadn't seen Berym since they left Molner together, and she was happy to have their little reunion. Berym saw her clutching herself and stopped smiling.

"What's this about an attack? Are you hurt?"

"They beat her up pretty badly," Rinn said.

"Call for Father Meral!" Berym shouted.

One of the villagers ran off.

"What happened?" Berym asked.

"Goblins," Rinn said. "A big tribe attacked us about a day's ride outside of Havnor."

The villagers started murmuring amongst themselves, and Elody saw worried looks pass between them all. Berym leaned in closer.

"Let us speak more of this later. For now, let's get you to the hall where you can settle in, and Father Meral can tend to you."

Elody climbed up onto the wagon next to Eliath. She was done laying in the back like a patient. It hurt a little more to sit up front, but she instantly felt better being near Eliath.

They followed Berym and the villagers into the village.

***

Elody winced with every bounce as they followed Berym through the village. A few people came up to greet them and say hello, but Berym was quick to pull them through the crowds. Eventually they all went back to work, some back to the fields, and others back to the rebuilding efforts.

"Where is Jalthrax?" Berym asked. "Flying off somewhere?"

"He's the donkey," Elody said, pointing.

Berym looked wide-eyed at Jalthrax who obliged him with a musty snort.

"He's still learning to control his powers," Elody said.

"Well, he's got the smell down perfectly," Berym said.

Jalthrax craned his neck to bite at Berym but only managed to get his teeth into the knight's chainmail. Berym just laughed and rubbed Jalthrax's neck. Elody had missed his laugh. So big and jovial. Infectious her aunt had called it. When Berym laughed, you simply had to laugh with him.

As they reached the crossroads in the center of town, a portly man in brown robes came rushing from one of the only intact buildings in the village.

"Who is hurt?" he asked, looking around at everyone. "I was told someone had been attacked by goblins."

Elody slid down from the seat and groaned as she hit the ground.

"Where are you hurt, my dear?" he asked.

"My chest, I think."

"She has some broken ribs," Eliath said. "Pretty badly bruised in the stomach as well."

The older man put his hands on her stomach and pushed in slightly, making her cry out.

"I'm sorry," he said. "You will feel better in a moment."

He placed his hand gently on her again and then, with something clutched in his other hand, he began to whisper. Elody couldn't make out what he was saying, but she knew he was praying to the goddess Threyl. She could see a disc of wood clutched in his other hand and knew it would have the engraved tear of the goddess.

Elody's stomach felt warm then. Her breath caught as it spread through her, touching every part of her chest, touching her heart. Elody had never felt the healing touch of a priest until now. Her mother and her aunt were witches and had always tended them when they were little, and by some miracle, she'd never been seriously injured.

The healing power from the priest's hand flowed through her, and instantly her pain was gone. The old priest stopped praying and opened his eyes. He pushed on her chest to check his handiwork and smiled brightly when she didn't recoil.

"There, that should do it," he said.

"Thank you, Father," Berym said. "May we use the church for a bit? We have some things to discuss."

"Of course," Father Meral said.

He led them just down the street to the church. While the rest of the village was mostly plots of charred dirt and ash, the church of Threyl was a solid stone structure that looked brand new. Across from it was a long hall that looked to be made of sticks and mud. Smoke poured from a hole in the roof of the structure, and Elody could smell meat cooking.

Father Meral opened the doors to the church, and they all followed him in.

"Tell me what happened," Berym said.

"A band of goblins ambushed us from both sides," Eliath said.

"Maybe twenty warriors," Rinn added.

"I had heard talk of bandits," Berym said, "but I thought the knighthood had worked to clear any goblins from the West Road."

"Well, they forgot some," Eliath said.

"It is good to see you doing better, Eliath," Berym said. "I had not heard good things."

"There was nothing good to tell," Eliath said. "But I'm better now."

Berym nodded, and Elody saw Rinn shake his head.

"What are you all doing here?" Berym asked. "I certainly did not expect to find you three when I came to see what the commotion was about."

"I came to find Eryninn," Elody said.

"You came for me?"

They all turned to see Eryninn standing to one side of the church door, a smile pasted on his half-elven face. Elody went right over and gave him a big hug, which he returned.

"I need your help," she said.

"I heard about Kalus," Eryninn said.

"What news of the Eldest?" Father Meral asked.

They all talked over each other, but between them all, they managed to get the whole story out.

"When did this happen?" Berym asked. "And how did you know this?"

He looked at Eryninn who only shrugged.

"I hear things," the half-elf said.

Elody went over to stand in front of him.

"I need you to take me west," she said.

"There is nothing west of here. Nothing worth seeing."

"Well, west is where I need to go."

"What is west?" Berym asked.

"I don't know, but that is where Jalthrax says we need to go."

"The lands west of here belong to the the elves."

"I need you to take me through them. Or possibly to them. I don't know yet."

"The elves have offered sanctuary to any dragonmages," Eryninn said. "I can see you safely to them."

"I don't think that's where I'm going," she said.

"That is where you *should* go," Eryninn said. "It is not safe here or anywhere on Gondril right now. Not for you and Jalthrax."

"Then you'll take me?"

Eryninn sighed and then nodded.

"I will take you. But I am not staying. I will get you as far as within the borders. I have some friends who can take you the rest of the way."

Elody hugged him again.

"Thank you," she whispered.

"Don't thank me yet. You'll find the elves, while offering refuge, are not known for their hospitality toward humans."

Elody saw the others in a quiet conversation of their own and turned to join them when a shout from outside broke everything up. Father Meral headed for the door when a man burst in.

"Dragons," he said.

They all exchanged a worried look.

"We have seen them flying overhead all day," Berym said. "Now we know why."

Other villagers poured through the door and formed a group.

"If your friends are in any kind of trouble, we need them gone," a man said to Berym.

"We must hide them," Berym said.

"Why?" another man asked. "What business is it of ours?"

"We will not turn out those who need help," Berym said.

Another man poked his head through the door.

"It's coming around again!"

"We have to get Jalthrax inside," Elody said.

Elody ran for the door and returned a moment later with Jalthrax, still a donkey, in tow.

"There's a basement you can all hide in," Father Meral said.

Jalthrax began to shift, and before Elody could stop him, he stood and stretched the wings of his true form. All twenty feet of his wings. Then he tucked them back against his side and stretched his long, silver neck.

"What is this about?" one of the villagers asked Berym.

"The dragons are at war with dragonmages," Eryninn said bluntly. "We have to protect her, or that dragon will probably kill her."

"And what of us?" one of the women asked. "What if he attacks us for hiding her? We can't risk that!"

"Get them to the basement," was all Father Meral said. "Close the doors up tight and bolt them from the inside. I will do my best to conceal them."

The villagers looked ready to protest again, but Berym was already marching for the door.

"Stay in here if you must," he said to the villagers, "but stay silent."

Berym and Eryninn marched outside while Father Meral ushered them all down through a trapdoor in the floor of the main altar room. Jalthrax had to tuck in tightly to get through, but he managed to get down the stairs with some grace. He was far more agile in his true form than that of a donkey.

"Stay quiet and do not open the door no matter what," Father Meral said.

The door swung closed, and they were enveloped in darkness.

"No lights," Elody said, as much to herself as to the others.

"Did anyone say what kind of dragon it was?" Eliath asked.

"No," Rinn said.

They waited in silence. Elody slowly stroked Jalthrax's neck, occasionally brushing against Eliath's hand as he did the same. The darkness was unsettling. The basement was quite large, but they all still huddled together near the door. No one wanted to stray too far from each other, least of all Elody. The only sound they could hear was their own breathing, Jalthrax's most of all.

Minutes passed in silence.

Finally, there was a knock on the trapdoor.

"It's all right," they heard Father Meral say in a muffled voice.

The door opened from the other side. Berym and Father Meral were there to help them out of the cellar, Jalthrax coming up last and straining the wooden stairs under his claws.

"He was looking for dragonmages," Berym said. "We told him our village did not have one."

"What did he do?" Rinn asked.

"He poked around for a bit and then left in a hurry."

"What kind?" Eliath asked.

"A brass," Eryninn said as he came inside. "He's gone. I watched him until I could no longer see him, which is a considerable distance."

Elody sighed.

"What do we do now?" she asked.

"We go west," Eryninn said. "And fast. I will take you to the elves."

Rinn and Eliath were back on their horses in no time.

Elody opted to ride Jalthrax as a donkey. It may not have been glamorous, but if they were going to be moving fast, it wouldn't do to be pulling a wagon.

She stepped close to Berym and gave him a big hug, one he returned with his crushing strength, but Elody was glad to feel it this time.

"Stay safe," he whispered.

"I have Eryninn to keep me safe," she said.

"Yes, but who will keep him safe without me?"

"You could come with us," she said.

"My place is here," he said. "Just be careful."

She squeezed him again, and then he helped her onto Jalthrax's back. Eryninn had saddled a horse as well, and with a kick of his heels, he sped off west into the forest. Even though he was a donkey and not a horse, Jalthrax had no trouble keeping up with everyone else.

As fast as they could, they raced for the elven lands.

Chapter Eight

The Crystal

CYTHYIL CRIED OUT in pain as his broken body hit the ground. He tried to move, to stand up, but all he could do was lie there, his cheek pressed against the warm stone beneath him. His eyes opened slowly, and he looked around.

They were on an island, he remembered that much from the air. Some distance away he saw a single mountain stretching high into the sky. A long plume of smoke wound its way out of the top, reaching even higher. They had flown for almost a week it seemed. Where on Gondril were they?

The stone beneath him was polished, not natural. Cythyil moved his head slightly, just enough to see more of his surroundings, and the stone went on as far as he could make out. Out of the corner of his eye, he saw Kalus, still in his human form, standing near Vaylin, now a bronze dragon.

There was no way out.

The whole flight here, maybe a week or more, he couldn't remember, Cythyil had tried to come up with a plan to free himself. When they stopped outside of

Havnor for one night, he'd tried to run for it. After that, Kalus had made sure he couldn't run. The steady beatings had broken his body and his spirit. He was dead already, he knew it.

"Get up," Kalus said from behind him.

"I… I can't."

"You want to end up like him?"

He saw Kalus's finger point at something out of his sight and lifted his head just enough to see. It was a body. A headless corpse lying about ten feet away. The head was a few feet away from the rest of the body.

"Velanon outlived his usefulness," Kalus said. "You help me, and you may avoid joining him."

Velanon. Cythyil knew the name well. It was the name of the wizard who had hunted the dragon mothers for months, killing so many of his friends. He had heard that the wizard was killed, but that was over five months ago. The body before him looked as though it might have just been killed yesterday. The soulless eyes of the pristine head stared into him.

"I… am not a wizard," Cythyil said, his words halting and slow. "I cannot help you."

"Oh, you can help me. And if you do, there might be something more than your life in it for you."

Kalus pointed again, and Cythyil tried hard to focus his eyes and follow him. When at last he saw it, his breath stopped cold. Kalus was pointing to a small, pink crystal lying off to the side. Cythyil's eyes fixed on it. He knew instantly what it was.

The dragonbane crystal.

Possibly the last one on Gondril. One of the most powerful artifacts ever made, the elves had crafted the dragonbane crystals to protect them from evil dragons.

But they were also imbued with a more sinister power. They could destroy a dragon, any dragon, with nothing but a thought.

That was his way out.

He looked down at his hands, broken and bloody. He could barely close his fingers they were so badly crushed. For days he had felt nothing but pain. But now he felt a glimmer of hope.

"What... do you want from me?"

"I want you to pick up that crystal, if you can, and then I want you to do as I say. You follow orders, and you may just live to count another day."

Now it was all clear. He had fed him and given him water, enough to stay alive, enough to get him here. Kalus had taken him from the school, but not before making him watch as he and Vaylin killed his students. His children. Everyone killed except for him, and now he knew why. Kalus could not touch the crystal himself, it would destroy him.

"Pick it up," Kalus said.

"I won't help you," Cythyil said.

He had to play this right. If he was too eager, Kalus might kill him right here and now and never give him the chance to get to the crystal. Even if he did get his hands on it, he might end up dead. The crystal was said to be powerful enough to destroy its wielder if they weren't strong enough to control it. Still, it was his only chance.

"You help me, and I will help you," Kalus said.

"You have nothing I want."

"Oh? What about your precious school?"

"You... you murdered everyone."

"Yes, but the school is still there. What if your school

were the only place on all of Gondril that could train and bond dragonmages. I can make that happen for you."

Lies. It was all lies, but Cythyil didn't care. He was only playing at resisting.

"I can heal you," Kalus said. "I can take away all of your pain in an instant."

Cythyil wanted to cry. He would give almost anything to make the pain go away. But it would cost him his soul.

"Or," Kalus said, "you can die a very slow and painful death right here. If you think I hurt you in the last week, you have no idea what I'm capable of."

Cythyil pushed himself up and got his knees under him. He sat there, on all fours, for what felt like minutes before he could speak.

"If I help you," he said, "I want my school back."

"Done."

"And I want my pick of dragon eggs from any mothers of my choosing."

"Well, I have no control over the dark dragons, but I'll do what I can. Done."

"And I want to be healed."

"After you have the crystal," Kalus said.

Cythyil pushed through his pain and managed to stand. It was excruciating. His knees trembled, trying desperately to keep him upright. Every breath was punctuated by a stabbing pain, no doubt from a broken rib. His hands were so swollen he could barely close his fingers.

One step at a time.

He shuffled one foot forward and then the other, not even lifting them from the ground. The stone in the circle, he now saw he was in some great circle, was even enough that it made the going easier. Slowly, inch by inch, he tried to reach the crystal.

Kalus was tense, watching his every move. Cythyil could feel his eyes boring into him with every step. And then he was there. His toe nudged the little crystal, and he took a deep breath to steady himself. Soon he would be free.

Cythyil bent down and snatched the crystal up. His whole world went dark. His mind went blank, and he felt something eating at his thoughts, trying to worm its way into his mind. This was the power of the crystal, he knew. He pushed back, forcing it out, trying to wrest back control. The darkness receded. Cythyil opened his eyes and saw Kalus smiling.

The dragonbane crystal was his.

"Excellent!" Kalus shouted. "I had a feeling you would be strong enough. Not like the others."

Kalus jerked a finger to the side, and Cythyil looked over to see three other corpses, all as pristine as Velanon's, in a pile. His stomach felt sick.

"Now let's be off. We have some work to do to get that school of yours back up and running."

Cythyil laughed. He laughed so hard he thought he might fall over, but he held himself up. He stood strong and laughed in Kalus's frowning face.

"You do as you're told," Kalus said, "and we can all get what we want here."

"You can't touch me!" Cythyil shouted. "You think I don't know what this is? You think I don't know what it can do?"

"I think you don't know as much as you think you do."

"So long as I hold it, you cannot harm me, dragon."

Cythyil held up a finger and smiled.

"But I can harm you."

"You'll be dead before you can try," Kalus said. "You live up to your end of the bargain, and I'll live up to mine."

Cythyil wasn't listening anymore. He closed his eyes and pushed his thoughts into the crystal, just as it had tried to do to him. Only now he was the one in control. He knew nothing of how to use the crystal, but he knew what it could do. What kind of power it held.

The stories had spread far and wide after the Battle of Molner. How the wizard Velanon had used the dragonbane crystal to destroy the previous Eldest without a word. A single thought was all it had taken to destroy the most powerful dragon on Gondril. And now Cythyil would to do it again.

Somewhere in the distance he heard someone speaking. Kalus was yelling at him, but it sounded as though he was shouting underwater. Then he heard something else entirely. A song. Someone was singing nearby. Cythyil ignored it and pushed deeper into the crystal.

He didn't even feel the lightning bolt hit him.

As his mind separated from the crystal, his eyes blinked open, and he found himself flying through the air. He landed with a thud several feet from where he was just standing, the air forced from his lungs by the hit. Cythyil struggled to breathe, to draw even a single breath. But even as he did, he became aware of the real danger.

The crystal was gone.

It must have flown from his hand when he was hit. He looked around frantically trying to find it. He saw it there, lying a few feet away, but his body wouldn't heed his call to move. He hadn't felt the lightning as it hit him, so lost was he in the crystal, but he felt the pain of it now. His body was finished, unable to even raise his arms.

Then he heard another sound. One he was very familiar with. A sound he'd heard many times in his former life. Bones snapped and cracked, skin stretched tight as it grew and pulled itself into a new shape. Cythyil just managed to open his eyes to see Kalus finish his transformation.

The Eldest towered above him in all his golden glory. Kalus was massive in his true form, as big a dragon as Cythyil had ever seen. He stood over him looking down. Cythyil never imagined that his life would end at the hands of a gold dragon. He had spent his life serving beside them, working together to better all of Gondril.

"Who knows," Kalus said. "I might have actually kept my promise."

The dragon leaned his head down, his jaws open wide.

"I guess we'll never know now."

CHAPTER NINE

JOURNEY

GORTOGH CHECKED HIS traveling gear for the dozenth time, not really sure why he was checking. He only owned a handful of things, and all of them were on him now. He had spent a few days gathering food for his journey. Some nuts and berries from the surrounding forest as well as breads and smoked meats stolen from the nearby goblins. He felt bad about stealing but comforted himself knowing that Kurgh would just summon more food if they needed it.

He was ready to go.

Gortogh marched out of his little cave, hoping it was the last time. Picking his way down the mountain trail, he breathed easy for the first time in what seemed like years. It was the first time he could recall being truly free since he was a child. No one was here to tell him what to do. No one could tell him where to go. He was on his own.

Before becoming chieftain of his goblin tribe, Gortogh had led a miserable life. Tall, thin, with not much muscle, he was never a specimen of the desired goblin traits. He was a terrible hunter. He could gather food in the woods, which put him on par with the women in the tribe. He could fight well enough, but he was weak. In short, he was worthless.

And his chief, a typical strong male name Hogar, made sure he knew it. He fetched water for the cook pots. It was his job to skin the animals the hunters brought down. He was even made to mend loincloths for a time. And they all laughed at him. Gortogh could have run away, maybe joined another tribe, but he most likely would have ended up dead. He was a prisoner to his weaknesses.

Then came the day he met the elf. The wizard Velanon. Everything changed for him that day. The wizard gave him power, a magical ring that could weaken his enemies and slow them. His skill with a blade was good but never quite strong enough. Suddenly, with a single thought, he could make even the strongest goblin as weak as he was.

He cut off Hogar's head with ease and thought he was finally free.

Free to do as he pleased. He was chief of his tribe, and no one could tell him what to do. But the wizard's leash was short, and tight. It was not at all what he'd dreamed of. The tribe became his responsibility. His burden. They all looked to him for direction. He became a prisoner of his strengths.

But now all of that was gone. The wizard was dead. The tribes wanted him dead. No one looked to him for anything. And with the wizard's magic still in his hands, he was strong enough to survive on his own. He'd been doing it quite successfully for months now.

Gortogh was truly free.

Free to go where he pleased. Free to do whatever he

wanted. And he knew what he wanted to do.

Prove to his brothers what fools they all were.

So, Gortogh went west. To find Ogrilon. To find answers. Was the city even real? Did he care? If he found no city at all, could he prove to them that it didn't exist? Or would it just continue to be a legend?

Gortogh didn't know. But the amulet had told him to go west. It had been noticeably silent since that moment, but it still hummed with power in its dark little pouch. He could feel it in there. He wasn't sure why it had told him to go west, but he knew what *he* was going to find.

And he hoped that he did find it. A collection of huts and caves somewhere in the mountain where the great goblin society once sat. Gortogh laughed at the picture in his head of the great goblins of the past huddled around a fire discussing philosophy. Fools, all of them.

He would find Ogrilon, whatever and wherever it was.

Praise Ogrosh!

With a small pack in place on his back, Gortogh set off. He went south first, skirting the territory in the forest now claimed by the remnants of a hundred goblin tribes. The less contact with his fellow goblins he had, the better. His face was instantly recognized by most of his brothers, and they wouldn't hesitate to kill him on sight.

Once he was far enough out, he turned west. Gortogh had no idea where he was going, but he knew from Kurgh's stories that Ogrilon was supposed to be somewhere in the westernmost Twin Crest Mountains. If he kept Ilothen's Crown over his right shoulder, he could keep to the deep forest, away from any potential settlements, and find his way there.

It'll be a lonely journey.

Gortogh had gotten used to being lonely. He had wished for it every day when he was younger. Growing up among goblins meant you were almost never by yourself. Goblin tribes stuck tight together, never friendly with one another, but never far from each other. When he was alone as a child, he could be himself. He didn't have to hear how weak he was. How useless he was.

Being alone didn't bother Gortogh. Much. As the hours passed though, Gortogh began to realize he was not alone. He glanced over his shoulder and saw movement through the trees. Close enough that he could see them moving and see them stop when he looked back, but far enough away that he couldn't make out who or what it was.

One thing was for sure. He was being followed.

Gortogh turned back around and kept walking. Whoever it was, he didn't want them to know that he knew. Probably just a goblin patrol that caught his scent and started tracking him. Chances were good they didn't even know who he was. Just a goblin from another tribe who crossed through their territory.

Or maybe they knew exactly who he was. Maybe they caught sight of him and recognized him. Decided they would hunt him down and make a name for themselves. Whoever was after him, he wasn't going to make it easy on them.

Gortogh kept walking, reminding himself constantly to avoid looking back. He thought for a moment of stopping and confronting them. Whoever they were, chances were good he could send them running. But things could get out of hand quickly. He didn't want to have to kill another goblin if he didn't have to. He'd done quite enough of that for one lifetime.

When he finally stopped for the day, Gortogh made a small camp in a clearing between some trees. He lit up a fire and waited, his sword resting on his lap. Closing his eyes, he appeared to sleep, but really he just wanted to heighten his hearing.

He didn't have to wait long.

He heard a twig snap. They were close. Close enough to see him there, he was sure. But what did they want? If they wanted to kill him, he was presenting them with an easy opportunity. Maybe too easy. If they were smart, they wouldn't fall for the trap. Gortogh certainly never would.

A crunch of leaves, closer this time. Gortogh opened his eyes just a slit and lolled his head to the side, pretending to be asleep sitting up. Slipping into his innate night vision, he scanned the forest beyond his little campsite. He caught some movement on his left side, right in his line of sight.

It was also in line with the tip of his sword.

Gortogh's weapon was a magical blade given to him by the wizard as part of their deal almost a year ago. It's greatest power lied in its ability to bestow him with ungodly strength. The strength of ten goblins, it felt sometimes. Enough to best even the strongest of ogres, which Gortogh had, in fact, done.

But the sword carried another power as well. With a thought, Gortogh could release the energy stored within the blade in a great arc of lightning. A bolt would shoot from the tip of the sword and fly, unerringly, toward its target.

Whoever was following him was right in line.

Gortogh didn't even have to move his head to release the bolt. Just raise his sword a little so that the lightning didn't touch his leg. It blasted out with a crackling sound, flying straight at the shadow hiding in the trees.

The bolt flew wide, just missing them. Gortogh wasn't trying to kill them, only scare them. When they jumped in surprise, clambering away from the tree, Gortogh heard an all-too-familiar sound.

The clacking of bones.

"Kurgh!" he shouted.

Silence.

"Come out, Kurgh, or I will hunt you down!"

The shaman walked around the side of the tree and threw his shoulders back. Even almost being killed wasn't enough to humble him. Gortogh kept his sword pointed at him, ready to release another bolt if he had to.

"Greetings, *Mighty One*."

Now Gortogh stood up. He would not be lower than Kurgh.

"Why are you following me?" Gortogh asked.

"That was quite an unsettling speech you gave the other night."

"I spoke the truth."

"As did I."

"We cannot both speak the truth."

Kurgh snickered.

"Why are you following me?"

"Because I know where you are going. Where you are trying to go."

"And where am I going?"

"Ogrilon."

Gortogh was silent. How did Kurgh know? He hadn't told anyone where he was going. He didn't even *have* anyone to tell.

"Where I go is my business. I am no longer a part of the tribe, so I am no longer beholden to you or your power."

"You are beholden to *Ogrosh*!"

Gortogh held his blade in front of him.

"Ogrosh does not own me. I go where I please."

"Then I am going with you."

"No. You're not."

"You cannot stop me."

Gortogh pointed his sword at the shaman and held the blade perfectly still.

"We could kill each other," Kurgh said, "but it will do neither of us any good."

"Why do you want come with me?"

"Because you do not deserve to find the great city!"

"Who says I'll even find it?"

They were both shouting now, something Gortogh didn't even realize how little he'd missed all those months in solitude. He hated fighting and yelling with Kurgh. They had been doing it for far too long it seemed.

"I have faith you will find it," Kurgh said. "Ogrosh has shown me."

"There's nothing to find. I am going to find whatever is left and prove you wrong."

"And I am coming along to prove you wrong."

Gortogh glared.

"This is foolish. We'll kill each other."

"For once, we have the same goal. Maybe not the same intent, but the end is the same for us both. We want to find Ogrilon."

"Maybe that's not what I'm looking for," Gortogh said.

"But it's where you're going, yes?"

Gortogh couldn't deny it.

"You can use my help," Kurgh said.

"I don't need anyone's help."

"Do you even know where you're going?"

"West. To The Anvil. Then south."

"Is that it? That's your map?"

"That's all you ever said in your stories!"

"I know the way to Ogrilon. You will wander in the mountains for the rest of your life without me, or at least until you starve to death."

"If you knew the way, you'd have found it already."

"I don't know the exact way, but I have Ogrosh with me. He will show me the way."

"Then he can show me the way too."

Kurgh laughed.

"Ogrosh owes you nothing, Mighty One. He will do you no favors."

"No, just send you along. Maybe you're right, Ogrosh does hate me."

Gortogh sat down and leaned his back against the tree. He closed his eyes and sighed.

"We leave at first light," he said. "If you slow me down, I will leave you behind."

"If we get into trouble, I'll make sure you die first."

He heard Kurgh sit close to the fire and then lay down. Gortogh opened one eye to look and saw Kurgh watching him as well.

This would be a long journey.

Chapter Ten

Into the Troll Marsh

GORTOGH STARED ACROSS the wide, open swamp in front of him. There was no end to the place. Only more and more water, its surface broken only by the occasional island of dry land and a few trees. It was a wasteland.

Kurgh fidgeted by his side.

"How far across?" Gortogh asked.

"I don't know."

"What do your legends say?"

"Only that the Troll Marsh is an evil place."

"How can a swamp be evil?"

"Trolls are abominations. The legends say when Ogrosh punished the wicked, he turned them into trolls and threw them into the marsh."

"I remember the children's stories about trolls."

"Trolls rarely leave the marsh if legends are to be believed."

"Can we go around then?"

"To the south the river widens, and the humans are too many. We would be spotted and most likely killed. The mountains to the north are treacherous. We would have to climb high to go around."

"Then this is the only way?"

"According to legend, yes. Ogrilon was almost impenetrable by army from the south. The north provides easier access, but we are not on the north side of the range."

Gortogh sighed and rested his hands on his hips, looking out over the marsh. The sun was dipping low, already having mostly disappeared behind the mountains in front of them. It would be dark soon. And they were standing on the edge of a swamp full of trolls.

If legends were to be believed.

"We should camp for the night and try to cross in the morning," Gortogh said. "We would at least have a chance of seeing something coming."

"We'll light a huge fire."

"Won't that draw attention?"

"This close to the marsh? Other than you and I, there are only the trolls out here. They'll smell us no matter what. And they hate fire. The bigger, the better."

Gortogh nodded and began looking around for something to make a fire with. They'd left the forest behind a day ago, which meant there was very little wood around. The ground beneath his feet was soggy. The air smelled damp and rotted.

"Where are we going to find wood?"

"I can keep a fire going through the night, but I will not be of much use in the morning."

Gortogh silently wondered what use he was at all. In the three days they'd traveled together, Kurgh had hardly done anything. Each night they camped, it was up to Gortogh to do all of the work. He gathered the wood. He made the fire. Kurgh barely even spoke. He just sat there with his eyes closed.

The only thing the shaman was good for was getting food. Gortogh had never been much of a hunter, but then he didn't need to be. Their first night camping he'd made a big show of collecting enough for them both to eat. Kurgh opened his eyes a bit and then scoffed. Then he summoned a deer that walked right into their camp and waited to be slaughtered.

"What about food?" Gortogh asked.

"There is little we can summon to feed us here. Perhaps your gathering skills will come in handy after all."

Gortogh clenched his fists and took a deep breath.

"And what will you do while I take care of all the work?"

"I will pray to Ogrosh to keep us safe through the night."

Gortogh growled and stomped off toward drier ground. The same answer, every night. Pray. Praise Ogrosh! Kurgh was going to pray for them. That should keep them safe.

Gortogh found himself muttering the whole time as he gathered plants and roots they could eat. He found a few small bushes with some berries on them he didn't recognize and picked those as well. He popped a few in his mouth, not caring too much whether they were poisonous. Goblins were not affected by poisons in the same way the fragile humans were.

When he thought he had enough, Gortogh trekked back to their little camp. It wasn't difficult to find even though the sun had set. A giant, blazing fire stood out in the darkness like a beacon in the night. Gortogh looked all around, expecting someone or something to come charging at them any moment. He tripped over the uneven ground in the dark and stumbled back into camp.

"All you've done is let every troll within a mile know exactly where we are."

"They may approach, but they will stay to the darkness. They will not come near the fire."

"So say your legends."

Kurgh closed his eyes and went back to praying.

Gortogh took his meager findings and divided them, setting half down in front of the oblivious Kurgh. It took less than a minute for Gortogh to finish his supper, and it did little to satisfy his appetite. He'd gotten used to eating meat again. Kurgh was good for that at least.

As usual, Kurgh's prayers seemed to go on forever. Maybe it was just because Gortogh was so bored. He'd grown used to being alone and having no one to talk to, but now here was someone to talk to. Kurgh just didn't do much talking.

Gortogh sighed, loudly.

"Are you going to eat?" he asked.

Kurgh opened his eyes, and his gaze drifted down to the offering in front of him. He didn't even bother with a response. Just went back to his praying. Always another prayer.

"I gave you half," Gortogh said.

"Half of nothing is nothing."

"Well, then I'll eat your nothing for you."

Kurgh breathed deeply and waved his hands across his chest. Gortogh wasn't going to wait for his answer. He snatched up the leaf with all of Kurgh's dinner and quickly devoured it. It was just as unsatisfying as the first half.

"Why do you pray for so long?"

"Why do you practice with that silly sword for so

long?" Kurgh asked without opening his eyes.

"To hone my skills. To keep them sharp."

"Then you have your answer."

"You can't practice praying. You just do it."

"You can't practice a sword, you just swing it."

Gortogh huffed and laid back onto his bedroll. The ground beneath him was dry enough, but the air around still felt damp. It was making him sweat, and he almost dared take off his armor. The fire made him even hotter, and he inched away from it, but its glowing presence reminded him of how vulnerable they were out here. Best to keep the armor on.

"When I pray, I am close to Ogrosh," Kurgh said, breaking the silence. "If you felt his presence the way that I do, you would pray too."

"Then why don't we all feel him in that way? Wouldn't it be better for us all if we had that connection?"

"It might be better for us all to wield a sword as well as you do too, but we don't all practice long enough and hard enough to reach your level of skill."

"So you're saying if I prayed all the time, I would feel a closer connection to Ogrosh?"

"For you? No. Ogrosh would not hear your prayers."

Gortogh bolted upright.

"Who are you to say who Ogrosh will hear?"

"I follow his teachings. I carry within me his power."

"I carry his power too," Gortogh said.

He yanked on the pouch around his neck and pulled from it the bronze amulet. The shaman immediately closed his eyes and turned his head.

"Put that away!" he yelled.

"I thought you wanted this for yourself," Gortogh

said.

"I will not let you sway me the way you once did!"

Gortogh shrugged and put the amulet back into its pouch.

"It's gone," he said.

Kurgh peeked from between his hands and then turned back, his face a rolling, boiling pot of anger.

"If Ogrosh hates me, why did he give me his amulet?"

"That was not Ogrosh's doing. Had he given you the amulet himself, you would not have used it to lead so many of our people to their deaths."

He might have had a point. Velanon had only given him the amulet so that he could gather an army. The wizard couldn't use the amulet himself, so he'd enlisted Gortogh for the job, promising him great power and strength. Velanon made good on his promise. If only Gortogh had known how high the price would be.

"No one should have it," Gortogh said at last. "It was made to enslave our people. If I could destroy it, I would. I've tried, but it cannot be broken."

"Then keep it hidden from sight," Kurgh said. "At least then it can't hurt anyone."

Some sound off in the distance made Gortogh reach for his sword. It sounded like water sloshing. Someone or something was moving through the marsh.

"Trolls," Kurgh said.

"How do you know?"

"I can feel them."

Gortogh glanced sidelong at the shaman.

"I told you that I can sense life. Ogrosh is keeping watch over us. Why do you think we've set no watch the last three nights?"

"I didn't know you could actually feel them."

"I can sense all creatures whose blood flows," Kurgh said. "These trolls are different somehow though. I have never known or seen one in my life, but I know that's what I feel now. They are close, just beyond the firelight."

Gortogh turned away from the fire and let his eyes fall into night vision. Peering out through the darkness, he could see them now. Three or four of them maybe, it was hard to tell. They were all huddled together, moving in circles around the firelight.

They were huge. Ten feet tall. As tall as an ogre, maybe more. Gortogh felt a shudder course through his body. If they got up enough courage to attack, there was little he could do to stop them.

"What do we do come morning?" he asked.

"We carry torches and march through the marsh as quickly as we can."

"You think torches will keep them at bay?"

"I don't know, but there is no other way."

Gortogh kept watching them. One of them broke off from the group and took a few steps forward. Gortogh saw a green, bloated foot appear at the edge of the light and gripped his sword tighter.

"The fire will not keep them back all night," Gortogh said.

He glanced back and saw Kurgh muttering another prayer. Only this time the shaman had his bone knife in hand, which meant he was calling on Ogrosh for magic. Kurgh sliced his arm, biting deep enough that Gortogh could see bone through all the blood.

The blood dripped down Kurgh's arm and pooled in his hands where it swirled around his fingers, forming an almost solid ball in his palm. The sight always amazed Gortogh, though he would never let Kurgh know it. He had seen the true power of what Ogrosh could do, and he had to admit that it frightened him at times.

Kurgh finished chanting and flung his hands at the trolls. The blood flew in little droplets, each one passing through the fire with a sizzle. But as they came out the other side, the drops of blood were on fire. On fire and streaking toward the trolls who were scrambling to get out of their way.

The tiny drops of fire struck the trolls in the back as they ran, screaming, from the light. Gortogh watched them all bumbling into each other and smiled a little.

"That should keep them back," Kurgh said.

Kurgh was good for something at least.

Praise Ogrosh.

CHAPTER ELEVEN

IMMORTAL BLOOD

GORTOGH SAT UP for what felt like the hundredth time that night and stared out into the dark. He could hear them out there, sloshing around through the muddy waters in the swamp. A glance over at Kurgh told him that the shaman hadn't moved since the last time he'd looked. If Gortogh didn't know any better, he would think Kurgh had fallen asleep sitting up.

The trolls hadn't come close enough for him to see them clearly, but he could see movement in the dark. Something very tall. Many somethings. The fire Kurgh had flung at them earlier was enough to keep them from getting nearer, but Gortogh had a nagging feeling they weren't going to stay away all night. And what happened with the dawn, when their fire went out?

The fire burned as high and bright as when it was first lit, even though there was no obvious fuel. Kurgh had told Gortogh to dig out a fire pit, but the fire just burned in the middle of their camp as though it rested upon the dirt itself. Gortogh felt silly, but he said a silent prayer to Ogrosh to keep the fire burning through the night.

A splash sounded close by.

"Kurgh," Gortogh whispered.

The shaman didn't move or respond.

"Kurgh!" he said, a little louder.

"Go to sleep," Kurgh said without opening his eyes.

"They're out there."

"Of course they are out there. They will not approach."

"How long can you keep that fire going?"

"As long as we need it."

Gortogh didn't feel very secure in that answer. He peered out into the swamp, waiting for something to move. He didn't have to wait long. They were everywhere, and getting braver.

"There must a be twenty trolls out there," he said.

"Ten," Kurgh said.

"How can you tell?"

"I told you, I sense their blood. Ogrosh watches over us. He will not fail us the way you have failed him."

Gortogh turned to say something back but decided to let it drop. He was tired of arguing with Kurgh about who failed what.

"They're getting closer," Gortogh said. "What do they want?"

"Your blood," Kurgh said. "They crave it."

"Don't they have enough of their own?"

"An endless supply, yes, but they always want more."

Gortogh chuckled. It sounded familiar.

"Go to sleep," Kurgh said.

"I can't sleep like this."

"Then we will both be dead tomorrow. When my strength is sapped, I will need you to keep us safe. If you get no sleep, we will both surely die."

Gortogh laid his head down and closed his eyes. He

didn't truly think he would be able to sleep, but he had to try. Rolling to one side, he opened his eyes and watched Kurgh as he sat perfectly still, legs crossed and arms open. Gortogh caught some movement, just a little, and saw for the first time that Kurgh had his bone knife in one hand.

As he watched, Kurgh took the tip of the knife and twisted it into his other arm. A trickle of blood flowed from the wound and then was pulled to his hand where it leapt into the fire. The hole in his arm was almost closed when he moved the knife over and repeated the process, never letting the wound close as it always had.

"Do you have to do that all night?" Gortogh asked.

"If I am to keep the fire going, yes."

Now Gortogh could see why Kurgh would be so weak tomorrow.

"How can you lose so much blood and still live?"

"Ogrosh gives me new blood. He heals my wounds and keeps me alive. But I can still push too far."

"Don't do that," Gortogh said. "If that fire goes out, we're both dead."

"If I become too weak, I'll just take your blood. It's all the same."

Kurgh opened his eyes and let a smile creep across his face.

"You'll find my blood not so easy to get at," Gortogh said.

"If I become too weak, you'll have a choice. You can give your blood to me or the trolls."

Gortogh was about to respond when a spear flew between the two of them and cut him off. He was on his feet in a second, sword in hand. He heard hooting from the darkness and saw the trolls gathered together in a group just beyond the firelight. They had gotten closer.

A lot closer.

"I don't think the fire is going to hold them off," Gortogh said.

"We could try and capture one," Kurgh said.

"Are you crazy?"

"If we can capture and hold one, we'll have an almost endless supply of magic. The blood of a troll is very powerful, and they never run out of it."

Gortogh had heard the scary stories about trolls as a child. They cannot be killed, except by fire, so they say. Even taking their heads off will only cause them to grow a new head. It was like they were goblin shamans with an infinite ability to heal their wounds. Immortal almost.

Another spear flew into their camp, this one closer to Gortogh, who was now a standing target. He hurried around the fire to the side farthest from the trolls and ducked down behind it. A roar cut through the night, joined quickly by others. Then the sound Gortogh had strained to hear all night.

Giant feet splashing, running through the marsh.

"Get up!" Gortogh yelled.

Kurgh must have sensed they were coming, because he was already on his feet when Gortogh looked back. Gortogh squeezed the hilt of his sword and felt the magical power of the blade course through his body. Instantly, he felt stronger. His muscles bulged, stretching his pocked, green skin to its limits. He gritted his teeth through the pain and ran to meet the charging trolls.

"Stay back!" Gortogh yelled. "I'll hold them off!"

He came around the fire in time to meet the first one into the firelight. He swung his sword, and was surprised when the troll didn't even try to block. His blade came down hard, opening a big gash across the troll's chest. Gortogh danced back and waited for the creature to fall, but it only kept coming. Before he could even bring his sword up for another strike, the wound on the troll's chest had already begun to close.

"Kurgh!" he shouted.

He could hear the shaman praying and hoped it would be more fire. Two more trolls were charging up behind their friend here, but many of them were still holding back. The troll he had cut stumbled back a bit as the other two pushed forward. At least they could be hurt, even if they healed quickly. Gortogh's only hope was to push these few back and do enough damage that the rest might think twice before trying it themselves.

The two new trolls came on together. Gortogh didn't waste time waiting for them. With a yell, he charged in. The trolls were almost twice his height, so reaching their heads would be too far of a reach. He went for the legs instead.

Chopping down with all his magical strength, Gortogh sliced through a leg. The troll lunged forward to try and grab him. He dodged to the side, and the beast fell forward with a shout, splashing into the muck. Gortogh smiled a bit as he stepped on its head and leapt for the next one.

This one was ready for him though.

The troll reached for him, trying to grab his sword. The dumb creature could not have known the power in that blade. Gortogh brought his sword down in a chop that severed the arm just above the elbow. He felt no resistance as the blade went through, it was so sharp.

The troll howled and then lunged again. Gortogh stabbed out, lancing it through the stomach. The troll whooped and reached for him, expecting him to be caught. With a thought, Gortogh released the lightning stored within his magical blade. The magic coursed down the length of it, right through the troll's body. A look of shock crossed the beast's face just before the magic blasted it ten feet back into the water.

Gortogh only had time for a single breath before another troll appeared. It was the first one he had cut open, completely healed now. The one behind it had managed to find and reattach its leg and was now getting up. Gortogh felt something tickle his foot and leapt back when he looked down and saw a severed arm grabbing for his ankle.

The children's stories were true!

They really could heal any wound. Gortogh hacked the arm on the ground, cutting it into two pieces, but the end with the hand just kept coming. The fingers stretched and dragged along the ground toward him. The troll in front of him now reached out to grab him. It was trying to drag him into its waiting mouth.

"Kurgh!" he shouted again.

"Push them back!" Kurgh shouted over the fire.

Gortogh pulled away, but the troll refused to let go. They tumbled back, Gortogh landing in the mud. The troll was on top of him now. Gortogh pushed with all his strength, which was considerable with his magic. He shoved the troll back as hard as he could. The creature was tall, more than ten feet maybe, and its arms and legs were thin and gangly. It was thrown completely off balance and tumbled back into the two trolls who, now healed, were now running up behind it.

All three fell back, hitting the ground with a sucking thud as they tumbled into the mud. With them healing this fast, there was little he could do to hold them off. He had no other choice. Gortogh charged in to hack at them while they were prone.

"No!" Kurgh shouted. "Get back!"

Gortogh had seen enough of the shaman's magic to know to do exactly as he was told. He shuffled back a few steps and waited with his sword drawn for the spectacular magic show he hoped would follow.

He wasn't disappointed.

Small, sharp blades of blood appeared in front of them and began to swirl. Gortogh had seen this spell before, had been on the receiving end of it, and it wasn't pretty to watch. The blades whirled faster, more joining the first few, as the spell picked up power.

Gortogh looked over his shoulder to see that Kurgh had opened both of his arms. The knife was lying forgotten on the ground as blood gushed from the wounds, leaping from Kurgh's arms and into the air to form more blades.

"Enough!" Gortogh yelled over the sound of the whirlwind.

Kurgh pushed out with his hands, and the blades obeyed. Spinning farther out from the two of them, they quickly caught the trolls who were only now beginning to get back on their feet. The blades struck the three of them, and now they did yell in pain. The horrible pain of a hundred cuts at once.

It was the most gruesome thing Gortogh had even seen.

When the blades sliced into the trolls, they seemed to explode like sacks of blood. It gushed from a hundred wounds on their rotten skin and poured down their bodies. But just as it did with Kurgh's, the troll blood leapt up to become more blades, joining the ones still swirling. Gortogh dared a look back when he heard Kurgh cackle behind him.

The more the trolls bled, the more knives leapt into the air to join the others. Even with their unholy ability to heal, the wounds couldn't close fast enough. There were just too many blades. And more joining them each second. Soon the swarm was so thick that Gortogh could barely see the trolls through it.

Kurgh pushed farther, the wall of whirling, swirling death moving out until it licked at the group of trolls waiting beyond the others. Kurgh had said there were ten trolls all together, and only three had charged. Leaving seven beyond the melee.

When the swarm of blades hit them, the whole night exploded.

Gortogh hit the ground. There were blood blades flying everywhere now, so thick that they blotted out the moon. He ducked down and covered his head, afraid to look up lest it get cut off. Through it all he heard Kurgh cackling like a madman.

"Your blood will be your own unmaking!" he shouted. "Ogrosh will consume you all!"

The whirling, scraping sound of metal continued for another minute and then just stopped. Gortogh dared a look around and saw nothing. The blades were gone. Only Kurgh remained, standing with his head high and arms folded.

Gortogh stood and looked at the carnage. What was left of the trolls, and there wasn't much, was lying in piles in the marsh. Even now, each one in hundreds of pieces, he could see all the little bits pulling toward each other to stitch back together. The one closest to their camp was mostly intact, though it still wasn't moving.

Kurgh went over to this one and began chanting. As he did, the remaining wounds on the troll's skin opened wider, and blood oozed out. As Kurgh chanted, the blood leapt to his hand. He held it out toward Gortogh, and the fire jumped from where it was still burning in the pit and into his waiting palm.

Then he turned it on the trolls.

One by one, he threw fire at anything that twitched or moved until nothing did. When he was done, he dropped the flaming ball at his feet, and the last troll burst into flames. It took only a minute for the entire body to be consumed by the fire.

"Get some sleep," Kurgh said.

Walking back to the same spot, he picked up the bone knife and tucked it into his belt as he sat down. With a deep sigh, he closed his eyes and went back to his silent prayer.

Gortogh didn't know what else to say, so he laid down and closed his eyes.

CHAPTER TWELVE

THROUGH THE DARKNESS

THE NEXT DAY, they began their march across the Troll Marsh. Gortogh had awoken refreshed and invigorated from the fight the night before. Kurgh was not looking nearly as well. The shaman had stayed up all night praying, which was not unusual for him, but it was the loss of blood that was getting to him now. Gortogh didn't even know how he was still standing.

Which was only barely.

"Slow down," Kurgh said again.

He'd already said it so many times that Gortogh had lost count. He couldn't help his speed. His feet were soaked through with swamp water, making them feel slick and slimy. The smell of this stagnant place was that of death and rot, nearly making him gag in places. But more than that, it was the sheer desolation.

The Troll Marsh was dotted with the occasional tree to mark the passage of time, but beyond that, there was nothing to see in every direction. Just warm, stagnant, stench-filled water as far as he could see. His every instinct told him to get out of this place as quickly as he could.

"Slow down!" Kurgh shouted.

"You speed up!" Gortogh said.

"I can't," Kurgh said.

Gortogh looked back and saw the shaman panting. Being goblins, they weren't the tallest of creatures, and that left them both in water up to their thighs. The trolls probably had a much easier time trudging through this place. When he saw Kurgh struggling to even move his legs, Gortogh softened a bit.

Just a bit.

Up ahead, Gortogh could see one of the lonely trees growing from the swamp. It was a sad, twisted thing sticking up from a small patch of land like some gnarly hand reaching for life above the muck.

"Come on," Gortogh said. "We can rest up there."

He pushed on and made it to the tree to wait for Kurgh. The shaman was giving it his all, but it wasn't getting him there very quickly. This was going to be an even longer trip than Gortogh had originally thought.

Finally, Kurgh reached the little tuft of land poking through the swamp and collapsed with a groan.

"I cannot go on," Kurgh said.

"Then we're in real trouble," Gortogh said.

He looked in every direction and was thankful that he saw no other signs of life. They'd only been in the swamp an hour, but already he was paranoid. He jumped at every movement. Every swish, every splash, every croak. Who knew how many things waited out there to kill them and eat them.

They would die in this swamp if they didn't keep moving.

Gortogh leapt up and pulled on Kurgh's arm.

"Come on," he said.

"I can't," Kurgh said.

Gortogh heard the whine in his voice, like some child being told to rise early for a hunt. He yanked the shaman's arm, though without the strength in his sword, it barely moved him.

"Get up!" Gortogh said.

"I can't," Kurgh said.

"Can't you just heal yourself? Give yourself more energy? Make yourself stronger? You can use my blood."

"Even with your blood, my body is too weak. I pushed too hard, and this is the punishment."

The sound of something plunking into the water drew Gortogh's attention, made him reach for his sword.

They had to get moving.

He drew his sword and held it over the shaman. Kurgh opened his eyes, and his face hardened.

"We have to move," Gortogh said.

"Are you going to kill me out of mercy?" Kurgh asked.

Gortogh squeezed the hilt of his magical sword and felt the energy flow through him, strengthening every muscle in his body. With one hand, he reached down and picked the weakened shaman up and pulled him over his shoulder.

"We can't stay here," Gortogh said.

With that, he marched on.

His sword in his right hand, Kurgh over his left shoulder, Gortogh trudged through the Troll Marsh as fast as his magically enhanced legs would carry him. After a time, they reached another scraggly tree and another patch of land. Gortogh set Kurgh down as gently as he could and sat beside him.

"Leave me," Kurgh said.

Gortogh laughed.

"And then where would I be? Stuck in some swamp alone? Not knowing where to go?"

"Wasn't that your plan in the first place?"

Gortogh nodded.

"It was a stupid plan," he said.

Kurgh chuckled.

"What?" Gortogh said.

"I must admit, I admire your conviction."

"What does that mean?"

"When you come up with a stupid plan, by Ogrosh, you see it through."

"How else am I to learn how stupid the plan was?"

Gortogh stood and stuck the tip of his sword in the ground. He lifted Kurgh again, who could only groan, and put him on his back. Kurgh got the idea and put his arms around Gortogh's neck. Gortogh picked up the shaman's legs and then grabbed his sword in one hand.

"Ready?" he said.

Kurgh nodded against his back.

The going was a little easier with Kurgh on his back, but it still wasn't quick. The journey was going to take a week if Kurgh didn't get some of his strength back.

"Why didn't you just take one of the trolls for their blood?" Gortogh asked. "Then we wouldn't be in this mess."

"Even if I had, I would not have had the power to wield it. Even with an infinite source of blood to draw, the magic must still pass through *me*. I am Ogrosh's faithful. He lends power to me, *through* me."

"Still. You might not be so bad off if you'd used someone else's blood."

"It would have made no difference. The blade wind I conjured grew too large, beyond my control. It took too much of my strength. Keeping the fire burning through the night, though a small task, was enough to sap all that I had left."

Kurgh laid his head against Gortogh's pack and slackened his grip. The talking was taking more energy than the shaman had, so Gortogh kept silent as they walked. After a while, he felt the shaman lift his head.

"I am sorry," he said.

"Sorry about what?" Gortogh asked.

"I am not used to being a burden. It is not a feeling I enjoy."

"You're the shaman, I'm the warrior. We each have our job to do in the tribe. And since we're the only two out here, we have to rely on each other. You kept us safe during the night, now it's my turn to get us through this."

"In my tribe," Kurgh said. "Before I... before I found you, I was always fighting with the chieftain. In most of the tribes, the high shaman receives the most respect of any. But Brogok hated my strength and devotion. He created a power struggle between the shamans and the warriors."

"What did you do?"

"I killed him," Kurgh said. "I slit his throat and stole his lifeblood to summon the most wonderful feast the tribe had ever known. Then I made sure the next chief was more faithful to Ogrosh."

Gortogh tensed. The way he spoke the words, it sounded as if the shaman was just talking about a lazy afternoon. It wasn't that Kurgh's story was shocking. Sadly, tales of violence *within* goblin tribes was almost more frequent than violence *between* them. Someone always had more power, and someone else always wanted it. Even Gortogh.

"My tribe was so small we didn't even have a shaman," Gortogh said at last. "Just a cruel chieftain."

"And you killed him," Kurgh said.

"I did."

It was true. Gortogh had killed his chief to become chief himself. It was the start of all of this. With that single act, he'd been set on a path he never expected to find himself on. Certainly not sloshing through a Troll Marsh with a half-dead shaman strapped to his back.

"You did what any stronger warrior would have done," Kurgh said.

"I only had strength because of the wizard. I did not deserve to be chief."

"You had more strength than he did. You took his strength from him. Just as if you'd taken his own blood the way I did. It matters not where your strength came from. That is the way of the children of Ogrosh."

The way of the children of Ogrosh.

Gortogh had always hated hearing that. And he'd heard it a lot. From chiefs, from shamans, from warriors. Even his own mother. The strong kill the weak, so never be the weaker one. But he was always weak.

"And now look at me," Kurgh said. "I would not blame you for killing me as I am now."

"I'm not going to kill you," Gortogh said.

"I know that. But I would not be shocked if you did."

"I hate the way of the children of Ogrosh."

"We do as he commands," Kurgh said.

"He does *not* command me."

"He gave you life."

"Well, *praise* Ogrosh! He can have it!"

Gortogh spit on the ground.

"Do not mock him! You owe him your life."

Gortogh climbed onto a small patch of sandy ground that jutted out of the water and dropped the shaman hard. He bent down to get in Kurgh's face.

"Ogrosh does not own me. He does not tell me what to do. You may choose that as your life, but it is *not* what I choose."

"You think you can choose?"

"No one owns me. I choose for myself."

With that, Gortogh left. He sank down into the water and marched on, leaving Kurgh slumped over on the little hill.

"You're just going to leave me here?" Kurgh shouted.

"*That* is my choice!" Gortogh shouted back.

He trudged on through the water, no longer paying attention to the shaman's shouts at his back. No one owned him. No one commanded him. Not anymore. And *never* would it be Ogrosh. He had never needed Ogrosh before, and he certainly did need him now.

When Gortogh returned an hour later, he found Kurgh kneeling on the little hilltop where he'd left him, his face in the dirt. He threw down the pile of sticks he'd carried back from the tree he cut down.

"I thought you'd left me to die," Kurgh said without looking up.

"If I had, it would be because I hate you and not because Ogrosh demands it."

Gortogh plopped down and began tying the sticks together with some rope he pulled from his pack.

"What are you doing?" Kurgh asked.

"We'll never make it through this swamp with you on my back. I need the strength of my sword to carry you and everything else, and I cannot draw the power forever.

Then where will we be? I'm making a raft I can drag you on. It will make the going easier."

Kurgh stared into his eyes. Gortogh could feel the shaman watching him, but he kept his attention focused on the rope and sticks. Eventually, Kurgh rested his head on the ground. It was a sight Gortogh had seen many times before.

He chuckled.

"I haven't seen you like that since you were running around kissing my feet and calling me Mighty One."

Kurgh's head sprang up so fast, Gortogh actually jumped.

"Never mock me!" Kurgh said.

His face was a bubbling cauldron of rage.

"You tricked me! You made me believe you were Ogrosh!"

"That wasn't my doing," Gortogh said.

"Do you really take no blame for your part in all this?"

"Of course I do! But I am not solely to blame. Wasn't it you who called the other shamans? Wasn't it you who brought them to join me?"

Kurgh hung his head.

"I was tricked," he said. "When I looked at you, I saw Ogrosh. I believed you were his champion. I believed you were Ogrosh made flesh on Gondril. That cursed amulet showed me a lie, and I believed every word."

"No one else was affected like that. Not as quickly as you anyway."

"You cannot know the depths of my faith," Kurgh said. "You said yourself, no one owns you. You owe nothing to anyone. You will never feel the power of true faith. That is why I believed you. When I looked at you, I saw his blood. And I gave myself to it."

"Is that why you groveled around in the dirt?"

"What would you do if you met Ogrosh in the flesh?"

"I would have a thousand questions for him."

"When I meet him, I will bow and grovel at his feet, and pray to him that I am worthy to remain in his presence."

Gortogh finished tying the last knot on his little, makeshift raft and stood to admire it. He plopped it into the water, and it floated. It looked sturdy enough to hold Kurgh's weight.

"Let us hope you don't meet him soon," Gortogh said.

CHAPTER THIRTEEN

OUT OF THE MARSH

THEIR JOURNEY ACROSS the Troll Marsh took three days.

The raft had made things easier, and after the second day, Kurgh got some of his strength back. Gortogh had insisted he stay on the raft and recover, and the shaman hadn't argued.

They had seen no trolls since that first night. Kurgh took the credit for that of course. Gortogh didn't care why they had stayed away, he just went as fast as he could. When the ground finally began to dry up, he pulled the raft onto land and fell to the earth to just lay in the scruffy grass and enjoy its touch.

"Well, that was an adventure," Kurgh said.

Gortogh opened his eyes to see the shaman's feet next to him.

"I'm just glad to be out of that accursed place," Gortogh said.

"As am I. I have a bad feeling in that place, but I'm not sure why."

"Because there are hundreds, possibly thousands, of trolls waiting in the dark to kill us."

"It's more than that. I think I'll explore it more on our return."

Gortogh groaned. They'd only just left the damn place behind, and already Kurgh had to remind him of the trip back. Gortogh didn't even want to think about that. He was secretly holding out some hope they could find another way home. Though he didn't count on it given how great this trip was going so far.

Right now he was just happy to be back on solid ground again. They had been without a fire the whole trip across the marsh, and he was ready for warm, dry feet and a hot meal. He pushed himself to his knees and looked ahead.

They were in the foothills of the Twin Crest Mountains, near one of the twin spires known as The Anvil. A cluster of smaller mountains surrounded it to the west and south, but The Anvil towered above them. Somewhere in its shadow was their destination. At least if the legends were true.

"Think you could summon us up some food?" Gortogh asked.

"You provide the wood for the fire, and I'll provide the meat."

Gortogh couldn't help a little smile as he went off in search of firewood. He could see some trees off in the foothills that wouldn't take him long to reach. His legs were tired from the march through the marsh, but there was still a little spring in his step now.

They had survived the Troll Marsh. Just the two of them. The hardest part of the journey, and the part Gortogh had most feared, was over. Finding Ogrilon should be easy after going through all of that.

When he returned to their little camp, Kurgh was

waiting with dinner. Two rabbits lay in front him, their skins already removed. Gortogh did little to hide his disappointment.

"That's all you could find?" Gortogh said.

Kurgh did little to hide his annoyance.

"I did not want to tax my strength."

"We haven't eaten a real meal in days! I'm sick of dried meat and moldy bread."

Gortogh dumped the small pile of wood he'd managed to gather. He reached into his pack and pulled out a small pouch.

"I found some berries a few hills over," he said. "Might help to round out the *feast* you've prepared."

"I provided two conies, you bring some berries, and you think *I* have not given enough? Why don't we just eat our own catches then."

"No!" Gortogh said. "Let's just get the fire started and get those two roasting."

Kurgh smiled and handed over the two rabbits. The shaman used a little magic to get the fire going quickly, and Gortogh had the rabbits on a spit seconds later. The smell of roasting meat was enough to have them both drooling as the meat turned and turned over the fire.

They both went to bed that night with full bellies and high spirits.

***

Their high spirits didn't last long.

They made it through the foothills and into the mountains the first day. The second day, they found a pass through the mountains that looked as though it hadn't been used in a long time. It was wide enough to let an army through, but very few people traveled near The Anvil anymore.

Kurgh had warned Gortogh to keep alert. The mountains in this area were claimed by the Erutharen. One of the three elven kingdoms, and the nastiest of the bunch to hear the shaman tell it. Eruthen was the son of Ilothen and the god of vengeance, and his worshippers took the job seriously. Especially against the children of the other gods.

Gortogh was cautious but still optimistic that they would soon find Ogrilon. Kurgh had taken the lead and was now guiding them on the path. He prayed night and day to Ogrosh to show them the way, and then he would march off deeper into the mountains.

Gortogh was starting to feel glad the shaman had come along.

"I don't know where to go," Kurgh said out of nowhere.

They had made a small camp in a shallow cave at the base of a mountain. The wind through the pass was chilled and cut right through them, so they had stopped for the night when they found the cave. Gortogh was snuggled up close to the fire for warmth and was feeling quite cozy up until Kurgh's little announcement.

Gortogh opened his eyes and looked around, not even sure if he'd heard correctly. He sat up and turned his head. Kurgh was looking right at him.

"What do you mean?" Gortogh asked.

"The legends don't say where we go from here."

"Well, what do they say?"

"Very little."

"I thought you said that you knew how to get there because of your damn legends."

"I lied."

Gortogh sat up, wide-eyed.

"Then what about all the praying nonsense?" Gortogh said.

He was straining to keep his voice down. Out here, exposed to the world, they didn't know who could be listening. It wasn't Ogrosh, apparently.

"I thought I could pray to Ogrosh, and he would show us the way," Kurgh said.

"Then where have you been going for the last two days? You've been praying and then walking off, and I've been following you thinking you knew where you were going!"

"I was waiting for Ogrosh to show me."

"Ogrilon has not been seen for thousands of years, if it even exists at all! And you thought Ogrosh would just point the way?"

"It exists."

"How do you know? You haven't seen it!"

"The legends tell of it."

"Yes, but apparently not how to get there. What good are your legends and your god now? We're out in the middle of nowhere, days travel across a troll-infested swamp. I knew I shouldn't let you come!"

"You would have died in that marsh without me. You probably would have run out of food before ever reaching it."

"I can take care of myself. I don't need you."

"You have always needed someone. You are strong now because of the wizard, but you have always been weak."

"Not anymore."

They stared at each other in silence, neither willing to look away.

"Well, we're stuck here together, so what do we do

now if Ogrosh won't just show you the way?"

"We go into the mountains. That much of the legend is clear."

"We could wander these mountains our whole lives and never find a damn city!"

"You must trust that Ogrosh will show us the way."

Gortogh threw his hands up and screamed. He wanted to yell, to curse Kurgh and his stupid god. But since he didn't have a better plan, he just rolled over and went to sleep.

CHAPTER FOURTEEN

UNWANTED HELP

THEY STUMBLED THROUGH the mountains for another two days.

Gortogh had taken the lead again, cursing Kurgh and his worthless god. Sometimes silently, sometimes not so silently. But mostly to himself. Gortogh was finding it less and less fun to tease the shaman, and he didn't want to provoke him further. Where would he get his dinner if Kurgh decided to leave?

Kurgh mumbled something behind him, but Gortogh ignored him. The shaman had become more and more erratic in his behavior with each passing day. Every night when they camped, he would throw himself to his knees and pray for all he was worth. Gone was the pose of silent, thoughtful prayer. Now it looked as if Kurgh was praying to the dirt itself.

The journey had not been without hope though. They had come across a few roads in the mountains. Though they looked old and in serious need of some repairs, they were there. Gortogh and Kurgh had followed a few of them, but they had only led to more roads.

On second thought, they were hopelessly lost.

Thankfully, these mountains were carved up like old, mouse-eaten bread. They'd found a cave every night to sleep in. Some were shallow, nothing more than a few feet of rock. Others went deep into the darkness, but they had each resisted the urge to explore.

It had rained the past two nights, and the two of them were thankful for any shelter. They had run out of firewood after leaving the foothills, but Kurgh kept a small fire going each night with his own blood. With nothing really to gather, and nothing to fight, Gortogh was starting to feel a bit useless. He wanted to help in some way.

On the third day, he got his wish.

Following yet another broken road along a ravine, Gortogh stopped and held his hand up. Kurgh was mumbling and not paying attention when he bumped into Gortogh's back.

"What?" Kurgh said impatiently.

"Something's not right," Gortogh said.

"Where shall I begin?"

"No, I mean here. Something is odd here."

The ravine was deep, cut between two mountains like the wedge of an axe head. A few large boulders dotted the road ahead and looked like a good place for an ambush. In fact, Gortogh had seen a place just like this before. He'd used it to ambush an elf who was following him once.

"I don't like this," he said.

"This is the only road that has shown any promise at all," Kurgh said.

He held up a piece of a broken pot they'd found and waved it around. At least, they thought it was a piece of a pot. It could be anything really, but it didn't look natural.

Someone had to have made it.

"I just don't like it," Gortogh said. "If I were going to ambush someone, this is where I would do it."

"There is no one out here!" Kurgh yelled.

Gortogh flinched as the echo of his voice danced down the ravine, bouncing from wall to wall.

"You said these are elven lands," Gortogh said.

"Have you seen an elf anywhere? Whatever was once here, they are long gone now."

Before Gortogh could argue again, Kurgh shoved past him and stomped off into the ravine.

"Wait!" Gortogh called.

He jogged to catch up and tried to grab Kurgh by the shoulder, but the shaman just shrugged him off. He reached out again and yanked back just in time to save Kurgh from losing his head. The sword appeared around the edge of the boulder and clanged into it right at the level of Kurgh's neck, leaving a huge gash in the rock.

Kurgh was stunned and sputtered something, but Gortogh had already shoved him back and drawn his sword. He was ready when the elf came around the boulder.

"Think you stand a chance with that thing, goblin?" the elf asked.

Gortogh silently sized him up. Elves were usually a bit taller than goblins, but this one was shorter than any he'd met before. He wore black from head to toe. Black leather armor, black boots, black cloak. Even his hair was black, though it had a purple sheen in the sunlight. It was a stark contrast to the perfectly pale, white skin of his face.

But it was his sword that drew Gortogh's focus. It was thin, barely half the width of Gortogh's own sword. The blade was a little shorter than a longsword, but not by much. With the way the elf weaved it back and forth in front him, there was no doubting his abilities with the thing.

"Can you even swing that?" the elf asked. "It looks a bit heavy."

Gortogh buried his smile beneath a growl. So many had underestimated his strength and skill with that sword. He was used to it by now, but it took everything he had to not reveal himself. He held the sword in two hands before him like he would a club, playing the part of the dumb goblin.

"I've been watching you for days," the elf said. "I had hoped you would leave without causing trouble, but I think this is more fun, don't you?"

Gortogh grunted. It was all he could to keep his mouth shut.

The elf leapt in, his sword aimed for Gortogh's heart. Gortogh swept it aside, but only because he knew it was coming. The elf was impossibly fast. He danced back a step and looked at Gortogh again.

Don't smile. Show no emotion. Give nothing away.

"Interesting," was all the elf said.

He lunged again, the same strike. Gortogh batted it away again, though it got a little closer that time. The elf smiled and lowered his sword. He was testing him.

With a shrug, the elf spun and slashed at Gortogh's face, forcing him back a step. It was a showy move, and Gortogh made note of it. The elf seemed more about making an impression before he killed him than making the kill. Which was probably good, because when the elf decided to fight for real, Gortogh would be dead.

He knew right off that he could not match the elf.

Gortogh's strength was immense when he expended the full energy of his sword, but it did little for his speed. His legs were strong, and he could move a bit more quickly, but he would never match the elf in quickness or skill. And that would be the death of him if he didn't find another way to end this.

But Gortogh had other tricks.

The elf slammed him with a brutal flurry of strikes. Gortogh barely got his sword up to block them all. He fell back with every hit, trying to get away. But really, he was leading the elf. When it looked like Gortogh was pressed to his limit, the elf moved in for the kill.

Gortogh released the power in his ring.

The ring Velanon had given him more than a year ago. The ring that had saved his life and made it so that he could defeat another faster, better foe. The effect was instantaneous. As the magic washed over the elf, Gortogh saw his movements slow. The elf's sword dipped just a bit as the weight changed in his hand.

Now it was Gortogh's turn to attack.

He lunged, the elf now on the defensive. Gortogh chopped and chopped at him knowing that the elf could not bear his strength. Without his dexterity, the elf was at his mercy. And he knew it. Gortogh could see it in his eyes.

Behind him, Kurgh was chanting.

The elf panicked and tried to retreat, but Gortogh was right there on him. He followed the elf's every step, never allowing him distance. The elf's swings were nothing more than slow swipes now. His strength was sapped, and with it his confidence.

Gortogh kicked out and caught the elf in his unguarded stomach. He went tumbling back to land hard on the ground. His sword went flying from his weakened grip. Gortogh held his sword over the elf's throat.

"Surrender," Gortogh said.

"He is alone," Kurgh said, ambling up.

"How do you know?"

"I spread my senses over the area and found no one else."

"That's what you were casting back there?"

"You seemed to have things well in hand."

"He was about to kill me!"

"And yet here you are."

Kurgh stepped slightly in front of him and looked down at the elf.

"Listen to me carefully," Kurgh said. "We know you are out here alone. There is no one who will come for you. That leaves you at my mercy."

Gortogh gave an annoyed look, but Kurgh paid him no attention.

"Since I am in a merciful mood, I will offer you a bargain."

The elf looked back and forth between the two of them. The elf still refused to speak. Not so chatty now that he was on the ground.

"You know these mountains, yes?" Kurgh said.

He looked pointedly at the elf and waited for an answer. After a few seconds, the elf nodded.

"Good," Kurgh said. "We are looking for an ancient goblin city. It is here in The Anvil region. Do you know what I speak of?"

The elf looked around, up and behind them. Gortogh turned to look but saw no one.

"There is no one here," Kurgh said. "You will answer

me, or I will drain the blood from your pathetic body and feast on it."

Kurgh drew his knife and cut his arm. He let the blood flow easily down his forearm and drip onto the elf. It must have been a shallow cut because it closed over after only a few seconds.

"*Your* wounds, I'm afraid, will not heal so easily. Yours will remain open long after your heart has ceased to beat. Until I have all of your life in my hands."

Gortogh saw the panic in the elf's eyes. He was younger than Gortogh had first thought. Elves always looked like young boys to him, but it was something else. The fear in his eyes was stronger than he would expect from a warrior. This elf was young, at least by elven standards. Maybe even a boy still, though Gortogh wasn't sure how many years old that made him.

"Tell me what I want to know," Kurgh said.

"And if I do?" the elf said.

Gortogh was surprised to hear him speak, but Kurgh only smiled.

"I have no reason to kill you. As I said, you have caught me in a merciful mood. Lead us to the goblin city, and I will simply let you go."

"You are a liar," the elf said. "All goblins are filthy liars."

Kurgh chuckled.

"I was told the same thing of the elves," he said. "I could have killed you already if I wanted to."

"But then you wouldn't have me to show you the city."

"So then you *do* know where it is," Kurgh said.

The elf closed his mouth, but Kurgh had already gotten what he wanted.

"Take me to it, and no harm will come to you," he said.

The elf's eyes darted to his sword lying a few feet away. The effects of the ring had probably worn off by now, and he was trying to decide if he could make it or not. Gortogh held his sword out and pointed it at the elf's chest in case he decided to try. The elf swiveled his back around and glared at Kurgh.

"Swear on your blood," he said.

Kurgh chuckled.

"What do you know of blood swears?"

"I know that if you swear on your blood, you cannot go back on your word. Swear on your blood that you'll release me once I take you to the city, and I will believe you."

Kurgh smiled and looked at Gortogh who could only shrug. His knife still in hand, Kurgh sliced into his arm once more and let the blood drip down to his waiting palm.

"I swear by the blood of Ogrosh, we will not harm you once we reach the city."

He held the blood in his palm for a second, then it dissolved back into his hand.

"There," Kurgh said. "Now take us there."

The elf stood slowly but a little more confidently. He started for his sword, but Gortogh stopped him with a look. He went over to pick it up and placed it in the scabbard on his back. He wouldn't be sheathing his own sword while they traveled with the elf. Never trust an elf, his old chief had always said.

Or another goblin for that matter.

"March," Kurgh said.

CHAPTER FIFTEEN

THIS IS IT

THE ELF LED the way down the path they were already on, taking them deeper into the mountains. The road they walked on was in bad shape and could barely be called a road anymore, but it seemed to be getting better as they went. Gortogh noted a few places where it had actually been repaired.

"Where does this lead?" Gortogh asked.

"To the city," the elf said.

"Does someone live there now?" Gortogh asked.

"No," the elf said.

"How long has it been abandoned?"

"I do not know."

Not much of a talker it seemed. Not that Gortogh would have been very chatty if he was being forced at sword point. He would be looking in every direction for an escape. Gortogh moved a little closer to the elf, sure that he was thinking the same.

"Where do you live?" he asked.

The elf kept walking.

"You must live near here somewhere. I see no provisions for long travel, so you can't have come far."

"He lives in the caves," Kurgh said.

"How do you know?" Gortogh asked.

"He is Erutharen. The southern elven kingdom."

The elf looked over his shoulder at the shaman who could only smile. He turned back and kept walking.

"How can you tell?" Gortogh asked.

"The symbol he wears on his chest is of Eruthen, son of Ilothen."

"What do you know of elves?" Gortogh asked.

"Very little other than they live in caves," Kurgh said. "But I know a lot about the gods of Gondril."

The elf stumbled ahead of them, and Gortogh raised his sword. He thought at first that the elf was trying to run, but he had truly just tripped. Too busy looking back at Kurgh to watch where he was going.

"You know nothing of my people," the elf said.

"Yes, I believe I just said that," Kurgh said. "Perhaps you could tell us about them."

"You asked me to take you to the city. I'm taking you to the city."

"Your choice," Kurgh said. "But it might be a long journey."

"Another hour," the elf said.

Gortogh and Kurgh shared a glance, and Gortogh knew they were thinking the same thing. They were almost there. After only a little more than a week, they were about to reach their destination. Just one more hour, and they would see it for the first time.

The city of Ogrilon was within their reach.

***

Ogrilon was nothing like Gortogh had imagined.

"This is Ogrilon?" he said.

Kurgh was silent beside him, but Gortogh could see

that the shaman had his doubts as well. They stood on the edge of a settlement, that was plain to see, but it looked small. Nothing like the legends Gortogh had heard his whole life.

The elf stood in their path for a moment before spinning on his heels and pushing between them. Gortogh turned and pointed his sword.

"Where are you going?" he said.

"I have fulfilled my end of the agreement. I am leaving."

"This is not Ogrilon!" Gortogh said.

"You asked me where the goblin city was, I showed you. This is the only goblin city I know of in these mountains. My sword?"

He held out his hand and waited. Gortogh looked at Kurgh, but the shaman wasn't paying attention. Gortogh shrugged and pulled the sword from his back and handed it to the elf. He immediately began walking again, but Kurgh stepped in front of him.

"This can't be it," Kurgh said. "There must be another."

"I have lived my whole life, one considerably longer than either of yours, in these mountains, and this is the only goblin settlement I know. *That* is it. That must be what you came looking for as there is no other."

Gortogh turned to look at the settlement again. It was small. Not much bigger than the village of Jornath his goblins had ransacked when he first became chief. A few huts lining the roads. A couple of small, squat buildings carved into the mountain. It was a bit sturdier than the typical goblin settlement but not by much.

"Is this truly it?" Gortogh said.

"Wait!" Kurgh called.

The elf kept walking. Gortogh pointed his sword.

"Stop or we will make you stop," he said.

The elf slowed and then came to a halt and turned. He folded his arms and glared at them.

"What other settlements do you know in these mountains?" Gortogh asked.

"The only others I know are buried within the rock itself. That is where my people live and a place I suggest you avoid. You will find our little arrangement flipped should you choose to go down that path."

"Why would one tribe of goblins settle all this way into the mountains without others?" Kurgh asked.

"Are you asking me to give you a goblin history lesson?" the elf said.

"It just doesn't make sense," Kurgh said.

The elf smiled and shook his head.

"From what I remember, different goblin tribes were always trying to kill one another. Perhaps one decided it was best to run and hide in the mountains than face their betters."

Kurgh sneered.

"Is that why you and your brothers left the other elves?" he asked.

The elf's face tightened. His hands fell to his belt.

"Don't," Gortogh said.

"Save your judgement for your own people," Kurgh said.

"We are done here," the elf said. "Though you are disgusting goblins, I expect you to honor your promise and let me go. If you do not, your blood is worthless."

Kurgh glared hard, holding the elf's stare. Then he waved his hand. The elf spun around and walked away.

"Come on," Kurgh said.

They walked deeper into the little settlement though it didn't take them long to reach the other side. No more than a hundred goblins could have lived here, and there was no telling how long ago. Everything was broken or destroyed. Some by nature and time, some by previous occupants.

They found evidence of several groups of inhabitants who must have, at one time, called this village home. Goblins, for sure, but also ogres and possibly humans at one time. Each one left some piece of their history behind to mark their passage through, but no one remained today.

It was empty.

"Where do we go now?" Gortogh asked.

"Exactly where we were headed before. To find Ogrilon."

"What if this *is* Ogrilon?"

Kurgh's head dropped.

"Then there is no hope for us."

And like that, he picked his head up, and marched on.

CHAPTER SIXTEEN

OGRILON

GORTOGH AND KURGH wandered the mountains for another two days with no sign of anything. It was starting to feel like the boondoggle Gortogh had suspected it would be all along. He was growing tired and frustrated, but not nearly as much as Kurgh. Ever since they had found the village, he had taken to openly complaining, sometimes yelling at their surroundings.

He was losing his mind.

They sat across a low fire from each other. Gortogh had cooked a mountain ram last night that Kurgh managed to summon and was now warming more of the meat for breakfast. The sun came over the mountains to his back and shined right into Kurgh's closed eyes. He growled and moved to the other side of the fire, right beside Gortogh.

Kurgh closed his eyes and tried to settle in, but he couldn't seem to get comfortable.

"This is impossible!" he yelled. "I can't concentrate like this!"

Gortogh had learned quickly not to talk back or ask questions. It would only enrage him further. So, he quietly turned the meat, enjoying the smell and the sizzling sound of the fat falling into the fire.

"Quiet that damn noise!" Kurgh yelled.

Gortogh pulled his stick out of the fire. It looked cooked enough. He blew on it a few times and then proceeded to eat. He laid a long strip of the meat over a rock nearby for Kurgh. If he would even eat it. Kurgh had also taken to punishing himself by not eating or drinking. The less he ate, the crazier his actions became. Perhaps the two are related.

Kurgh was taut, his body tightly compressed into position instead of his normal, relaxed pose. He looked ready to lash out at anything near him. Gortogh carefully got up and moved to the other side of the fire. The sun in his eyes didn't bother him nearly as much as sitting next to the disturbed shaman.

Kurgh screamed, startling him.

"This is hopeless!"

Gortogh didn't take the bait.

"We can't just stumble around these mountains forever!"

Still not biting.

"This is all your fault! Ogrosh has forsaken me because I am with you!"

He bit.

"Is that what you think this is?"

"There can be no other explanation!"

"What if there is no Ogrilon to *find*? What if that village really *was* it?"

"*That* was not Ogrilon. The legends do not lie."

"How do you know? No one has seen it or been to it in maybe thousands of years."

"I have faith. If you had the same faith, we would

have found it. Ogrosh is punishing you."

Gortogh sighed and shook his head. He tried to ignore the shaman's words, but something gnawed at him. What if Kurgh was right? What if Ogrosh really was punishing him? It seemed like a foolish way to do it. Why not just kill him or cut his legs off? He was a god after all. But making him wander around the mountains? Maybe Kurgh was his punishment.

No, this wasn't Ogrosh's doing. This was his own doing. A stupid quest to find something that doesn't even exist. All to prove a point to someone he didn't have to prove anything to. What in the nine hells was he thinking?

Still.

What if Kurgh wasn't crazy? If Ogrosh was truly punishing him, they might very well wander these mountains forever. Or at least until the elves got tired of their snooping and decided to take care of the problem. If Ogrosh had the power to punish him from afar, why not just help them instead? Wouldn't he want them to find Ogrilon?

Kurgh's eyes were closed when Gortogh opened the pouch around his neck. He pulled the amulet from its hidden home and held it tightly in his hands. If Ogrosh wanted to help them, perhaps he could find a way with this. Gortogh squeezed the amulet tightly in his hands and then did something he hadn't done since he was a child.

Gortogh prayed to Ogrosh.

Really prayed. He prayed to find the way. Or, if the city didn't exist, he prayed to find some way to know that. He wasn't sure if praying to prove someone wrong was something Ogrosh would frown upon, but he didn't care. He came out here to find something, and by Ogrosh, he was going to find something. Even if it was nothing.

The amulet hummed in his hands. Not like it had in the past though. It was a different kind of feeling. A low buzzing sound. A tingling in his skin that he felt spread through his whole body.

"What are you doing?" Kurgh shouted.

Gortogh ignored him. The amulet was doing something, and he wasn't about to stop.

"Put that away before you make things worse!"

Gortogh blocked him out. He let himself hear only the amulet. With energy coursing through his body, Gortogh stood and began to walk.

"Ogrosh will strike us both down for this!"

Gortogh kept walking.

"Where are you going, you fool?"

He walked north and felt the power dim just a little. He turned east and felt it get even weaker. When he went back to the west, it grew stronger. He understood.

The amulet was showing him the way.

"What?" Kurgh asked.

He sounded more intrigued than angry now.

"The amulet is telling me where to go," Gortogh said.

"I could have told you we needed to go west."

"Gather up our things," Gortogh said. "We'll follow it."

And they did follow it. West, and then north. Deeper into the mountains.

Walking all day and sleeping only until the sun came up, they followed the humming power of the amulet. When the power became weaker, they turned in a new direction. When it became stronger, they went that way.

West and north. The amulet continued leading them west and north.

On the third day, they found a trail. Buried over by rock and mud, it led lower into the mountains. They followed the trail, the amulet practically leaping from Gortogh's hand. He could feel the excitement, the anticipation coming from it. More than that, he could feel it from Kurgh. And his own, if he was honest with himself.

Would they truly find the lost city? Was the amulet leading them to Ogrilon or someplace else? Did Ogrosh really want them to find it? Is that why he led them here? Gortogh didn't know, but he knew in his heart this was the way.

The trail led them down through a narrow pass and into a valley below. As the trail rounded the mountain, they saw the first tower. The amulet hummed loudly for a moment and then stopped. They both stood silent, neither one daring to move as their eyes took it all in. The gates before them were gone, crumbled to piles of stone and metal. But beyond that lay the real treasure.

They had found Ogrilon.

CHAPTER SEVENTEEN

RUINS

"IS THIS REALLY it?" Gortogh asked.

They stood on the edge of the valley. Before them was a short, narrow pass that led right to the gates of the city. What was left of them anyway. It took up the whole valley, it seemed. Ogrilon spread out in every direction before them, more than they could even see from their vantage point.

Kurgh just stared up, his eyes flitting from place to place. Gortogh looked past the crumbling gates to what was beyond. The edges of the city were cut into the mountains themselves with buildings and towers that seemed to climb the rocky peaks. While most of those looked to be somewhat intact, the rest of the city was nothing but piles of rubble.

A building here, a building there, most collapsed to broken blocks of stone. Gortogh didn't know what he expected to find, but this wasn't it. By the look in Kurgh's eyes, it wasn't what he had hoped for either.

"It's destroyed," Gortogh said.

"Ogrilon has not been touched in thousands of years," Kurgh said. "Of course it would be crumbling."

Gortogh wasn't even sure that it was Ogrilon they were looking on, but he had to admit that it was unlikely to be some other forgotten city of legend.

"This is not crumbling," Gortogh said. "This is destroyed."

Kurgh shuffled forward toward the gate.

"Wait," Gortogh said. "We don't know what attacked this place. They could still be here."

"After thousands of years?"

"Dragons live a long time."

"Not that long."

Kurgh kept walking. Gortogh shrugged and fell in behind him. The gates, once mighty walls of stone as thick as four ogres, were now, like everything else, a pile of rubble. Gortogh kicked a stone that clattered off the wall to tumble down amongst the others.

"What could have done this?" he asked.

"Dragons," Kurgh said.

He pointed to some of the stone where blackened scorch marks were still visible.

"That could have come from anything," Gortogh said.

"Do you know of another force which could level gates of stone this thick?"

"Wizards. I have seen what their magic can do."

"No," Kurgh said. "You can see great claw marks in the wall. This was the work of dragons."

"Why didn't we hear that story in your legends?" Gortogh asked.

"Perhaps because no one survived to tell it," Kurgh said.

From the level of destruction, that was looking likely.

Gortogh admired the walls as they passed through the gates. They were six feet thick, at least, and they went from one side of the mountain pass to other, as though they had grown from the living rock itself. If he didn't see its destruction with his own eyes, Gortogh would have thought the wall impenetrable.

They moved through the city, from one crumbled building to the next, with slow ease. They were both taking everything in. Gortogh still couldn't believe the city was real. No doubt Kurgh had believed it all along, but Gortogh couldn't help thinking the shaman was a little disappointed. Ogrilon, if it was that, was not the great, shining city he had spoken of so often.

Kurgh bent down and picked up the broken piece of some clay pot. He squatted on the ground, holding it in his hand and turning it over. With a deep breath, he tossed it aside where it shattered.

"There is nothing left," he said.

Gortogh looked around. He had to agree.

"Those towers look intact," he said, pointing up. "Perhaps we'll find something in there."

"Too risky. They could collapse."

"They look sound. They're carved into the mountains themselves."

Kurgh knelt in silence, staring up at a broken column of some building that might have once been important.

"I didn't come all the way out here to just turn around and go home," Gortogh said.

Kurgh stood and spun on him.

"Why did you come out here?" Kurgh asked.

"To show you that Ogrilon was a myth."

No reason to lie about it now.

"Well, you were wrong."

"I was wrong."

"That should make me feel good," Kurgh said.

"It doesn't?"

"No. Ogrilon is here, we're standing in it, but what good is it? There's nothing left of it."

"What did you think we would find? Why did *you* come all this way?"

"I don't know," Kurgh admitted. "I thought we would find… something. Anything about our history, about our people. Something to tell us where to go."

Gortogh scoffed.

"History will tell you nothing about your future."

"You're wrong. History can tell us we were once great. This city, though it's in ruins, tells us that. Goblins once had a city like no other I have ever seen. Perhaps the greatest city ever built."

They looked around, turning in a circle to take it all in. Gortogh closed his eyes and imagined it.

Ogrilon.

The gates stood before him, magnificent and formidable. Beyond lay the shining city, cut from the gray and white rock of the mountains around him. Spires grew upward like fingers stretching to the heavens. A bubbling fountain stood in the center of the city, its waters sprung from the cold depths of the rock below.

"It was beautiful," Gortogh said. "I can see it."

"You didn't even believe it was here," Kurgh said.

"But I see it now. You are right, it is an amazing city."

"Once, perhaps."

Gortogh sighed.

"There must be something left."

Kurgh made a show of looking around. Gortogh could see just as well as he could there was nothing left. The towers of the city were still standing only because they were part of the mountain, but he could see giant holes in the sides where they were falling apart. Or perhaps where they were torn apart.

"Well, what do we do now?" Gortogh asked.

"The sun will set soon," Kurgh said. "We can maybe try searching in the morning."

"Search for what?"

"For anything!"

Gortogh thought it best to leave the shaman to his thoughts and decided to make camp. He made a fire with the last of the firewood and laid some of his dried venison in front of Kurgh. They stared silently across from each other. Gortogh had so many things he wanted to talk about, but he actually preferred the silence to crazy Kurgh shouting at him. Hours passed, but the boredom eventually got the better of him.

"You must at least be glad that it's here," Gortogh said. "Perhaps your legends aren't lies after all."

"No one but you ever thought they *were* lies. What good does a destroyed city do me?"

Gortogh shook his head.

"I found what I came looking for," he said. "What did you hope to find?"

"I told you. Our past."

"And you've found it. Maybe it's all true. Maybe the war with dragons really happened as you say. Only it didn't end the way your legends tell it."

"That still doesn't explain what happened."

"What happened to what?"

"To us! I want to know what happened... to us... to our people. How did we go from this once-great city to living in caves and huts?"

"I don't know."

"*No one* does. That is why I'm here. You ask what I

want? I want to know what happened."

Kurgh turned away from the fire and laid his head down. Gortogh didn't know what to say. He had never thought of the question before. He had always believed that goblins simply were who they were. He never believed the stories of Ogrilon and the great civilization.

They were all just goblins.

What did happen? He had never asked himself the question, but now it was staring him in the face. The goblins were once a great and, by the looks of it, powerful civilization. Where did it all go? How did they end up as warring savages living under the boots of the other children of the gods?

It was with this weighing on his mind that Gortogh fell asleep.

CHAPTER EIGHTEEN

SEEKING

WHEN HE AWOKE the next morning he was alone. Gortogh sat up in his bedroll and looked around, but Kurgh was nowhere to be seen.

"Kurgh?" he called softly.

No answer.

"Kurgh?" he shouted.

Still no answer.

Gortogh stood and cracked his bones, feeling very sore from the night on the hard ground. Most of his nights had been hard lately, but it seemed to be getting worse. Maybe it was wearing on him. Maybe he was getting old. Probably both.

Where was Kurgh? And how could he just walk away without Gortogh hearing? The shaman was sneaky, that much was true, but Gortogh was not that hard a sleeper.

"Kurgh!" he yelled again.

The name echoed from the stone around him, floating across the little valley of Ogrilon as though the mountains themselves were calling him. Gortogh picked up his things and started walking. He couldn't have gone far, it was only... midday? Gortogh checked the sun again to be sure. How could he have slept that long?

Perhaps the trip really was starting to wear on him. Or maybe it was the peace he'd come to know in the last few days. He didn't know if it was the amulet or Ogrilon, but something had changed. Gortogh felt different somehow.

He set about exploring the ruined city. There wasn't much to see, really. He poked his head in a few of the nearby buildings and called out for Kurgh again, but there was no answer. Not even a sound except the ones he made.

There was nothing.

What remained standing of Ogrilon was empty now. When the goblins abandoned the city, they must've had time to take everything with them. Not a pot or bed remained. Just rock and rubble as far as he could see.

Gortogh heard a rock click off another and tumble to a stop. He looked up, hoping it was Kurgh, but found someone else instead.

"Don't move," the elf said.

Gortogh stood up straight and folded his arms in front of him. He stared as the elf picked his way down from behind the rocks.

"You knew," Gortogh said. "You knew this is what we were looking for."

The elf looked the same as when he'd left them days ago. His sword was drawn and pointing straight at Gortogh's chest. He could probably draw his own sword before the elf could reach him, but there was no reason to hurry. If the elf had wanted him dead, he would have crept close and done it before Gortogh had even heard him.

"I wasn't about to just lead you here at sword point,"

the elf said.

"Why not? What do you care what we're looking for?"

"What *are* you looking for?"

Gortogh eyed him appraisingly. So, that's why he didn't bring them here. He wanted to know what they wanted with the place first. He wasn't sure what they would find. Not that Gortogh or Kurgh knew either, but he must have *thought* they knew. Boy, was he in for a surprise.

"What *is* there to find?" Gortogh asked.

"Nothing," the elf said. "Just broken homes and statues."

"Then why not bring us here in the first place?"

"Because I should have killed you where you stood."

"You tried," Gortogh said.

He smiled and puffed out his chest.

"You got lucky, goblin."

"Is it so hard to believe a goblin can best you at swordplay?"

"You are not better than me. You used some trick on me."

"I did," Gortogh said. "Does that mean I didn't defeat you?"

"Not fairly."

Gortogh laughed.

"Oh, you wanted a fair fight? Then you should have picked another opponent. I didn't realize we were in the Valley of Fair Fights, my apologies."

The elf raised his sword and took two steps closer.

"Will you fight me fairly?" he asked.

The confusion on Gortogh's face must have been evident.

"Draw your sword and let us see who is better," the elf said. "No tricks this time."

"No," Gortogh said.

"No?"

"No. To fight you would be stupid. We have no reason to fight."

"You are a goblin, that is all the reason I need."

"Why? What have I done?"

"I don't know what you've done, but I know who you are."

Gortogh laughed.

"Praise Ogrosh! If only you'd joined me weeks ago. You could have just told me who I am, and I could have saved myself the trip out here."

Now it was the elf's turn to look confused. Gortogh spun and started to walk away.

"Go home, boy," Gortogh said.

"I am no boy!"

"I don't know how old you are, elf. You're probably a great deal older than me, but I know a boy when I see one."

Gortogh turned back.

"What is your name?" he asked.

The elf sputtered.

"You do know your own name, yes?"

"Arnem," the elf finally managed.

"Let me give you some help, Arnem. When you get in a fight, you win. However you must, you win. If you don't win, you die. This strange way you think fighting should be does not exist outside of play. If you fight me again, I will use everything I have to kill you. You should do the same."

Gortogh walked away and continued his search for

Kurgh.

***

Gortogh opened his eyes and found the sun quite stinging. He'd slept longer than he'd intended, and it was late again. He had gone to bed the night before after hunting for Kurgh most of the day and finding no trace of him. The elf had gone as well, though Gortogh was thankful for that. He'd had quite enough fighting lately.

"Morning!" Kurgh said.

Gortogh bolted up and saw the shaman sitting across from a low-burning fire. Something about him unsettled Gortogh. Kurgh was smiling. A big, toothy grin that made him look even crazier, if that was possible.

"Where have you been?" Gortogh asked.

"Searching," Kurgh said.

His smile widened even further

"Did you find something?"

"Nothing!" Kurgh said.

"Then… why so happy?"

"That's just it. Don't you see? We haven't found what I came here for."

"Which is what?"

"The library! The legends speak of the library of Ogrilon as one of the largest and greatest collections of knowledge amassed on Gondril. It holds all the history of the goblins and much of the history of the rest of the world."

"Then it is lost now. Maybe a few books survived, but we're not likely to find anything."

"That's just it. I've been all over the place. I've been from one side of the city to the other, and I can find nothing that looks like the great library from the legends."

"One pile of rubble is the same as another," Gortogh said.

"No. The library is not here. But it must be somewhere."

"Then where would it be?"

"In the towers? Underground?"

"Inside the mountain? Doesn't seem likely."

"Why not? The dwarves made their homes deep in the mountains, why not our ancestors?"

Gortogh looked at the ground with an appraising eye. It didn't seem likely.

"If it is beneath us, then it is most likely buried there. We wouldn't even know where to begin looking for an entrance."

"All I know is that the library must be here somewhere. There would be books, tablets, something. We have to find it."

How long would all that take? Though he didn't relish the thought of their journey back, Gortogh had no intentions of digging through this rubble for the rest of his life.

"Give me the amulet," Kurgh said.

Gortogh took a step back, his hand clutching instinctively to the pouch around his neck.

"No," he said flatly.

"The amulet brought us here, to the city. Ogrosh wanted us to find it. But this can't be all he wanted us to see. There must be something else here he wants us to have. The amulet might show us the way."

Gortogh took the amulet from its dark hiding place and clutched it in his hand. He looked at it, as he had done a hundred times before, and wondered why he had it. Was this what it was all about? Had Ogrosh truly led him here to find something?

"Give it to me," Kurgh said.

"No," Gortogh said again. "I have seen what this can do in the hands of someone like me. I fear what it would do in the hands of someone like you."

Kurgh's hand inched for his knife.

"What do you mean someone like me?"

"I hold no love for Ogrosh, and still with the amulet I was able to lead thousands. What evil could it do in the hands of someone who believes with all his heart?"

"You ask the wrong question. What good could it do?"

"This is not a tool of good. It was made for evil, and that is all it can do."

"It led us here. I do not think that was evil or a mistake."

Gortogh turned the disc over and over in his hand. He felt the hum of its power now stronger than he ever had before. The amulet felt at home in this place, he could feel it. Here in Ogrilon, and he had no doubt now that is where they stood, the amulet was truly awakened.

"Is this what you wanted?" he asked.

He felt silly talking to the amulet, a thing, yet somehow it felt natural. The amulet felt alive in his hand, and he spoke to it as if it were. Kurgh was watching him closely, but he didn't care.

"What do you want us to see?"

He felt a tingle in his fingers. The same he had felt before when it led them here. Gortogh turned in a circle, taking a few steps in each direction, and noted where the amulet's power felt strongest.

"There," he said.

He pointed away from their camp, into the heart of

the city. Gortogh took the lead, and Kurgh scurried up to walk beside him. Side by side, they walked to the center of the city where the remains of a great fountain stood. Water still collected in its basin, but Gortogh could hear it flowing out through a crack somewhere and back into the mountain.

"Where now?" Kurgh asked, impatient.

Gortogh walked around the fountain in each direction.

"That way," he said, pointing west.

"Away from the city?" Kurgh asked. "But the library would be near the center."

"I don't know that we *are* going to the library," Gortogh said. "The amulet is telling us to go that way."

He walked on without waiting to see if Kurgh would follow. He knew that he would. The crumbling, pitted street took them away from the fountain and away from the remains of the city. Soon they were beyond the buildings and the city proper. The cobbled street became a rocky path leading deeper into the mountains.

Still the amulet guided them on.

CHAPTER NINETEEN

THE GREAT LIBRARY

THE AMULET PULLED them west, beyond the city. They passed another gate that was destroyed like the first they encountered and followed out into the mountains. Gortogh held the amulet tight in his hand and moved it back and forth as they walked, moving where the amulet's pull was strongest. Around a bend, the path split off behind a rocky outcrop and seemed to lead up.

"It says we go up," Gortogh said.

Kurgh pushed past him and looked to where he pointed.

"There is a staircase," he said.

Gortogh looked closer. There was, indeed, a staircase. Carved into the mountain itself, it led up around the outside of the cliff face. But toward what?

Kurgh didn't wait to find out. He took the stairs two steps at a time without bothering to look back. Gortogh chuckled. The shaman didn't like playing second to him. Wherever they were going, Kurgh wanted to be the first to reach it.

The stairs went higher. The steps were cut into the mountain in such a way that there was a waist-high ledge on the outside that could be grasped to rest and take a breath. Gortogh didn't stop often, but Kurgh seemed determined to reach the top without a break. With a deep breath, Gortogh climbed up after him.

When he finally reached the top of the stairs, he stood in stunned silence.

There before them was the grandest structure Gortogh had ever seen. Granted, he'd spent most of his life in caves and forests, but even the spires of Ogrilon could not compare to what was before him now. Carved from the mountain, like so many other structures of the goblin city, the place was massive. It stood almost sixty feet tall, lined with great, white columns in front that looked as though they couldn't possibly hold the thing up.

Yet here it was. Intact and untouched. The building had not only managed to escape whatever destruction befell Ogrilon, but it was actually pristine. Even the hand of time seemed not to have touched it. There was not a speck of dust on the white steps before them. Not a single crack in the perfect columns.

"This is it," Kurgh whispered.

"What?"

"The library. This has to be the library."

"How do you know?"

"Because it's what I always imagined it to be."

Gortogh scoffed.

"Well, what else could it be?" Kurgh asked.

Gortogh shrugged, but Kurgh wasn't looking. His eyes never moved from the doors in front of them. Twenty feet tall and made of solid bronze, the two double doors stood closed before them. Kurgh inched forward a step and then stopped. Gortogh slipped the amulet around his neck and followed.

"How do we get in?" he asked.

"Knock?"

Kurgh marched up the steps, and Gortogh followed behind him, though he stayed a few steps back. What if something lived in this place? Something that needed, say, twenty foot doors and sixty foot ceilings? If Kurgh wanted to knock, let him knock. Gortogh wasn't about to.

Kurgh knocked.

His bony knuckles clacked on the door, but the sound that emanated out was like a gong. The clanging sound echoed out from the door for several seconds. Kurgh was reaching up to knock again when they heard a loud grinding sound.

Gortogh immediately reached for his sword and leapt back from the doors, but Kurgh didn't move. The shaman raised his arms to the heavens and waited. Together, as if by magic, the doors swung inward in harmony with one another. A musty smell, like wet wood, wafted through the big opening and hit Gortogh in the face. Kurgh stepped inside.

"Wait!" Gortogh said.

Kurgh turned to look.

"You're not going in there," Gortogh said.

"I have waited my whole life for this moment," Kurgh said. "You can stay out here if you want."

And with that, he disappeared into the darkness beyond. Gortogh growled and bounded up the steps. With his sword still in hand, he followed Kurgh inside. He found him only twenty feet from the door, staring at the wall with his mouth agape. Gortogh turned to see what he was looking at and felt his own mouth fall open.

The wall in front of them was as high as the building, painted from floor to ceiling with the most beautiful image Gortogh had ever seen.

Ogrilon.

The great goblin city stood before him now just as he'd imagined it when they first arrived. Golden and white, one with the mountain. He could almost hear the sparkling water as it flowed in the fountain. He even thought he saw it move in the painting.

The city was painted with what must have been thousands of goblins. They walked and ran and played through the streets of Ogrilon without a care on their intricately painted faces.

"It's beautiful," Gortogh said.

He turned to say something to Kurgh, but the shaman was facing the opposite direction. Gortogh looked over his shoulder and saw another painting encompassing that wall. But this one was not of a peaceful city. This was a painting of a great battle.

A war.

Goblins and dragons fighting each other. Blood raining from the sky, forming into fire and ice as it struck the flying dragons. At the center of the painting, taking up most of the wall, was a golden dragon, wings stretched between two columns. And riding the dragon was a goblin shaman. Dressed much like Kurgh, the shaman had one hand on a long set of reins and the other holding a sphere of blood.

Around the shaman's neck was an amulet. But not the bronze disc that Gortogh now wore. Not an amulet made of Ogrosh. The amulet was a tiny pink crystal dangling at the end of a gold chain. Gortogh had seen that crystal before. It was the crystal worn by the wizard

Velanon.

The dragonbane crystal.

They both looked at each other when a voice broke their silence.

"Praise Ogrosh, you have finally come!"

CHAPTER TWENTY

THE MONK

"I HAVE WAITED so long for you to come!"

Gortogh gripped his sword and felt the magical strength flow through him. Kurgh had his bone knife in hand once the shock wore off. They both stood facing this new figure.

A goblin. Gortogh was too stunned at finding someone here to speak. All he could do was hold his sword at the ready in case the other goblin attacked.

"But which of you is it?"

The man stepped closer, and they both tensed and raised their weapons. The goblin didn't seem to notice. Gortogh looked him up and down for a weapon but saw none. He was dressed in simple white robes that covered his entire body. Gortogh saw no pockets, not even a belt, but that didn't mean there was nothing concealed beneath the robes.

"It must be you," he said, moving closer to Gortogh.

Gortogh pointed his sword menacingly, but the goblin wasn't even looking. He had fallen to the ground in front of Gortogh and was laying with his arms outstretched.

"Bless me, Giver of Blood, that I might fulfill my last wish and go to you."

Gortogh cocked an eye at Kurgh, but the shaman only shrugged.

"Who are you?" Gortogh managed to ask.

"But… you know who I am," he said. "You know and see all."

"What is your name?" Gortogh asked.

The goblin looked up, his face a mash of confusion and hurt.

"I… I don't understand, Father of Fathers. You know me. You must."

"Have we met?" Gortogh asked.

"Only ever in my prayers, Mighty One."

Kurgh grabbed Gortogh by the shoulder and pulled him close enough to whisper.

"It's that damn amulet," he said, pointing but not touching the disc around Gortogh's neck. "He thinks you're Ogrosh."

Gortogh pulled the amulet over his head and stuffed it back into the pouch he wore there.

"There has been a mistake," he said. "I am not Ogrosh."

"But… but I can feel it," the goblin said. "I can feel you here in my heart."

"Get up," Kurgh said. "The amulet he carries only makes you think you feel Ogrosh. He is no more Ogrosh than you are."

Kurgh pulled the goblin's arm, trying to yank him to his feet, but he wouldn't budge. Instead he began to weep. Quietly at first and then getting louder. Kurgh looked at Gortogh, but he could only shrug.

"Get up!" Kurgh shouted.

The goblin wailed.

"Leave him be," Gortogh said.

He pushed past the robed goblin crying on the ground and moved beyond the painted murals they had seen when they first came in. Deeper into the hall he went, though he could still hear the muffled cries of the goblin echoing around him. Kurgh glided up alongside him.

"What do we do with him?" he asked.

"Nothing," Gortogh said.

"But what is he doing? How can he be here?"

"Perhaps he lives here."

"But how? I see no one else. No wife, no family. How can he just live here?"

"Perhaps when he stops blubbering we can ask him."

More paintings covered the halls beyond the entry, each one depicting some great event in Ogrilon's history. The two of them found a stone bench in the middle of the hall and sat down. After another few minutes, the crying died down, and they heard the goblin get up. Gortogh was impressed at how quiet he was as he walked over to them.

"I am sorry," he said. "I did not mean to lose control of myself like that."

"Who are you?" Gortogh asked for the third time.

"I am Targhal, keeper of the library."

"Then this *is* the library?" Kurgh asked.

"The great library of Ogrilon, yes."

"What are you doing here?" Gortogh asked.

"I am waiting. And while I wait, I care for the books."

"Waiting for what?"

"For Ogrosh. I am sorry I got so upset earlier. When I thought you were him, I thought my wait was finally over. When you were not him, I... I lost control of myself. It is unlike me."

"What makes you think Ogrosh is coming?" Kurgh asked.

"Because this is the only place he *can* come," Targhal said. "This library is the only place on Gondril where Ogrosh can appear."

Gortogh and Kurgh exchanged a glance.

"How do you know this?" Kurgh asked.

"It says so in the texts," he said, waving his hand behind him into the library. "This library is Ogrosh's home on Gondril. It is where he can speak to his children."

"Ogrosh has appeared here in person?" Kurgh asked.

"Not for many thousands of years, no," Targhal said, "but he can."

Gortogh could hear the optimism in his voice, but something else he said stood out even more.

"How long have you been here?" he asked.

"A little over four thousand years," Targhal said.

Gortogh's mouth hung open.

"But... how can that be?" Gortogh asked, stunned.

"I told you. I am waiting for Ogrosh."

"You cannot have been here that long," Kurgh said. "You would have died millennia ago."

"The library keeps me safe," he said. "I need no food, no water, nothing. I do not age, I will not die. Everything within these walls has the protection of Ogrosh himself. That is how it has stood for so many thousands of years. No war can destroy this temple. This is Ogrosh's home on Gondril."

"But... you just stay here?" Kurgh asked.

"I am waiting for him to appear. When he does, I will

go home with him."

"What if he never comes?" Gortogh asked.

"I will wait until he does."

Gortogh looked at Kurgh and could tell the shaman was thinking the same thing. Targhal was insane. Insane and smiling cheerfully.

"Come on," he said. "I'll show you the library."

Chapter Twenty-One

Still Searching

GORTOGH PICKED HIS way down the steep staircase to the valley floor below. It was their third day in the library, and while Kurgh was having a good time, Gortogh could hardly stand it. He couldn't read or write the way Kurgh could, so the library held little interest for him.

Kurgh had learned to read at a young age. Gortogh, though weaker than most goblins, never cared for reading. It was not something that warriors did. Kurgh, on the other hand, had always wanted to be a shaman. Gortogh had tried looking at some of the pictures on the first day, but Kurgh got annoyed at his constantly asking what was going on in the book.

Targhal had followed them around at first, but Kurgh made it very clear that he didn't want the monk around. That's what he called himself, a monk. Before Ogrilon fell, he had been part of an order of monks who stayed within the library and kept it perfect for the day Ogrosh would arrive.

Thousands of years ago, a visit from Ogrosh was not so uncommon a thing, but ever since the fall of the city, he had not been seen. Gortogh tried to talk to the monk about the city and what happened to it, but he quickly disappeared into the stacks of books and didn't show his face again. It was all very strange. And very boring.

Gortogh couldn't stand it.

That was when he left and started exploring the city. It was a bit more satisfying at least.

He also wanted to find food. Not because he needed it, the library really did keep them from being hungry at all. He just needed to eat. All those months alone in his cave, the meals were the one constant. He marked his days by them. Measured his life by them.

Foraging around in the city didn't yield much, but he did manage to find some things to eat. Mushrooms grew up from some of the cracks in the mountains. The fountain in the center of the city still had flowing water, probably from an underground spring. He had to reach down beneath the surface to get it, but it was there.

He'd even managed to hunt a few lizards. Big lizards the size of his leg, which made for a pretty tasty meal once they were cooked. A bit stringy though. But today it was only mushrooms.

Why was he doing this? He didn't need to eat if he stayed in the library. It was stupid to sit out here and eat bland, dry mushrooms just to satisfy some silly sense of self. He was used to it though. The loneliness gave him time to think.

But he wasn't alone today.

He felt the tingle in the amulet that told him something was amiss, and he knew who it was.

"If you're going to hide and watch, you might as well come and join me," Gortogh said.

A minute passed in silence, and Gortogh couldn't help but smile. From behind a mound of rocks, Arnem stood up and brushed himself off.

"How did you know I was here?" he asked.

"We are not as dumb as you think we are," Gortogh said.

Gortogh waved his hand, but the elf stayed where he was.

"I'm not going to bite you," Gortogh said.

"I would kill you first," the elf said.

Gortogh laughed and nodded his head.

"Probably," he said. "But let's not find out. Come, sit."

The elf eyed him for another moment but then finally relented and came over. He kept his sword out though. Gortogh pointed to a rocky seat across from him. He held up his hand and offered some of his mushrooms.

"Are you going to kill me?" he asked, pointing to the sword.

"I won't need to," he said. "Those mushrooms will do it for me. We use them to make a potent poison."

Gortogh looked at them in his hand, shrugged, and popped the rest in his mouth.

"They're a little dry" he said.

He chewed a few more times and then swallowed. The elf looked stunned, which was what Gortogh had wanted. Still eyeing him, the elf took the rock across from him and sat down. He kept his sword beside him.

"Sure you don't want some?"

"No," the elf said. "You'll be dead in just a few minutes."

Gortogh shrugged and took a swig from his waterskin.

"Where is your friend?" the elf asked. "In the library?"

Gortogh chuckled.

"Why did you lie?" he asked.

"Lie about what?"

"You said there was nothing in the city. Did the library just slip your mind?"

"No, I knew it was there. I just didn't think it was worth mentioning."

"Not worth mentioning?"

"It's as empty as the rest of this place. Just another relic of a lost tribe of savages."

Gortogh hid his confusion as he looked around. Did the library hide its true nature from anyone but goblins? Or maybe just those would do it harm. Whatever it was, the elf couldn't see what he and Kurgh saw. Which is probably why its contents were still there. Otherwise, the elves would have taken everything millennia ago.

He'd been studying the city for days now, and one thing was for sure. Ogrilon was not built by some race of savages. If he hadn't seen the murals himself, Gortogh would have never believed it was his own people who had made it. It was far too beautiful to be made by goblins. Yet here it was.

"You didn't find anything in the library?" Gortogh asked.

"Did you?"

"No. But Kurgh is determined to keep looking until he does."

It wasn't exactly a lie.

"They weren't savages," Gortogh said.

"What?"

Gortogh waved his arm around at the ruins of Ogrilon.

"This does not look like the home of savages," Gortogh said. "This place, Ogrilon, was once a beautiful, shining city."

"And now it is nothing but rubble. What good is it?"

"A diamond that is covered in dirt is still a diamond. It only waits for someone to come along and dust it off."

"And what if the diamond is broken? What then?"

"It can still sparkle as it once did. If only in pieces."

The elf folded his arms and glared.

"Are you some sort of goblin prophet?"

Gortogh laughed. If only.

"Just someone who has spent most of his life alone, thinking."

"You are not like any goblin I have ever met."

"How many have you met?"

"None," the elf admitted. "But I have learned enough about them to know that you are different."

Gortogh sighed.

"Sadly, you are right about that. It may be that I know as little about goblins as you do."

He waved his hand around, gesturing at the city.

"I never believed in this place, you know. Maybe when I was a child, but it was always just stories to me. Yet here it stands. Perhaps what we both know of goblins is wrong."

The elf looked doubtful, but he did uncross his arms and relax a bit.

"Do your people know of the city?" Gortogh asked.

"It's just another ruin," the elf said. "One among many. No one comes here if that's what you mean."

"Why are you here?"

"I'm under orders to watch you until you die or leave."

Gortogh chuckled.

"Did you do something wrong to get this assignment?"

He looked confused.

"No," he said. "I volunteered."

"To traipse around after two goblins?"

"I like being alone in the mountains. Where I am from, you are never alone. You always watch your back."

"Sounds like a goblin tribe."

"We are a bit more civilized than that," the elf said.

Gortogh waved his hand in an arc.

"So were we once. Might be your turn just hasn't come up yet."

The elf seemed to think about that a bit.

"Do you have any food?" Gortogh asked. "Mushrooms have never done much for me."

"They should have killed you by now."

Gortogh patted his stomach and grinned.

"Strong constitution," he said.

The elf pulled a small pack from his shoulder and set it down. He dug around a moment and then produced a small loaf of bread. He handed it to Gortogh with a shrug. It felt hard, but he took a bite anyway. He was right, it was hard. Like eating gravel.

"What is your name?" the elf asked.

"Gortogh."

"That sounds odd."

"Not if you're a goblin."

"How long are you going to stay, Gortogh?" the elf asked.

"Trying to get rid of us?"

"Ready to get home."

"I thought you liked the solitude."

"I do for a while. But it starts to affect me after too long."

"Yeah, it'll do that."

Gortogh took another bite. The bread was hard, but at

least it had some substance. He'd grown tired of mushrooms. The lizard was the last real thing he'd eaten, and it had been pretty scrawny for its size.

"I'm just waiting for my friend to find whatever he came for, and then we'll go. Can't say I'm anxious to get home though."

"You don't miss it?"

"They want to kill me probably more than you do."

"Sounds like my home after all."

"Kurgh called you Erutharen. Said you worship some god."

"Eruthen," the elf said. "Son of Ilothen. He is the god of vengeance."

Gortogh scoffed.

"Sounds lovely."

"Better than the *Blood God*."

He had him there.

"Your friend won't find anything in that library. I've been all over it."

"Won't stop him from looking," Gortogh said. "Kurgh can be a bit determined."

"What is he looking for?"

"Answers."

"What is the question?"

"Isn't it always the same? *Why* are we here?"

"I'm here because you won't leave. You are here because *he* won't leave. It seems the answer lies in always doing what others want."

"Ha! Now who's the prophet?"

The elf smiled a little. Gortogh found he liked this elf. He had never known one before, and Kurgh had been pretty clear that these Erutharen were not good people. But he liked this elf.

"Well, I suppose I'll go and see if I can help Kurgh. The faster he finds what he wants, the faster we can all go home. You sticking around?"

"I have to," the elf said.

Gortogh nodded.

"Goodbye, Arnem."

"Goodbye, Gortogh."

CHAPTER TWENTY-TWO

AN ANCIENT TALE

GORTOGH CAME BACK to the library to find everyone right where he'd left them. Kurgh had stacked a few more books around himself and was slowly peeling through them, but he was in the same spot. Targhal was hovering near the giant stacks, watching and tittering nervously from afar.

Kurgh was talking aloud like he'd been doing for days, telling Gortogh little details he found. Despite Gortogh telling him numerous times that he wasn't interested, Kurgh insisted on reading passages from the texts. Had he even noticed I was gone?

"The mountains south of The Anvil used to be filled with goblin cities," Kurgh read.

Gortogh grunted as he sat down, the only response he could even fake.

"The book doesn't say what happened to them. Nothing says what happened to them."

Kurgh had been looking for days for an answer to his question. What happened to the goblins? They had found Ogrilon. They had found the library. Everything Kurgh had ever dreamed of was here waiting for the taking, but they had no idea how to get it. They could spend a thousand years looking and never find the answer.

Or even four thousand, apparently.

Gortogh had even tried the amulet once, just to see if it would lead him to whatever Kurgh wanted. The only thing it led to was Targhal coming over as soon as he touched the amulet. Gortogh heard a shuffle and looked up to see the monk over near the first stack of books.

"He's watching us," Gortogh said.

"Ignore him," Kurgh said without looking up. "He's unstable, and probably dangerous."

Gortogh didn't think the little monk was dangerous. Just a little anxious at having Kurgh touch all the books. He had told them on their first day that they could read any books they wanted, but they could not remove them from the library. But as soon as Kurgh started grabbing things and stacking them up, the monk became nervous. He would disappear within the stacks for hours at a time and then return to stand near them and fidget.

"Agh!" Kurgh shouted. "I can't understand this!"

"What?"

Gortogh didn't mean to respond, but now he had.

"None of this is telling me what I want to know!"

"What do you want to know?" Targhal asked from over Gortogh's shoulder.

The monk was so quiet, Gortogh hadn't even heard him approach. He looked up and saw Targhal eyeing the pouch around his neck while trying not to look like he was looking at it. Kurgh slammed the book shut.

"I could live here for a thousand years and not find the answer!"

"I doubt that," Targhal said. "I read through all of the

books in the first thousand years I was here. I've reread most all of them at least three times now since."

"You've really read every book here?" Gortogh asked.

"Three times," the monk said. "Though some of them are very dry. I only read those the once."

"And you remember them all?"

"Of course. My order is here to read the books and commit them to memory should anything ever happen to them."

"I thought Ogrosh protected the library."

"Some things are out of even Ogrosh's hands."

Gortogh chuckled.

"Go on," Targhal said. "Ask me anything. I can tell you about that amulet, for example."

Gortogh closed a hand over the pouch at his neck when he saw Targhal staring at it again.

"I already know about the amulet," Gortogh said. "Dunatis cut Ogrosh in some heavenly battle and stole a drop of his blood. He forged it into the amulet to try and control Ogrosh's people."

"No, no, no," Targhal said. "That is not it at all. Ogrosh created the amulet himself. A gift to his champion on Gondril so that they would always feel his presence. Though he could not communicate with them, through the blood amulet, Ogrosh could help his champion and help guide them."

"But why does it control other goblins?"

"It does not," Targhal said. "But every goblin can feel the presence of the blood and feels as though Ogrosh is beside them. It gives the champion the power to lead all of his people. I can feel it even now. It overwhelmed me when you first arrived, but I am very sensitive to his presence in this place."

"Would you both be quiet?" Kurgh shouted. "I am trying to read."

"I can help you," Targhal said. "Tell me what you are looking for."

"I don't *need* your help," Kurgh said.

"What happened to us?" Gortogh asked.

"I said I don't need help!"

"Do you want to be here forever? He's read every book in this library and has actually *lived* for the last four thousand years when everything happened."

"You want to know what happened to the city, yes?" the monk asked.

"More than that," Gortogh said. "What happened to *us*? To Ogrosh's people."

Targhal sighed and paused. It seemed to take him a long time to work up to speaking again.

"I do not know what you know, so I will start from the beginning."

Gortogh leaned back and couldn't help noticing Kurgh had abandoned his book and was now listening to the monk.

"Five thousand years ago, the two great wars were fought. The first between Dunatis, the dwarven father, and Ilothen, the elven father. The second between Anarr, father of dragons, and Ogrosh."

"We know this much," Kurgh said.

"You know of the war, but not what happened."

"Ogrosh defeated Anarr with dragon blood magic," Kurgh said, "and nearly wiped the dragons from the face of Gondril."

"That much is true," Targhal said.

"That's true?" Gortogh asked.

"Yes, but it is only the beginning of the story. It is

what happened next that began the downfall of the children of Ogrosh."

"What happened next?" Gortogh asked.

"Anarr was the eldest of Aeos's children. Surrendering to his youngest brother was almost too much for him to bear. But he had to in order to save what remained of his dragons. He brokered a peace with his brother, offering a bond between their peoples."

"Anarr offered to bond dragons to goblins?" Kurgh asked, intrigued now.

"Yes. But only the most powerful goblins. The five shamans who ruled over all the goblins. Anarr would grant them each one of his dragons as a sign of peace and cooperation. To bond our two races together, Ogrosh and Anarr crafted five crystals of their own energy. Each one putting a small part of themselves into the crystals, giving them immense power. They were called the dragonbond crystals."

Targhal pointed to the wall behind them and the goblin shaman riding high on the dragon's back. The pink crystal around his neck seemed to twinkle in the daylight pouring through the windows.

"I thought the crystals were meant to destroy dragons," Gortogh said. "I heard the wizard call it a dragon*bane* crystal."

"An unfortunate mistranslation by the elves who took the crystals when the great unmaking was done. Though not entirely incorrect by the time they found them. The elves took many of the artifacts from Ogrilon and the other cities of the goblin empire after its fall."

"Where are the other crystals?" Gortogh asked. "You said there were five of them."

"They have been destroyed through the ages. And

with each one, Anarr and Ogrosh lost a piece of themselves and a bit of their hold on Gondril. Only one remains now. And it is under Anarr's constant watch on the Isle of Dragons."

"What is the great unmaking?" Kurgh asked, interrupting.

"That is what you came to know," Targhal said. "That is what happened to our people."

"How do you know that is what we seek?" Kurgh asked.

"I would want to know," Targhal said.

Kurgh nodded and took a deep breath.

"Tell me," he said.

"There were once only five great and powerful tribes among the goblins, each with a mighty city, though Ogrilon was the greatest and the strongest. The five shamans ruled their tribes with the immense power of the crystals. The first dragon riders of Gondril. No one, not even the elves or dwarves could stand up to their might. With the dragons at their side, the high shamans of Ogrosh could rule over all the realms. But the power and the dragons would corrupt them. The shamans turned from the teachings of Ogrosh."

Gortogh looked sidelong at Kurgh, but the shaman was transfixed on the monk.

"It was the dragons, you see," Targhal continued. "Through the crystals, they were bonded to the shamans. And they used that bond to poison their hearts. It began first with a single shaman preaching the new word of Ogrosh. They corrupted his teachings to their own ends."

"Which teachings?" Kurgh asked.

Gortogh leaned in a little.

"Do you know why Ogrosh is called the Blood God?"

Targhal asked.

"Because he demands blood in his name," Kurgh answered immediately.

"No!" Targhal yelled. "That is what led to the unmaking! That was the poison they spread. Ogrosh's teachings were about brotherhood."

The monk was getting worked up and paused to calm himself.

"Ogrosh's teachings were about the bond of blood. Everything was possible through that bond. That is why he is called the Blood God. It was the high shamans who corrupted his word and turned it into a declaration of war."

"But why?" Gortogh asked.

"Because their minds were poisoned by the dragons. They didn't know it, but I know it. I have had thousands of years to think on it, and that is what I know now. The dragons were strong, and with their blood, the high shamans were more powerful than any being the world had known. The dragons convinced them they could rule over all of Gondril."

"I have never heard this story," Kurgh said.

"Because no one was left to pass it on," Targhal said. "The high shamans launched their crusade against the other races of Gondril. Starting with their closest neighbors and friends. The elves had won their war against the dwarven children of Dunatis, but in the heavens, Dunatis had killed Ilothen, his own brother. The elves were strong in numbers, but they had no god to protect them."

Gortogh was on the edge of the bench now. Elves and goblins as friends? Goblins riding dragons? Gods killed in the heavens? Kurgh's stories were never as interesting as this.

"The elves would have been destroyed too, if the high shamans had worked together to fight them. But the promise of power whispered in their ears was too great. They turned on each other. Instead of fighting together, in blood, they went to war against one another in Ogrosh's name."

"Is that what happened to Ogrilon?" Gortogh asked.

"And all the other goblin cities. Destroyed. A civilization wiped from the lands, though many goblins survived. It took less than a decade for the high shamans to destroy what Ogrosh had built. It was his greatest failure."

Gortogh widened his eyes and looked at Kurgh, but the shaman was staring at the floor.

"It was you," Gortogh said.

Kurgh glared at him, but Gortogh was just getting started.

"You wanted to know what happened to us? Well, praise Ogrosh, now we know! It was you. You and your kind. Ogrosh demands *blood*? You destroyed what he made!"

Kurgh looked up, his fists tight, his face quivering.

"It is not Kurgh's fault," Targhal said. "Nor the fault of any of his kind. They only preach what they were taught. The corrupted teachings that have been handed down since those days. He did not know better."

Kurgh opened his mouth to shout, to scream, but nothing came. Gortogh could see the pain and confusion all over his face. This was not what he came to learn. Kurgh seemed to lose all will to hold himself up and fell to his knees. The monk went over and laid a hand on his shoulder, and Kurgh lifted his head. Gortogh could see the tears in his eyes.

"It is not your fault, Kurgh," Targhal said.

"I have failed Ogrosh," he said. "I have corrupted his teachings and killed in his name. Given blood in his name."

"You did what you thought he wanted, he knows that. It was not you who failed him, it was Ogrosh who failed all of you."

Kurgh shook his head.

"Ogrosh has never failed me," he whispered.

"All the gods have failed us. Though they are the makers, it was wrong of them to interfere in our world," Targhal said. "Ogrosh saw the destruction done in his name, and he knew what he had done. And so he left the world. That is why he has not appeared here since that time. He is ashamed."

"How do you know this?" Kurgh asked.

"Four thousand years is a long time to think on things," Targhal said with a little smile. "Ogrosh's meddling cost the lives of hundreds of thousands of goblins, nearly all of his children, just as it cost Anarr his. But Anarr does not see it that way. That is why he does as he does now. Anarr has still not learned his lesson after all these years."

"What does Anarr have to do with this?" Gortogh asked.

"Do you know what is going on in the world today? In this place, I can feel the ills of Gondril as though they were a weight on my shoulders. I sense the whole of Gondril around me. The history is still being written. Anarr has been playing this game for a very long time. For a thousand years he has bonded his dragons with humans and elves, ensuring their survival and power in the world, letting them grow in numbers. Now he meddles once more. He is using the crystal to poison the world, just as he did long ago. And all of Gondril will be made to suffer before he is done."

Gortogh had been right all along. It was always the gods.

"What can we do?" Gortogh asked.

"Why do you think it lies with you to do something about it?" Targhal asked.

Gortogh put his hand around the pouch on his neck.

"Because I am guilty of doing the same."

Targhal thought for a moment and then shook his head.

"I have no easy answer for you," he said. "I do not know what can stop all of this from coming to pass. It would seem Gondril is doomed to its fate. Ogrosh has left us already."

"But we still have his blessing," Kurgh said. "He blesses me every day with my magic."

"And you give of your blood as well. You are a part of him. You share blood with Ogrosh himself, and he blesses you with his power. It is the bond between you both. A promise he made long ago, and he keeps it always. Even as he watches from afar, no father would abandon his children completely. Especially when they are lost and stumbling and in need."

"What of the other gods?" Gortogh asked. "What of Anarr?"

"Dunatis has stepped away from the world, but he still watches over his children. The dwarves are few in the world now, but he is there. Ilothen is gone. Threyl has never interfered with her humans. She got it right, I think. Ogrosh has stepped away as well, but Anarr...

Anarr has never stopped. His dragons are strong and in great numbers now. He showers them with his brilliance and makes them stronger than all his siblings' creations. He is poised to wreak a terrible vengeance on Gondril. Especially on his youngest brother."

"How do we stop that from happening?" Gortogh asked.

Targhal shrugged but then thought on it a moment.

"To be truly free, one must first remove the chains," he said. "That which was made must be unmade."

Gortogh could barely contain his smile. He stood and walked over to shake the monk's hand. There was a tingle in his touch, but Gortogh gave it only a passing thought..

"Thank you," he said.

"For what?" the monk asked.

"For showing me what I have to do."

"I have told you nothing," Targhal said. "I wish I had an answer for you."

"You've done enough," Gortogh said.

He turned and left the library without looking back. He could hear Kurgh saying something to the monk, but he didn't stop. He knew what had to be done now.

"Stop!" Kurgh shouted behind him, but he kept going.

Kurgh grabbed his shoulder and spun him around.

"Where are you going?"

"To clean up your mess," he said.

"This is not *my* mess!"

"You and your god. You wanted the truth, well you found it. Ogrosh did this to us."

"Ogrosh is not to blame for our fall, nor is he to blame for yours."

Gortogh yanked the amulet from its home and held it in Kurgh's face. The shaman flinched away as though it might burn him if he touched it.

"I know the truth now," Gortogh said. "*This* is Ogrosh's influence. This is *his* doing."

"You see the truth as you wish to see it. Did you not hear the monk? It was not Ogrosh who gave you the amulet. Who did?"

Gortogh put his hands on his hips.

"The elf," Kurgh said. "Who told you to gather an army? The elf. Who ordered you to war? You can blame Ogrosh all you like for your problems, but it has always been mortals who destroy the world."

"What about now? Did *you* hear what the monk said? It was the gods and their games that nearly destroyed us all. Anarr is meddling even as we stand here arguing. They have their hands in all of it. I know now what I have to do?"

"And what is that?"

Gortogh turned and marched off.

"I have to rid Gondril of the gods."

CHAPTER TWENTY-THREE

THE ELVES

WHEREVER ELODY LAID her bedroll, Rinn would lay his right beside it. If she waited for him to put his down first and then put hers somewhere else, he would move. And where Rinn put his bedroll, Eliath would be on the opposite side of the fire. After a week traipsing through the forest, Elody was reaching the limit of her patience.

She sat away from the fire, Jalthrax on one side of her. In the summer heat and humidity, the dragon's cold, metallic scales cooled her down. Rinn was beside her, like always, and Eliath and Eryninn were on the other side of their little campfire.

Eryninn insisted they were safe within the forest, but Elody hadn't felt safe since they left Derne. Many times they had seen dragons flying by overhead. Eryninn would call a stop, and everyone would hide until it had passed safely out of sight. None of that felt very safe to her.

"We should leave the forest behind in another few days," Eryninn was saying.

Elody turned her attention back.

"Where do we go from there?" Rinn asked.

"From there it is a straight march west to the sea. If we are, indeed, to continue west."

Elody rested her hand on Jalthrax's back, but the dragon didn't stir. She knew that was where they had to go. Thrax was more insistent than ever that they needed to keep going west.

"We keep going," Elody said.

Eryninn nodded, but she could tell he didn't like the idea. Truthfully, she didn't like it either. Where were they going? Jalthrax couldn't say, and she doubted he even knew. All they could do was follow where he led.

"It will take us almost a week to reach the sea," Eryninn said. "From there we can, perhaps, find a boat or someone to take us out."

"We can't just sail a boat aimlessly across the sea!" Rinn said.

He looked at everyone for support but found none.

"You're right," Elody said. "Eryninn is the only one I asked to come along, and all I asked him for was to lead me through the elven lands. Once we reach the sea, I will go alone."

"No, you won't," Eliath said.

"I'm not going anywhere," Rinn said. "I just want to know where in the nine hells we *are* going."

"I wish I could tell you," Elody said as she stroked Jalthrax's neck.

"It's settled then," Eryninn said. "I'm going to patrol."

Eryninn stood and was gone before anyone else could speak.

The half-elf had been nervous ever since he noted their crossing the border into the elven homeland. He was trying to put on a face of control for them all, but Elody had been watching him. He liked to keep his feelings hidden, but she could see his eyes darting everywhere. His *patrols* were getting more and more frequent the deeper they got.

Rinn laid back and rolled away from her with a huff. Elody sat there a while longer, staring at Eliath across the low fire. His eyes were closed, and his breathing was getting heavier, she could tell. She wanted to get up and move her bedroll closer to his, but she knew Rinn would only object. Or worse.

So, she settled for just laying down and rolling over herself. Jalthrax's deep, rhythmic breathing beside her lulled to sleep in no time.

***

Elody tried to stay close to Eryninn as they traveled. The half-elf was being evasive about his plans and concerns, and she was looking for signs of the truth. He was nervous and moving faster today than he had before.

"Can you keep him quiet?" Eryninn asked over his shoulder.

Jalthrax was still in his dragon form and making a lot of noise. He couldn't help it, really. He was bigger than they all were and made a lot of noise when he walked. He squawked in response to Eryninn's question, which earned them both a stern glance.

"Be quiet, or you'll have to turn back into a donkey," she whispered.

He went to snort at her, but she stopped him with a glance. Eryninn had said it was safe for Jalthrax to remain in his true form, but Elody didn't like it. Ultimately, she liked the fight with Jalthrax about it even less, so she let him do it. But they had seen dragons flying overhead several times in the last week. Eryninn insisted they were safe, but his actions said otherwise.

Rinn and Eliath hung back a few steps from the three of them. Though they walked almost beside each other, neither spoke to the other. Elody would look over her shoulder every few minutes, and they would both give her a little smile. But just as quickly, they would go back to frowning at her back.

This was not the trip she had hoped for.

She wasn't really sure what she had hoped for, but her original plans didn't call for two dour men trailing behind her. Three if you included Jalthrax, who was none too happy that he couldn't fly. Four if you counted Eryninn, but she had always expected him to be solemn. It was just his way.

The chirp of a bird pulled her from her thoughts. Hearing a bird wasn't so uncommon in the lush forest, but this one sounded different. Louder. More urgent. Eryninn stopped fast in front of her, his head whipping around in all directions. She knew in an instant that something was wrong.

"Hide!" Eryninn said.

Jalthrax and Elody were already moving for the cover of a large tree and some bushes. They had done this a few times already in their journey, and they all knew what to do. Elody glanced back to see Rinn and Eliath duck behind some trees and out of sight. Her fears were confirmed a moment later when a dark shadow covered them from above.

They waited, breathless, for the dragon to pass over.

Glinting in the sunlight, Elody saw a belly of brass. Was it the same one they had seen a week ago? It couldn't be. Despite Eryninn's assurance, she was getting paranoid. With a few loud flaps of its wings, the dragon disappeared from sight, and they all let out a breath.

"How many does that make?" Eliath asked as he neared.

"Fourth in as many days," Eryninn said.

"I thought you said they wouldn't come this far," Rinn said.

"The elves have offered asylum, but they will not openly attack a dragon just for flying over the trees. We don't even know that one was looking for trouble."

"We have to believe every dragon we see is trouble," Eliath said.

Elody nodded, though she hated to admit it. In all her years of training, the dragons she met had been nothing but nice. Some even friendly and funny. A brass she once knew had stayed for days at Master Cythyil's school entertaining everyone. She had spent hours chatting with him.

Now, brass dragons were her enemy. Not all, perhaps, but she couldn't assume any were safe. Deep in her heart, she secretly hoped the dragons would all rebel against Kalus's evil rule and find a new Eldest. As Eryninn told it, that's what the silvers and golds were doing even as they traipsed through the woods. With the help of the elves, they were planning a rebellion. But that put all the brass, copper, and bronze dragons on the wrong side. On Kalus's side.

"We should keep moving," Eryninn said.

Everyone nodded, and they continued on. Elody stayed closer to Eryninn now.

"What are you looking for?" she asked.

"I am just being cautious," Eryninn said.

"You're nervous."

"These woods are crawling with trouble."

"I thought we were safe here."

"From elves, perhaps, but despite what you humans think, there are far worse things than elves in the shadows of the trees."

"I don't think elves are scary."

Eryninn scoffed.

"You haven't spent enough time with your elders then."

"I only know you, and you've done nothing but help me since I met you. If that is any measure of elves, I think I'd like them very much."

"My brethren are nothing like me. Whether you would like them or not, they would despise you."

"Why?"

"You are human. That is all the reason they need."

"You make them sound like goblins."

"They wouldn't harm you with blades. Their weapons are far more subtle and cut much deeper."

Eryninn continued scanning the trees, and all she could do was sigh. She ran her hand down Jalthrax's neck as she walked. Goblins, ogres, high priestesses, red dragons, gold dragons, wizards. Her life had certainly changed since her simple days in Jornath. The village seemed so far away now, and not just because it wasn't there anymore. It felt like a whole other world.

Eryninn stopped short, and she bumped into his back with a grunt.

"Sorry," she said.

But he wasn't listening. He waved his hand frantically, and everyone stopped. Elody was about to hide behind a tree when Eryninn snapped his bow from his back and nocked an arrow. She almost asked what he saw, but only a moment later her unasked question was answered.

The thick tree branches ahead of them groaned and

cracked as two lumbering creatures burst forth. Eryninn loosed his arrow and had another one nocked seconds later. Elody only had time to turn her head and see the commotion.

Ogres.

Two of them charging straight for them.

"Get back!" Eryninn shouted.

He fired another arrow, hitting the same ogre in the chest a second time, but the ten-foot-tall creature only yanked it out and ran on. Elody had seen ogres fight before. Had seen the power they wielded in those massive wooden clubs. Her mind was reaching for Jalthrax before her body had even reacted. Jalthrax crouched low in a fighting stance and drew a breath.

"Four more!" Rinn shouted.

She chanced a look over her shoulder and felt her stomach fall. Four more ogres were coming from one side straight toward Rinn and Eliath. The two of them were already casting. She didn't know who to help.

"Help Eryninn!" she said to Jalthrax.

She spun her body to face the other four ogres. The magic was already in her hands, though she barely remembered taking it. She weaved the blue threads between her fingers, forming a crisscrossing web between them. Jalthrax loosed his freezing breath beside her, and she heard a roar of pain in response.

Elody threw her hands wide, pushing them at the charging ogres. Eliath finished his spell in the same moment. A bolt of lightning flew from his fingertip to strike the first, then a second ogre. Both of them flew back and landed on the ground with a thud. They lay there, twitching like eggs in a frying pan.

The threads of magic left her hands and grew. Bigger

and wider until they turned white and hardened. A web of sticky strands stuck fast between two trees just as an ogre charged between them. In an instant, the beast was stuck fast. It roared, pulling with all his strength, but the web would not budge.

Rinn finished his spell and fanned his hands across his body. An arc of flame spread out from his fingers, catching the last ogre who hadn't had sense enough to stop charging. It caught the full blast in its face, screaming in pain. The flames flew past it, licking the webbing holding the other ogre in place. Immediately they began to burn, and the ogre was free.

So much for that spell.

The two on the ground were starting to recover. Eliath was already casting another spell. Rinn had drawn his dagger and was dancing back against a tree. Jalthrax roared and breathed again. Elody noticed the twang of Eryninn's bow had stopped and glanced back to see him, sword drawn, fighting the two ogres.

Elody had never seen the half-elf in a sword fight. Had never seen how gracefully he danced with the blade. The ogres had never seen its like either. The clubs descended in rapid fire, but Eryninn just skipped out of their way. As each club passed, back in went his blade. It was small and thin, but the damage to the ogres was bloody. Every opening, every vital spot, the blade found its target. Stab after stab, they were bleeding from dozens of wounds. She could see Eryninn smiling through it all. Elody was enthralled.

Until she heard the roar.

"Dragon!" Eliath shouted behind her.

She looked up as a shadow passed overhead. Even through the trees she could see the brass belly of the dragon. It was coming for them.

"Stay out of sight!" Elody said to Jalthrax.

It wouldn't do any good. Jalthrax was not about to leave in the middle of battle, and she knew it. The brass came down in a small clearing about thirty yards away. For a brief moment, Elody wondered what its intention were. Was it here to help them?

She got her answer in a burst of fire.

The dragon breathed out, a line of fire pushing through the trees straight at them. Eryninn rolled to the side. Elody dove behind a tree. Jalthrax managed to just get out of the way. She couldn't see where Rinn and Eliath were, she only prayed they were safe.

The dragon seemed to care very little for the ogres. They were caught in its line of fire, several of them dying in the flames. They screamed a few seconds before falling silent. As soon as the dragon's breath died off, Eryninn was around the tree and firing.

"Aim your spells at its head!" he shouted.

He loosed, the arrow catching the brass in the neck. The dragon roared and pushed through the trees. The ancient oaks and maples of the elven forest bent aside like sticks, some snapping in half. Eryninn fired, again catching it in the neck.

Rinn shouted something just as a cone of ice and frost burst from his hand. It struck the dragon in the face. It roared in pain, blinded by the cold.

"We can hurt it!" Rinn shouted to Eliath. "Use your spells on it!"

Elody could do nothing. Not against a dragon. Her spells could not harm the beast, she knew. She could weave the dragon magic from Jalthrax, but the spell would not affect another dragon. If she could draw some of her own magic like Rinn and Eliath, she could do something. But her own magical well was too small for any real spells.

Jalthrax's breath could certainly hurt the brass though. Dragons of fire and cold were mortal enemies. Their breaths could easily kill each other. But it would put Jalthrax in serious danger against a much larger, much older dragon.

"Stay back," Elody said.

She rested her hand against the silver dragon's back and held him fast behind the tree where they'd taken up cover. There was little else they could do.

Though the brass roared in pain, the dragon was far from finished. Elody put her back against the tree as another blast of fire flew past. But the dragon had gotten tangled up in the thick trees and couldn't maneuver its neck enough for a clear shot. The rest of the men were wasting no time in taking advantage of the brass's predicament.

Rinn fired another blast of frost, eliciting another roar. Eryninn continued to fire arrows at its neck and head. Eliath, however, did nothing. He just stood there, like he was waiting for the right moment. The dragon was stuck fast between two large oaks, its head and neck exposed. Still he waited and did nothing.

"Eliath!" she shouted.

He glanced back. She saw the fear in his eyes. Was it fear?

The dragon broke loose, and everyone scrambled. Eryninn fired one last arrow before diving behind a tree. Rinn and Eliath did the same.

"We'll never defeat it!" Eryninn shouted. "We have to try and run!"

They all looked at him and then each other. How could they outrun a dragon? The dragon had pulled back behind a copse of trees and stopped. They all knew it might be their only chance for escape.

Over the trees and the thudding of her heart, she heard a bird call. It was a screech, like an eagle or a falcon. A bird of prey.

The forest exploded with motion.

A blast of frost flew from the trees to one side. The dragon roared, louder than it had before. The soft twang of bowstrings filled the air as a rain of arrows fell on the beast. The brass burst from its cover, sucking in a deep breath and then breathing all around as its neck circled. The trees caught fire everywhere it hit, but still the arrows came.

A bolt of lightning struck the creature in the head. Its face contorted in pain as the energy flowed through it. Then the dragon fell. Its body and head crashed to the ground with a great thud that shook the forest. Shouts in a language she didn't recognize seemed to come from the trees themselves. Torrents of water blasted them, extinguishing the fires the dragon left behind.

Rinn and Eliath looked at her with confusion, their hands in the air. Eryninn was the only one who seemed calm. He slung his bow across his back and stepped out from his tree to wait. Elody approached, not knowing what to say. A few trees away, an elf stepped out with a smile on his lips.

"I warned that you would need our help," the elf said.

"Then it's a good thing you came when you did," Eryninn replied.

The elf walked to stand in front of Eryninn just as Elody reached his side as well. She knew her mouth must be open, but she couldn't help staring at the elf. She had never met one in person. Eryninn was half human, half elf, but he had always seemed rough to her. Not elegant and perfect as the elves were often described.

The one before her now looked like what she had always imagined. He was a little shorter than Eryninn, a little thinner. She would call him frail if she didn't know better. Long, brown hair fell across his shoulders, parting just slightly at his pointed ears.

"Do you like what you see?" he asked.

She looked up to see he was talking to her.

"No, I— I mean yes. I don't know. I've never seen an elf before."

Eliath and Rinn moved in behind her.

"What's going on?" Eliath asked.

"We were just saving you from certain death," the elf said. "And it looks like we arrived just in time."

"Who are you?" Rinn asked.

"Eryninn has not mentioned me?" he turned his attention to the half-elf. "You wound me."

"Thank you, Alranir, but your help was not needed."

The elf laughed.

"Not from where I stood."

"Wait," Elody said, "you know him?"

"We are old friends, Eryninn and I."

"We are not friends," Eryninn said.

Behind the elf, Elody saw more of them filtering out from the trees. And beyond, the dead dragon. The elves surrounded the body, some still holding their bows. Without a thought, she pushed past to watch. She approached slowly as an elf in a dark blue cloak looked on.

"Over a hundred years old, she was," the elf said as

she neared.

"How do you know?" she asked.

"Her size. The length and width of her fire breath."

"You watched her fight?"

"I threw the killing blow."

The elf laid his hand on the dragon's head and took a deep breath.

"Did you know her?" she asked.

"No. Just one of many I have fought and killed in the last week."

"You're a dragon hunter?"

The elf sighed.

"I am now."

He turned and walked away. As he did, Elody counted at least a dozen other elves around the body, all dressed as Alranir. Supple leather armor, long cloaks, and longer bows. The body of the dragon was filled with arrows from all sides, each one wedged between two plates of her shining, metal scales.

She heard an argument behind her and hurried back over to see what was going on.

"He's been here the whole time!" Rinn said to her.

"Who has been where?" she asked.

"This guy!"

Rinn pointed at Alranir.

"He's been watching us from the trees!"

"It is my task to do so, boy, and I do as I am ordered."

"Then where were you when those ogres first came on?" Rinn asked. "Were you waiting to make a grand entrance?"

"I was ordered not to interfere unless it would cost Eryninn his life to do otherwise."

"Why?" Eliath asked.

"Why what?" Alranir said.

"Why are you watching Eryninn? He is a half-elf, not one of you."

The elf eyed Eryninn and shook his head.

"It matters not. I follow orders, that is all you need know. I must deliver this latest news, but I shall return this evening."

"Don't bother," Eryninn said.

Alranir's response was to turn and walk away. He gave a whistle, like the chirp of a bird, and the elves all turned and disappeared back into the trees.

"What is this all about?" Eliath asked.

"I will tell you more once we're away from here," Eryninn said.

***

Elody, Rinn, and Eliath stared around the fire. After getting as far away from the dragon fight as they could, they had all collapsed from exhaustion. Eryninn had made a brutal pace, and despite their questions, he remained silent or just kept telling them he would explain when they stopped.

Now he was gone. On another patrol, though Elody hardly saw the point. If the elves were watching them all as they claimed, they were perfectly safe. She saw what they did to the brass dragon. They would make short work of anyone coming to harm them. If they were watching.

"He's hiding something," Eliath said.

"So what if he is?" Elody said. "He is our friend, and he is allowed his secrets."

"He is no friend of mine," Eliath said.

"I want to know," Rinn said.

They nodded at each other. *Now* they were going to

be friends? Elody had to admit she was curious as well, but she trusted Eryninn enough to know that he would tell them when the time was right. But there was a nagging feeling in the back of her mind that she couldn't shake. He had lied to them all. He knew the elves were watching, were following them, but he said nothing.

There was no doubt he was hiding something. Eryninn silently slid into camp and sat down in the spot left for him by the fire.

"All clear," he said.

As if that was going to do it. He poked the fire with a stick and then stood.

"We need more wood," he said.

"Stop," Eliath said. "You can't keep avoiding this."

"We need more wood."

"Eryninn, please," Elody said.

The half-elf sighed and sat back down.

"What's going on?" Rinn asked. "Why are the elves following us? Do they want us out? Because we'll gladly leave. We've wanted out of this damn forest ever since we got here."

"As do I," Eryninn said. "That is all I am trying to do. Get us through safely and continue west."

"Why are they following us?" Eliath asked.

"To see us safely through," Eryninn said. "I told you all that we were safe, and I meant it. The elves have been tracking our movements and watching us from the safety of the trees."

"Why?" Eliath asked. "Why do they care? Are they afraid we might harm something while we're here?"

"The elves protect their own," Eryninn said.

"Of which you are not," Eliath said. "I have known elves in my life, and none have ever spoken well of half-breeds."

Elody saw Erynnin stiffen at the name. She rested her hand on his leg and gave him a smile.

"Just talk to us," she said softly.

"How long have they been watching?" Rinn asked.

"Since we left Derne," Erynnin said.

"So, from the very beginning," Eliath said. "They knew we were coming through the forest. As does every other dragon on Gondril it seems. Have you stopped to think for a moment that maybe they are reporting our movements?"

"They would not do that," Erynnin said.

"You don't know that," Eliath said. "How long have you known this Alranir?"

"Since the Battle of Molner," Erynnin said.

"And why has he taken such an interest in you? You must have something that he wants. You've spent your life away from the elves, so maybe you don't know, but they don't care about you."

"I know this," Erynnin said.

"It doesn't matter how good or how strong you are. They don't care simply because of what you are."

"I know!" Erynnin shouted.

"Then why are they watching you?" Eliath asked firmly.

Erynnin hesitated.

"Tell them."

They all turned to see Alranir step into the light, looking hard at Erynnin.

"He is the nephew of the king," Alranir said. "My orders are to bring him home if he will come."

"I will not," Erynnin said.

"Then I am to watch you and keep you safe. For as

long as you are within our borders at least."

Elody's eyes were wide as she looked at the half-elf beside her, but he wouldn't look back. He just stared at the elf.

"Why didn't you tell us?" Elody said.

"Tell you what? What difference does it make. An uncle I have never met is important somewhere. They are not my people."

"Your uncle is not just *someone*, he is the *king*!" Alranir was shouting now. "And you show him *great* disrespect by not accepting his invitation."

"What invitation?" Elody asked.

She was looking at Eryninn who had finally met her eyes.

"My grandfather is dying," he said. "My uncle wants me to be there."

"You should," she said. "Why don't you want to go?"

"Because I don't care," he said.

"The true king is dying, and you don't care?" Alranir said.

"He is not my king, and he is not my family," Eryninn said. "My family was my mother and father, and they are gone. Your *true king* banished them to live without help or family. My father told me plenty about my grandfather."

"You speak of things you know nothing about," Alranir said.

Eryninn leapt to his feet and stood just inches from the elf.

"*You* are what I know, Alranir. The dripping disdain in your voice. The way you order me around as though I'm nothing. You are everything my father said his people were. *You* are why I was told to stay away."

"I have no love for humans, it is true, but your uncle, *the king*, is not like me. And he is nothing like your grandfather was. The true king entered twilight not long before you were born, so he never got to tell his son how much he missed him. But it was your father who left, not your grandfather who threw him out."

"Why should I believe you?" Eryninn said.

"Because the central players in this little game are all but dead. I have no reason to lie to you. Your father is gone, his father is nearly gone. Only your uncle remains, and all he has ever wished for is to meet you."

Elody stood and walked over to Eryninn.

"You should at least meet him," she said. "He is your uncle. Your father's brother."

"My father loved his brother," Eryninn said, "but he hated his people."

"Your father may have hated his people," Alranir said, "but his hate was not returned. For years your grandfather waited for his son to come home."

"Eryninn," Elody whispered. "Your grandfather is dying. Don't you want to at least see him? Maybe talk to him before—"

"The true king cannot speak," Alranir said. "He is in twilight and only awaits the death of his mortal body."

"Oh," Elody said. "Still. You should go and see him. Meet your uncle. What harm can it do?"

Eryninn turned to look at her.

"I thought we were going west," he said. "This is not my quest we are on, but yours."

"Well, it's Jalthrax's quest I suppose, but I don't think he'd mind stopping for a day or two."

Jalthrax screeched behind her and she smiled.

"I am here because you asked for my help," Eryninn

said. "If you wish us to go with the elves, I will go. But I think it is a bad idea."

"This is your family, Eryninn. You should know your family. I lived most of my life thinking my aunt was some kind of gruff old monster."

"She is," Rinn said quietly.

Elody ignored him.

"It wasn't until I went to stay with her after... after my father died. I was wrong about her. She's not as gruff as I thought. And she loves us. She's all the family we have left, and now I can't imagine not having her."

Eryninn stared long and hard at her, and all she could do was hold his hand and smile. Everyone else stood still and waited. It was Eryninn's decision.

"We will go," he said. "But I do not want to stay long. We still have somewhere west to go."

Jalthrax squawked again.

"I think he approves," Elody said.

They all turned to Alranir who couldn't hide a little smile.

"Very well," he said. "We leave at first light."

And with that settled, he joined their fire.

Chapter Twenty-Four

Family

"How far is it?" Elody asked.

She had moved alongside Alranir, who was leading their little procession through the forest. It felt odd not having Eryninn at the front. He had taken up a position in the rear, a few yards behind everyone else. Elody wanted to go back and comfort him, but her curiosity won in the end.

"We should be there by nightfall," he said.

He didn't look at her when he spoke, which felt a little weird, but she decided it must be an elven thing. He was shorter than she was. Not something she was used to. Eliath and Rinn were both several inches taller. Even Eryninn had an inch on her. She had always heard that elves were shorter than humans, but she didn't think they were shorter than her. And she wasn't done growing yet.

A bird chirped in the distance.

"Is that one of your scouts?" she asked.

"No, it was a titmouse. Please be quiet."

"Oh. Sorry, I just thought you signaled by bird calls."

The elf lengthened his steps and tried to get ahead of

her, but Elody jogged to catch up. Jalthrax walked beside her, occasionally snorting at her for not letting him fly. Though she felt safer in the presence of the elves, Alranir, like Eryninn before him, had forbade the dragon from flying.

"Can you keep him quiet?" he asked. "I have seen dragons four times his size tiptoe through this forest without making a sound."

"He's not very good at tiptoeing."

The elf sighed and shook his head.

"Where are we going?" she asked.

"To Nirorn, the capital of our kingdom."

"How many kingdoms are there?"

"There are three elven kingdoms, though you would do well to avoid the others."

"Are they not as friendly as you?"

He turned to say something to her, but her wide grin told him she was teasing him. He didn't take it well.

"Can't you go and walk beside your brother and beloved?"

"He's not my beloved."

Alranir scoffed.

"You look at him as such."

"How do you know how I look at him?"

"Don't worry, he is entirely oblivious to your stares. I, however, see everything."

She looked down and stroked Jalthrax to avoid the look of satisfaction on his face.

"Do not tease when you cannot take it yourself, my dear."

"He really doesn't see?"

"He sees nothing. Too busy playing with whatever is dangling from that chain around his neck."

Elody looked back to where Rinn and Eliath were walking behind them. They both gave her a smile and waved. It didn't seem to matter who was in charge, at least they kept up their feud.

They walked for a while in silence. Elody didn't want to be a bother, but she had so many questions. She tried hard to refrain from asking about Eryninn. It didn't feel right prying into her friend's life like that. If he wanted her to know, he would tell her himself.

"Why do you have two kings?" she asked, finally.

"There is only one king."

"But, last night you said Eryninn's grandfather and uncle were both kings."

"Taernalys is the true king. He will remain so until the day he passes, which will not be long from now. But his son, Tarathiel, became king when his father fell into twilight."

"What is twilight?"

He gave her an annoyed look but no answer. Bringing his hand to his mouth, he cupped it and made a perfect bird call. Elody didn't recognize what kind of bird it was, but it was answered a moment later by the same call.

"What was that?" she asked.

"A titmouse," he said.

Elody laughed, eliciting a strange look from the elf.

"What is twilight?" she asked again after a time.

"I do not wish to be rude, but I should keep an eye out for trouble, and I find you very distracting."

"Oh, I'm sorry. I was just curious. I've never met an elf before, and I have so many questions."

"I'm sure you can find someone to answer your questions when we reach Nirorn, but now is not the time, and I am not that someone."

Elody nodded and fell back to walk beside Rinn and Eliath. Mostly Eliath. She hadn't noticed him touching the chain around his neck before, but now that Alranir pointed it out, he did seem to have it wrapped around his finger a lot. She also noted that she must have stared at him for a full minute before he turned to look at her.

She sighed and looked at Jalthrax who could only huff.

***

Their path through the forest turned sharply at one point, though Elody could see no trail they were following. But, Alranir must know the way to his own home, and he was tired of her questions, so she stayed quiet. Several rests were called throughout the day, but the elf always looked in a hurry to get moving again, so they didn't rest long. They had been walking for weeks already and were used to the pace.

After walking for hours with nothing but trees to see and birdcalls to hear, Alranir came to a sudden stop.

"We wait here," he said.

"Wait for what?" Elody asked.

"I was told to wait here, that is all I know."

Rinn and Eliath caught up once they stopped, but Eryninn still stayed to the back.

"We don't need another rest," Rinn said. "We can keep going."

"We are not resting, we are waiting," Alranir said.

"Waiting for what?" Eliath asked.

"I asked him that already," Elody said. "We're waiting because they told him to wait."

Alranir groaned, no longer able to hide his displeasure at his assignment. Curiosity winning out, Eryninn joined them.

"What are we doing?" he asked.

"We are waiting!" Alranir said, his patience gone.

"Don't ask him for what," Elody said.

Not knowing what else to do, Elody sat down with her back against a tree. Jalthrax joined her a moment later and laid down beside her. The rest just stood and watched, waiting for something to happen.

Elody heard another bird close by and looked around for its source. A moment later, an elf walked up and went straight to Alranir. They spoke for a moment in that same, strange language she didn't understand. Whatever the newcomer was saying, Alranir didn't like it. He began yelling at the other elf, but cut himself short when he saw everyone looking at him. He said one final word, and the new elf disappeared, heading back the way he came.

"We are waiting for a royal guard," he said.

"Why?" Eryninn asked. "Can't we just walk in quietly?"

"Apparently not," Alranir said.

"Why do we need a guard?" Eliath asked. "Do you not trust us?"

"Of course I don't trust you," Alranir said, "but that is not what the guard is for. A royal guard is sent to escort heroes through the Dawn Gate on their return."

They all looked at each other, and Elody saw the confusion on all their faces.

"Can we just sneak quietly in?" Eryninn asked.

"I would like nothing more, but the king has ordered it."

"I do not want some kind of heroes' welcome."

"You do not deserve one. The honor is reserved for true heroes and the dead returning from war. Sadly, you are neither."

"I don't like this either," Eryninn said. "I don't want it."

Alranir spun on him.

"Nor do I! But I, and you, will not disobey the king!"

Eryninn shrunk beneath the words. Elody had never seen him back down from an argument before. He turned his back on the elf and stormed away, coming to rest against a tree next to Elody.

"Is it so bad?" she asked him.

"You heard him," Eryninn said. "This is an honor for heroes, not for me."

"I have seen you do heroic things in battle. At least twice you've saved my life and Rinn's. You saved the women of Jornath. Berym told me that everyone in Derne is alive because of you. Because you saved them."

"I am not a hero."

"I don't know what you think it takes to earn that title, but you are certainly one in my eyes."

Eryninn turned away and went silent. Elody tried to think of something else to say, but it was obvious Eryninn wasn't in the mood to hear it. So, they waited.

Half of an hour passed before they heard more birdcalls.

"Get up," Alranir said. "The guard is here."

Elody never heard a sound as they approached. She could see them plainly enough, there were at least two dozen elven guard. All dressed in bright, silver chainmail and covered head-to-toe in dark blue cloaks. They marched in perfect order, as she had seen the knights do so many times, but unlike the knights, they made no sound. Their boots touched the ground as any marching soldier's would, but she could hear nothing.

"How do they do that?" she asked.

"Magic," Alranir said.

The guard came to a stop in front of their little group and then turned as one to create a path down the middle. Without waiting, and unable to hide a sneer, Alranir walked between the guards and took the lead. He stood at the head of the columns and waited.

Eryninn was the first to move, walking up behind Alranir. Elody and Jalthrax moved in behind him, and Rinn and Eliath followed. Once they were all together, Alranir began marching, and the columns of guards followed. Several guards at the rear closed in around them as they moved.

"Never thought I'd live to see this," Rinn whispered.

"I can't believe we're going into an elven city," Elody said.

"I've been to a few smaller villages," Eliath said, "but never a city. And certainly never the capital."

Eryninn glared over his shoulder, and they stopped talking. Ahead, the city was coming into sight. The gates and wall of the outer city were small at this distance, but they could easily see three spires rising above. Gleaming white in the sunlight that filtered through the thick trees, they towered above the forest like ancient guardians.

There were two smaller towers, one close to them and one in the distance. But the largest of the three, the one in the center beyond the gate, was as beautiful as anything Elody had ever seen. The stone was so white that it actually glowed, rays of sunlight bouncing off of it and sparkling as they fell down on the city around it.

"What is that?" she whispered.

"It is the God Tower," Alranir said. "The brightest and most beautiful of all creations. It is the home of Ilothen on Gondril."

"I thought Ilothen was dead," Rinn said.

Alranir's hands clenched, and Elody saw his face tighten.

"That's what my aunt told me," Rinn said.

Eryninn gave him a stern look as Alranir turned back and kept marching.

"What?" Rinn said.

"Perhaps best not to mention that again," Eryninn said.

"It's true, isn't it?" Eliath asked.

"Just because something is true does not mean you *have* to say it," Eryninn said.

They marched on in silence. Elody couldn't take her eyes from the tower. The dancing light from its surface was enchanting, and she wondered how something so beautiful could be built. What was it made of? What made it shine like that? But she saved her questions, hoping someone might actually answer them later.

As they neared the city, the gates swung inward to let them pass. The guards high on the wall gave a salute as they entered, and Alranir and each of the guards in their procession returned it. It was all very formal, and Elody was starting to feel the weight of it all. Even though she wasn't the one being honored, she began to understand why Alranir would be angry at them receiving this gift.

Beyond the gates, a wide street led straight through the city and to another wall surrounding the God Tower in the center. But it was the path there that made Elody's breath catch. Lining the road were hundreds of elves. Each one dressed in beautiful clothing like Elody had never seen. They watched from the sides at attention as they entered through the gates.

As they passed, each and every elven citizen bowed

their heads in salute. Now she understood. This was the welcome of heroes, of the fallen. Solemn, silent, powerful. She stared at Eryninn's back and saw his head dip low, unwilling to look into the eyes of those they passed. From the whispers behind her, Rinn and Eliath felt it too.

Ahead of them, Elody saw the end of their walk. Down a garden path that ended at the wall around the central tower of Nirorn stood the king. Eryninn's uncle if it was to be believed. While the rest of the crowd around them had their heads bowed with solemn faces, the elven king wore the biggest smile.

Eryninn had not even looked up to see him.

He actually reminded her of Eryninn. They shared the same long, light brown hair, but it was more than that. Something about his face that was reminiscent of Eryninn. They favored each other. Though Eryninn usually wore a beard that covered his chin and mouth while the elven king had no hair across his face at all.

The king was dressed in a dark blue silken shirt with pants to match. He stood on a small platform that Elody imagined must have been built just for this purpose. As the dappled sunlight above cascaded down the white tower behind him, the light haloed around the king. Elody's breath caught, and Eryninn finally raised his eyes to see for himself.

Their eyes locked for the first time, and the king's smile brightened. He raised his hands to usher them forward, and Alranir marched the last few steps with a little more speed. When they finally reached the edge of the stairs leading to the platform, Alranir stepped to one side where the guards had made an empty spot.

That left Eryninn standing alone before the king.

Elody thought for a moment of going to him and standing beside him, but she could feel that it wasn't her place. This was his moment, and she couldn't interfere. Even if he might have wanted her to.

The king took a tentative step down without a word. Two more steps, and he stood right in front of Eryninn at about the same height. The final step brought them to the same level but made Eryninn just a few inches taller. Elves were much shorter than she had always imagined somehow.

Eryninn stood perfectly still and silent.

Elody thought to tell him to bow or salute or something, but before she could consider her words, the king took another step forward and wrapped Eryninn in a hug. Alranir, to his credit, remained perfectly still and silent, but the rest of the crowd was not so reserved. Many of the gathered elves gasped. Whispers filled the silence.

But no one was more stunned than Eryninn.

Elody could only imagine his face, but as the king stepped back, Eryninn took a step back himself and nearly bumped into her.

"My nephew has returned to us from the grave," the king said.

The crowd quickly quieted as he spoke.

"And he has brought guests with him. For as long as they are here, they are honored guests. Show them the same respect you would show me."

He took another step toward Eryninn who instinctively took another step back, bumping into her. He grunted some apology, but the king was there beside him, whispering.

"Will you walk with me?"

Eryninn nodded.

The guards parted to let the two of them through, and they walked away into the garden. Elody looked back at Rinn and Eliath who could only shrug. Beside her, Jalthrax gave a squawk, and she reached down to touch him.

What were they supposed to do now?

Chapter Twenty-Five

The King

ERYNINN WALKED A step behind the king, even though he kept ushering him forward.

"Come," he said, "I want you to talk with me."

Eryninn moved up, but with each step, he fell behind again. Though he was used to always being out in front in the forest, this was not the forest. Not in the way that he had grown to know it. This was a far more dangerous place to someone like him.

"Alranir told me of the dragon attack," the king said. "I hope that the rest of your journey here was safe."

"It was."

The king nodded, and they both walked in silence for several minutes. Eryninn could think of nothing to say, so he just admired the garden and the city. It was bigger than he had ever imagined. His father and mother told him very little of Nirorn growing up, and what little they did share was tainted with talk of the people. Though Eryninn's mother was never one to speak ill of the elves, his father held no such reservations.

"My mother always said nice things about you," he finally said.

He thought it was a nice thing to say. It felt awkward. Eryninn had to remind himself that he was speaking to the king. He wanted to yell and scream and fight, so strong were the words of his father in his heart, but he could not forget where he was.

"I loved your mother very much," the king said. "She was a wonderful woman."

"My… my parents never spoke about their life here."

"I doubt that very much," the king said.

A knowing smile crept onto his face, and Eryninn couldn't help a little chuckle.

"My brother was not known for holding his tongue in check. It could be as sharp as any blade when he wanted it to be."

"He spoke of his people often," Eryninn said.

"I can imagine he did. Not all of it is true, you know."

Eryninn nodded but said nothing.

"Do you know how my parents met?" he asked after a time.

"Your mother was a priestess of some power. We often called on her to aid us in times of great need."

"I thought most elves hated humans, my grandfather most of all."

"Hate might be a bit strong, but I admit that my father did not care much for humans, that is true."

"Then why ask them for help?"

"Because I was sick," the king said.

"Sick?"

"Of an illness that could not be cured by herbs and poultices. Nor by the magic of wizards and witches."

"There were no priests who could help?"

"The elves count a great many among their priests, but they do not have the power of the gods. They pray to a god who is long dead."

Eryninn looked sharply at him and then around to see if anyone had heard.

"Does it shock you to hear me say so?"

"Alranir did not appreciate Rinn asking about Ilothen."

"It is a sensitive subject for some, but that does not make it false. It is well known that Dunatis killed his twin in celestial battle. Ilothen is no more in this world, and his priests receive none of his blessings."

"Then why pray to him if you know he is not there?"

"Because we do not know. No one knows, not for sure. After all, what is death to a god? Is he truly dead, or merely too distant for us to touch? Perhaps he will return some day, and most of his people await that day."

"My mother came to heal you?"

"She did. I am alive today because of your beautiful mother."

"What happened?" Eryninn asked.

The king sighed.

"My father was not fond of humans, I have said as much. When Tarin fell in love with your mother, he did not take the news well. When he learned Aliri was with child, he was furious. Things were... complicated. He told Tarin that he must abandon her and you. But Tarin would not."

"So your father threw them out."

"No," the king said.

He stopped and stepped in front of Eryninn to face him.

"My father was not the kindest man, but he would never have thrown his son and his wife out into the world. Whatever your father told you, know that he left of his own will. He and Aliri left to raise you on their own, away from this world. But it was their choice to leave."

"But… why?"

"Because my brother was strong and stubborn and had far too much pride to stay here and be looked down upon by his own people. There were some, are some still, who believe that half-blood elves are an abomination that should not be. But there are those, like myself, who would welcome them."

Eryninn's chin had dropped, but his uncle took it in his fingers and forced his eyes up to meet him.

"You are my blood, Eryninn. Tarin was my brother, and I loved Aliri like my own sister. This may be the first time we have met, but it is not for my lack of searching. Kiranoth came to me and told me when my brother died, but she had promised not to tell me where you were. I begged her to tell me, but she would not."

"She never told me," Eryninn said.

"She would not, no. My brother made her promise long ago never to reveal his location to his family. I counted the Silver Queen among my closest friends, but she would never tell me that. Not in a hundred years would she have."

"You heard that she died?"

"Yes, I heard. We all did. It was a sad day in Nirorn. She was known to many of us, and we called her a friend. She returned often once my brother died and told me that you were well and that you were safe. When she died, I sent people to find you. When I couldn't, I assumed you were dead."

They continued walking, and Eryninn saw that they had rounded one side of the tower and were walking through another set of gates toward the tower itself.

"Where are we going?"

"To see my father," he said.

Eryninn stopped. His uncle turned to face him.

"I don't want to meet him," Eryninn said.

"There is nothing to meet. Only a still-living form."

"No."

"He can't hurt you, Eryninn. I have no doubt that if my brother had not been so stubborn, he would have seen my father differently. But he fell into twilight shortly after Tarin left, and whatever chance they had was lost. You should at least see him and say goodbye. Whatever you think he is, he is that no more."

Eryninn stared a moment longer, his uncle waving his hand toward the door. Taking one step and then another, he reluctantly followed him into the tower. Once inside, they took a set of pure white stairs up to the very top of the tower. It was a long walk, but he never even thought of the soreness in his legs. He was walking to meet the man his father most hated in this world.

Even if his uncle was right, and his grandfather wasn't as bad as he had always thought, he couldn't shake the feeling of dread. As though some great and powerful monster waited for him. The top of the stairs spilled out into a short hallway leading to two golden doors.

His uncle continued without pause, but Eryninn stood stiffly at the top of the stairs.

"He cannot hurt you," the king said. "His time is almost done. Do you not at least want to see him?"

Eryninn hesitated a moment longer and then followed his uncle to the doors. With the lightest touch from the king, the doors swung inward. They opened to reveal a white chamber filled with light. The windows that surrounded the top of the tower let the sunlight flow from every direction, no matter the time of day, and bathed the entire room in bright daylight.

At the far end of the chamber was a raised dais with a golden throne resting on it. Between the doors and the throne, beneath a golden, glass window in the ceiling of the tower rested a bed. And lying in the bed, covered in white, silken sheets, was the true elven king.

His grandfather.

Eryninn forced himself to approach beside his uncle.

The true king looked old. Eryninn had never seen an old elf. The few he had met in his life always looked flawless and perfect. Ageless and timeless. But the elf before him was very old. The skin on his face was wrinkled and sagged, falling to either side down his jaw. His eyes were closed, and his mouth was open just a little. The only sign he was even alive were the little breaths he drew in and out through that tiny opening.

His uncle reached out to take his father's hand.

"He is almost gone," he said.

"I don't understand," Eryninn said. "How long has he been like this?"

"He fell into twilight just after your birth. Almost thirty-seven years."

"Like this?"

"Just like this."

"But why?"

"Because there is no one to take his soul," his uncle said. "His soul was ready to go home long ago, when he entered his twilight. At that moment, his spirit left his body. But Ilothen was not there to receive it. So it is tied here, bound until his body takes its last breath."

"Is that how all elves die?"

"Those who make it to the end of their years, yes. Most die in battle or long before they reach that time."

His uncle took his hand then and put it on top of his grandfather's. Eryninn tried to pull away, but his uncle held him fast. The old man's skin was cold. It felt just as it looked. Without life. But Eryninn could still see his chest rise and fall with each breath.

"How much longer will he be like this?"

"A few more days, maybe. A few weeks."

"And then what?"

"Then he will be consumed in dragon fire, as all the great kings were. For many millennia that was done by the Eldest. A rite of passage for the elven kings of old. But not this time."

For a brief moment, Eryninn felt like this was his grandfather. Not a monster. Not an evil man. Just a man who made mistakes.

"Why did he wait so long?" Eryninn whispered.

"He was a stubborn old man. He thought that Tarin would come home after a while, and they would talk the whole thing out. He was even ready to accept you and your mother."

"How noble," Eryninn said.

His uncle chuckled.

"You have only half of my blood but all of our stubbornness, Eryninn. We elves have the luxury of far too much pride. When you live hundreds of years, it seems there is always time to reconcile. But sometimes we wait too long and lose the chance."

He put his hand on Eryninn's shoulder.

"Let us not make the same mistake," he said. "None of us knows how much time we have. I would like you to stay a while. I want to know you if I can."

Eryninn nodded, but he wasn't sure. He had so many conflicting thoughts rolling through his head, and he didn't know which were right or which were wrong. His uncle smiled and patted his shoulder.

When Eryninn looked at him, he saw a genuine smile of affection. And something else. He looked at his uncle and saw something he had not seen since his mother died seventeen years ago. Something he never thought he might have again.

Family.

CHAPTER TWENTY-SIX

JALTHRAX'S FATHER

ELODY KNOCKED SOFTLY and waited. The long, white staircase going up and down the tower was empty, but still she was quiet. She knocked again and knotted her fingers. After what seemed like minutes, but was probably only seconds, the door opened and Eliath peeked out.

"Oh," he said, "hello."

"Is your room really nice?" she asked.

He stepped aside and waved his arm, and she saw it was just like her own. Large, white, and beautiful. A wide bed made of what she could only guess were feathers lay in the center surrounded by white stone in every corner. The floor was polished, white stone. The walls were the same. Everything looked perfect and serene. The sun pouring through the window, with white curtains of course, gave everything an unearthly glow.

"Just like mine," she said.

"I know. Pretty nice."

"Have you seen any guards?"

"Only the one who showed me to my room. He said if I needed anything to just come down and find someone."

"Doesn't that seem odd to you? That they would just let us stay in these amazing rooms with no guard?"

"Well, I don't know a lot about the elves, but I do know they are very cautious when they feel they need to be."

"I know!" she said. "Eryninn is always so cautious. And they just drop us off here like untended children?"

"Do you want a guard?" Eliath asked. "I'm sure if you ask for one, they'll appoint one."

"Of course not. I just thought it was odd, that's all."

"Where's Rinn?"

"Upstairs," she said. "Next one up. We all got east-facing rooms, the guard said. He said they were the most beautiful rooms in the whole city."

"Mine said the same."

She looked into his room again while he stood still and watched. It was the first time they'd been alone together since the night he'd burst in on her campsite. She had so much she wanted to say to him, but she just hadn't had a moment. Now was her chance.

"That was a really long trip," she said.

"Yeah," he said.

Not the opener she was hoping for.

"Where's Jalthrax?" he asked.

"The guard told me there was a roost at the top of the tower where he would stay. He's probably up there."

"Do you want to go up and take a look?"

"Sure."

He reached out for her hand as he took a step up, and she couldn't hide a little smile behind his back. They walked up the stairs to the next door where Eliath stopped.

"Did you want to ask Rinn?"

"No," she said quietly. "He's tired and cranky, and I don't want to bother him."

Eliath just nodded and continued on. Truthfully, she'd seen enough of her brother for a while. It felt like he'd been stuck to her side the entire trip, and she really needed a break from it. Walking up, holding Eliath's hand, was just the kind of break she was thinking of too.

The tower was much taller than it had appeared from the outside. Their long journey had already left Elody's legs tired and sore, and these stairs weren't helping much. Each step burned like fire, but she pressed on. Eliath didn't seem bothered at all, or at least he was good at hiding it. When they finally reached the top, she couldn't suppress a groan and a sigh.

"Tired?" he asked.

"Just sore. I don't know how Eryninn can keep that pace and still walk the next day."

"Elves are sneaky," he said with a smile.

The stairs spilled out onto a stone floor that led to a single door. Eliath pulled it open without stopping, and the sunlight in the western sky flooded in, blanketing them both in its warmth. The sound of flapping wings greeted them as their eyes adjusted to the brightness.

Eliath tugged her hand, and Elody gripped it tighter as they stepped out. The entire top of the tower had been built as a huge dragon roost. Bigger than the one at the actual Dragon's Roost back in Havnor from what Elody could see. And unlike that one, which had remained empty most of the time she'd seen it, this one was teeming with life. The sun up here wasn't blinding because of their proximity to the sky, it was blinding because of all the shining metal.

Dragons of gold and silver stood tall on the ledge of the tower, their wings spread to the heavens. The light reflected off their polished metal scales and lit the roost like it was awash in flames.

"Wow," Eliath said.

Elody had to agree. She could only see a half dozen dragons from where she stood, but that was more golds and silvers than she'd ever seen in her life. Certainly in one place. One by one they leaned forward and seemed to fall from the tower. Their roars cut the air as large wings spread, catching the air and sending them back up and across the treetops.

"Amazing," Elody said.

"They're huge," Eliath said. "I've met a few silvers and golds in my life, but none so big as these."

"I wonder how old they are," Elody said.

"Very old," a voice said.

Their attention snapped away from the flight of dragons and back down to the roost where a single elf was standing at the far ledge. Eliath and Elody looked at each other, shrugged, and then walked over to stand behind the elf.

"Where are they going?" Elody asked.

"To watch over the forest," the elf said. "Our world is not as safe as it once was."

Elody and Eliath watched the dragons, each headed in a different direction, disappear into the distance.

"You are Jalthrax's bonded," the elf said plainly.

Elody's eyes widened a bit, but the elf turned to face her with a gentle smile.

"He told me a lot about you," he said.

"You can speak dragon?" she said.

The elf chuckled.

"Do you know where he is?" she asked.

"Flying around somewhere."

Eliath looked at her, alarmed.

"He can't be flying around out here!" she said.

"He begged and begged me," the elf said. "I had no choice but to let him. He said he'd been grounded for weeks."

"I couldn't risk him flying. It's too dangerous."

"And he said before that you made him be a donkey."

Eliath laughed.

"I was trying to protect him," Elody said.

"Well, you have done a fine job of it," the elf said. "You two take good care of each other by the looks of it."

"Thank you," she said, pulling her shoulders up a bit.

"Is it safe for him to fly?" Eliath asked.

"I told him to stay near the city."

As if on cue, Jalthrax swooped up suddenly from below the tower ledge, climbing straight into the sky. With one last flap of his powerful wings, his body twisted in midair to face straight down in a dive. He rushed past them with a screech, and Elody ran to the edge of the tower where the elf was looking over. Just as he neared the ground, his wings stretched out and snapped taut as the wind filled them. He soared over the garden below and then began to climb again.

The elf laughed, but it took all Elody had to push her heart back out of her throat.

"I hate when he shows off," she said.

"He's just stretching his wings," the elf said.

"You never told us your name," Elody said.

"Ilyaren," the elf said.

"How did you learn to speak dragon, Ilyaren?" Eliath asked. "I tried to learn once, but it was impossible. I had to wait for Tark to speak to me first."

The elf chuckled again.

"You're a dragon," Elody said.

The elf laughed.

"What gave it away?" he asked.

"The silver hair," Elody said. "The Silver Queen told me that when dragons take a form, they usually keep some part of themselves their true color as a matter of pride."

The smile faded from the elf's face, and he hung his head and nodded.

"The queen was correct, as she almost always was."

"You knew her?"

The elf sighed and looked out across the forest.

"She was my mate before she died."

"Your... mate?"

The Silver Queen had a mate?

"For a time, yes."

"Tark once told me that, for dragons, it's the females who choose their mate."

"That is true."

Jalthrax flew by again, screeching as loud as he could as he passed them. Elody and Eliath both laughed. It had been weeks since she had seen him so happy. She knew it was for his safety, but she had no idea how much not flying would affect him. Within minutes he had disappeared into the distance.

"Are you sure it's safe for him to fly here?" she asked.

"He is safer here in Ilothar than anywhere else on Gondril. I promise you, I will not let any harm come to him."

"What is Ilothar?" Elody asked.

"It is where you are standing," Ilyaren said.

"I thought we were in Nirorn," she said.

"You are in both," he said. "Ilothar is the kingdom of the elves, and Nirorn is its capital city."

"Alranir said there were three elven kingdoms."

Ilyaren scoffed.

"Alranir doesn't say much of anything to anyone."

"No," Elody said with a laugh, "I suppose he doesn't."

"He is correct though. Once there was only a single kingdom of the elves, all united under their maker, Ilothen."

"But then he died," Eliath said.

"Yes," Ilyaren said, "then he died. The Ilotharen await his return one day, but some of the elves are not as patient. When Ilothen died, they found a new god in his son, Eruthen. Others turned to the father of the gods and sang their praises to Aeos himself."

Eliath snorted.

"Trading a dead god for an absent one," he said.

"Perhaps," Ilyaren said, "but who is to say what the gods will do. The Aeotharen, as they called themselves, split from the kingdom and formed their own to the north where many of them found peace in other gods. They are most like you humans with your plethora of higher beings, but they are not welcoming to outsiders. The Erutharen are even less so."

"You live with enemies on all sides?" Eliath asked.

"It has always been so for the children of Ilothen," the elf said. "Brothers to the north, brothers to the south, goblins to the west, humans to the east, and all of them hostile. You learn to protect what you have. So when I say that Jalthrax is safe here, I mean it. The Ilotharen and the dragons here will see to that."

"It doesn't seem like anywhere is safe anymore," Elody

said. "We were attacked several times on the way here. Once by a brass dragon."

"I heard," Ilyaren said. "Gondril has once again become a place where dragons must fear for their lives. Even from their own kind. The dark dragons have never been called friends, but neither have we been at war for a thousand years. It is the War of Ways all over again."

"My master Cythyil taught us about that," Elody said. "Wizards and dragons killed each other for a hundred years until most of both sides were gone."

"It wasn't just the wizards. They managed to turn the dark dragons against us as well. They turned dragon against dragon, something which had never happened before in Gondril's history."

"You say it like you were there," Eliath said.

"I was," Ilyaren said. "You may not know it to look at me, but I am the oldest living dragon on Gondril. I fought for a hundred years in the War of Ways. I remember it all too well."

Eliath and Elody stood slack-jawed and staring.

"The oldest dragon on Gondril?" Elody said. "Even older than Kalus?"

"By a hundred years, yes."

Elody brightened.

"Then you should be the Eldest! You can take it away from Kalus and stop all of this!"

Ilyaren looked down and shook his head.

"I cannot. By Anarr's decree, only a gold may become Eldest. Anarr has blessed me with a longer life than most of my kind, but Eldest is something I can never be."

"But that's not right," Elody said. "Eldest means the oldest. You're the oldest."

"I have tried that argument myself, but Anarr's decree

is clear. Kalus is the Eldest."

"Who would be Eldest if not for Kalus?" Elody asked.

"Thalaras is the eldest gold on Gondril after Kalus."

"Can't we just kill him?" Eliath asked. "Kalus I mean."

"The mantle of Eldest cannot be taken by blood."

"Does that mean Thalaras can't fight Kalus, or that none of you can?" Eliath asked.

"The decree only says that none shall become Eldest by blood."

"But what if Kalus dies and Thalaras has nothing to do with it?" Elody asked.

"It would certainly be breaking the spirit of the decree if not the exact words."

"But you can stop it," Eliath said. "You can stop all the madness that Kalus is creating. This can't be what Anarr wants."

"Only Kalus can decide the will of Anarr. That is his right."

"But that doesn't make sense!" Elody said. "Kalus is destroying everything you have built! He's creating another war that is likely to get thousands of your kind killed."

"I know this," Ilyaren said.

"Then do something about it," Elody said. "Stop Kalus before he does any more harm."

"It is not my place!" Ilyaren said, spinning to face them. "And it is not your place to question me."

"You're a coward," Eliath said.

Ilyaren moved so fast Elody barely had time to yelp. His hand shot out and grabbed Eliath by the front of shirt, pulling him face to face with the silver-haired elf.

"Out of respect for you and your loss, I won't throw

you from this tower, but you should be mindful of who you are speaking to. I have lived for more than a thousand years on Gondril, and I have the scars to prove it."

With that, he shoved Eliath backward and then pushed past Elody to leave. She ran to Eliath, who still looked a bit stunned.

"Are you okay?" she asked.

"I'm fine," he said.

He straightened his shirt a bit and drew his shoulders up.

"They sit and wait for someone else to do something," Eliath said. "The gold and silver dragons could end this right now, but they do nothing. All for some decree made by Anarr thousands of years ago."

"That doesn't mean *we* have to do nothing," Elody said. "Jalthrax keeps telling me we have to go west. Something is pulling us there, and it has to have something to do with all of this."

"What if it doesn't? What if it's all just a trick?"

"Then at least we tried. If the dragons of light will do nothing to stop this, at least we can try."

Eliath nodded his head and looked out over the trees. She wanted to go to him, to embrace him. She took a step forward and heard a screech from above where Jalthrax was gliding in for a landing. As gentle as a leaf, he landed in the middle of the roost. Then he stretched his wings as far as they would reach and flapped them several more times, beating the wind up around them.

"I take it you liked stretching your wings then," Elody said.

She walked over and put her arms around the silver dragon's neck. She could feel the joy returned to him. He nuzzled her back and rubbed against her, growling long and low as a cat purrs.

As she held onto him, the tower door swung open and a guard appeared. Elody pulled back from Jalthrax as Eliath came to stand with her. Had Ilyaren called the guards on them? The guard came right up to them and stood at attention.

"The king has requested your presence at a banquet tonight in honor of his nephew."

"Oh," Elody said. "That sounds wonderful."

The guard spun and left back the way he came.

"In honor of his nephew?" Elody said. "He'll love that."

CHAPTER TWENTY-SEVEN

THE BANQUET

ELODY LOOKED AT herself in the mirror and tried to smile. The elves had offered her a beautiful gown to wear to the banquet in Eryninn's honor tonight, but she had wanted to wear her formal dragonmage robes just like all the other mages. She hadn't realized how it would feel to have them on again. Now that she was wearing them, they felt stifling.

A knock at the door drew her out of her thoughts. It opened a crack, and Rinn peeked in.

"Can I come in?"

"Sure."

Rinn stepped into the room, and Elody was taken aback. The elves must have loaned him some clothes, because she had never seen him like that. A simple, white silk shirt covered his chest and was tucked neatly into a clean, simple pair of brown leather pants. Long, black boots covered his calves all the way to the knee, but it was the cloak that made her breath catch.

It was a dark purple, and as he moved, it seemed to shimmer with starlight. As he stepped into the room, the fading light in the window touched the fabric and sent sparkles dancing across the walls. Rinn pulled it in front of him and twirled it a little for effect.

"Like it?" he asked. "The elves said it was what all the wizards wear. Which, I guess I'm one of now. It's odd not having to hide it. Wizards are treated like royalty here, not hidden away like criminals."

"Did you tell them?"

"No. A guard just showed up with clothes and told me what the cloak was for. I was surprised at first, but I think these guys have a way of knowing things. They're a little scary like that."

He twirled the cloak again and smiled the biggest smile.

"It's beautiful," Elody said.

She looked down at her dirty, wrinkled robes and frowned.

"You look great," he said. "I haven't seen you in your robes since..."

"The day Dad died."

"I was going to say since the day you got Jalthrax, but yeah."

"It feels so long ago," she said.

"I know."

Elody turned back to look in the mirror again. Her once-shiny robes now seemed so dull and flat. They never sparkled like the elven cloak Rinn was wearing, but did they always look so plain? True, she never wore them, so they were always packed away in a trunk or a bag, but they just looked so plain to her now. So... lifeless.

"How long are we going to stay, El?" Rinn asked.

"I don't know. Jalthrax has had the freedom to fly for the first time in weeks, and now it seems like he doesn't want to leave."

"Maybe we should stay then. Even without Eryninn, the elves offered to let us stay in order to keep you safe. I heard there's a camp for dragonmages who have taken refuge. They're all coming here for protection."

"I didn't come all this way just to hide out."

"But maybe that's what you need to do. You know, until this thing passes."

Elody spun on him, her whole face tight.

"Passes? You think this is just going to pass? I'm being hunted, Rinn! Every dragonmage on Gondril is being hunted!"

"And this is the safest place for you to be right now."

They were both shouting. Elody was afraid they would alert someone, but she couldn't control it. All the frustration just boiled over.

"I didn't ask you come with me. No one did."

"If you don't want me here, just say the word. I'll be gone in the morning."

"I never wanted you here!"

"Fine! You've been miserable ever since we left Derne, and I'm tired of it. All I tried to do was help."

"I don't need your help. I don't want your help."

Elody couldn't control herself. She could see the pain on Rinn's face, the hurt she was causing, but she couldn't stop the words from coming. Rinn opened his mouth to say something else, but instead turned and left. His sparkling cloak disappeared as the door closed, and the room was once again dull and lifeless.

***

Elody smoothed her robes again for the hundredth time before stepping into the grand hall. The beauty of it made her pause in the doorway, blocking the line of people behind her. All around her, the room glowed a bright white. It was made of the same polished, white stone the rest of the towers were made of, but in here it seemed even more beautiful. More grand.

The ceilings were as high as the trees outside with long, white curtains stretching like flowing vines all the way to the top. In front of her, long tables had been set around the outside of a lowered floor in the center of the room. A single table sat at the far end of the hall with three long tables facing it, making a square.

A polite cough from behind her broke her reverie, and she noticed a young elf standing in front of her bowing with his hand out. She looked down with a smile and took the proffered hand as gracefully as she could and was led around the left side of the room.

"This way, Lady Elody," the elven boy said.

He looked even younger than her, but the elves always did from what she understood. He was probably four times her age even as he was only a boy among his own people. People flowed in behind her toward the long tables. Some were led to their seats, and others seemed to know just where to go.

The elf pulled her along and had to give her a gentle tug every few steps to remind her to keep moving. Elody couldn't help admiring everything in the hall. It wasn't garish or loud, no gold or gems anywhere. Just the purest white she had ever seen. She saw no torches, but everything was so bright. The light in the room seemed to come from everywhere and nowhere all at once.

The elf came to a stop, and she looked to see him gesture to an empty seat. She smiled feebly and tried to hide her disappointment. Elody found herself in the same place she'd been the entire trip. Between Rinn and Eliath. With a muffled sigh, she took her seat, and the young elf bowed and was off.

She smiled at Eliath and then turned to her right. Rinn wouldn't even look at her. After she'd calmed down, she regretted the things she'd said. She wanted to apologize, but the way he was acting now only made her mad all over again. She talked to Eliath instead.

"Amazing, isn't it?" he asked.

The great hall was located in the base of what the elves called the God Tower. Elody wasn't sure why, she'd just heard it mentioned. From the looks of the place, it must be where the king held his most formal occasions. Though, knowing very little about the elves, they might do this once a week. It didn't feel like it though. It all felt very... official. And elegant.

But now that she was near the head table, Elody couldn't take her eyes off of Eryninn. The half-elf was standing next to his uncle and looking very stiff. He was dressed in some sort of formal attire like his uncle and didn't look very comfortable in it. While his uncle stood perfectly still and smiled at everyone who entered, Eryninn shifted from foot to foot and fidgeted with his clothing. He had even shaved, looking as smooth as the elves around him, though a bit more burly. It would be comical if he didn't look so miserable.

More than the clothes though, it was the attention he was getting that most likely had him on edge. Eryninn was used to being alone. He preferred to hide away from others when he could. Since being in Derne, he had become a bit more open, but Elody could see the pain on his face at having to be the center of attention.

As the room filled, everyone stood at their chairs and waited. The king raised his hand, and the room quieted.

"My nephew has returned home to us," he said,

pausing a moment. "Those of you who know me know that I loved my brother very much."

He put his hand on Eryninn's shoulder, and he smiled in spite of his obvious discomfort.

"The last time I saw Eryninn, he was only a babe. Not even old enough to remember me. But I thought of him every day over the years. When I learned of my brother's death, I…"

The king paused and steadied himself with his hand on Eryninn's shoulder. Elody had never seen a king before, but she was surprised at his actions. Should a king show so much emotion in front of his people?

"When my brother died, I searched and searched for Eryninn. When I could not find him, I thought him dead."

The king turned to face Eryninn, and they both looked at each other.

"But now he has returned to me. Tonight, we honor my brother. I am so happy to have a small piece of him with me again."

The king raised his glass, and Elody did the same when she saw everyone else raise their own. The king pulled Eryninn close and hugged him. To Elody's surprise, Eryninn hugged him back.

"Let us eat!" the king shouted.

Everyone took their seat, and Elody did the same. Eliath leaned over and whispered in her ear.

"Eryninn looks a little nervous."

"He's not one for crowds," she said. "Especially not where he's the one everyone is looking at."

Just then, she caught Eryninn's eye and smiled. She waved, and he gave a curt nod. It can't be easy sitting with the king. Elody felt much better at her table to the side and had no doubt Eryninn would rather be sitting there with them. Or maybe even outside. Up a tree somewhere.

Elody had never attended a meal with any kind of ceremony. Everything was all new to her. Even though she'd been eating her whole life, she suddenly felt like there was a right and a wrong way to do it. And she was surely doing it the wrong way. She watched the others around her and tried to mimic what they did.

"Just watch what I do," Eliath whispered.

He picked up a small fork and waggled it in the air for her to see. She picked up the same fork and started eating the small salad of field greens in front of her. In a minute she had finished the whole thing and suddenly felt like a pig.

"Is this all we get to eat?" she whispered to Eliath.

He laughed and then tried to suppress it.

"No, this is just the first course. They'll most likely bring a soup next. Don't fill up on everything, the good stuff comes later."

"What kind of good stuff?"

"I don't know. I've never been to an elven banquet before. Only the ones my father held. But the dessert is always the best, and it always comes last. Save room for that."

Elody smiled and leaned over to Rinn.

"Save room for dessert," she said.

Rinn shot her an annoyed look and took another bite of his salad.

"Fine," she said and turned back to her plate.

But she had no more food in front of her. She took sips of her wine to pass the time and silently vowed to slow down a little when the soup came. The wine was good. Really good. Sweet, like summer berries. Not bitter like the beer her father had always made. She felt a tap on her shoulder and turned to find Eryninn.

"Eryninn!" she whispered excitedly.

"I just wanted to come over and see how you were all doing."

"This is wonderful," she said. "But how are you?"

"It's all a bit overwhelming," he said. "It's not at all what I expected."

"Your uncle seems very happy that you're here," Eliath said.

"I'm… getting to know him a little better now. I was told that after the dessert course there would be dancing."

Elody tensed, and her eyes went wide.

"Don't worry," he said, "I'm not dancing. And I don't think you're expected to join in unless you want to. Perhaps we can meet outside when the dancing starts."

They all nodded, and Eryninn returned to his seat with an awkward smile at his uncle. The courses came a bit too slowly for Elody's taste, and she kept having to remind herself to take little nibbles to make each one last longer. Apparently the elves had much smaller mouths than she did. Or maybe it was just that they were all talking between bites, and she wasn't. A nearby elf with a pitcher refilled her wine goblet every time she drained it, so that gave her something to do with her hands.

When the dessert finally arrived, after five previous courses, she could hardly enjoy it. It was delicious, whatever it was. Rich, creamy, and sweet. Elody gobbled it down in two bites and quickly stood to excuse herself.

"You can't leave yet," Eliath said.

"Why not?" she said, sitting back down. "I'm

finished."

"The meal isn't over just because you've finished."

Elody sighed and leaned back in her chair.

"Sit up straight," Eliath said.

She glared at him.

"Sorry," he said. "Didn't mean to do that, it's just an old habit. I hated when my tutors did it to me."

"When can we leave?"

"When the king orders the tables cleared."

She reached for her wine again.

"You should slow down on that," Eliath said.

Elody sat staring at her empty plate for what felt like an eternity before the king finally waved a hand, and dozens of elves came and cleared the tables. Once the food was gone, only the wine remained. And it was being consumed quickly. A moment later, a band started playing a beautiful song filled with strings and flutes, and some of the gathered elves got up to dance.

"Now we can go," Eliath said.

Elody couldn't get out of her chair fast enough. Rinn gave her a look, but she ignored him. Perhaps it was the wine she'd drunk, be she really cared very little for what Rinn thought of her at that moment. Eliath took her by the hand and led her around the table to the other side of the room. Large, floor-to-ceiling windows occupied the far wall, and the glass doors on bottom had been opened to let the cool night air in.

Elody stumbled a little as they passed the other chairs.

"How many glasses of wine did you have?" Eliath asked.

"Well, they wouldn't hurry up with the food, and I had to keep my hands occupied somehow."

Eliath put his arm around her to steady her, and she had the sudden thought that being a little drunk might not be so bad. Before she knew what she was doing, she had laid her head against his shoulder and pulled in closer.

For his part, Eliath smiled politely at everyone they passed and made some gesture to her that she couldn't see.

"What are you telling them?"

"That you're young and can't hold your wine," he said.

"I'm a grown woman!"

"A grown woman doesn't get stumbling drunk at an elven banquet."

"I'm not drunk, I just had a little too much. I can walk on my own just fine."

But she made no move to extricate herself from Eliath's arms. Instead, to her own surprise, she tucked in tighter.

***

Eryninn felt a little better as he returned to his seat. He wished he could go and sit with his friends, but Alranir had made it clear it would be inappropriate for the guest of honor to leave the head table.

"You should not have left the table," Alranir whispered.

The elf was seated directly to his right, which had made the whole meal that much harder. It was bad enough his uncle, the elven king, was seated to his left. At least he'd been occupied speaking to his generals. Alranir said little, and when he did, it was usually to correct Eryninn on some inappropriate behavior he was unaware he was doing.

It had made for scintillating dinner conversation.

"Straighten your back."

Alranir had mastered the elven art of criticism. He could point out a flaw in everything Eryninn did without so much as anyone else hearing. And all with a perfect, polite smile that never left his lips. The smile was still better than his usual scowl though, Eryninn had to admit that.

"You are not my mother," Eryninn said.

"No, the one you had apparently felt it unnecessary to teach you table manners."

Eryninn could barely contain himself. He crushed his hands together under the table to keep from striking the elf. It wouldn't look good to start a fight at his own banquet.

"Everything all right?" his uncle asked.

"Fine," Eryninn said. "Just trying to relax."

"You're doing great. Far better than Alranir did at his first banquet."

Eryninn laughed. He hadn't meant for it to be so loud, but his uncle joined him. Soon the whole table was laughing, though they had no idea what it was about. All except for Alranir. He wasn't laughing.

The king turned back to his generals again. Eryninn kept an eye on his friends and tried to ignore Alranir.

"Enjoy it," Alranir whispered. "Be the king's new plaything for a while until he grows bored with you. You will eventually end up like every other shiny new toy. Thrown in a box and forgotten."

Eryninn rounded on the elf and glared.

"Now I know why my father hated this place. You are everything he warned me about."

They were both keeping their voices down, but their smiles had disappeared, and it was starting to draw attention.

"Your father was not welcome here anymore than you are now. He left, and he should have stayed gone, just like you."

With that, the elf stood and left. Eryninn was about to chase after him when his uncle leaned over and put a hand on his arm.

"What was that about?" he asked.

"I don't know," Eryninn said.

And truly, he didn't.

CHAPTER TWENTY-EIGHT

A New Quest

ONCE AROUND THE table, Elody and Eliath exited the first open door and out onto a large balcony that overlooked a garden below. Eliath walked her to the stone rail at the edge and leaned her against it.

"If you feel sick, lean over the railing. It'll be less embarrassing for everyone that way."

Elody was about to reply that she didn't feel the least bit sick, but as she leaned over to get a better look at the railing, she found that wasn't exactly true. Her stomach did feel a little queasy now that he mentioned it.

"What's going on?"

It was Rinn. She could hear him marching over in his very clompy boots.

"She's fine," Eliath said. "She just needed a little air."

"Oh, yeah, you'll do just fine on your own, El."

Elody spun, all regrets of their earlier argument gone. She was ready to fight.

"Go home, Rinn. Go back to Aunt Jelena and study to be a great and powerful wizard. I don't need you, I have Eliath to take care of me."

"Keep your voice down," Rinn said.

"*Both* of you keep your voices down," Eliath said. "This is a party for your friend in a place where we are all guests."

"It would really matter very little."

She looked up to see Ilyaren smiling and coming over to their little gathering.

"Elves have superior hearing. Everyone in that room can probably hear your conversation. And dragons, well, we hear even more."

"She had too much to drink," Eliath said.

"I saw," Ilyaren said. "You must be Rinn."

He bowed slightly, and Rinn nodded in return.

"I am Ilyaren. Jalthrax's father."

"Wait," Elody said, "you're Jalthrax's father?"

"I… thought that was clear when I said I was Kiranoth's mate."

Elody's head was fuzzy. Jalthrax's father? She had never even thought about Jalthrax having a father, much less that she might be standing in his presence one day. Ilyaren did say he was the Silver Queen's mate though, so it made sense.

"I didn't think about it," she said.

"Eliath, would you excuse us for a moment?" Ilyaren said.

"Of… course," Eliath said.

Elody scrunched her eyes and looked at Eliath, who seemed a bit confused himself. He pulled his arm out from behind her, and she immediately had to grab the stone railing for support. Rinn stepped up to hold her, but she shrugged him off.

Eliath looked at her again and then went back in to the party.

"What was that for?" Elody asked.

"I needed to speak with the two of you," Ilyaren said. "I've spoken with Jalthrax some about this journey that you're on, and I thought it was time we talked."

"Well, it's his journey," Elody said. "I feel like I'm just along for the ride. And Rinn just followed me."

"I came to help her," Rinn said.

She could hear the edge in his voice.

"I believe I know where it is you are going," Ilyaren said.

"Where?" Elody asked, standing up straight.

She moved a bit too quickly though and immediately regretted it. Rinn steadied her, but she didn't protest this time.

"The Isle of Dragons," Ilyaren said. "I believe that is where Jalthrax is going."

"What is that?" Rinn asked.

"It is Anarr's home on Gondril. An island far out in the ocean, reachable only by dragon."

"How do you know that's where he's going?" Elody asked.

"Because he told me he feels pulled there. He doesn't know where, of course, but he feels a pull. Something tugging him west. It could only be the isle."

"What is tugging him?" Rinn asked. "What if he's being pulled into some trap by Kalus?"

"Kalus does not have that kind of power. To send a magical pull over such great distance and sustained for so long requires more power than any mortal holds."

"Wait," Elody said. "So who's pulling him?"

"Anarr," Ilyaren said. "Anarr is calling him home."

Elody had to lean back to steady herself again, even with Rinn holding her on one side.

"What does Anarr have to do with this?" she asked.

"Anarr is all things dragon," Ilyaren said. "I do not know why he is calling Jalthrax, only that he is."

"Then we have to leave," Elody said. "We have to go tomorrow."

She stood, but Ilyaren put a hand to her chest.

"I will take Jalthrax to the isle," he said. "It is not a place that you can go."

"What?" they both said together.

"You're not taking him away from me," Elody said.

"I must. You cannot walk on the Isle of Dragons, it is forbidden. I must take Jalthrax myself. The journey is too long for him to make alone, and he will have to ride on my back at least part of the way."

"Then we'll go with you," Rinn said. "We don't have to go to the island, you can drop us off in a boat or something, but you're not separating them. Not with everything going on in the world."

"I did not tell you this to debate the subject," Ilyaren said.

"Good, because there's no debate," Rinn said. "You're not taking Jalthrax without me and Elody."

"You would deny the will of Anarr?" Ilyaren asked, his voice rising.

"Wouldn't you? Kalus is the will of Anarr, yes? Yet here you stand, leading a rebellion against him."

"That is a different matter and one that does not concern you, wizard."

"But Jalthrax *is* my concern. He's not going anywhere without us."

Ilyaren stared hard at Rinn, who stared just as hard back. Elody suddenly felt ill. Not because of the wine, though that probably wasn't helping, but because of all the things she had said to Rinn. For weeks she had been ready for him to leave, had treated him so badly. Yet here he was standing up to a thousand-year-old dragon for her. She hugged his arm close to her and stared Ilyaren down with him.

"Jalthrax can make his own decisions," Ilyaren said. "We will let him decide."

"And you will let Elody talk to him first," Rinn said firmly.

"Very well."

Ilyaren turned and stomped off. Elody saw movement from the corner of her eye as Eliath came out from behind a door and walked over.

"That didn't sound great," he said.

"You heard?" Elody asked.

Eliath nodded.

"What are you going to do now?" he asked.

Rinn pulled his arm away from her, and she instantly wanted it back.

"I'm going to my room," he said. "If you see Eryninn, tell him I'm sorry for not saying goodbye."

He left without looking back, leaving Elody and Eliath alone.

Feeling very sick to her stomach, Elody wished again that he would come back.

***

The bright, white corridors of the Dawn Tower, brightened even more by the rising sun, were not as beautiful through Elody's bleary eyes. The sunlight cascading off the polished stone actually stung a bit, and she felt tears welling up.

Her head was faring no better.

It pounded to the rhythm of her slow footsteps as she trudged to the dragon roost at the top of the tower. The climb had seemed painfully long when she wasn't feeling sick. Now it felt impossible.

With several stops to rest and recover along the way, Elody finally reached the platform at the top of the tower. With a deep breath, she pulled the door and stepped out into the morning air. And immediately regretted it.

The sun blasted her in the face, the Dawn Tower living up to its name. The rising sun in the east had crested the trees and was now bearing down on her from its heavenly perch. Her eyes blinded, she could only hope that it was Jalthrax screeching and coming toward her. A moment later, she was hit with his big head rubbing against her.

"Hey, Thrax," she said.

He pushed against her chest, and she rubbed his head and neck.

"Okay, I got it."

She leaned over and rested her head on his, thankful for a moment to breathe. Her eyes slowly adjusted to the morning sun, and she was finally able to open them.

"Did you go flying this morning?" she asked.

The dragon growled, and she took it for a yes. As the sun warmed them both, Elody laid her head on top of Jalthrax's and held him for a while. What would his answer be? Would he go to the island without her? The thought of being apart from him made her heart hurt, but she knew how important this journey was for him. Though he couldn't talk to her about it, he had made his feelings clear ever since he felt the pull.

Now she had to ask him to choose.

Ilyaren was not going to bend and let her go to the island. It was up to Jalthrax to decide whether he would go without her or whether he would abandon his quest and stay. Elody hated not knowing the answer, but the longer she held him, the more she wanted to stay just like that. For his part, Jalthrax seemed content to remain there as well.

"Did you talk to Ilyaren about our journey?" she asked.

She really meant *his* journey, but she used the word our to make it clear that she considered herself a part of this. Jalthrax pulled away and nodded.

"He came and talked to me last night. Did he tell you where you have to go? What it is he thinks you're feeling?"

Again he nodded.

"Did he tell you that I can't come with you?"

The dragon cocked his head to the side and furrowed his scaly brow.

"The place you're going, the Isle of Dragons, is not a place I can go. None but dragons can set foot on its surface."

Jalthrax snorted, blasting her in the face.

"I know, but that's the way it has to be."

Jalthrax looked down, and she stepped forward so that he would look up at her.

"You have to decide whether you want to go on this quest without me, or—"

A roar from above startled them both, and they turned to the sky. Dragons, dozens of them, were circling above and flying in from across the trees toward the Dawn Tower. Big dragons. Golds and silvers. So many that Elody was sure they could never all fit in the roost. But as they touched down, each one began to shift and change, taking an elven form with silver or gold hair.

Elody immediately recognized Ilyaren.

"Kalus is coming," he said bluntly as he pushed past her.

"What?"

But Ilyaren was already gone, having leapt from the side of the tower. Elody ran to the edge to see him drift lazily toward the ground. As each of the other dragons landed, they did the same, leaping over the edge of the tower and falling slowly to the courtyard below.

Across the city, she could see a procession from the God Tower marching through the garden. At its head was the king, dressed in simple clothes and not looking much like a king. Beside him was Eryninn.

"We have to go, Thrax," she said. "Fly down there and join them. I'll take the stairs."

Jalthrax leapt into the air with one beat of his powerful wings and circled around the tower. Elody was already running for the door. She took the steps two at a time in a run. Below her, she could see Rinn just coming out of his door.

"What's all the commotion?" he asked. "I saw a gathering from my window."

"Kalus," she said. "He's coming."

Rinn fell in step behind her without a word. Elody ran right past Eliath's room, but she heard Rinn hit the door twice as he passed.

"Kalus is coming!" he yelled.

As they made the rest of the way down, she could hear Eliath's door open and slam shut and then his footsteps above them. They passed through the great, double doors of the Dawn Tower, opening east into the rising sun and saw a gathering of dozens of elves. Most of them dragons. The king's procession arrived just after them, and they all stood waiting at the eastern gates of Nirorn.

The Eldest was coming.

Kalus was coming.

Chapter Twenty-Nine

Eldest

THE ELDEST ARRIVED in Nirorn with all the fanfare of a beggar.

The king stepped in front of the gathered and ordered the gates open. As they swung wide, there stood a golden-skinned elf wearing nothing but traveling clothes and the biggest grin his face would allow. Beside him, a stern-faced elf with long, bronze-colored hair stood perfectly at attention.

The golden-skinned elf waltzed through the gates as though he had a royal honor guard at his back and a parade at his front. His arms swung freely back and forth as if to some music only he could hear. The wide grin never left his lips.

"Really, your majesty," Kalus said coming to stand before the king. "This kind of greeting wasn't necessary. Though I must admit I waited almost an hour for my royal escort. I was aware that the Eldest always received such an honor when visiting Nirorn. The kingdom seems to have slipped in its manners since your father's passing."

"Eldest," the king said through gritted teeth. "My

kingdom is always open to friends. And I am happy to report that my father has not passed."

"Really? By Anarr, the old buzzard must be older than me by now."

The elven king stiffened, and the guards behind him moved their hands to their weapons. Kalus seemed unconcerned.

"What do you want here?" the king asked, his voice tight.

"Nothing from you," Kalus said. "I came to speak to my people, and I hear you're practically flush with them."

The king looked over his shoulder to where a group of five elves, each with golden or silver hair, stood watching.

"You may go," Kalus said to the king.

The elven guard drew their swords, but a wave of the king's hand stayed them. With a slight bow to Kalus, the king stepped back and away, moving to stand near Eryninn. The group of five elves moved up to stand before Kalus.

"Eldest," one of the golden-haired elves said.

"Thalaras," Kalus said. "I take it you call yourself leader of this little rebellion?"

"There is no rebellion, Eldest," Thalaras said. "The golds and silvers have always lived among the elves. This is our home. You yourself have spent most of your years in the elven kingdoms as I recall."

"Yes, but I preferred to spend my time with the Erutharen. I find them more to my liking. Not as weak-willed as your friends."

"What do you know of wills, Kalus?" the other gold asked. "Your time is consumed bending others to your own."

"Yes, Olania, and I found the Erutharen much harder

to bend. But since you brought it up, I am, in fact, hear to *bend* you to my will. I want to know, why do you insist on defying Anarr?"

"We would never defy Anarr," Ilyaren said, stepping forward.

"Yet here you are," Kalus said, "protecting dragonmages when I have ordered them all dead."

He waved a hand at Elody and then stopped when he looked at her.

"Young Elody there should be dead, yet here you stand. You defy Anarr with your every breath."

He knew her? He knew her name? How did Kalus know her? Could he have remembered her from the Battle of Molner? Even then, how would he know her name?

"You're wrong," Olania said.

"*I* am the will of Anarr," Kalus said. "When you defy me, you defy him, by his own word."

"Do not play the part of the pious, Kalus," Ilyaren said. "We know all about your visits to the isle. It is forbidden for any but dragons to walk there, you know this. It was bad enough that you took that wizard to Anarr's home, but now you have brought even more men to the island."

"I was simply trying to remove that accursed crystal so that I could have it destroyed. It is an affront to Anarr and a horrible stain on his home."

His words sounded sincere, but Kalus could barely contain the wide grin on his face.

"You spit in Anarr's face with your every act," Ilyaren said.

"And yet I am his word on Gondril," Kalus said. "Boys and their fathers just never will get along, I suppose."

Kalus looked to the other two silver-haired elves who had, thus far, remained silent behind the lead three.

"And you?" Kalus said. "Alyniryn? Evranon? You would deny Anarr as well? You would choose to protect dragonmages in direct defiance of your god?"

"You are not Anarr," Alyniryn said.

"No," Kalus said, "but while Daddy is gone, big brother makes the rules. And you will all follow them, or I will have to put you back into line."

"Are you threatening us?" Ilyaren asked.

"Yes, I am. Continue to defy Anarr, and you will pay the price. Don't think I don't know about your plan to go to the isle yourself. What are you looking to do, Ilyaren? Get the crystal for yourself? Ask Daddy for permission to be the big boy?"

"Leave, Kalus," Thalaras said.

Kalus glared at the assembled elves and dragons, his gaze meeting everyone in the crowd.

"Very well," he said. "Know that anyone caught harboring dragonmage fugitives will be marked a traitor to Anarr and be killed. You will follow my law, or I will see you all undone."

He smiled the most innocent of smiles.

"Anarr wills it," he said, almost charmingly.

Ilyaren started to say something, but Thalaras held up a hand to stop him.

"Just let him go," Thalaras said.

Kalus took a few steps back and then began to change. His skin stretched painfully tight, the cracking of his bones filled the air. His body grew larger and larger until he had reached his true size. Before them all now was a massive gold dragon. His scales were a bit dull from age, and even burned in a few places, but his shadow fell over everyone there, drenching them all in its darkness.

"Your highness," Kalus said, addressing the elven king. "If your lands are used to harbor dragonmages, know that I will no longer respect the peace our peoples once shared."

"You do what you must, Eldest," the king said, "and I shall do the same."

The man who'd come with Kalus climbed up the side of the dragon's scales and seated himself between two spikes on his back.

"The isle is no longer your place," Kalus said, looking pointedly at the five changed dragons. "You defy Anarr, and you are no longer welcome in his home. This is my decree, and it is law."

With his last words spoken, Kalus leapt into the air with a beat of his powerful wings. A moment later, he had disappeared from sight.

***

Elody was nearest the dragons when the king marched over to them.

"May I have a word with all of you?" he asked.

Thalaras nodded and turned to follow with the others falling in behind him. All except Ilyaren. As the crowd dispersed, they were all left standing together. Ilyaren watched and waited as everyone went their separate ways and then marched calmly over to them.

He grabbed Eliath by the shirt and slammed his back against the Dawn Tower.

"Who have you been talking to?" Ilyaren yelled.

"What?" Eliath said, trying to push the elf off of him. "I haven't been talking to anyone."

"You lie!"

Ilyaren put his arm against Eliath's neck, pushing hard against the unbendable stone at his back. Elody was already in motion, running hard toward them.

"What are you doing?" she shouted.

She grabbed Ilyaren's arm and tried to pull him off.

"Let go of him!"

"He has betrayed us!" Ilyaren said.

Elody yanked Ilyaren's arm away and stepped between the two of them.

"What are you talking about?" she yelled.

"The plan to take Jalthrax to the isle," Ilyaren said. "I only made it yesterday, and I told *you* about it last night. And Kalus already knows about it. He came here just to let us *all know* that he knows!"

"Eliath wasn't even part of that conversation," Elody said. "You sent him inside."

"Because I didn't trust him, and I was right not to. But you heard everything didn't you? Did you tell him about it?"

Eliath was looking straight at her. She had told him about it. He had heard the entire conversation, and they had talked about it after Rinn had gone to bed. She swung her gaze around to where Eliath was still firmly against the wall.

"Eliath?" she said meekly.

"I would never betray you," he said. "I... care to much about you and Jalthrax to do that."

"But you told someone," Ilyaren said. "Who did you tell?"

They were all watching him now. Rinn, Elody, Ilyaren, even Jalthrax. Eliath was against the wall, Elody's hand against him, and she wouldn't let him go until they learned the truth.

"I…" Eliath started to say. "I'm working for the dragonmage conclave. I've been sending them updates about what I see and hear."

Ilyaren moved forward.

"The dragonmage conclave?" he said. "And how are you communicating with them?"

He reached under Eliath's shirt and yanked the chain out. A golden amulet hung on the end of the chain.

"With this?" Ilyaren asked.

He let the amulet fall to Eliath's chest where Elody could only stare. She jerked her hand away as though it had touched fire and held it against her chest with her other hand. She began to tremble.

Eliath looked at her, spoke only to her.

"A man named Selex recruited me when I was at my lowest point," he said. "He asked me to send him updates about dragonmages and things going on in town."

He held up the amulet, and Elody recoiled.

"He gave me this so that I could use my magic to send messages back to him."

Elody felt a stone in her stomach. A stone that threatened to come back up. She turned away from him, the words caught in her throat. She grabbed Rinn who stood shaking, his fists clenched.

"I was only trying to help," Eliath said. "To be a help to the dragonmages."

"That amulet," Rinn said, his voice quivering.

Eliath picked it up and held it out. Elody looked up from Rinn, and studied it as it hung there. Maybe she was wrong. It couldn't be.

"There is only one I've ever seen like it," Rinn said. "It belonged to Master Cythyil."

Rinn knew it too. It had to be Master Cythyil's amulet. But how did Eliath get it? Did the dragonmage conclave really give it to him? How did they get it?

"Kalus," Ilyaren said. "You've been sending your updates directly to Kalus. He gave you the amulet after he killed Cythyil."

Eliath looked at the golden disk again before ripping it over his head and throwing it to the ground.

"I didn't... I didn't know," he said. "How could I have known?"

Ilyaren shook his head.

"You thought that the dragonmage conclave would just invite you in to help them? A half-dead dark dragonmage?"

"He told me they needed help," Eliath said. "They needed eyes to watch over mages."

"You are a fool," Ilyaren said. "And you may have doomed us all."

"I didn't know," Eliath whispered. "I just wanted to help."

"Kalus knows everything," Rinn said.

***

Elody stood on top of the Dawn Tower watching Jalthrax fly. Streaking up into the sky, he flapped his wings once, twice, and then flipped and dropped down to swoop over her head with a screech. She couldn't help laughing a little, even if she really didn't feel like laughing. He was so happy to be flying again.

How long would he be free to do it now?

While everyone had stood glaring at Eliath, she looked into his eyes and saw the fear and guilt. And all she could do was run. She couldn't look at him and think about anything but betrayal. Even if he hadn't meant it, that's what she felt.

Kalus would come soon. Then there would be no more flying. Not for Jalthrax and the other bonded dragons. Not for her. If Kalus has his way, they will both be dead before this was all done.

She heard the door click open and sighed with relief when she saw it was Ilyaren. Though she didn't really want to see the elf, she was just glad it wasn't Eliath. She couldn't face him now. The elf slid up next to her a moment later without a sound.

They watched in silence as Jalthrax did tricks in the air. More daring now that his father was watching, Elody noted.

"I used to love flying as much as that," Ilyaren said.

"I've only flown once. With Eliath on Tark before..."

"I saw Tark fight at the Battle of Molner," Ilyaren said. "He gave his life to try and stop Kalus."

Elody nodded and closed her eyes at the memory. So many things were lost that day.

"I believe that Eliath didn't know," Ilyaren said. "Kalus tricked him. But that doesn't change what is done. Kalus knows about Jalthrax and the isle."

"It doesn't matter," Elody said. "He refuses to go without me."

"You knew that he would."

"Honestly, I didn't. I hoped. I can't imagine being separated from him. Not now."

Ilyaren stood in silence watching Jalthrax loop through the air.

"I will take you to the isle," he said after a time.

Elody looked at him. Even as a dragon in elven form, he chose to be the height of a normal elf, which put Elody a good inch taller than him. She looked down at him now, and he turned to meet her gaze.

"I thought humans were not allowed," she said.

"I will not flaunt Anarr's laws so easily as Kalus, but I believe that if he is calling Jalthrax, he must know that you would come. Anarr knows all things."

"But Kalus knows that was our plan. We can't go now. He'll probably have the place guarded by a hundred dragons."

"It is likely. But I trust in Anarr, and you must trust in him too."

"How would we get there?"

"The flight takes several days, but we cannot fly straight there. I have made it many times, but I cannot take you all on my back for so long a distance. We'll need a boat to take us."

Elody shook her head.

"It's too dangerous," she said. "And Jalthrax is young. I've seen what that monster can do."

"As have I," Ilyaren said. "But that is exactly why we must go. We have to stop him somehow, and I believe you and your brother can do it."

"Rinn? What does he have to do with this?"

"I believe that he may be able to do what neither you or I can do."

"What?" she asked.

"Retrieve the dragonbane crystal."

Elody stared hard at him and shook her head again. They couldn't. That crystal was evil, she had seen it with her own eyes.

"That crystal should remain safe where it is," she said.

"But don't you see? Kalus has already made several attempts to retrieve it. It is only a matter of time before he succeeds. The crystal is not safe where it is."

"Then why haven't you gone to retrieve it already?"

"Because none of my kind can touch it, and the council all agreed that we could not take a human or elf to the isle."

"But now you will?"

"One who is called by Anarr? Yes, I will. I will take the risk that I am right about this. But we have to leave now while everyone is still distracted with the commotion Kalus has caused."

Elody still wasn't sure, but she nodded after a moment. What Ilyaren was saying felt right. It's what they had to do. Pulling a bit of energy from within herself, she weaved the tiny, blue threads of magic between her delicate fingers into a spell. As she finished casting, the magic seeped into her hands, and she cupped them to her mouth and whispered.

Half a minute later, Jalthrax came soaring in over the treetops to land gracefully in the middle of the roost. Casting the same spell again, she whispered something else and then turned to Ilyaren.

"Rinn will meet us here," she said.

"Then we're ready to go," Ilyaren said.

With a deep breath, his body began to stretch and crack into its magnificent true form.

CHAPTER THIRTY

A MEETING OF ELVES

ERYNINN SHIFTED TO the left of his uncle. Alranir stood on the king's right. The three of them stood silently in the king's council chamber, a long, lonely table stretched out in front of them. Eryninn had been in the room a couple of times while the king spoke of smaller matters, but this was different.

Ever since he arrived, his uncle had taken him everywhere with him, but this was the first time Eryninn felt awkward about it. He didn't belong in these proceedings. A glance at Alranir told him the elf agreed.

One by one, a row of elves filed in. Eryninn knew they were all dragons in elven form, which only made it more intimidating. He stood in a room with an elven king and four of the most powerful dragons on all of Gondril. As if he needed a reminder of how this was not his place, the king's war council filed in after.

One king, an elf who hated him, two generals, four dragons.

And Eryninn.

"Perhaps I should wait outside," he said to his uncle.

"Stay," was all the king said.

So Eryninn stayed.

No one sat. The long table in front of them had enough chairs for all of them and twice as many, but everyone preferred to stand it seemed.

"What are you not telling me?" the king said.

The two generals turned with him to stare at the four elven dragons standing on the other side of the room.

"I have given all dragons and dragonmages safe harbor within my lands on your assurances that Kalus's petty war would not come to my door. Yet I find him at my gate this morning."

A golden-haired elf, Thalaras, stepped forward.

"I am sorry, your majesty. Kalus is… unpredictable, as you can plainly see."

Olania put her hand on his arm. Eryninn had actually met all of the dragons, and knew them all by name, though he had never seen them in their natural forms.

"And where is Ilyaren?" the king asked.

"Cooling off somewhere," Olania said. "He is the oldest among us, but sometimes I think he acts the youngest. His temper causes him no end of trouble."

The king paused for an uncomfortably long time. Even Eryninn began shifting again and reached out for the chair in front of him to steady himself.

"Well, it seems Kalus is determined to bring this war to us whether we would engage in it or not."

"His behavior is escalating, yes," Thalaras said.

"Can we do nothing about this?" the king asked.

"Put a stop to it!" one of the generals said, slamming his fist on the table.

His name was General Ilaran, Eryninn remembered. They had shaken hands briefly at that accursed banquet his uncle insisted on throwing. The other general was

General Valen, a quiet man that the king trusted implicitly, by his own word.

"Our information says that Kalus has a few hundred dragons at his command, your majesty," Valen said. "Brass, bronze, and copper all. The gold and silver have all sided with us or remain out of it entirely."

The king looked at the dragons for a response.

"You would have us go to war with our own brothers and sisters?" Thalaras asked.

"I would have you end this before more of your brothers and sisters are killed," the king said. "You know that to be the inevitable end here. Kalus is not simply going to roll over like some remorseful dog and wait for you to rub his belly."

"Your majesty," Thalaras said, "what would you have me do?"

"Let us retrieve the dragonbane crystal," the king said. "I know your answer in the past, but I ask you once again. My wizards are prepared to use the crystal now, and only once, to kill Kalus without any further bloodshed."

"And what of the next dragon you disagree with?" Alyniryn asked.

The silver dragons had remained mostly silent without Ilyaren. In truth, Eryninn had met them all but had rarely heard any of them speak outside of Ilyaren. Alyniryn and Evranon both reminded him a lot of himself. Ready to step up when needed, but preferring to remain in the shadows.

"What of when Thalaras becomes Eldest?" Alyniryn continued. "Will you use the crystal on him when you disagree with his laws as well?"

"Thalaras has been a friend to my people and my

family for centuries," the king said. "I would never harm him."

"You cannot promise that," Alyniryn said. "Not absolutely. That crystal deserves to be at the bottom of the ocean somewhere, but barring that, it is far safer where it is, out of the hands of men."

"Until Kalus retrieves it," Olania said. "He has tried several times already."

"If we cannot defeat Kalus with the crystal," Ilaran said, "then we must do it another way. One that will entail far more blood, I fear."

"I cannot be party to this," Thalaras said. "I should be punished by Anarr for even hearing it."

"The decree says only that you cannot take the mantle by blood," Evranon said. "It says nothing of what you hear or think. Anarr does not convict you for your own thoughts, Thalaras."

"This cannot be the only way," Thalaras said. "Anarr cannot have meant for us to war with each other this way."

"I cannot fight Kalus with only my wizards," the king said. "We have more than most, and we have weapons against dragons that have not been used for many centuries, but we cannot do this alone."

"Will the gold and silver fight against Kalus?" Eryninn asked.

Alranir glared at him from beside the king. He wasn't even sure why he spoke up. The thought of the dragons of light fighting against each other gave him chills. There was some part of him that hoped they would fight so that all this could end. But there was another part that hoped the dragons would refuse to kill their own.

"They will fight," Olania said. "Not for dragonmages,

but for themselves. We cannot live the coming centuries under Kalus's rule. This is but his first plan. I fear to know what else he has cooked up in a hundred years of slumber."

"Is this truly the only way?" Eryninn asked.

What was he doing? Why couldn't he keep his mouth shut?

"It is the quickest way," his uncle said. "With the help of the gold and silver dragons, we can defeat Kalus and stop all of this bloodshed."

The king looked at Thalaras who stood shaking his head.

"You know this is the only way," the king said.

"What if we destroyed Kalus with the crystal and then destroyed it?" Eryninn asked.

"It cannot be destroyed," Olania said.

"Not true," Ilaran said. "There were once believed to be five dragonbane crystals on Gondril. Now only the one remains."

"We have no assurances you would destroy it, and we could not stop you once you have it," Alyniryn said.

"You would have my word," the king said.

Olania shook her head. Her long, silver hair danced over her shoulders.

"The crystal will remain where it is until we can find a way to destroy it," she said.

"Then it must be war," Valen said. "There is no other way."

The king nodded.

Eryninn knew what his uncle was planning before they ever walked into the room. They had discussed the situation with Thalaras over dinner the previous evening, and he knew his uncle was ready to take the fight to

Kalus. He only needed the dragons to agree to go along. Kalus's little visit this morning might just have been the push they needed.

"I cannot fight Kalus," Thalaras said. "I must remain out of the fighting if I am to keep my own head."

"Very well," Valen said, "Thalaras does not fight. What of the others?"

They looked at Olania and the two silver dragons. The thin smile on her lips told Eryninn they had been waiting a while for this. Perhaps Thalaras was the only one standing in their way this whole time.

"We will fight," Olania said.

The two silvers nodded, along with the generals, the king, and even Eryninn. If Kalus would bring war on them all, then they would take the war to him.

"Begin preparations," was all the king said.

The room cleared in seconds, leaving Eryninn with the king and Alranir. Alranir always seemed to be near when he wasn't off on some request of the king.

"You knew they would fight," Eryninn said.

"They have no other choice," his uncle said. "I hated forcing Thalaras's hand, but we cannot continue to look away blindly from what Kalus is doing. Thalaras does not want to kill his brothers, yet Kalus has been killing dragons all over Gondril."

"What will we do then?" Eryninn asked.

"Kalus has been doing all the fighting so far," his uncle said. "Now let us take the fight to him."

* * *

Eryninn felt good standing in the warm sunlight. Nirorn always seemed to be the perfect amount of warmth. As though the sun were trapped by all the white stone and made to serve the elves alone. He had been cooped up inside for too long, and it was starting to get to him. He had decided to go for a walk when he felt someone yank him from behind.

"Who do you think you are?"

Alranir looked ready for a fight.

"I am going for a walk," Eryninn said. "Is that a crime?"

"You need to learn to keep your mouth shut," Alranir said. "You had no right to speak in that meeting."

"My uncle asked me to attend. I don't think he did so just so that I would stand and be silent."

"*The king* invited you to be polite. Stand still and be silent is *exactly* what he expected you to do."

"Well, I notice that you follow the etiquette quite well. I shall look to you next time I need to be weak and keep my opinions to myself."

Alranir reached for his sword, but Eryninn just folded his arms.

"You do not belong here," Alranir said.

"I never wanted to be here," Eryninn said. "But now that I am, I'm learning to like the place."

"You need to follow your friends and leave."

"My friends? They left?"

"While you were inside playing general."

"Where did they go?"

"Why would I know or care?"

Eryninn turned and skipped down the stairs.

"Sorry," he said, "we'll have to continue this lovely debate later."

He could hear Alranir cursing his back. Eryninn had no idea why he made the elf so angry all the time, but he had to admit that he liked getting to him. Just being a half-elf was enough to upset some of these people. But

Eryninn could make sure it wasn't the only reason.

Perhaps he was more like his father than he cared to admit sometimes.

CHAPTER THIRTY-ONE

VOYAGE

ELODY HAD NEVER seen the ocean before. But there it stood in front of her. From a hilltop far away, she could already smell the salty air as it wafted in from the west. The road they were on led down a ways and on to the coast. But between them and the sea was a large, dirty town that gave her a bad feeling.

"I don't understand why we need to go in," she said.

Rinn nodded beside her. She looked down at Jalthrax for added support, but the little dragon gave no hint of his feelings. He just looked on at the little movement in the city they could make out. On the other side of Rinn, Ilyaren sighed.

"Because we need passage."

"I still think we can just fly," Elody said. "The flight here wasn't that bad. We can make it to the island."

"The flight here took less than a day. The trip to the isle will take almost two weeks there and back again. You cannot ride for that long, it is too dangerous. And I do not think Jalthrax could make the trip."

Jalthrax growled something next to her.

"You are strong," Ilyaren said. "But the trip is too

long, and you have never made it before. You will have plenty of time to fly once we procure passage on a ship."

"Lot of ships going to the Isle of Dragons this time of year?" Rinn asked.

"They would not even be able to approach it," Ilyaren said.

"Then how do you plan to book passage there?" Rinn asked.

"Once we are aboard, I will steer the ship where we need to go."

"What ship?" Elody asked.

"Whatever ship will take us for the money we have."

"What if they're pirates?" she asked.

Ilyaren chuckled.

"I will not book us on a pirate ship."

"What if we're attacked by pirates?" she asked.

"Do you have a fear of pirates?" Ilyaren asked.

"We grew up with our dad telling us stories of the pirates of The Buckle.," Elody said. "We lived north of there and often traded with boats coming up the river."

"The pirates of The Buckle are a different lot," Ilyaren said. "No, we'll be perfectly safe here."

Elody wasn't convinced. The tales she had heard of pirates was enough to make her swear off ever getting on a ship. But if that was the only way to get them all to the island, she had no real choice.

"Come," Ilyaren said.

He stepped in front and marched off down the street without waiting to see if they were coming. Elody looked at her brother.

"What do you think?" she asked.

"We'll be all right," he said. "We have the oldest dragon on Gondril with us, and we're no slouches with the magic either."

He smiled, and she couldn't help but return it.

They hurried to catch up to Ilyaren.

***

The city of Rockport smelled nothing like the sea. Elody wasn't entirely familiar with the smell of the ocean, but she knew it shouldn't smell like this. Rockport smelled more like a dead sea of bloated, rotting fish. The cool, salty breeze she felt high on the hilltop above this wretched place was long forgotten now.

"Why did we come here?" she asked.

"Because we need a boat," Ilyaren said.

"Yes, but why here?" she asked. "Why this place? Surely there must be someplace a little... nicer."

"Rockport is the closest town to the isle. Sailing out from here will save us a day on our journey at least."

"Who would live in a place like this?" Rinn asked.

"People who want to hide from the world," Ilyaren said. "Which are the kind of people we need. Anyone with enough respect wouldn't take us out into the middle of nowhere and just trust that everything will be fine. The sailors of Rockport are a bit less discerning."

Elody moved closer to Rinn who took her by the hand. Her other stayed on Jalthrax at all times. It made her feel stronger to know the dragon was there. The people of Rockport didn't look as though they cared much for dragonmages.

The streets were crowded, nearly bursting with people, but they moved aside as she and the others came through. Many scowled at them, more at Jalthrax it seemed. Ilyaren either didn't notice or didn't care.

"These people are not very friendly," she said under her breath.

"They probably think you are here as some sort of law. Dragonmages of light are not well-regarded in cities like Rockport. You will find few friends here, but they shouldn't make trouble for us."

"We should have made Jalthrax turn into a donkey," she said.

"I asked him," Ilyaren said. "He did not want to."

"Well, maybe he should have anyway."

"It is not my place, or your place, to make him."

"I wouldn't *make* him."

"Come," Ilyaren said.

He picked up the pace and actually started waving his hand for the people in front of his path to move. With the three of them right behind him, they made it to the docks much faster. You would think being the oldest dragon on Gondril would have taught him some patience.

Once down on the docks, Ilyaren stopped and turned on them.

"You stay here. I will go and find us a ship."

"What are we supposed to do?" Rinn asked.

"Just stay out of trouble," Ilyaren said.

He left the three of them there and then walked off down the dock. As soon as he was out of sight, Elody felt a little less safe. The sailors down on the docks were even less friendly than the other citizens of Rockport. And she and Rinn and Jalthrax were standing right in the middle of them.

"I don't like this," Rinn said. "We should find another way."

"Ilyaren says there is no other way."

"Then another town. We should have gone someplace a little... cleaner."

Even as he said it, a sailor shoved past him, snorted, and spit on the ground. All they could do was wait and hope that Ilyaren found something soon.

They stood for almost ten minutes, watching and waiting.

"You need a boat?"

Elody jerked her head and saw a man standing a few feet away leaning against the dock.

"What?" she asked

"Do you need a boat?" he said.

He looked about Rinn's age if Elody had to guess, but a lot dirtier. He wore a tar-covered tunic and pants that hung loosely from his skinny frame. The whole look was tied together with a knotted length of rope around his waist that seemed to be the only thing holding it all up. Though his smile was friendly enough, Elody had to keep from recoiling at his rotten teeth.

"Our friend is getting us passage," Rinn said.

"I have a boat," he said.

"*You* have a boat?" Rinn asked.

"Truly. Well, not me, but I'm on a boat. Good captain. Good crew."

"What is your ship called?" Elody asked.

His smile widened.

"The Golden Goose," he said.

"Well, our friend will find us a ship," she said.

"All the same to me," he said. "You just looked a little too clean to be standing around these docks."

"Does your ship allow dragons?" Elody asked.

"El," Rinn said.

"Captain likes mages," the man said. "Used to keep one on board for weather working before the damn Eldest went all wacky. You work the weather?"

"I have never tried," she said.

He nodded.

"Be nice if you did. Truly. Makes the going a lot easier."

Elody could see Ilyaren coming back down the dock.

"Away," he said.

He waved his hand at the man who bowed and shrunk back.

"I've found us a ship," Ilyaren said.

"What's it called?" Elody asked.

"The Sea Dragon," he said.

"Bad ship," the man said over Ilyaren's shoulder. "Captain Harken has a reputation for robbing his fares once they're out at sea with nowhere to run."

"That would be unwise of him," Ilyaren said.

"My captain is a good man," the man said. "Talk with him, he'll cut you a fair deal."

Ilyaren turned to face him.

"What is your ship, boy?" he asked.

"The Golden Goose, sir," the man said. "Captain Jonas's boat."

"I saw your ship, but the captain was not aboard."

"Sir, here's Captain Jonas now."

The boy waved his hand, and they all turned to see an older man coming up behind them.

"Captain Jonas!" the man yelled.

The man straightened himself as he saw them looking and nodded as he passed.

"Sir, these good people are looking for passage," the man said.

Captain Jonas looked the four of them up and down a moment before responding.

"Where to?" he asked.

"Into the middle of the Anarrian Sea," Ilyaren said.

The captain looked to the man and then back at them again.

"What's out there?" he asked.

"That is none of your concern," Ilyaren said.

"Where my boat goes concerns me, stranger," the captain said.

"It does not matter. Captain Harken has already agreed to take us."

Captain Jonas laughed.

"You sail with Harken, you'll get what you deserve, friend."

"And I should trust you more?"

The captain pulled his shoulders back and looked Ilyaren straight in the eyes.

"I'm no thief," he said firmly.

Ilyaren stared hard back at him until Elody thought they would fight right there on the dock. She pulled her hands out of her robe and let them hang loosely just in case things went sour.

"Very well," Ilyaren said. "But I cannot tell you where we are going."

"I need maps," the captain said. "I need to know where in the nine hells we're going."

"There is no map for where we are going," Ilyaren said. "But I will guide you there."

The captain scoffed.

"And what if you fall overboard and drown, and we end up stranded on the open sea?"

"The likelihood of my dying is very, *very* low."

"All the same…"

"I will pay you fifty gold suns per passenger," Ilyaren said.

Whatever objection the captain had on his lips dropped pretty quickly as they clamped shut. He looked back at his man and then to the four of them again.

"The dragon counts as a passenger," he said.

"Fine. Two hundred gold suns."

The man tried hard to hide his grin, but he wasn't very good at it.

"Let's see 'em," he said.

Ilyaren took a pouch from his belt. Everyone on the dock, even some not invited to their chat, could see how big and full it was. He opened the strings just a bit and showed the glittering gold coins inside.

"You should be careful flashing that around," Captain Jonas said. "Could get you in a lot of trouble down here."

"That would be *very* unwise," Ilyaren said.

The captain shrugged.

"Never been paid elven coin," he said.

Ilyaren pulled one from his pouch and slapped it into the captain's hand.

"It is made of the same gold as your crowns," Ilyaren said. "Now, do we have a deal?"

The captain had his hand out before Ilyaren could even finish. They shook, and the captain turned down the dock and waved for them to follow.

"I guess we have a deal," Elody said.

***

Elody's legs dangled over the side of the boat with her eyes closed and tried to calm her roiling stomach. It felt like everything she had eaten, which was very little, could come back up for revenge any moment. She found that if she took slow, deep breaths, she could keep everything down for just a little while longer.

She also kept her eyes closed so no one would look at

her.

They had only been at sea for a day, and here she was, feeding the fish her breakfast. The snickering of the sailors as they passed behind her was all she needed to hear to keep her head down and breathing.

"Hey there," someone said.

She opened her eyes just a crack and saw the man from the dock. His name was Gavin, and he and the crew and captain of the Golden Goose had turned out just as friendly as he had said.

"It happens to a lot of people their first time at sea," he said.

She took another deep breath.

"Did it happen to you?"

"Probably. I don't remember my first time. My first memories were on a boat, so they've always just felt like home to me."

Elody opened her eyes and looked at him. He was smiling as usual, something she noticed he did quite a lot of. She couldn't say the same for most of the other men on the boat though. Not that she blamed them. She wasn't having much fun on this voyage either. Certainly nothing worth smiling about.

"I feel awful," she said. "Everyone is laughing at me."

"Bah. I've seen every man on this boat in the same spot you're sitting in at one time or another."

"Really?"

"Truly," he said. "Every man, 'cept maybe the captain. So don't let it get to you. Just keep your head down and breathe."

"That's what I'm trying to do," she said.

"Your dragon there seems to be having a fine time," he said.

She looked up to where he was pointing out over the water. Jalthrax was a ways out from the boat, but the sun glinted off his silver scales so much that it was hard to miss him. As they watched, he did several spins in the air and then dove down to skim across the tops of the little wave crests.

Elody had to smile, in spite of her stomach.

"He hasn't had much of a chance to fly lately," she said.

"Your brother looks about as sour as the rest of these sailors," he said.

Elody looked around Gavin to watch Rinn sitting ten feet away. He was cross-legged on the deck next to a short, scrawny old man who was showing him how to tie knots. Every time Rinn got it wrong, the old man would slap his hand without saying a word and then go back to his own work. Rinn looked up and caught her with a glare.

"Knots aren't really his thing," she said.

"Every man works on a boat," Gavin said.

"What about me?"

"I said every man. Last I checked, that wasn't you."

"You've been checking me?" she asked.

Gavin grinned and then looked away. They sat in silence for several minutes just watching Jalthrax glide along above the water. He looked so at home out here over the ocean. Like he could just glide for days without ever so much as beating his wings. Just ride the air all the way across Gondril.

"The men have been wondering where we're going," Gavin said.

"Me too," Elody said.

"You don't know where we're going?"

"It's not really my journey," she said.

"You're just traveling with the elf?"

"Actually, we're all just traveling with him."

She pointed out to where Jalthrax was doing loops in the air again.

"Truly?"

She nodded.

"Then where is he leading us?" he asked.

"I don't think he's leading," she said. "I think he's following just like the rest of us."

"Never heard of a bunch of people just following before."

"You follow your captain wherever he goes."

"Yeah, but I trust Captain Jonas knows where he's going."

"Well, I trust Jalthrax. This is his journey. I am only here to follow."

Elody heard footsteps and looked up as a shadow passed over her.

"Come with me," Ilyaren said.

"I don't feel so well," she said. "Where are we going?"

"To practice," he said.

He turned and walked off toward the back of the ship. Gavin had told her to call it the stern so the others wouldn't snicker behind her back. Elody couldn't hold back a groan as she stood and felt her whole world begin to rock. She grabbed the railing for support and stood for a second to take another deep breath.

"Need some help?" Gavin asked.

"No," she lied. "I'm fine. I need to go and practice."

Ilyaren had told the captain that he was her teacher and was training her in the art of dragon magic. It provided him a way to hide his own magic through her.

Though she didn't know whether Captain Jonas believed him or not. She had seen something in the captain's eyes that told her he always seemed to know more than he let on.

She found Ilyaren just behind the wheel of the ship and staring forward. She went over to him and then stood waiting for him. His eyes were closed. She almost tapped his shoulder, but she had learned early on that the dragon was not fond of being touched. Soon, he opened his eyes and looked at the sails.

"We need to speed our journey along," he said.

"How can we do that?"

"By working the wind in our favor."

"Can you do that?" she asked.

"Just pull some magic from Jalthrax and cast a spell."

"What should I cast?"

"Anything that won't harm anyone."

Elody crooked her lip and looked around. What could she cast?

"Just pick something," Ilyaren said.

Elody sighed and shook her hands out. Pushing her mind out, she sought Jalthrax out over the water. She could feel his presence, just as she always could. No matter how far he got from her, she could always feel him in a general direction. But he was definitely too far away for her to draw magic this time.

"I can't reach Thrax," she said.

Ilyaren turned on her with a look that reminded her an awful lot of her former teacher.

"Do they teach you *nothing* in these school?"

"I have only had Jalthrax for a year now," she said.

"No wonder your village was destroyed," he said.

Elody opened her mouth to respond but found her

words frozen in her throat. She sputtered and tried to speak, but he cut her off with a wave of his hand.

"Use your own magic," he said. "We cannot wait for Jalthrax to get close enough."

"I… I don't know if I can."

"Try," he said. "They did teach you that, yes?"

"Yes," she said.

Her blood was rising now, and her fists were like tight little knots.

"Then take some magic and cast," he said.

Elody started to say something but couldn't think of anything. She was at a complete loss. Instead, she flung her hands out and shook them to loosen her tight fingers. When she was ready, she closed her eyes and reached down inside of herself.

She could feel the pulse of the magic within her almost instantly, but it felt distant. Not as distant as Jalthrax was, with him she could feel no magic right now. No, she could feel her own magic much more intimately. It was just so hard to grasp.

It was hard to concentrate with Ilyaren sighing loudly beside her, but she finally managed to draw enough magic to her hands for her spell. Ilyaren saw the blue energy pooled in her hands and nodded. As she began to weave the threads of magic, he cast his own spell next to her. Elody pulled and stretched the stuff in her fingers and then put her hands to her mouth just as Ilyaren finished casting.

"Ilyaren is an arse," she whispered so low that not even the dragon could hear her.

But Rinn did. The simple spell she had cast carried her whisper on the wind. Across the deck, down the ship to where Rinn was still being slapped for tying knots wrong. His head snapped up, and he looked right at her and smiled. They both nodded, and she laughed a little.

Ilyaren seemed not to notice. He tried to be inconspicuous as he twitched his hands and pointed at the sails. As he did, the wind behind them whipped into a gust and blew Elody's hair in front of her face. She brushed it back and looked up to see the sails of the Golden Goose straining against their rigging. The boat lurched beneath her, not a great feeling, as it was propelled forward at an even faster pace. Elody stumbled and grabbed the nearest rail to keep from falling.

Captain Jonas joined them a moment later as the men scrambled to tighten things up.

"This your work?" he asked.

He was looking at Elody, and she almost pointed at Ilyaren before she remembered their ruse. She managed to stand up straight and look the part for almost a whole second before grabbing the rail for support again.

"Yes," she said.

The captain looked at the sails and nodded his head.

"I used to have a mage who was brilliant at weather working," he said. "Lost him when the dragons started attacking their own."

"Was he attacked?" Ilyaren asked.

"No. Just left. Said he didn't want to put us all in danger."

"He was probably right," Ilyaren said. "These are dangerous times to be a dragonmage."

"Aye," the captain said. "I don't expect any trouble out this far though."

"Nor do I," Ilyaren said.

But Elody saw his face when she caught his eye. He was lying.

"Well, keep up the wind if you can," Captain Jonas said. "The quicker we get you where you're going, the quicker we can get you back off the boat again."

"I believe that is something we all want," Ilyaren said.

The captain wandered off leaving the two of them mostly alone again.

"We must come back every few hours and replenish the spell," Ilyaren said.

"Do I have to keep coming?"

"*You* are the mage, not me. I am just pretending to be a teacher."

"Well, you've got the act down pretty well," Elody said.

Chapter Thirty-Two

Attack at Sea

JALTHRAX FLEW ALONG behind the ship as it sped through the open waters. Though he wanted to scout out farther, Elody had forbade him from getting too far ahead of the Golden Goose. So, he opted for flying behind her and watching Elody. Mostly it was just nice to feel the wind lift his wings.

Elody and Ilyaren were on the aft deck doing their teacher and student routine. Jalthrax found the whole thing very amusing, and he let out a squawk to get her attention. She looked back over her shoulder and smiled at him before going back to pretending to cast a spell.

Jalthrax braced himself as Ilyaren finished casting. The wind kicked up behind him, and he had to angle up to avoid crashing into the back of the boat. The sails filled once more, and the Golden Goose sped on toward her destination.

The Isle of Dragons.

Ilyaren had said they would be able to see it within a day. They had already been at sea for three days, and even though he had the freedom to fly a little, Jalthrax was growing bored. The sailors on the ship weren't openly hostile toward him, but neither did they like him being around. They seemed to like Ilyaren even less.

Probably his cheerful demeanor.

Jalthrax chuckled to himself. It was nice having someone he could actually talk to. Even if that someone rarely spoke without something condescending to say. Maybe that was just a part of being over a millennium old.

"Skyward ho!"

Jalthrax heard the call and looked to the top of the mast. The crow's nest, as he'd learned it was called, looked like little more than a barrel hanging from the mast, but the man in it had an important job. To scan the surrounding waters for enemy ships. Jalthrax was still getting used to sailor jargon, but he was pretty sure the man hadn't spotted a ship.

Ilyaren didn't think so either. The older dragon looked straight at him and waved an arm up. Jalthrax nodded and flew higher to get a better look. If the human in the crow's nest could see something this far out, his superior sight should be able to get an even better look.

Jalthrax flew high above the mainmast and scanned the horizon. He wasn't sure which direction the man had spotted something, but his instinct was to look toward their destination, toward the isle. His instincts proved correct. What must have been only specks in the distance for the human in the crow's nest could be seen quite plainly by Jalthrax's eyes.

A bronze and a brass dragon. Their shiny scales glinted in the sunlight and gave away their positions quite clearly. He flew down to land on the deck next to Ilyaren and relayed the information.

Ilyaren looked to the distance and shook his head.

Jalthrax growled out something in the dragon tongue. They could be friendly. They didn't have to be an enemy.

"No," Ilyaren said. "Bronze and brass are no longer friends to us."

"A bronze and a brass?" Elody asked.

Ilyaren spoke in her own language, so she could understand quite clearly. Jalthrax hated that he couldn't talk to her. He felt like he was leaving her out when she was the person he most longed to tell everything. He could hear the fear in her voice and wanted to comfort her, but all he could do was nod or squawk and wait for Ilyaren to translate.

Jalthrax grumbled something at Ilyaren. He wanted them to wait, to see if maybe the two dragons were friendly. Or maybe they would just fly by without bothering them.

"If we wait, they will surely destroy this ship," Ilyaren said.

"Why wait then?" Elody asked.

"Jalthrax wishes us to treat them as friends until they show otherwise."

Elody looked straight at him.

"You know they aren't here to make friends," she said.

Of course he knew it. Still, he hoped it wasn't true. His life had been short on this world, especially given the lifespan of his kind, but he had already seen so many of them die. Now they openly killed each other, and he had chosen a side based solely on the color and sheen of his scales. More like a side had been thrust upon him.

"We must meet them in the air before they reach us," Ilyaren said.

"We?" Elody said. "You can't take Jalthrax with you."

"I need him," Ilyaren said. "He may need to distract

one until I can take care of the other."

Her panic was rising. Jalthrax could feel it coming off of her just as she must feel his power when they were close. Her every emotion was projected, and he could feel even the slightest one. He had felt it from the very first day they had bonded and ever since.

"You want to use him as a distraction?" she shouted.

"He is my son, and he is silver. A warrior of his kind. His place is not to hang back by your side as a child on his mother's skirt."

"He's not big enough to face a full-grown dragon," she said.

Her voice was raised, but she kept most of her fear hidden from Ilyaren. Jalthrax could feel her suppressing it though. She kept herself steady, but on the inside she was trembling.

Jalthrax moved closer and put his head against her. It had the immediate effect of calming her just a little. Her hand fell to his head, and he closed his eyes and sighed.

"He must learn to fight," Ilyaren said. "We do not live in a time where he can be spared this lesson."

"But... he's too young."

"Jalthrax is strong. I will do my best to see that no harm comes to him."

He opened his eyes to see Elody staring into them. A quick breath, and he blew a puff of cold into her face that made her smile. He knew she was only putting on a brave face, could feel it within her.

"Get back!" Ilyaren shouted.

The two of them looked up from each other to see that some of the sailors had gathered on the deck below. The captain pushed his way through the crowd and climbed the steps to the aft deck where they stood.

"What is going on?" he asked. "My man says there are dragons in the sky and coming this way."

"Two of them," Ilyaren said. "A bronze and a brass."

"They looking for them?" he asked.

He pointed at Elody and Jalthrax.

"Yes," Ilyaren said. "But they will not make it that far."

"You have a plan for fighting two dragons?"

"I will take care of them myself," Ilyaren said. "Now stand back and join your men."

The captain started to protest, but Ilyaren wasn't listening. Jalthrax and Elody stepped back instinctively as the elf's body began to change beside them. The smooth, pale skin strained as the bones within began to grow and change. The captain stood staring in horror a moment longer before charging down the stairs away from them all.

Ilyaren's elven form stretched and snapped, growing impossibly large. Soon the smooth skin sprouted scales of silver, small at first, but growing larger as his body continued its change. As he grew bigger and bigger, the back end of the ship began to dip lower into the water.

Claws curled where hands once were. Wings exploded from Ilyaren's back and stretched far beyond the little boat. When they were fully extended, he launched himself into the air to finish the change. The ship could have sunk from his weight if he hadn't.

When the change was complete, he swung his great, silver head down toward Jalthrax.

"Come," he said.

Jalthrax looked at Elody and wanted to say something. To tell her to be safe or tell her how much he loved her, or just tell her not to worry. He had to settle for a squawk and a puff of cold air. With that, he leapt into the air behind Ilyaren and flew to meet his kin in battle.

Ilyaren was waiting for him as he flew on, and together they sped in the direction of the approaching dragons.

"You will take the bronze," Ilyaren said.

Jalthrax growled back. The bronze would be the biggest. Why should he take the biggest?

"Yes, but his lightning breath will not harm you near as much as the brass's fire. That said, you should avoid getting hit by either if you can."

Jalthrax felt a shiver as he thought about it. He had never fought another dragon. Had never even thought about it really. Now he was going into battle against two. Even with the oldest dragon on Gondril at his side, he felt the fear creep into his heart.

"Do not fear," Ilyaren said. "He is older and bigger, which makes you younger and faster. Your job is not to fight him, only to keep him occupied until I can kill the brass. Once that is done, I will take the bronze as well. Use your superior speed and young reflexes to lead him away and stay well clear of his breath and claws."

Jalthrax growled. How could he keep track of Ilyaren in the roar of battle?

"Don't worry about where I am. You need to worry about where the bronze is and keep him chasing you. I will come as soon as I am able."

Jalthrax growled, a hint of fear in his voice. What if he couldn't keep him away?

"Then try and find me," Ilyaren said. "Whatever you do, don't fly into the water. Bronze dragons are most at home in the water. You have no chance of escape if you meet him there."

Jalthrax nodded and felt his stomach lurch. They were close enough now to see the two dragons flying straight for them.

"You will do fine," Ilyaren said.

Jalthrax nodded again, but the words were little comfort. All he could think of was Elody. What would she do if something happened to him? What would happen to her if they failed to stop the two dragons? Would they leave her alone after he was gone? Could they even know she was a dragonmage?

"Get ready," Ilyaren said. "They will both come for me, so you will have to breathe and claw at the bronze until he breaks off and chases you."

Beside him, Ilyaren took a long, deep breath. Jalthrax did the same. This idea was suddenly sounding very stupid indeed. He was supposed to take on a bronze dragon that was more than seven times his size and *make* it chase him. But for now, he had no more time to think about it. Within seconds, the dragons were on them.

The brass and bronze dragons roared at them both. Ilyaren loosed the breath he had been holding in, blasting the two of the straight in the face. Their roars turned to screeches as the storm of ice and frost stung at their eyes and mouths.

The brass veered off quickly, trying desperately to get away from the freezing cold. The bronze roared back in defiance and flew straight for Ilyaren just as his breath died out.

Jalthrax hesitated only a moment.

Just long enough to gather his courage.

He flew straight for the bronze, breathing out with everything he had. His breath was small next to his father's but just as cold. It hit the bronze on its exposed underside. The bronze screeched and turned to snap at him. Jalthrax was already through his legs and on the other side.

He turned in the air and flew back again. Ilyaren was right. The bronze was a slow, lumbering giant next to him. The dragon tried to bite at him as he neared again, but he was far too slow to catch him. Jalthrax tucked his wings in and flew like an arrow straight for the bronze's belly.

All dragons, no matter the color of their scales, shared a similar weakness. The scales on their bellies were softer than the rest. It was a weakness that could sometimes be exploited by men. But in an aerial battle, it was the best place to sink your claws.

The bronze blew out a breath. A huge lightning bolt crackled from his open jaw and flew at Ilyaren. Jalthrax shouted, but Ilyaren wasn't looking. He was too busy chasing the wounded brass to see.

The lightning struck his silver scales. Ilyaren's whole body spasmed and jerked. He roared like an animal. He began to fall, his wings still spasming.

"No!" Jalthrax cried out.

But his father was much stronger than he looked. His wings spread wide, catching the wind. In an instant, Ilyaren was rising again. Coming back to the fight.

Jalthrax had to distract the bronze.

He saw now what his father had meant. If the bronze and brass attacked together, Ilyaren would be in real trouble. The bronze was above him now. It was ignoring Jalthrax completely. Which only made him angry.

He flew at the bronze's belly again. As he neared, Jalthrax pivoted in midair and threw his claws up. He found purchase under one of the bronze's scales and grabbed hold. With all his strength, he ripped and tore at the bronze's belly.

The dragon screamed.

Its claws grabbed at Jalthrax, but he was small enough to avoid them. The bronze swatted at him like a horse does a fly. Jalthrax would fall away and then rake his claws into the bronze again. Ilyaren was right. With his speed and agility, he stayed one step ahead of the bronze.

But this was no horse he was pestering. The bronze sucked in a breath and blew out beneath him. Jalthrax tucked in. The bolt passed mostly over him. Mostly. He felt a jolt as an arc of blue energy whipped out and struck him. His body jerked. He tried to hold on with his claws, but he had no control over his muscles.

Then he was falling.

Fast.

He tried to regain control of himself. Tried to get his muscles to answer his call. When he could finally move again, he spread one wing out. The wind caught it and flipped him over. Then the other wing shot out to catch the air. He stopped falling. But he still felt the pain.

His whole body hurt. The clear, blue water below was calling him to just fall in and rest. And he needed it. He needed to rest and regain his strength. He had only caught a little of the lightning, but it was enough.

No.

There was no time for rest. Jalthrax looked up and saw the bronze and brass dragons both tearing at Ilyaren. Fire, lightning, and ice filled the air. And the screams. Many came from the two dragons, but Jalthrax could hear Ilyaren too.

He had to get back in there.

Jalthrax flew straight up. Straight for the bronze's belly again. Another bolt, even a little one, would probably kill him. But he didn't care. Ilyaren would die without his help.

Jalthrax crashed into the bronze's underside right where he had attacked before. The scales were already weak there, a couple just hanging on. Jalthrax ripped into the leathery flesh beneath them. He tore with all of his strength and was rewarded with blood and a scream of pain from the bronze.

The dragon turned his neck beneath him again, but Jalthrax was wise to that trick now. Letting go, he dropped quickly as another lightning bolt crackled over his head. He couldn't help a little smile as he reversed his flight and sped back up.

The bronze was bleeding from a hole in his stomach now. A hole Jalthrax had made and was working on making bigger. Jalthrax raked at the wound again and again. He may have been small, but allowed to continue, he would no doubt kill the bigger dragon.

The bronze had no choice but to break off from Ilyaren and confront him. Jalthrax let go as the bronze clawed at him. He caught the wind and flew out fast. The bronze was right behind him.

Only, now what?

The bronze was chasing him. That part of the plan had worked. But what was he supposed to do now? He might be able to outrun the bigger dragon, but could he outrun lightning? The intake of breath behind him told him he was about to find out.

Jalthrax broke to the side. His only hope was to dodge, but he couldn't even look back to see where the dragon was. The now-familiar crackle of lightning filled his ears. He pulled his wings in tight and fell. The bolt of lightning flew right above his head.

From somewhere, Jalthrax heard a scream. It didn't sound like Ilyaren. Jalthrax dared a look and heard a great splash as the brass dragon's body plummeted into the sea. The bronze was right above him and bearing down, but even he stopped when the brass hit the water.

Ilyaren's roar filled the air as he raced toward the bronze. Now it was the bronze's turn to panic. The dragon banked hard and tried to fly back the way it had come. In the direction they were all heading. Back toward the isle. The bronze was making a run for it.

But Ilyaren wasn't going to let him.

With another blast of Ilyaren's great breath, the bronze curled into a ball and dropped into the ocean. Ilyaren didn't hesitate as he hit the water right behind him. Though tired, Jalthrax flew closer to see if he could get a look.

The waters roiled and frothed beneath him, clouding everything. Ilyaren had said that bronze dragons were great swimmers. Why did he go in after him?

The blue sea below was turning pink. There was blood in the water. A lot of blood. But whose was it? The ocean burst up as a body broke the surface and flapped into the air once more.

Dripping with water that was quickly turning to ice against his scales, Ilyaren took a long, deep breath. They were both panting from the fight. Jalthrax looked at him questioningly, and Ilyaren just nodded.

"Dead," he said when he could finally get a breath.

Jalthrax growled. What about the brass?

"Dead," Ilyaren said.

The ancient silver dragon turned back toward the ship

and flapped his wings with tremendous effort. Jalthrax could barely move. His wings were moving on their own now, just enough to keep him aloft. Still, he forced himself to move, to fly back to the boat.

Back to Elody.

CHAPTER THIRTY-THREE

WAR

BARELY THREE DAYS later, Eryninn found himself in a sadly familiar place. The battlefield just outside the city gates of Molner. Only three months ago, Eryninn stood atop the city wall before him and commanded troops against an invading horde of ten thousand goblins. Now he was here again, at war with a different enemy. And on the side of some he once considered an enemy.

A lot can change in a few months.

Eryninn was surprised at how quickly the elves were ready to march, but he soon learned that his uncle had been planning an attack on Kalus for months. Ever since the dragons and dragonmages had begun flooding into his kingdom. Kalus hadn't even declared war on the mages at that point, but his uncle knew what was to come. And he had planned for it.

The four dragons of the inner circle had delivered the news to the rest of the dragons taking refuge among the Ilotharen. They were ready to fly within hours. It seems everyone knew this day would come.

Ilyaren was still nowhere to be found. Even Eryninn didn't know where he'd gone, but he did have a pretty good idea who was with him. Elody, Rinn, and Jalthrax had all disappeared at the same time. Eliath had remained, but he would not tell them where the others had gone.

Eryninn sat beside him beside one of the many campfires.

"Not hungry?" Eryninn asked.

Eliath picked his head up, his contemplation broken, and looked confused. Eryninn pointed to the full bowl of soup sitting in his hands.

"No," Eliath said.

Eryninn didn't need to ask why. Molner was not a happy place for Eliath. This was the place where half of him had died. This was where he lost Tark, his dragon.

"Do you want to talk?" Eryninn asked.

"Do you?" Eliath asked.

"No, but I will."

Eliath nodded and went back to looking at his soup. They sat in silence for a long time, Eryninn staying beside him just in case he did want to talk. Eryninn was glad for the silence. Their campfire was empty except for the two of them, all of the elves having chosen to eat with each other rather than the morose human.

"I was only a bit older than you when my father died," Eryninn said, breaking the silence.

He wasn't even sure why he'd said it. He loved silence. Preferred it to all other forms of communication. His uncle was turning him into quite the talker.

"How did he die?" Eliath asked.

His eyes never left his soup, but at least it was something.

"Fighting in a war that had nothing to do with him."

Eliath scoffed.

"Tark didn't even want to be here," he said.

He waved his arm at the wall as he said the word *here*.

"I begged him not to go," Eryninn said. "He wouldn't listen. My mother had served under King Dornan and said he was a good man. In truth, I think my father had just grown to like helping people. It is not something my people do often, but it was something my mother was born to do."

"What about this?" Eliath asked, motioning towards the elven army.

"My uncle is… different than I have known many elves to be. He cares about his people most of all, but he also seems to care about non-elves, which is rare."

"Tark cared about everyone and no one. He acted haughty and tough, but he would throw himself into any harm to save someone in trouble. That's just who he was."

"That was my father," Eryninn said. "You know, I used to think he was a fool. A stupid hero willing to give his life for so many who didn't deserve it."

Eliath looked up.

"And now?"

"Now… now I see that maybe I was wrong about him. Or maybe I was right, but I'm just becoming more like him."

"Well, let's hope you don't end up like him," Eliath said.

"There are worse things to be than a hero," Eryninn said.

"I suppose," Eliath said.

Eliath went back to staring at his soup, and the silence dragged on for a while. They both looked up when they heard shouting from the wall. It was lit up like a celebration, lined with torches in every direction as men marched back and forth.

"They look nervous," Eliath said.

"You would think *they* were the ones fighting tomorrow."

"What are they doing?"

"Watching us. Waiting for us to leap up and strike at any moment."

"Do they really fear the elves so much?"

"The whole city was built on just that fear, yes. Molner used to be a small outpost. The human kings built it here on the edge of Ilothar to keep watch over the elves in case of war. It has been here for a hundred years and grown into quite a bit more than just an outpost now."

"Have the elves ever attacked it?"

"Not even once," Eryninn said.

They both chuckled.

"How did you get them to let you camp here?" Eliath asked.

"My uncle went and spoke to the mayor personally and explained why they were here. The humans were in quite a tizzy to see us. Their scouts had reported a large movement of elves, and they were already preparing for war. When we walked in to see the mayor, he thought we were delivering our terms for their surrender."

"Did he surrender?"

"He looked ready to, but my uncle smiled and shook his hand before he could say a word and launched into his explanation for our troops. You could feel the wave of relief roll off the man. After that, he became very genial. It's not often a human, even one of his considerable wealth, gets to meet an elven king."

They both chuckled a little and then fell back into silence. Above them, the moon occasionally disappeared behind the wings of a large dragon flying past. The skies were filled with them. The golds and silvers that had answered their call had numbered in the hundreds, possibly even a thousand. Most were young, but many were quite old.

Elven dragonmages had come to fight as well, though most of their spells would do no good. They were here to support the ground troops and help operate the dragon fighting machinery. Their dragons would still fight in the air, even without them using their magic in combat. Eryninn looked at Eliath and wondered how many of them would go home tomorrow without their dragon.

How many of them would lose half of themselves?

"Stay close to me tomorrow," Eryninn said. "My uncle has asked that you be with us in the command tent."

"Why?" Eliath asked.

"You have proven yourself useful these last few days. Also, there's really no place else for you to go."

"I should have stayed behind."

"And miss seeing Kalus fall?"

Eliath thought for a moment and then nodded.

"I suppose that would bring me a little peace."

Kalus was the one who had killed Tark. Eryninn forgot sometimes that Eliath had such a personal stake in all of this. Nothing would bring Tark back, but Eryninn held out some small hope that seeing Kalus burn would give Eliath something.

"Get some rest," Eryninn said. "We march to the mountain at dawn."

Eryninn stood and left the warm glow of the

campfire. He stepped into the darkness a ways and stared off into the distance at the lone mountain that stood tallest against the smaller, jagged formations. Even at this distance, he could make out their shapes against the moonlight.

Anarr's Teeth they were called. The largest was simply known as Dragonhome. The birthplace of dragons on Gondril and home to the Eldest. Eryninn watched as fire lit up the sky in the distance. Kalus knew that they were here. He knew what they were coming to do, yet he did nothing.

He was probably laughing about it all.

***

The sky was filled with dragons.

So many dragons that it was hard for Eryninn to find the sun amidst them all. The light was there, reflected in a thousand, shiny metal bodies, but the sun itself only appeared in glimpses through the mass of flying beasts. Golds and silvers on one side, brass, bronze and copper on the other.

"This is how it begins," his uncle said.

The two of them stood with the two elven generals, Ilaran and Valen, in a circle of elven wizards. Eryninn could feel the magic around them, pulsing like a living thing encasing them in its protective energy. The wizards had cast many spells on as well as over them all. They were well protected from anything the dragons could throw.

He hoped.

Eliath stood beside him, wavering like he might fall over at any moment. He looked ill, but he was doing his best to hide it. Eryninn pretended not to notice.

"How what begins?" Eryninn asked.

"The downfall of a race," his uncle said. "This is just how it began for our people. A battle over who was right and who was wrong. Over who should be king."

"My father was not fond of giving history lessons."

"Nor was he fond of receiving them," his uncle said with a smile. "My brother made quite a game of evading his tutors whenever possible, much to our father's disappointment."

Eryninn smiled at the thought. In their little home, his father was known for skipping out when it came time to do chores. He always had some part of the forest he needed to look in on or someone he swore needed help.

"We were once one nation," his uncle said. "Blanketed in Ilothen's love and grace, we had no reason to fight. We built a shining city to his glory and lived in peace throughout the land. Then Dunatis attacked his brother, and his dwarves attacked our realm."

"Why?" Eryninn asked.

He knew bits of the history from his mother, but his father didn't like discussing things that happened thousands of years ago. Too many problems going on *right now*, he used to say.

"The same reason it always happens," his uncle said. "Love. They both loved the same woman."

"Who would two gods fight over?"

"The goddess Threyl."

"They fought for their own sister?"

"Gods do not share relations the way we do. Ilothen and Dunatis both loved Threyl. Ilothen won her heart, but Dunatis would not let it end at that. He ordered his dwarves to war. And when it was over, and Ilothen was gone from the heavens, we were a broken people. In faith and in life."

Eryninn saw Ilaran and Valen hang their heads and sigh. They must have heard the story a hundred times in their lifetimes, and still it made them sad to hear it again.

"The king tried to hold his people together, but it was no use. Too many differences, and no one above to settle it. The kingdom was fractured into three, and it remains so today."

Eryninn had learned quite a bit about the three kingdoms now. He had grown up with very little knowledge of any of them, let alone his own. Footsteps from behind made him turn to see the four dragons approaching, still in their elven forms. The king turned to regard them, and Thalaras pointed back over his shoulder where something was happening.

The dragons that hovered and flew near Dragonhome parted like a great, flowing, undulating river, clearing a path. And through them all, the Eldest emerged. From a large opening cut into the heart of Dragonhome, Kalus and his bronze lieutenant flew out in a straight line toward them.

"He wishes to speak," his uncle said.

"He always does," Olania said.

"Stay here and mind the troops," his uncle said to the two generals.

Then he waved his hand at three wizards behind them and walked onto the field to meet Kalus. Eryninn, Eliath, the four dragons, and the three wizards were right behind him. The wizards muttered soft enchantments as they walked, casting any spell they thought would keep their king safe.

Kalus landed in front of them, halting their march, and the bronze dragon landed beside him.

"Eldest," his uncle said.

"Tarathiel," Kalus said with a sneer.

In the week he'd spent in Nirorn, not a single person had ever called his uncle by his true name. Eryninn only knew it because his father had called his brother by it, but no one spoke it to him. It was always your highness, or your majesty, or my lord.

"You can end this," his uncle said. "End your crusade against dragonmages, now, and we can all leave here without bloodshed. It is your prerogative to make laws banning dragonmages, I grant you, but you do not have to kill your own kind and others."

"I am the Eldest!" Kalus screamed. "I make the laws for my people just as you do for yours, and I doubt that you would stand there and let me dictate morality to you, *your highness*."

The king pulled his shoulders back and stood up straighter.

"End this," he said plainly. "You are clearly outmatched, and you cannot win. Your forces are small, and your dragons the weaker."

"Yes," he said, looking at Eliath. "You just can't count on reliable information these days."

"The elves have always had a bond with the dragons of light," his uncle said. "Do not end a thousand years of peace for your foolish pride."

"You think this is my pride?" Kalus said. "You are a small, little elf."

Kalus leaned closer, his neck craning down to almost eye level with them all. The wizards behind him began to titter nervously, but the king only waved his hand. He was not intimidated in the least. Or, if he was, he hid it well.

"This is not about me, Tarathiel. This is about Anarr. I am his word on Gondril, and he speaks to me. He has told me what I must do. Anarr came to me. He spoke to me and told me to remain strong. The enslavement of my people will not go on. Not for humans, and not for you."

"This is madness," Thalaras said.

He stepped forward, but only to stand beside the king, not in front.

"You claim to hear the word of Anarr yourself now, Kalus? You're as mad as they've always said!"

"You…" Kalus looked down at him. "Is this what it's come to, Thalaras? You cannot wait your turn, so you take the mantle by blood? I have no doubt there will be no objections when it comes time for *you* to be anointed. Surely they won't attempt to steal it from you as they did me. What's a little murder among cronies?"

"I will not fight you, Kalus," Thalaras said. "This is not my fight."

"Is that what you will tell Anarr when you meet him?" Kalus asked. "Anarr knows what you are doing here, Thalaras, and he will punish you for your treachery."

Eryninn knew in his heart that Kalus must be lying about hearing the word of Anarr, but even so, he saw Thalaras take a step back at his words. There was doubt on his face, on all of the dragons' faces.

"You will all pay for this betrayal," Kalus said. "This is not a fight you can win."

Olania scoffed from somewhere behind him, but even to Eryninn it sounded weak.

"Anarr is with me," Kalus said. "And because of that, I cannot lose. So bring your war to me if you must. I am confident Anarr will see me through."

He looked to the four dragons.

"Are you so sure you are right?" he asked. "Are you so sure you know the will of Anarr better than I?"

The other dragons just looked on with nothing to say.

"When this is done," Kalus said, "know that I will come for you all. I will send my loyal dragons against all the races of Gondril who do not obey me. You know that I will."

"Last chance, Kalus," his uncle said.

"Yes," Kalus said, "it is. Last chance for all of you. But, since no one likes to get all dressed up for the ball and then miss it, I suppose we should get on with it."

Kalus leapt into the air, and the bronze dragon silently followed. The dragons above parted once more, letting Kalus return to the cave perched high on Dragonhome. Once there, he turned and stood on the ledge, looking out across the skies.

His uncle turned and marched back to his generals and the protective spheres of his wizards. Eryninn, Eliath, and everyone else fell in behind him. Once there, his uncle pulled just Eryninn and the generals to the side.

"Is this folly?" he whispered.

Eryninn hid his surprise. His uncle had seemed unshakably sure throughout this whole campaign. Even in the face of what may be the most powerful dragon on Gondril, he did not back down. And now he doubted they could win?

"There will never be a better time," Ilaran said. "Kalus gains followers with each passing week, but his forces are still small now. We are, perhaps, even in our dragon numbers, but we have the golds and silvers."

"And our wizards, many of them trained as dragon hunters," Valen said. "We have superior numbers and superior firepower, your majesty. We may not have that advantage forever."

His uncle turned and looked Eryninn in the eyes.

"What do you think?" he asked.

Eryninn didn't know what to say. He looked to the generals for some roll of the eyes or some indication that he was not welcome here, but he saw none. The king had asked his opinion, and he was staring at him now, waiting for him to give it. They were all looking at him.

Eryninn shrugged.

"Like Kalus said, we didn't get all dressed up for the ball for nothing."

His uncle smiled and patted his shoulder. With a wave of his arm, he called the four dragons over.

"Thalaras will remain under protection here with us," he said, "leaving the three of you to command the dragons from the sky. We have wizards back here to provide cover and many more waiting to strike."

The four dragons nodded. Thalaras stepped to the side and stood waiting with them while the other three moved away from the crowd and began to shift. When they had finished, they all climbed into the sky and to the head of the columns of gold and silver dragons.

"It begins," his uncle said.

Olania, at the point of the dragons, gave a roar so loud that it seemed to shake the ground where he stood. The other golds and silvers took up her call and joined her, blanketing the world with a deafening sound.

On the other side, the brass, bronze, and copper dragons roared in return. It was a sound never heard before on Gondril. So many dragons ready to die and kill each other. Eryninn knew then that they would win. Kalus could not have Anarr's blessing in this. Anarr could not want this.

It began so suddenly, Eryninn didn't know where to look.

He wasn't sure who was the first to move, but in an instant, the sky was churning and roiling with dragons. They flew so close together that they did actually block the sun, casting the ground and all of the elves in darkness. From the black below, Eryninn saw great bolts of lightning. Some flew from the ground up into the dragons, others came from the heavens themselves to strike from above.

Ilaran shouted something over his shoulder, and Eryninn heard the crack of a catapult. The elves had many weapons for fighting dragons, though most had not seen use in centuries.

"I need eyes," his uncle shouted.

A wizard behind them began casting, his voice almost like a song as the words flowed from his lips. Blue threads of magic leapt between his fingers, and he reached out in a fan, the threads spreading between them all. As the spell took effect, Eryninn found, to his amazement, that he could see far into the distance. The spell had enhanced his vision so that he could see all the way across the field.

All the way to Kalus smiling on his rocky perch.

"Something is not right," his uncle said.

Eryninn felt it too. The dragons were only just beginning, but already Kalus's forces seemed woefully outmatched. The ground shook nearly every minute with the force of a falling dragon, crashing one by one to the earth. A few of the gold and silver dragons had fallen, but there must have been more than double the amount of brass, bronze, and copper.

Kalus stretched his wings out. Eryninn watched it, couldn't take his eyes off of it. With a beat of his wings, he lifted into the air and flew straight up, heading for the summit of Dragonhome.

"What is he doing?" Valen said.

"Surveying the damage?" Ilaran asked.

"No," his uncle said, "this is it. This is what he had planned."

They looked at each other and then back to Kalus. They could barely make him out now, he was so high up the mountain. But they could hear his roar. And roar he did. Many of his forces looked to him and roared in answer.

Then they saw it.

"What is that?" Valen asked.

From behind the mountain they came, flying fast toward the raging battle.

"Reserve forces?" Ilaran asked.

But there were too many to be a reserve. They were far off, but even at this distance, Eryninn saw more dragons than Kalus currently had on the field. Maybe double. But something was different. He couldn't make them out clearly, but Eryninn knew something was off.

There was no glint of metal on their forms.

The sun poured over the oncoming dragons, but none of it was reflected back. Instead it was swallowed in their colored hides.

"Dark dragons," he whispered.

"What?" his uncle said.

"The dark dragons," Eryninn said more confidently. "Kalus has enlisted the dark dragons to fight for him."

They all looked again, straining hard to see. One by one, they saw what he saw. The dark dragons, thousands of them, flew in over Dragonhome and joined the battle.

The effect was instantaneous.

The brass, bronze, and copper dragons roared a greeting while the silvers and golds looked on in shock. The whole battle ground to a halt for the instant it took everyone to recover.

"Call the retreat," his uncle said.

"Your highness," Ilaran said, "we can—"

"Call the retreat!"

Valen turned and shouted to the troops, his voice amplified by magic.

"Pray we can get out of this with what lives we have left," his uncle said.

Kalus had played his hand perfectly.

They never stood a chance.

CHAPTER THIRTY-FOUR

THE ISLE OF DRAGONS

ELODY SAW THE plume of smoke rising from the sea before the land came into sight. She didn't know what she had expected to see, but it was nothing like this. As they drew nearer, the Isle of Dragons towered above them.

The island jutted more than a hundred feet up from the water. Other than the constant smoke that drifted lazily into the sky, the only part of the island to be seen were the massive cliffs. They stretched up to the sky, daring anyone to try and climb them. The top of the island was completely hidden from below.

Rinn, Elody, Jalthrax, and Ilyaren stood and stared from the foredeck. They heard clomping coming up the short steps behind them.

"That where you're headed?" Captain Jonas asked.

"It is," Ilyaren said.

"Any port on that island?" the captain asked.

"There is no approach to the island except by air," Ilyaren said. "And even that would be unwise if you are not a dragon."

Captain Jonas scratched at the back of his neck.

"The men don't like it," he said at last. "We thought we'd have time to get off the boat a bit wherever we were going."

"I never said we would land anywhere."

"It was assumed."

"Then that is your problem to deal with, not mine."

The captain scratched his neck again.

"How long we supposed to wait here?"

"Until we return," Ilyaren said.

"The deal was we bring you out here and back. We can't stay here forever. We'll run out of food."

"We will not be gone long."

"What if you don't come back? How long should we wait?"

"If we do not return in two days, you may return without us. If you are still here upon our return, I will give you *another* hundred golden suns."

The captain nodded solemnly, but Elody could see the smile tugging at the corners of his mouth. The matter settled, Ilyaren ushered the captain away and turned to the three of them.

"I will have to carry the two of you," he said. "It might be uncomfortable, but the flight will be short."

"I've ridden a dragon before," Elody said.

"You will not be riding. I have to carry you in my claws."

She and Rinn exchanged a look.

"I cannot change in my true form on this ship," Ilyaren said. "It will surely sink under the weight. I must transform in the air, but there is no way after that for you to climb onto my back."

"What about a rope?" Rinn asked.

"It is a short trip," Ilyaren said. "I will carry you."

Having settled the matter himself, Ilyaren turned away and began to change. His skin and bones stretched and popped until he had taken shape and then leapt into the air. The remaining transformation complete, he flapped his giant wings lazily above the ship. Jalthrax was beside him a moment later.

Rinn and Elody shared one more look and then moved as close to the front of the ship as possible. Ilyaren the silver dragon stretched his talons down and closed one over each of them. Elody grabbed on for her life as she lifted off the deck. The dragon's claws formed a perfect little cage around her, locking her in from every side.

The two of them in hand, Ilyaren beat his wings and flew toward the isle.

***

They flew above the cliffs as they neared, and Elody could see the true island for the first time. A forest of trees ringed the outer edge, stretching from the very edges of the cliffs all the way to the center. They flew without stopping over the trees and straight to the eye of the island.

A large ring of black stone was laid in the middle of the island and surrounded on all sides by pillars. In the distance, Elody could now see what had made all the smoke they saw from the sea. A volcano grew out of the forest like a great, grey wart climbing high into the sky. It never made so much as a sound, but the stream of smoke and ash from its top was constant.

Ilyaren flew to the edge of the stone circle and flapped lazily until he was just above the ground. Opening his claws, Rinn and Elody slid down and felt their feet touch the stone. Ilyaren flew a few feet away and touched down with Jalthrax beside him. Elody moved to go to him but then stopped when she saw the little dragon's face.

Jalthrax said nothing and barely moved. His eyes flitted in every direction, from the volcano, to the circle, to the pillars. Perhaps he felt the majesty of this place more than Elody did. The volcano was incredible, and not something she'd ever seen in her life, but it still just felt like an island. She couldn't even hear the waves crashing against the cliffs, they were so high up. It was quiet and calm.

Too calm.

"Wait," she said, "where are the dragons?"

"No one lives here permanently," Ilyaren said. "We only come here when a council is called."

"She's right," Rinn said. "Kalus wouldn't just leave this place empty and unguarded. Where is everyone?"

"I sent them away."

Elody whipped her head around, her hands raised to cast, and expected to find Kalus waiting for them. Instead, she found something she did not expect. It was a gold dragon, that much was obvious, but he was bigger than any she'd ever seen. Bigger than Kalus. Bigger than Ferin, the previous Eldest, even, and she had been huge. But it wasn't the size that gave her pause, it was the feeling she had looking upon him.

Peace.

She was not afraid of this dragon, though she had no idea if he was a friend or an enemy. She could not bring herself to even ponder that he might be anything more than a friend. Her hands dropped to her side. She could see Rinn felt the same. But if that is what *they* felt, the presence of the gold dragon affected Ilyaren and Jalthrax tenfold.

Ilyaren bowed his head low, his nose scraping the stone, his eyes closed, afraid to look up.

"First Dragon," he whispered. "I am unworthy of your presence."

Elody looked at him and at Jalthrax, silent beside him, and wondered for a moment what they were doing. As it sunk in, she fell to her knees and looked at the ground.

"Forgive me," she said. "I did not know."

She looked up, and the gold dragon smiled.

"You're him, aren't you?" she asked.

"I am, child," he said. "I am Anarr. First of Aeos's children. First son of Gondril. First dragon. Father of dragons."

Rinn was on his knees now too. None of them knew what to do, so they all just stayed like that.

"Rise," Anarr said. "I cannot speak with you if you will not stand and look at me."

As one, they looked up. The sun at their backs peeked over the tops of the trees behind them and glinted off Anarr in a hundred directions. His golden brilliance lit every inch of the stone circle, and Elody could feel it wash over her. That peace that she felt, it came from him.

From Anarr.

"I do not fear you," she said. "Dragons exude fear to most humans, but I do not fear you. Why?"

"Because you know me," he said. "You have known me since the day you bonded with one of my children."

The dragon nodded to Jalthrax.

"Come forward, Jalthrax'ul'Daltharr, and let me look upon you."

Jalthrax walked forward without a moment's

hesitation and stood, staring up at Anarr.

"You will be one of my strongest creations," he said.

His voice was soft, very unlike most dragons Elody had heard speak. Everything about him made her feel at ease.

"Come forward, Ilyaren'ul'Taratharr."

Ilyaren raised his head proudly and stood before his god.

"My oldest son," Anarr said. "I have wronged you."

"Never, Creator," Ilyaren said. "All I have, I owe to you. You gave me life, gave me twelve-hundred years on Gondril. You owe me nothing."

"The decree I made five thousand years ago has robbed you of what should have been yours. It is hard, sometimes, for a father to look beyond his favorite children to the second standing behind them. Even when they sometimes deserve the greater of his praise."

"I am grateful for my life, First Dragon. I am blessed now to stand in your brilliance."

"You have always trusted in me most, and that is why you are here now. It is why you have brought me these humans. I knew that you, above all my other children, would trust in me enough to bring them here."

Anarr turned to regard Elody and Rinn, and they were both forced to look away for all the light surrounding him.

"You are not my children," Anarr said plainly. "But you, Elody, are of my blood. It has been two-thousand years since I have spoken directly with mortals as I do now, but I could no longer stand by and watch the destruction of all that I have made. I will not be Ogrosh and watch my people destroy each other."

Elody waited, unsure of what to say.

"I need you and your brother," Anarr said.

"What…" Elody said. "What can we do?"

"You can help me make this right. If you will."

Elody turned to look at Rinn, and he gave a shrug.

"Tell us what we can do," Rinn said.

"For you, Rinn, your task is simple. So simple that it will change all of Gondril. You must kill my son Kalus."

Rinn's eyes went wide, and he looked at Elody who could only shrug. Rinn opened his mouth several times to speak before he managed to get the words out.

"I don't understand," he said.

"Kalus has betrayed me. The dark dragons denied me and were cast from my light. I offered them the light, my brilliance, but they refused me. They are no longer my children. And Kalus has made a deal with them to destroy my chosen children. For this, he cannot be forgiven. For this, he must die."

Anarr's gaze drifted to the side, and they all followed him until they stopped on a grizzly scene. Behind them, partly hidden by the overgrown vegetation, were the stacked, blackened corpses of six men. At least that's how many Elody could count there. The bodies had begun to decay and blend together as they decomposed.

Elody gagged and reached out for Rinn to steady herself. In the year since her father died, she had seen many dead bodies. Some in worse shape than these, and some of people she loved. She never got used to it. It still made her sick.

Rinn took a step forward, and she almost stopped him, but he pulled away from her arm and kept walking. When he reached the bodies, she saw him stop and look down at the ground. Elody took a few steps closer and saw what he was looking at.

The dragonbane crystal.

Just lying there in wait.

"Take it," Anarr said.

Rinn looked at him with confusion and doubt playing across his face.

"Ilyaren cannot touch it," Anarr said, "it will destroy him. Elody cannot touch it because it will rupture her bond with Jalthrax. Only you can take it, Rinn. Only someone who can control magic can control the crystal. That is why you are here."

"I can't control magic," Rinn said. "I'm terrible at it. I've only just begun learning wizardry, and I'm no good at it."

"Perhaps," Anarr said, "but I know that you can master the crystal. You can tame it, just as you have tamed the well of power within you."

Rinn looked down at the ground again and shook his head.

"We made that crystal together, Ogrosh and I. We poured our blood into it so that we would be bonded together forever. I see the same in you and Elody. I have seen it ever since she became bonded. The crystal is a part of me, and I give it to you, Rinn."

Rinn bent down slowly. His fingers touched the stone around the crystal and hovered there for half a minute before they finally closed around it and took it. Instantly, Rinn's eyes closed, and his body began to shake. Elody tried to run to him.

"No," Anarr said. "He must make the crystal his own, or it will master him instead."

"What does that mean?" she cried.

"He must exert his will over the crystal if he is to control it."

"What if he fails?"

"He will die," Anarr said.

"You never said he could die!" Elody shouted.

She tried to run even as Ilyaren reached out to put a claw in her path, but as she dodged around it, she stopped. It had only been a few seconds, but Rinn stood in front of her smiling.

"Hi," he said. "You weren't worried about me, were you?"

Elody approached slowly.

"Are you... okay?"

"Better than okay," he said. "It's amazing, El. I... I don't even know how to explain it. I can feel the dragons around me. I can feel their heartbeats in my mind."

"The crystal is stronger for you than most," Anarr said. "Because you were once bonded yourself, even if only a short while, you have the same connection to my children. You will be able to feel them everywhere."

"And you want me to kill Kalus with this," Rinn said.

"I want you to make right what I have nearly destroyed."

"What about when Kalus is dead?" Rinn asked. "What would you have me do with the crystal then?"

"I have watched you both," Anarr said. "I already know what you will do with it."

That seemed to settle the matter for him, so he turned his attention to Ilyaren.

"Ilyaren, my son," he said. "When Kalus is dead, you will become Eldest. From this day forward, I decree that when the Eldest passes, the oldest dragon of light will take his place."

"I..." Ilyaren stuttered. "I don't know what to say, First Dragon."

"Say you will rule wisely and keep peace among my children. Do not make war against your brothers and sisters. Do not do as the children of Ogrosh and Ilothen have done."

Anarr turned to Elody.

"I have a task for you as well," he said. "The most important one."

Elody and Jalthrax both bowed.

"You will become my champion on Gondril," Anarr said. "I have not had one in all my years, but it is time that I do. You will be my message to the world that the bond between dragon and mankind has my blessing. Wherever you go, spread my word. To my children, to the children of Ilothen, and to the children of Threyl."

"But…" Elody said. "Why me? There must be a better choice."

"Do you not wish this task?"

"No! I would gladly be your champion. I just… I'm just a young girl. Jalthrax is not even a full year old. Who will listen to me?"

"You are my champion," Anarr said. "You will have Jalthrax at your side. You must make them listen. And if they do not, your brother will be at your side to see that they do. You will have the help of the Eldest. Ilyaren will tell them all what I have told you here today."

Elody bowed.

"I am honored," she said.

"Now go," he said. "Every moment you are here is another moment for Kalus to destroy all that I have worked a thousand years to create. Put an end to his evil and begin the work of healing my children."

Ilyaren bowed low.

"It will be done, Creator," he said.

He laid flat on the ground and leaned a shoulder down for Rinn and Elody to climb onto his back. It felt odd sitting on the dragon's back without a saddle, but it was better than hanging onto his claws.

"I will speed you on your journey," Anarr said. "See my will done. End this madness and bloodshed. Bring peace to Gondril."

Ilyaren leapt into the air, Jalthrax beside him. Elody stared long at the giant gold dragon as they flew higher. Had she really just met a god? But she knew in her heart that she had. She could feel it. Anarr had blessed them all with a task, and now they had to see it done.

They had a lot of work to do.

CHAPTER THIRTY-FIVE

LOST

IT TOOK THEM two days to leave the mountains behind them, and another two to cross the Troll Marsh. They saw no sign of the trolls on their passage, but that had become the least of their concerns. With little food left from their journey, Gortogh had taken to foraging in the marsh itself. He'd come up with some toads and a few odd mushrooms, but the pickings were lean.

Kurgh had refused to use his magic at all. Keeping a fire was out of the question, but he could have used a spell to lighten their loads or refresh their feet. Gortogh had seen him cast any number of helpful spells in his time with the shaman. But none were forthcoming now.

Kurgh had stopped praying to Ogrosh completely.

The shaman had become quiet, distant. They had argued a few times the first day out from Ogrilon, but now Kurgh had abandoned even that pursuit. Gortogh didn't know what he was going to do, but he knew he had to do something.

When they finally reached the edge of the marsh, Gortogh let out a big sigh of relief. The flat, dry scrub land gave way to sparse trees and then eventually forest.

Gortogh felt at home once more, comfortable in the environment he'd known all his life.

Kurgh showed no sign of change. He only looked at Gortogh, the shaman's eyes flashing to his chest for a brief moment before looking away.

Gortogh wore the amulet openly now and silently dared Kurgh to challenge him. Gortogh would catch him looking, and he wondered if it still held the same influence now that Kurgh knew its powers. Perhaps its influence was even greater given what they knew of Ogrosh and his blood bond.

Gortogh gathered wood for a fire. He knew Kurgh wouldn't be convinced to start a fire with his magic, so it was up to Gortogh to get their feet dry. He had a fire blazing in no time. He smiled at Kurgh, but the shaman never lifted his head.

With a sigh, Gortogh went off in search of some food. They had managed to survive on some stale, moldy bread and the rest of Gortogh's dried meat and cheese, but it had been a hungry few days. He found himself wishing several times that they'd stayed in the library where hunger never found them.

He returned an hour later with only a few berries. Even though they were back in the forest, it was sparse, and he was having little luck finding sufficient food. Instead of eating the berries, he tried a different tact. He threw them at Kurgh.

The shaman looked up, annoyed.

"Summon us some food," Gortogh said flatly.

"No," Kurgh said.

"You would rather starve?"

"Yes."

"Well, praise Ogrosh. Let's all just wither away in his

name."

"Ogrosh owes you nothing," Kurgh said.

"I just walked across a troll swamp, into the great library of Ogrilon, and back out again to deliver his word to the people. He at least owes me a damn meal. So get to it."

Kurgh looked down and shook his head.

"We're already half starved as it is. Stop punishing yourself for believing in what you were taught."

"Everything I've believed is a lie."

"Then make it right. But both of us starving here is not going to help anyone. Least of all Ogrosh. Without you to spread his word, the lies you grew up with will continue to spread. The broken teachings will continue to poison our people."

Kurgh looked up. His eyes lingered on the amulet for a second before meeting Gortogh's gaze. The shaman knew he was right, he could see it as clearly as if it were written on his face. Gortogh felt bad for manipulating Kurgh all so he could get a decent meal, but he meant what he said. The poisoning of Ogrosh's people by men like Kurgh would go on if they didn't put a stop to it.

Also, he was really, really hungry.

Kurgh pulled his back up straight and rested his hands on his knees. Gortogh couldn't suppress a smile as the shaman began chanting. Eating meat supplied by Ogrosh had never been his favorite thing, but he was so hungry now he didn't even care who it came from. Kurgh cut his arm and drew his blood as he prayed.

When Kurgh finished chanting, they both stood still and waited.

Gortogh spun as he heard cracking branches behind him but relaxed a moment later when a young buck walked slowly into camp. It stopped just beside him and stood perfectly still. He couldn't help reaching out a hand to pet him. He could feel the strength in the buck's tight back. His antlers were small but had several points already.

It always made him a little sad to kill them this way. It wasn't a hunt. It wasn't a contest of hunter versus prey. They just stood silently waiting to die. His mouth was watering just looking at the buck, but as he reached for his knife, something stayed his hand.

"It feels wrong," he said.

He hadn't meant to speak it aloud.

"What?" Kurgh asked.

Gortogh cleared his throat.

"It feels wrong to kill them this way."

Kurgh scoffed.

"You like the meat don't you?"

"Yes, but don't you think this is a bit unfair?"

"Would you rather starve? You *made* me summon it."

"I know. But now it feels wrong."

Kurgh threw his hands in the air.

"I asked Ogrosh for meat, at *your* request, and he sent this for us."

"Yes, but… what if it was false?"

"What could be false? Don't let your quest to *destroy* the gods blind you to the truth. I know the truth now, and I will carry the word of Ogrosh to all our people. My faith is clearer than it has ever been."

"Yes, but… look how he stands. Staring at you. Waiting for you. What if he's not here to feed you?"

"Why else would he be?"

"Did you actually ask Ogrosh for food, and this is what he sent?"

"I asked for an animal. The deer appeared."

Gortogh shook his head.

"You don't see it, do you?"

"Do not question *my* vision, *Mighty One*."

"Ogrosh sent you the deer in friendship. You asked for an animal, and he sent you a companion. And now you want to kill it and eat it!"

Kurgh laughed.

"You are going to stand there and tell *me* Ogrosh's meaning?"

Gortogh ran his hand slowly down the buck's back. He continued to stand still, as though waiting for something.

"I heard what the monk said, did you? Ogrosh's magic is given for brotherhood. For blood. But not the way you have always preached. He sent you this buck because you asked for an animal. But not as food, as a friend."

"You know nothing of Ogrosh," Kurgh said. "I have lived my life dedicated to him! You have done nothing but spit in his face."

"He and I haven't always seen eye to eye, that is true. But what if it's you who has spit in his face?"

Kurgh leapt up, the glistening white bone knife suddenly in his hand. Gortogh resisted the urge to reach for his own sword, keeping his hand calmly on the buck instead.

"Ask Ogrosh for food," he said.

Kurgh's chest heaved, and he spoke through gritted teeth.

"I have already done that."

"No," Gortogh said. "Ask him for food and see what he delivers."

"I will not let you question his will," Kurgh said.

"I am not questioning him. I am questioning you. As you yourself should be doing. Isn't that why you've refused to use your own magic? After what we have learned, shouldn't you question everything you know?"

Gortogh saw it all so clearly now. At last he felt like he understood Ogrosh, and maybe even himself a bit more. Killing helpless animals under his spell had always felt wrong. Worshipping Ogrosh had always felt wrong. But perhaps it wasn't the worshipping but the *way* of the worship.

Kurgh couldn't see it. Gortogh saw the confusion in his eyes, but it was clouded by anger. How could he make him see?

"Pray for food," he said.

Kurgh stared a moment longer and then sat down in his meditation pose. He dragged the knife across his arm, wincing only a little at the cut as blood began to pour out. Closing his eyes, he whispered to the heavens as the blood pooled in his hand.

Gortogh watched closely, waiting for something to happen. What if he was wrong? What if Ogrosh really did want blood the way he'd always been told? The blood dripped from Kurgh's hand and plopped to the ground. Where each drop touched, a tiny mushroom poked through the dirt. They grew, slowly at first, until they were the size of a fist. Kurgh opened his eyes and stared in wonder.

"Praise Ogrosh," Gortogh said.

Kurgh shot him a look, ready to fight, but there was no malice in his voice. This time he truly believed Ogrosh had blessed them. Kurgh had asked for food, and Ogrosh had sent food. Gortogh bent down and plucked one of the mushrooms, popping it into his mouth.

It was warm and earthy, a flavor unlike anything Gortogh had tasted before.

"It's good," he said through his mouthful.

A few more bites, and the whole thing was in his mouth. He chewed each bite and swallowed, a big grin on his face. But as he finished the last piece, he found, to his amazement, that he was no longer hungry. The one little mushroom had filled him and satisfied him completely.

Kurgh had picked one and was eating it. Gortogh could tell by the look on his face that he'd discovered the same thing. Through it all, the buck stood motionless, watching them. Still waiting. Kurgh swallowed and stared down at the rest of the mushrooms. Dozens of them just waiting to fill a hungry soul.

"Praise Ogrosh," Kurgh whispered.

***

Gortogh woke with a start. He reached for his sword and found it beside him, right where he'd left it. What had woken him? He sat up and looked around.

Kurgh was in his meditation pose, but he looked strained. His face was contorted in a grimace, and his body jerked with small spasms.

"What's going on?" Gortogh said.

No response.

"Kurgh!"

The shaman's eyes opened, and he shot Gortogh an angry look.

"Do not disturb me when I am meditating," Kurgh said.

"I was trying to find out what was going on. And you looked like you were in pain."

"I was trying to feel the trolls more deeply."

Gortogh's sword was in his hand in an instant.

"What trolls?"

Kurgh pointed off into the darkness. Back toward the marsh.

"I thought we were well out of the marsh," Gortogh said.

"Perhaps they followed us," Kurgh said. "What is the farthest you've ever tracked a meal?"

Gortogh didn't want to tell him what a terrible hunter he was. He heard a heavy snort and nearly jumped out of his bedroll. The young buck was resting quietly on the ground next to Kurgh. Though his eyes were closed, the shaman was gently stroking its back.

"What are you doing with him?" Gortogh asked.

"Bonding," Kurgh said.

A little smile crossed his face. Gortogh shook his head and slowly stood. He kept his sword in one hand as he started to pick up some wood and throw it on the coals. Within a minute, the fire sprang back to life. More wood was added, and the small flames grew.

"They will not attack," Kurgh said.

Gortogh snorted.

"You said that the last time."

"I am going to meditate again. If they followed us this far, I want to see what they want."

"Can you do that? Sense their thoughts, I mean."

"Normally, no. Ogrosh lets me sense the presence of blood. Sometimes, if the bond is strong, I can learn who or what it is. But usually I can only sense a presence. But the trolls... they are strange to me."

Gortogh peered out into the darkness. The trees around them were sparse as they were still near the edges of the marsh. He caught the occasional flicker of movement, but he could not see any trolls. He turned to say something and found Kurgh had closed his eyes and was already meditating.

Gortogh stood watch and waited.

Kurgh's body jerked. First it was his hands and arms. Then his torso began to spasm and twist. Gortogh moved closer to him just in case he was needed. Not that he would know what to do anyway. Kurgh had left him no instructions. Only that Gortogh wasn't to disturb him again.

So he waited some more.

Kurgh cried out, making Gortogh jump. He swung around, his sword in hand, looking for an enemy, but he saw nothing. Kurgh was writhing now, barely able to maintain his pose. Gortogh crept closer, looking for some sign he should help.

Kurgh's eyes shot open.

"What?" Gortogh said.

"I know what they are," Kurgh said.

"What what are?"

"The trolls. I know who they are now. They are the five."

"The five what?"

"The five high shamans who brought about the great unmaking. The five who carried the crystals and rode dragons."

"How do you know that?"

"I was inside their heads. We had a connection I have never felt with another being. I heard all of their thoughts."

"They cannot be," Gortogh said. "They would be thousands of years old."

"Trolls are nearly immortal. That is part of their

punishment."

"But we killed more than five alone. How can there be more?"

"I don't know. The tales say that a troll can regrow its own head if you chop it off. Maybe a head can regrow a whole new body given enough time."

Gortogh shuddered and looked out to where he could hear more noise.

"What a cruel fate," he said.

"The punishment fit the crime."

"You think they should suffer an eternity for a mistake?"

"A mistake that cost hundreds of thousands of lives and an entire civilization? A mistake that destroyed the teachings of a truly great and noble god? I would punish them with no less."

Gortogh shook his head.

"Gondril would be a much better place without gods and their wrath."

Gortogh looked at Kurgh, ready for a fight. But the shaman looked as calm as ever, his hand rhythmically stroking the buck's back. They sat in silence for several moments, Kurgh with his eyes closed, and Gortogh watching for trolls.

"They will not attack," Kurgh said. "They think that you are Ogrosh."

Gortogh picked up the amulet and turned it over in his hand.

"They fear you, yet they want so badly to be near you again."

"Why fear me?"

"They do not fear you, they fear Ogrosh. He is the one who damned them to that life and that swamp."

"Then why hold him in awe? Why desire to be near him? If Ogrosh had done that to me, I would hate him. I would try to kill him with every drop of my life."

"Because he punished you? Only a child is angry at his parent for punishment when they are the ones who wronged."

Gortogh waved a hand and turned back to peer into the night. Ogrosh was just as cruel as the rest of them. Maybe he had learned a lesson, and maybe he did want to leave them to their own decisions. But he would always be there to punish them. Always the stern father.

"What do you plan to do?" Kurgh asked, breaking his revery.

Kurgh sliced into his arm, whispered a few words, and flung it on the fire. The flames exploded, leaping high into the sky, and Gortogh heard squeals and shouts disappear into the night.

He felt a sadness for the trolls now. No matter their crime, they had done their penance.

"You must know you cannot destroy the gods as you say," Kurgh said.

"I know that."

"Then what are you playing at?" Kurgh asked.

"No one can destroy the gods but themselves. But they hold the power to destroy us. To damn us to an eternity of their own hellish making. Why should they?"

"Because they are gods, and we are mortal. We are their creations."

"We can't let them control us."

"You cannot stop them."

"Maybe not, but I can try."

"Again, how?"

"You heard the monk. All that is going on in the

world right now, everything that is outside of our tribes, is the work of Anarr. Gondril is tearing itself apart, and it's all his doing."

"What do you care if the humans and dragons destroy each other? More for us, I say."

"No," Gortogh said. "If they want to kill each other, that is their own will. But not when they are made to do it. They do not know what they are doing. I have heard enough to know that whatever Anarr wants from this, it can't be good for any of us for him to get it."

"But why Anarr alone?"

"Because he is the cause of this. Don't you see? Ogrosh has left us to ourselves as was his will. Threyl has always done the same. Dunatis has vanished, and Ilothen is dead. Anarr is the meddler here."

"Was it not you who said we cannot stop dragons? Four dragons destroyed nearly ten thousand goblins, remember? What do you think you can do against Anarr and his dragons?"

"*You* can defeat them."

Kurgh arched an eyebrow and chuckled.

"Me? What makes you think I want to follow you into this folly?"

"Because you know I am right. If Anarr gets whatever it is he wants, it will be disastrous for us. Have no doubt that when he's done with the humans, he'll come for us. The gods seem to hold very long grudges. If Anarr becomes all powerful, who do you think he will wage war on next?"

Kurgh touched the symbol of Ogrosh carved into his chest. It sat there, always uncovered, for all to see. The fist of blood. Though Kurgh had a few small scars on his body from his younger years, the only one that never faded was his symbol of Ogrosh. Years of cutting himself had not left a single mark. He had once told Gortogh that the symbol was the last thing cut into a shaman's body before he was granted the power to heal. Once he was touched by Ogrosh, his body would never scar again.

"You know that I am right," Gortogh said, seeing Kurgh's face fall. "If Anarr grows even more powerful, he will come for Ogrosh. Dunatis killed Ilothen, his own twin, and now the elves have no god to pray to for magic or healing. What will you do, Kurgh, when there is no Ogrosh to pray to?"

Kurgh's eyes were wide, his hand clutching at the scarred skin on his chest. He finally saw the truth. Gortogh wanted to smile, he was so proud of himself, but he resisted the urge.

"What can we do?" Kurgh asked.

We. The word hit Gortogh like a bolt of lightning, and now he couldn't hold back his smile.

"We have to stop the dragons and whatever they are planning," he said.

"But how do we do that? The monk said that the shamans of old could summon powerful magic by using the blood of dragons against their own kind. We have no dragons."

"Then maybe we need to make friends with some."

Kurgh scoffed.

"You think they will simply fight beside us as equals?"

"If we tell them what we know. If they see what we see."

"Even with dragon blood magic, we'd need an army. The humans will not listen to two crazed goblins spouting nonsense about gods trying to end the world."

"I had thought about that," Gortogh said. "But I have

no good answer. We could call to the tribes and gather an army, but they are as likely to kill me as follow me. They might follow you, but we don't have the time for that."

Kurgh smiled and pointed to Gortogh's chest. He looked down and saw the amulet hanging there, staring back at him. He picked it up and dangled it in front of him.

"No," he said. "This is more influence of the gods. This amulet is no better than those damned crystals."

"But we have a chance to use it for good," Kurgh said.

"Velanon thought the same thing."

"It is the only way. We need an army. And we already know the amulet can get us one."

"Yes, but last time it took more than half the year to bring the tribes together. We may not have that long."

"But last time you didn't use the amulet. You just let it hang there. Now you know what it is, what it can do."

Gortogh closed his fist over the bronze disc.

"Use it," Kurgh said. "Walk as Ogrosh. Speak as Ogrosh. *Become* Ogrosh. They cannot disobey."

"But that's just it. They *cannot* disobey. You would have me use my own people? After what I did?"

"If we could convince them all that Ogrosh was in danger, they would all come willingly, but we don't have the time for that. We're only encouraging them to do what they would already have done."

Gortogh shook his head.

"I don't like it," he said.

"I don't see another way."

Gortogh continued to stare at the amulet. He could feel its power humming in his hand, even as it danced in front of him.

"I…" Kurgh started. "I believe the amulet came to you for a reason."

Gortogh let the amulet fall and eyed the shaman.

"Call it fate. Call it Ogrosh's hand. Call it luck. But I believe that you have that for a reason. You just let someone lead you astray before."

"And what if we fail?" Gortogh asked.

"We will not fail. Ogrosh may not move us directly as Anarr does, but this is his hand at work. The amulet is with you for a purpose. Use it."

Gortogh closed his hand around the disc once more and felt its power. Was this truly what Ogrosh wanted? Was that any better than what Anarr wanted? He didn't know. But he knew that Gondril would suffer if he did nothing. His people would suffer more than they had already.

"Then let us raise an army," he said at last.

CHAPTER THIRTY-SIX

GATHERING ALLIES

ERYNINN STOOD PERFECTLY straight to the left of his uncle. The king was seated on his throne, a place he rarely sat Eryninn had noticed. But this was official business of the kingdom. Alranir stood to the king's right, looking much straighter and more official than Eryninn.

He had certainly done this before though.

The rest of the throne room was empty. The generals and dragons all had other business to tend to. Today's business was the king's alone. Once again, Eryninn found himself wondering why he was invited.

Alranir, it seemed, was never far from the king. Eryninn wondered, not for the first time, what their relationship was. Was Alranir his uncle's personal bodyguard? He certainly had the skill for it. But Alranir rarely wore armor around the city, which seemed an odd thing if he were a royal guard.

Though he said little during official meetings, Alranir spoke very openly with the king. Something no one else seemed to do. Maybe that was his role. He provided the king with someone to speak honestly and frankly with.

Whatever he did, he never strayed far from the king unless ordered to.

The double doors at the end of the hall swung silently inward. The official throne room of Nirorn sat at the top of the God Tower, but that was not where they were now. With the true king still alive, any business of the sitting king was conducted in a secondary throne room at the base of the tower. No less grand than the true throne room, this one at least was a little easier to reach without growing winded.

One of the royal guard marched very formally down the long, white hall and stopped in front of the three of them.

"Your majesty, King Garnet of Anvil Hall has arrived."

"Send him in," his uncle said.

The guard bowed and left, pulling the doors closed behind him. Eryninn waited anxiously for the new guests. Since coming to Nirorn, he had seen many new sights. Things he had never thought he would see in his life. But he was about to see something few on Gondril would ever see.

The great doors opened, and the dwarven king marched in.

He was flanked on either side by a dozen dwarves. Thirteen in all, including the king himself. His uncle had told him the dwarves were superstitious and always traveled in odd numbers. They marched with such precision they sounded like one set of feet. Like a giant marching through the hall.

But these were no giants. They weren't even as tall as a goblin. His uncle had explained what dwarves looked like, but Eryninn did not expect them to be this small.

The king himself was barely four feet tall, if even that.

Each of the dwarves, the king included, wore a beard that was cropped short. Their hair was the same. It was course, not like fine elven hair, but it was golden yellow like most Ilotharen. They looked like the shorter twins to the elves.

Yet Eryninn had no doubt of the strength they possessed. Each dwarf was as thick as a stone block and twice as hard. They looked poised to attack at any moment. Each carried a weapon strapped across their backs, a concession his uncle was forced to make. Dwarves, it seemed, went nowhere without their weapons.

The weapons themselves were like nothing Eryninn had ever seen. They looked like a short-handled hammer, but the top of the hammer sloped up to a blade that swept back in a curve ending in a sharp point. They sparkled in the bright sunlight, made from a metal Eryninn didn't recognize. He caught himself staring and looked away.

"Your majesty," his uncle said.

He stood and waved a hand. The dwarves marched until their king came to a stop just below the raised dais of the throne. Then the dwarf bowed low. All of his men did the same.

When he stood, Eryninn's uncle bowed. Eryninn and Alranir did the same, just as they were told.

"King Tarathiel," the dwarven king said. "Been too long."

"A long time, King Garnet," his uncle said.

"You were just a prince the last time I saw you."

"I still am," his uncle said.

"You elves," the dwarven king said. "Never

understood your ways."

""Nor I yours, but that is no matter. Thank you for coming all this way. I know the journey was long. Truly, I was surprised when I learned you had come in person. I did not expect such an honor."

"You might not think it's such an honor when you have to throw me a feast," King Garnet said.

He laughed, and his guards laughed with him.

"What's this I hear about you having trouble with dragons?"

"Have you no eyes on the surface?" his uncle asked.

The dwarf scoffed.

"I'm no fool, Tarathiel, I know what is going on in the world. My question was what *you* are doing having trouble with dragons? I heard about your defeat at the hands of the Eldest."

"We are regrouping."

"You're sending out cries for help to anyone who'll listen."

"And I am glad that you did."

"I came to help. As much as I can. I don't have the warriors to spare that you'll need to see the job done, but we can help. What I want to know is why you've stepped in this mess."

"I count many dragonmages among my people. I will not stand by and let the Eldest decide to slaughter them."

"Fair enough, but why not just take the Eldest and leave the rest of 'em alone?"

"That is what we are trying to do."

The dwarven king scoffed.

"Bit late for a sneak attack," he said. "But we'll help where we can."

"Thank you," his uncle said. "I knew that we could count on you. Our friendship has remained strong through the centuries. My father always spoke very highly of you and your people."

"I doubt that," King Garnet said. "The old arse hated me. But, I hated him too, so it was all even."

They both laughed. Eryninn looked at Alranir, but the elf wouldn't look at him. He turned back and stood at attention. The dwarven king finished laughing and then got quiet as his face hardened.

"We need to talk about the Anvil," he said.

His uncle took a step back and sat down on his throne.

"We can talk more about that when *this* business is done," he said.

"We can talk about it now," King Garnet said.

His uncle sighed and shook his head.

"When the Eldest has been dealt with," he said. "I promise you, *then* we will speak more of this matter."

The dwarven king looked ready to continue when the doors swung open again. The royal guard marched toward the throne, stopping just beyond the dwarven guards.

"Your majesty," he said, "the Aeotharen await."

King Garnet looked at the guard and then back to his uncle and raised an eyebrow.

"You asked *everyone* for help that you could find?" he asked.

"Everyone who would listen," his uncle said.

The dwarf eyed him a moment longer and then turned and marched through his men and out the door. The elven guard followed and pulled the doors closed behind them all.

"What was that about?" Eryninn asked.

Alranir shot him a look, but his uncle just waved his hand.

"Trouble," he said. "If the Erutharen come, and I have no doubt they will just to cause problems, it could mean trouble."

"Then why did you ask them to come?" Eryninn asked.

"I do not know. Perhaps all this business with the dragons has sparked something. A hope that maybe all the elves can look at this and see what fools we've all been."

Alranir laughed but then quickly caught himself.

"You have something to add, Alranir?" the king asked.

"No, your highness. Just that... the Aeotharen will hear us, and I believe they have come to help. But the Erutharen? They want only one thing. Vengeance is all their god asks of them, and it is all they know."

His uncle sighed and slumped back against the throne. He looked tired. Older somehow, though Eryninn had only known him for a week now. The fight against Kalus has weakened him, both physically and mentally. Eryninn had seen him wandering sometimes now when everyone else was sleeping.

But there was no time for rest.

The doors swung open again, and a group of elves walked softly in. Counter to everything the dwarves were, the Aeotharen elves were as quiet and soft as Eryninn had always imagined elves to be. Each one was dressed in light blue robes that just brushed the ground when they walked, yet made no sound. Not a step, not a swish could be heard.

They approached in a group instead of a marching

formation and stopped before the king. The one in the lead stepped forward and bowed.

"King Tarathiel," he said.

There was nothing in his voice that Eryninn could hear. No malice or mischief. Eryninn hadn't known what to expect, but he thought there would be some underlying hostility. Something. But he heard and saw nothing from any of the elves.

"Father Uynari," his uncle said. "I thank you and your brothers for coming."

"We heard about your battle with the Eldest and came as soon as we could."

"Well, we could use the help."

"The Goddess would want us to," the priest said.

"There are still many wounded within the city, though the priests and priestesses of Threyl have been hard at work saving as many as they can. What we could really use are your talents in battle."

The priests shuffled their feet, and the one in the lead gave a halfhearted smile.

"I am afraid we cannot help you in your fight," he said. "We are only here to help the wounded."

"You can help them to not get wounded in the first place," his uncle said.

"This is what we can offer," the priest said. "I did not come here to join you in your fight against the Eldest."

His uncle opened his mouth to speak but instead just closed his eyes and nodded.

"We appreciate any support you can offer," he said. "There are many still wounded in the tents around the city if you can help."

"We will get straight to work," the priest said.

The others lined up behind him as he filed out of the

throne room. The king sighed and slumped back against the throne again.

"Why do I bother?" he asked. "Perhaps you are right, Alranir."

"I know I am," Alranir said.

Now it was Eryninn's turn to glare.

When the great doors swung open again, his uncle could hardly hide his displeasure.

"What now?" he whispered.

"Your majesty," the guard said. "The… Erutharen ambassador is here."

His uncle let out a deep sigh and rubbed at his eyes.

"Just what I need," he said. "Send them in."

"They are not *here*, majesty, they are waiting for a royal escort."

"No!" Alranir shouted.

The king stood and waved him down with a hand.

"Your majesty, you can't," Alranir said.

"How long have they been waiting?" the king asked.

"For almost an hour. They informed no one of their arrival, and it was not until a scout saw them that we even learned they were here."

"How did they get so close to the city without someone seeing them?" Eryninn asked.

His uncle sighed again.

"Eryninn will go and meet them," he said.

Alranir laughed.

"You are going to send *him*?"

"That is enough, Alranir," his uncle said. "Eryninn will go and meet them. Prepare a royal guard to attend him."

"Yes, your majesty," the elf said.

He turned and was gone as fast as he could. Alranir

tried to say something else, but the words looked stuck. After trying and failing, he turned without a word and stormed out, slamming the doors shut behind him.

"Thanks," Eryninn said. "As though he didn't have enough reasons to hate me."

"He does not hate you," his uncle said.

"Of course he does. Have you seen the way he treats me?"

"What my brother has told you of our people is not entirely untrue. Someone of Alranir's station is not looked upon favorably, and he has suffered for it. It has made him bitter and angry."

"I have seen others look at him with respect. Never the way he looks at me."

"Now, yes. But it has not always been that way for him. His mother and father never wed before he was born, which is deeply frowned upon in our world."

"No more so than being a half-breed."

"No, I suppose not, but you had something he did not. You had a mother and father who loved you, and you were never made to feel shame for who you are. Alranir carries a lot of anger from his earlier life."

"But why does he direct it at me? Because I'm a half-elf? All because my mother was a human?"

"It has more to do with *his* father than *your* mother," his uncle said.

Eryninn turned to face his uncle who had sat back into his throne.

"My brother struggled the same way when he was younger," his uncle said. "Always wanting to be something he was not. He did not want to be a prince. He hated doing things just because they were expected of him. He hated being in my shadow and always being the second son. Always a disappointment to my father."

"Is that how Alranir's father treated him?"

"No, but he was not much better. Thankfully, Alranir has taken a different path than my brother. Tarin spent a lot of time chasing women and throwing it in my father's face. All of that changed when he met your mother though. She changed his life. But... not before he had ruined someone else's."

Eryninn frowned.

"What do you mean?" he asked.

"When my brother ran off with your mother, he left someone else behind. A girl who had become pregnant. One he was not even in love with if his stories are to be believed. He left her to raise that child all on her own and left it to me to clean up his mess, as he so often did."

It took a second for his thoughts to register.

Eryninn stared hard at his uncle. His eyes had softened when he saw the look on Eryninn's face. His mind was reeling. His father had another child by another woman? How could he not know about this? How could he not have told him?

"I took the boy in and treated him as my own son," his uncle continued. "When his mother died years later, I was the only family he had left. Until now."

His uncle was there, then, with his arm on Eryninn's shoulder. He needed it to steady himself. He wasn't even sure of what he'd just been told. Did he hear it all clearly? Someone else in this world shared his blood. Someone who had been standing in front of him the whole time.

Eryninn stumbled for the door.

***

Eryninn yanked the big, white doors of the throne room

open and was immediately blinded by the sunlight. He threw his hand over his face and pushed out into the day. He didn't know where he was going, but he had to get some air. His uncle had just upended his whole world in a single conversation.

A brother.

Eryninn had a brother. And it was Alranir. Someone he'd grown to dislike more and more as time had gone on. Someone who obviously had nothing but disdain for him as well. The last person on Gondril he would want to be brothers with. Yet, if his uncle was to be believed, that is what they were.

Blinking through the light, he found who he was looking for. Alranir was standing with his back to the doors and watching the dwarven contingent. Eryninn didn't know what he would say, didn't know if this was the right time for it. He pulled his shoulders up and walked up behind his brother.

"You've known all along, haven't you?" he said.

Alranir barely glanced over his shoulder. Eryninn could see the smirk.

"Of course," he said. "Why do you think uncle sent me to find you?"

"Why didn't you tell me?"

"Because it changes nothing."

"It changes everything!"

"Nothing has changed. You know my past, that is all. It makes us nothing to each other."

"You... you're my brother."

"Half brother at best, and not a half I would care to know."

"I don't understand," Eryninn said. "Why do you despise me? What have I done to you other than being born half human?"

Alranir spun on him so fast he stumbled back and almost fell.

"You stole my father from me," he said. "You and that *human* mother of yours. We were a family before she came and took him from us."

Eryninn hardened.

"Do not speak of my mother. She was as close to a saint as you could ever meet."

"What a wonderful saint she was, destroying my family. You deserve them both. I hope you had a *wonderful* childhood filled with laughter and play. Mine was filled with ridicule and scorn because of what your father did."

"*Your* father as well," Eryninn said. "And he was a good man. He made some bad choices, but he was a good man, and a good father."

"If only he were here now. I would kill him myself for what he did to my mother."

"But why take it out on me? What have I done to you?"

"I owe you nothing," Alranir said. "You deserve the same treatment I received as a child here. Hated for what you are, for the way you were born. Others may look past your heritage or think you a prince because of your father. But all I see is your human mother and what she took from me. My mother died alone and ashamed."

"I... I didn't know. How could I have known?"

"You should have stayed away from here."

"You were the one who made me come!"

"Only because the king ordered me to. You do not belong here, and you will never be accepted. Uncle will name *me* his successor, *not* you."

"Is that what you think I'm here for?"

"I have seen the way he looks at you. You are the new, fluffy pet to trot around for the elite, nothing more. I have been here, by his side, for more than thirty years."

"I don't want your crown!" Eryninn yelled.

He hadn't meant to raise his voice. They were beginning to cause a bit of a scene in the courtyard. Thankfully, the only ones within earshot were the dwarves and some of the royal guard. Most of the citizens, even the upper class elite, didn't roam the gardens of the God Tower.

"I don't want anything from you," Eryninn said. "I learned only minutes ago that I have a brother. For twelve years, I have been alone with no family at all. And in a week, I have discovered an uncle who wants to know me and a brother who doesn't. I'm not even sure which makes me happier."

Alranir started to say something but stopped. Footsteps behind him made Eryninn turn. One of the royal guard was standing there with a dozen others.

"The king has asked us to escort you to meet the Erutharen, Ambassador Eryninn."

Alranir's face turned to stone. Eryninn sighed and hung his head.

"I don't want anything from you," he whispered. "Only to know you."

He stepped to the side and walked past the motionless Alranir. The thirteen royal guard fell into step behind him as he marched for the Dawn Gate.

When he glanced over his shoulder, Alranir was still watching him go.

***

The march to the eastern outpost took about thirty

minutes, but it was time that Eryninn desperately needed to himself. The royal guard were good for that, he'd found. Being the king's personal guard, they didn't speak much unless they were spoken to. Even then the answers were short.

All of which gave Eryninn time to think. His mind was buzzing, and he couldn't shake the thoughts. It was all just a jumble in his head. Everything had gotten so complicated.

He had a brother. Who hated him.

Actually, it wasn't that complicated, but it was all still very confusing. A week ago, Eryninn had no family that he cared to know. Now he had an uncle who had asked him to stay with him, and a brother who wanted nothing to do with him. Things were a lot simpler when he lived alone, hidden away from the world.

"Ambassador," the lead guard said behind him.

Eryninn turned with an odd look. Ambassador? Is that what he was now? His life was getting more complicated by the minute it seemed. The guard pointed ahead where he looked to see a waiting group of elves. Only they were unlike any elves he'd ever seen.

They were pale, paler even than regular elves. He would think them all sickly if he didn't know better. Living deep below the mountains made the Erutharen very different from their brothers, his uncle had told him. With little exposure to the sun, they had become whiter and whiter over the millennia.

But if their skin wasn't enough to shock him, their hair was. It stood in stark contrast to their pale skin, colored black and purple and shades in between. The Erutharen rarely cut their hair, preferring to let it grow down their backs in one long, silky river. Because there was no color to their skin, they colored their hair instead. Using what, no one really knew, but it wasn't natural.

The guard behind him coughed, and Eryninn realized he had gotten ahead of them in his haste to meet these new elves. He slowed his steps and fell into step in front of them. Ahead, a single elf stepped from the group to face him. He counted thirteen of them standing in two lines with what he assumed was the leader now out in front.

"We have been waiting an eternity," the lead elf said.

"You don't look a day over four-hundred," Eryninn said.

The elf narrowed his eyes while a few behind him chuckled. He silenced them with a wave of his hand and eyed Eryninn and the guards as they approached. Eryninn came to a stop in front of the elf and bowed before standing at a loose attention.

"Welcome to Nirorn," he said formally.

The elf looked him up and down with a sneer.

"A half-elf? They send a half-elf to greet us? Your king too busy to drum up a half-eaten ogre?"

Eryninn choked back his words. He was an ambassador now, much as he hated the idea. His words represented his uncle here.

"My uncle, *the king*, welcomes you."

"Your uncle? He only welcomes help after the Eldest burned up half of his army. Yes, I imagine your uncle is *very* welcoming right now."

Eryninn began to speak, but nothing he could think of would come out pleasant. In the end he settled on his name.

"I am Eryninn."

"Lord Vandar ul Malothen," the elf said.

Some of the Erutharen chuckled. Eryninn bowed and opted to say no more, instead turning on his heels to lead the way back.

"Come," he said.

His own guards parted to allow him past and then fell into line behind him. He didn't even know if the Erutharen were behind them, but he hoped someone would tell him if they weren't. He braved a glance over his shoulder and saw them all marching in step behind his own guards.

His first task helping his uncle seemed to be going well enough.

When they reached the Dawn Gate, it was already open and waiting for them. The guards along the top of the wall watched with some interest as they passed beneath. While this was only an escort and *definitely* not an honor guard, some of the citizens of Nirorn stood waiting in the streets for their little processional.

Eryninn heard chuckles and laughs from the Erutharen behind him.

"You would think they had never seen a cousin before," Lord Vandar said.

Eryninn ignored him and kept walking.

"Where I come from, the world is dark and scary," the elf said. "Yet we do not fear it. These Ilotharen stand in broad daylight beneath the warmth of the sun and cower in fear. They are like children scared of the dark, but in the light."

Eryninn marched on. He could feel the tension in his own guards behind him, but he kept walking, hoping to keep them focused forward. Within minutes they rounded the wall around the garden of the God Tower. Eryninn almost breathed a sigh relief before he saw what awaited them.

The dwarves.

All thirteen of them stood in a perfect, unbreakable line before the doors of the tower. And they had their weapons out. Eryninn was forced to stop at the foot of the steps.

"Step aside," he said in his most formal tone. "The king is expecting us."

"Oh, we've been expecting you too," King Garnet said.

Then came a sound Eryninn dreaded hearing. The sound of steel scraping leather. The sound of swords being drawn.

He spun and saw the Erutharen had drawn their weapons. The royal guard immediately drew their own. Eryninn held up both hands and tried to wave them all down.

"We came here to talk, dwarf," Lord Vandar said. "Truly, when the king called for help, I assumed your people could offer little."

"You're not here to help, Vandar" Garnet said. "You're here for some kind of trouble. Revenge maybe. That's what your kind is always looking for."

"It would appear we are not the only ones," Vandar said.

"Everyone, please calm down," Eryninn said. "What is this all about now?"

But Eryninn already knew. His uncle had told him this might happen. When the largest dwarven kingdom, the Anvil Dwarves, lost the war to the elves many millennia ago, some of the elves sought vengeance for the death of Ilothen. Which led them right to the doorstep of Anvil Hall, the mountain home of Dunatis's dwarves.

What few dwarves remained fled to save their race and were forced to make a home somewhere else. Many of the elves stayed, taking over the dwarven halls and tunnels as their own. Their love of vengeance led them to Eruthen, and a new elven kingdom was born.

But the dwarves never stopped wanting it back.

"Now is not the time for this," Eryninn said.

"Can't think of a better time," King Garnet said.

"Nor I," Lord Vandar said.

"This is not the time!" Eryninn shouted. "There are bigger things in the world than your petty arguments."

"Stand aside, son," Garnet said. "I respect your king. There's no need for you and your men to get hurt here."

"If you respect my king, you will respect my orders and stop this."

"Can't do that," King Garnet said.

The first shot cracked like a wooden barrel falling from a tower against the stones below. Eryninn saw the crossbow in the dwarf's hand rattle and shake as it loosed its deadly bolt. He only had a moment to react after hearing the shout from behind him.

Then the courtyard erupted into chaos.

Eryninn drew his own sword and jumped to one side as he turned. He felt someone grab his arm and started to fight when he recognized the lead of his royal guard. The rest of the guards had backed off as well, leaving the dwarves and the Erutharen to clash in the middle.

"We have to stop this!" he shouted above the din of battle.

"Yes, sir," the guard said.

With only a nod, the other guards waded into the fight. They kept their swords ready, but were trying as hard as they could to keep from hurting anyone. They were trying to break up the fight. Despite a look from the lead guard, Eryninn waded in to help.

He immediately regretted the decision.

Unlike so many fights before this, unlike the Battle of Molner, Eryninn didn't know who his enemy was supposed to be. Did he attack the Erutharen? Surely they were the evil instigators of this mess. But it was the dwarves who attacked first.

A scream to his right grabbed his attention as an Erutharen elf fell to the ground, bleeding and holding his stomach in. Eryninn instantly abandoned his sword and bent down to help. He tore the silly cloak his uncle had made him wear from his shoulders and pressed it hard against the elf's abdomen.

"Just hold on," Eryninn said. "We have priests who can help."

He was about to shout for a priest when he saw the elf's eyes look past him and go wide. Eryninn looked up and saw another of the Erutharen standing above him. Then he saw the blade coming down for his head.

Clang!

The blade stopped as another intercepted it. Only that blade didn't wait for the other to recover. It stabbed out, catching the Erutharen in the chest. With one deft motion, the blade slid in and then out again, leaving only the slimmest of holes. But blood poured quickly from the little opening, and within seconds, the elf fell, lifeless.

Alranir stood above Eryninn, his bloody blade in hand.

Eryninn was about to say something, to thank him, but the fight around him erupted in even more fighting as more of the Nirorn guard joined. It took only a minute longer for them, with Alranir leading, to gain control of the courtyard.

Through it all, Eryninn pushed on the dying elf's stomach and hoped it would be enough to keep him alive until help could come.

"Get the priests!" he heard someone shout.

The king, his uncle, was there then, shouting orders to everyone. His voice was filled with anger, but Eryninn could hear him saving it for later. When what needed to be done was done. His uncle had a way of getting things done when others could not have maintained their heads.

Elven priests, the Aeotharen that had arrived only hours before, raced into the courtyard of the God Tower to tend the wounded and dying. One knelt beside him and nodded. He took Eryninn's hands from the wounded elf and began to pray. A light spread from the priest's own hands, and he held them gently over the wound. It quickly closed, leaving the elf breathing slowly and comfortably.

"When they are healed, bring them all before me," his uncle said.

He looked at Eryninn and jerked his head toward the doors to the tower. As he stood, he saw the courtyard was filled with Nirorn soldiers now. At least fifty stood ready with swords drawn, all of them pointing at their visitors.

Eryninn stood and followed after his uncle.

***

"Tell me what happened," his uncle said.

For the first time since his arrival, he stood not beside his uncle but in front of him. Eryninn suddenly felt like a small child again, his father asking him what he had done. Alranir was beside him. The thought of having a brother there to face it with him was almost comforting. If it had been a different brother, maybe.

"We arrived in the city without incident," Eryninn said. "When we entered the gates of the tower, the dwarves were standing in a line and blocking our passage. King Garnet and Lord Vandar exchanged words, and then they attacked."

"Who attacked first?" the king asked.

"The dwarves shot a bolt into the elves, I believe," Eryninn said.

"You believe?"

The king shook his head.

"I need to know for sure," he said.

"The dwarves fired first," Eryninn said.

That was how he remembered it, and it would have to be good enough. Alranir remained characteristically silent during the whole exchange. He just stood at perfect attention, never even twitching. He must really be enjoying this. The king waved them both forward.

"Come," he said, "stand beside me."

They both took their places, Eryninn to the king's left and Alranir to his right. Then his uncle nodded to a guard at the rear of the room, and the double doors were opened. King Garnet and Lord Vandar alone entered the throne room, and the doors were quickly shut behind them. The two walked the length of the room with their heads held high and stopped in front of the raised throne.

"I want this dwarf restrained," Vandar said. "His kind is dangerous and should be put down like rabid dogs."

"Step outside again, elf, and we'll see who is put down."

"Stop!" the king yelled. "I should have you *both* taken into custody for what you have done."

"One of my men is dead!" Vandar shouted. "We came here offering our help, and *this* is what we are treated to?"

The king waved his hand dismissively.

"This is *exactly* what you came for, Vandar. Do not pretend as though you came to help us. You have no intention of doing so, and everyone in this room knows it."

Eryninn didn't know it. Why was he sent to retrieve the Erutharen elves if they weren't coming to help? Did his uncle know they would end up in a fight with the dwarves? Vandar opened his mouth to retort but could only shrug and smile.

"King Garnet?" his uncle said.

"If you won't help us take Anvil Hall, we will take it ourselves."

"Anytime you would like it back, just come and take it," Vandar said. "Though I warn you, it will not be easy. The previous occupants left the place *very* well defended. We had to demolish much of the old halls and artifacts though. They were not to our taste."

Eryninn could see the rage boiling in King Garnet's stubby face. His short-cropped beard covered most of it, but there was no mistaking the look in his eyes. His uncle and Alranir must have seen it too because Alranir took a step forward and pulled his sword just a few inches from his scabbard.

"Enough," his uncle said. "It was a mistake to ask either of you for assistance. You both live as though it were five thousand years ago. Our peoples are *not* at war any longer."

"No longer at war," King Garnet said, "but neither are we at peace. Not until our home is returned to us."

"Whose home?" Vandar said. "We have lived there longer than you now."

"Go," his uncle said. "Both of you, take your men and leave. I pray that Gondril does not follow you down this foolish road of vengeance and death you seem intent to remain on."

"We came to help," the dwarf said.

"I no longer want your help, King Garnet. We will talk another time, when the world is healed, if there is ever such a time. Alranir, see that the guards escort the dwarven and Erutharen envoys to our borders."

Alranir stepped off the dais and waved his arm toward the door. King Garnet bowed and said no more. Lord Vandar waved a hand over his retreating back. Eryninn could hear a little chuckle as he left.

His uncle slumped onto the throne and rubbed at his eyes.

"What a mess," he said.

"Did you know this would happen?" Eryninn asked.

"I knew it was a possibility, but I trusted King Garnet to be honorable. He has always been so in the past, and I have known him a very long time."

"Why did he do this?"

"Desperation. Dwarves live hundreds of years, but Garnet's time as king will end soon, and he wants to leave his legacy. He wants to reclaim Anvil Hall for the dwarves. And he wants me to help him."

"Is that what he's wanted to talk to you about?"

"It's all he ever wants to talk about."

"Why not help them? The Erutharen are your enemy as much his."

His uncle shook his head and then looked him in the eyes.

"The Erutharen are my brothers. They are not my enemy, though it is doubtful they would say the same of me. As much as I would like to help Garnet, I will not start a war with my own people."

"But they are not your people. They despise you."

"I believe they can be shown the light."

"Doubtful."

"You did."

His uncle sat up straight and stared at him.

"You hated us probably more than the Erutharen do. Do you still feel the same about us?"

"That's different. My father never told me the whole story."

"And you think they have learned any less? Hatred and judgement are the worst gifts we give to our children. It is something I have tried so hard to impart to my son."

His son. He truly considered Alranir his son, though this was the first time Eryninn had heard him referred to as such.

"Yet Alranir hates me," Eryninn said.

"He does not get that from me. Alranir has a lot to work out, but I am there to see him through it. We are making some progress."

"Better work harder."

His uncle smiled.

"We will keep at it," he said.

CHAPTER THIRTY-SEVEN

RETURN

THEIR RETURN FROM the isle was met with little fanfare, and that made Elody nervous.

Once they had reached Rockport, Ilyaren had taken a very different path on their flight back. They had all been worried that Kalus would send other dragons against them. But perhaps Anarr *had* blessed their journey. They made it back to the elven forest without incident.

Ilyaren called out to a few gold and silver dragons as they reached the western border of the elven lands, but whatever their response was, he didn't like it. They must know where we've gone and what we've done. And they don't like it.

"What are they saying?" Rinn asked.

"That we must get to Nirorn as quickly as possible," Ilyaren said.

"What's going on?" Elody asked.

"We will know when we arrive," he said.

Jalthrax flew up beside them and screeched, but Elody could only shrug. Ilyaren flew on faster, and Elody became even more concerned. What was going on?

They saw the tip of the God Tower peeking out over

the trees in no time, and Ilyaren breezed right past it and to the roost atop the Dawn Tower. He touched down gently, and Rinn and Elody slid off of his back as quickly as they could. Their feet only just touched the ground when Ilyaren began to shift into his elven form.

The roost was empty except for a single elven guard standing near the door.

"I am to take you to the king," he said.

He turned and waited for them to follow. They really weren't happy about them going to the isle it seemed. Elody started to come up with any number of explanations, but all of them seemed weak. In the end, she decided that it didn't matter. Anarr had blessed them all, and that was all they needed.

They followed the guard down the stairs, Ilyaren almost pushing past him to speed things up. Through the doors of the Dawn Tower, they went out across its courtyard and into the streets of Nirorn. Elody had never seen a town so empty. Ilyaren must have noticed it to.

"What is going on?" he said.

"I am to take you to the king," the guard said.

Ilyaren grunted and pushed past the guard, who marched faster to keep up. They were jogging now with Jalthrax flying above. Within a few minutes, they reached the outer gates of the God Tower. Ilyaren shoved his way in and pushed through the doors.

"They are waiting in the council chamber," the guard called.

Elody and Rinn jogged to catch up while Jalthrax came to an abrupt landing and tried to follow them in. The guards at the door to the tower stopped him.

"No dragons out of elven form," one said.

"But he can't take elven form," Elody said. "He's not

old enough yet."

"Then he'll have to wait here," the guard said.

Elody sighed and turned to Jalthrax.

"Wait out here, Thrax. I'll tell you everything when I get back."

She ran on to catch up and saw Rinn disappear around a bend in the stairs. Taking the steps two at a time, she managed to get close enough to see his back disappear into a large door on the inside of the tower. When she got there, she stopped short in the doorway.

The room was filled with very important-looking people who all looked very somber and serious. Rinn was against the wall just inside the room, and she slid softly up next to him and waited without a word.

The king sat at the head of the long table with Eryninn at his side. Elody gave a single wave of her hand, and he nodded, but that was it for their greeting. The rest of the room was looking at the three of them, Ilyaren standing in front of them, opposite the king.

"What has happened?" he asked bluntly.

"While you were off galavanting," Olania said, "we were fighting a war."

"What?" Ilyaren said. "What have you done?"

"We went out to face Kalus," the king said. "It was my decision, and the dragon council agreed."

"Kalus is dead?" Ilyaren asked.

Rinn looked at her, and she could see him rubbing the little pink crystal between his fingertips.

"No," Thalaras said. "Kalus has enlisted the dark dragons to his cause. We were forced to retreat."

"What madness is this?" Ilyaren said. "I leave for a week, and you run off to war with the Eldest?"

"Do not shout in this chamber, Ilyaren," the king said.

"As I said, I chose the course of action. It was my mistake."

"The better question is," Olania said, "where were you?"

"I went to the isle," Ilyaren said. "I took Jalthrax, Rinn, and Elody there with me."

The four dragons in elven form, one Elody had never seen before, stared hard at Ilyaren.

"Do not judge me," Ilyaren said. "I went because Anarr called me to."

"Kalus said the same," Thalaras said. "You are claiming to hear the voice of Anarr now as well?"

"We didn't just hear him," Elody said, feeling brave suddenly, "we saw him. He was there waiting for us."

Now it was not just the dragons whose mouths were open but most of the elves in the room as well. Ilyaren folded his arms across his chest and waited.

"You..." Olania said. "You spoke to Anarr?"

"He's very kind," Elody said.

They looked at Ilyaren who nodded his head only once.

"How can this be?" Thalaras said. "Anarr appeared before you... humans? You are not even allowed on the island!"

"The Creator said that he had called on us to make things right," Ilyaren said. "He told us that we must destroy Kalus and repair all that he has broken."

"Tell us everything," Olania said.

She was trying to remain calm, but Elody could see the tension in her eyes. All the dragons looked ready to explode, but they remained silent and let Ilyaren speak.

"What I tell you now, comes from the First Dragon himself. Rinn, Elody, and Jalthrax were all there to witness, but you all know that I speak truth."

He paused for a breath.

"Kalus is to be destroyed," Ilyaren said.

He waited for that to sink in a moment.

"Rinn has been given Anarr's blessing to end Kalus's life."

The whole room turned to look at them, at Rinn, who stood up tall and let the dragonbane crystal sparkle defiantly on his chest. Whispers floated around the room as they all saw what it was he wore.

"Anarr has given this piece of himself to Rinn to wield," Ilyaren said. "When Kalus is dead, I am to be the new Eldest. Anarr has decreed that when an Eldest passes, the oldest dragon of light on Gondril will ascend to replace them."

Thalaras appeared ready to object, but instead took a step back and said nothing.

"Anarr has blessed the bond between his children and the children of Ilothen and Threyl. The bond should be celebrated and encouraged, and for that, Anarr has tasked Elody with being his champion."

Everyone shifted where they stood. The whole room seemed to move.

"Anarr wants us to make this right. To make right what Kalus has destroyed."

"And what of the dark dragons?" the king asked. "How does Anarr propose we deal with them?"

"When Kalus is dead, and I am Eldest, I will once again unite all the dragons of light. And we will send the dark dragons scurrying back to their holes."

"How can we do this?" the king asked. "We cannot just walk up to Kalus and strike him dead. Even he is not that blind."

"We could sneak in behind his lines," Eryninn said. "Rinn is quite skilled in the art. He and I could sneak into Kalus's cave and kill him in a single breath with that crystal."

"And what if you're caught?" the king asked.

"The dragons cannot harm us so long as we have that crystal."

"They can still use magic," Olania said. "The crystal will not protect you from their magic, only their dragon forms."

"We will not be seen," Eryninn said firmly.

"No," Thalaras said. "We cannot kill Kalus while hiding in some cave. If we are to unite the dragons of light, they must see him die. They must know that Anarr has willed this."

"Thalaras is right," Ilyaren said. "This must be done in a way that lets the other dragons see Anarr's power. They must hear the message we have to deliver."

"Then what would you propose we do?" the king asked.

"March on him again," an elf beside the king said. "The clerics of Threyl and their paladins are with us now, and the Knights of Gondril are coming. We must draw Kalus out the same way that he drew Ferin out."

Elody didn't recognize the elf, but there were two of them sitting beside the king, and she guessed them to be some kind of advisers.

"Kalus is too arrogant not to meet with us on the field of battle," Eryninn said. "When he does, Rinn will be waiting for him."

"So the armies are just a ruse?" the king said.

"If we cannot sneak to him," Eryninn said, "we must make him come to us. We need a show of force that is strong enough that he believes it."

"We cannot afford to lose even more of our people," the king said.

"We don't have to," the other elf beside the king said. "Kalus won't be able to resist taunting us after our last encounter. When he does, Rinn and the others will be waiting."

"They must be far enough away that Kalus can't sense the crystal," Ilyaren said. "It's not easy to detect, but one who is looking for it can feel it. With Kalus's network of spies, he must know by now that we reached the island. We saw no one, but Kalus has been one step ahead of us the whole time. If he knows we have the crystal, he won't come."

"I would like to speak to Rinn and Elody myself," the king said abruptly. "We will discuss more of our plans after."

The king stood, and all the elves in the room rose as well. They filed out the door without a word of protest, and the dragons reluctantly did the same. When the movement had ceased, Rinn and Elody stood across the table from Eryninn and the king.

"Is this all true?" the king asked.

"Yes, your majesty," Elody said. "Anarr himself spoke to us and told us what we must do."

The king seemed to ponder that a moment, and Elody took the chance to smile at Eryninn who returned it.

"Are you sure about all of this?" the king finally said.

"Anarr has given me this task," Rinn said. "And, he has given me the power to see it through."

"What about your sister there?"

"She is Anarr's champion, your majesty. When Kalus

is dead, she must deliver Anarr's word to his people."

The king shook his head.

"I do not like these gods," he said. "They play at games with our lives. And now I must ask my people to go to war again less than two weeks after the last?"

"Killing Kalus is my task alone," Rinn said. "I will go alone and sneak in as Eryninn said, your majesty."

"I will go too," Eryninn said.

"No," the king said. "If Kalus detects the crystal, he will run. Or worse. You may be able to kill Kalus with that crystal, but I know of its powers. It will be drained once you do, and you will have no protection from the other dragons that would seek to harm you."

"I will manage," Rinn said.

"Thalaras is right," the king said. "If you are to stop Kalus without causing a war between the dragons of light, they have to see him die. They have to know that Anarr wanted him dead."

"What will you do, Uncle?" Eryninn asked.

The king sighed.

"I cannot ask my people to lay down even more lives," he said. "But I can ask them to march. With the help of the Threylian priests, the Knights of Gondril, and defensive magic from my wizards, we can keep everyone safe long enough to finish Kalus before there is more blood."

The matter settled, the king stood and bowed his head.

"I know your journey was long," he said. "Go and get some rest. We will speak again later when I have made plans with my generals."

Eryninn stepped around the table with a smile.

"Come," he said. "There are some people who've been

waiting to see you."

***

Elody and Rinn followed Eryninn out of the tower and to one of several large tents that had been setup in the courtyard and gardens surrounding the tower.

"The wounded," Eryninn explained.

Elody realized she hadn't seen Eliath anywhere, and the thought made her throat tighten. She had had a lot of time to think about it while on their trip to and from the island, and she had decided she wasn't mad at him. He didn't know what he was doing.

But where was he.

"Where's Eliath?" she said.

"Follow me," he said.

He pushed his way into one of the larger tents and led them on. Was Eliath wounded? Was he in here helping the wounded? She hoped it was the latter, but she feared the worst. He was nowhere she could see.

Women in robes and men in chainmail armor moved among the wounded, each one holding firmly to something in their hands as they prayed. The symbol of the mother holding her child. The holy symbol of Threyl, the Goddess.

Elody stumbled as she looked around the tent. It was full of beds, mattresses stuffed with hay or feathers, laying on the ground. All the beds were full. Filled with the wounded and the dying. She put her hand to her mouth and tried to stifle a cry. Fumbling along, she followed Eryninn deeper into the tent. All the beds were filled with elves except for one.

"He will be all right," Eryninn said. "He took a pretty bad fall when the dragon he rode was hit from the side, but they were low enough to the ground it didn't kill him."

Eliath lay there, unmoving.

"He told me what happened," Eryninn said.

He turned to look Elody in the eyes.

"He didn't know," he said.

"I know," Elody said. "I'm not angry with him anymore."

"I am," Rinn said.

"After you left, he went to the king and told him everything. How he'd been helping Kalus without his knowledge, how he'd been giving reports about our movements and thoughts. But my uncle was not angry. Eliath helped us so much leading up to the battle. He probably saved many lives."

"What did he do?" Elody asked.

"He fed Kalus a lot of bad information about our plans. When we finally arrived, Kalus was truly surprised. Though, he had a big surprise for us as well. But without Eliath, many more lives would have been lost."

Elody nodded, tears floating at the base of her eyes.

"He's resting now," Eryninn said. "Oryna set the bones and mended them all, but she said that broken bones take much more to heal than wounds of the flesh. He still needs sleep."

"Oryna?" Rinn asked. "Oryna is here?"

"She led the priestesses and paladins to our aid after the battle. The priestesses have been tending the wounded nonstop ever since they arrived."

Rinn looked all around the tent and then stopped on a figure standing in the distance, watching them. Several of the other priestesses came up to her, and she said something and then sent them away, her eyes never leaving Rinn.

"Go," Elody said. "I'm going to sit with Eliath."

***

Rinn approached slowly, not wanting to interrupt while Oryna was talking with another priestess. One by one, she sent them on their way and then stood waiting. She looked weak, shaky.

"I didn't know you were here," Rinn said.

"We do seem to bump into each other, don't we," she said.

"I should have known you would be here. So many people to help, you would be leading the charge."

"I did actually lead the charge, as you say. Word reached our temple from the priests in Molner the night before the elves marched on the Eldest. I had gathered everyone I could and was on my way before the battle even began."

They looked around at the rows and rows of wounded.

"How bad was it?"

"Not as bad as some I've seen," she said. "Worse than some others."

"So many," Rinn whispered.

A priestess standing off to the side bowed respectfully and interrupted.

"Forgive me, Orphan Mother," she said. "May I go and rest?"

The girl looked like she would fall over from exhaustion.

"If you have done all that you can," Oryna said.

The girl thought for a moment and then took a breath.

"I can heal one more, perhaps, Orphan Mother," she said.

"Do all that you can and then rest," Oryna said.

She smiled and touched the girl's cheek.

"Thank you, Mother," she said.

"I need to keep moving," Oryna said. "Will you join me?"

Rinn nodded and fell into step behind her.

"Why do they call you that?"

"All the high priestesses of Threyl are called Mother," she said and moved on.

She went from bed to bed examining each of the wounded and calling out to other priests and priestesses as she went. An elf beside her grimaced as she reached down to touch the wound in his side. It had been bandaged to stop the bleeding, but his body was chalky white.

Oryna put her hand on him and whispered a prayer. A warm glow extended from her hand and flowed out. Rinn watched, amazed, as the wound closed up, the skin stitching itself back together. When she was done, all that remained was the stain of blood on the skin. Some color had even begun to return.

"You'll be fine," she said to the soldier with a smile. "It may take a little time, but when you feel well enough to walk, please go and help someone else to your bed."

The soldier nodded and sat up, testing his side with his fingers. Rinn looked up, but Oryna had already moved on. She passed over some of the soldiers, calling out to someone else as she did. The ones in the most pain, the ones screaming or wailing, those were the ones she stopped at.

"If you can heal them all like that, why are there so many in here?"

"There are many more in the other tents waiting to

get in," she said. "We have priests going through the other tents as well, but there is not enough healing to go around. We make them comfortable as much as we can and then heal them when our strength allows it."

"Couldn't you just pray to Threyl to heal them all?" Rinn asked.

"I'm afraid even I haven't the strength for that. Threyl may grant me my power, but it still must flow *through* my hands. To heal everyone like you say would certainly kill me. Threyl would never grant me that, though I would do it if I could."

Rinn didn't doubt that she would.

"How do you decide who to help?" he asked.

"That is the problem," she said. "Threyl grants me the power to heal even someone who is close to death, but it takes so much more out of me. So, do you expend your energy to heal one who is almost dead, or do you heal three who are not as bad off but will certainly die without aid?"

"You save the three," Rinn said.

She hugged him and smiled a little.

"I have missed you," she said.

He wanted to kiss her, but he knew it wasn't the time. She had already moved on anyway. As he followed her through the tent, he watched her pray over almost every soldier she met. He could see her growing weaker with every one, and she was beginning to lean on him more and more as they continued.

"You need rest," he said.

"Just one more," she said.

But one more became another. And another after that. Oryna could no longer walk on her own and had to have Rinn hold her up as she went to the next soldier.

"Stop," he said.

"Just… one more."

She stumbled.

Just a little, but without Rinn holding her, she would have surely fallen. He bent down and lifted her legs, cradling her in his arms.

"One more," she whispered.

Rinn ignored her and went to find an empty bed. There were none. He looked to one of the other priestesses, and she pointed to a flap at the back of the tent. He carried her through, and she murmured deliriously with each step. One more. Just one more.

Through the flap, he found a smaller tent with more beds lined up, but instead of wounded soldiers, these were filled with the clerics of Threyl. Though they showed no outward wounds, some looked worse than the soldiers they worked so hard to heal. Their skin was pale, and beads of sweat had formed on their sleeping faces. Oryna began to shake in his arms.

"She will be fine," a man said, stepping forward. "Threyl will see to her."

The paladin reached for her, but Rinn pulled her back. With a bow, he stepped back to wipe a rag over a sleeping priest's forehead. Rinn found an empty bed and laid Oryna down on it.

"One…" she whispered.

"What can I do?" Rinn asked.

"Take a cool rag and wipe her face," the paladin said. "It will help. Threyl will not let her chosen come to harm, even if they seek to put themselves into harm's way."

Rinn took a rag beside her bed and wetted it in a bowl of cool water, then wiped her face. Her head shook back and forth like she was saying no, but no words escaped her lips.

When the paladin wasn't looking, he bent down and kissed her forehead.

"Rest," he whispered.

He stayed beside her bed the rest of the night.

Chapter Thirty-Eight

A New Day

"Hey."

Elody stirred, her eyes opening slowly. It took a few seconds for her to remember where she was. Someone was talking to her. Eliath. He was awake.

"Hey," she said.

"Where... where are we?" he asked.

"The infirmary tent. You got hurt bad in the battle."

"How long have I been here?"

"The battle was four days ago. I've been here with you for the last two."

"You've been here for two days?"

"Not even the king himself could drag me away."

She smiled, and that eased him a little.

"What happened?" he asked.

"What do you remember?"

"The dark dragons," he said. "They swooped in like a crazed flock of birds, attacking everything in sight. Even some of Kalus's dragons. The king called for a retreat, and the dragons with us changed into their true forms to fly us away."

He stopped to clear his throat, and Elody handed

him a cup of water which he gulped from. When he had finished, he continued.

"The king and his advisers climbed onto the golds and flew off. Eryninn and I got on the back of Evranon, the male silver, and we were right behind them. Then, out of nowhere, this red dragon comes from above and swoops down on us breathing fire."

He paused, and Elody took his hand. She had never known a red dragon other than Tark, had never even seen one, so it was hard for her to imagine one so savage. But that's exactly what people said of red dragons.

"Evranon flew as fast as he could, and Eryninn and I were both holding on for our lives. He avoided most of the blast and managed to get out ahead of it. The red chased after us, and Evranon flew below the other dragons fighting it out in the air. He swerved low and left to avoid another blast, and I lost hold. Tark always had a saddle, and I'm not used to riding without one. I remember falling, but then… nothing."

Elody squeezed his hand, and he took another drink.

"You nearly died," she said. "It's a miracle that you didn't. When you hit the ground, you broke nearly every bone in your body. Eryninn told me that he called out to the king and swung around to go back for you. The other silver, Alyniryn, came back with one of the king's wizards, and they fought the red off to get to you. The wizard used a spell to put your body in some kind of stasis so that you wouldn't die, and they flew you back here."

Eliath tested his arms and legs, gingerly flexing his joints.

"They kept you in stasis until the Threylian priests arrived. It took Oryna all of her healing for a day just to mend your body, but she was able to save you."

"What happened at the battle?" he asked.

"The retreat saved a lot of lives, but not all. The silver and gold dragons, along with the wizards, fought to drive back Kalus so that the elven troops could retreat. Many died, but many others made it. Eryninn told me little bits and pieces while sitting with me."

Someone wailed in pain nearby, and they both turned to find the source. There were still a lot of wounded, but most weren't life-threatening anymore. The priests and priestesses had managed to save many of the worst cases, though not all.

"What will happen now?" Eliath asked.

"They're planning another attack this very minute."

"Another attack?" Eliath asked, instantly tense. "Are they insane?"

"It won't be like the last time. Rinn and I... we retrieved the dragonbane crystal. Rinn is going to use it to destroy Kalus and end all of this."

She didn't tell him about meeting Anarr and the rest of it. The details didn't seem so important in that moment.

"When the armies go to draw Kalus out, Rinn and I will take a small group to meet him. When he comes, Rinn will kill him, and Ilyaren will become Eldest."

"You mean Thalaras."

"It's a long story, and I'll tell you later, but that's what is going to happen."

"I want to go with you," he said. "I want to be there to help."

She smiled.

"I wouldn't want you anywhere else."

He returned the smile and then pulled her hand

closer.

"I didn't know I was talking to Kalus," he said.

"I know that. I know that you would never risk mine and Rinn's lives like that."

"Well, maybe Rinn."

That earned him a slug on the arm. He cried out in pain.

"Sorry!" she said.

"I was only kidding, you don't have to beat me up," he said.

"Eryninn told me about how you helped after we left. He said you saved a lot of lives."

"I was only trying to make up for what I'd already done."

Elody reached over to the table beside his bed and picked up the golden sun amulet lying there. She held it out to him, but he pulled his hands back.

"Take it," she said.

"I don't deserve it."

"But think of the good you can do with it. Look at the good you've already done with it."

"It's not mine to take."

"Well, I don't know if it's mine to give, but Cythyil was my master, and he's dead now. So, I guess it doesn't belong to anyone now. I want you to have it."

She pushed it at him again, and he reached a hand up and took it. He looked at it in silence, clenched in his fist, for a while before he spoke again.

"When Selex... Kalus gave this to me, he said it was so that I could help the dragonmages. For everything I had done in the Battle of Molner. The conclave wanted my help. I... I just wanted to be useful again."

"I know," she said.

"When I put it on, and I felt that rush of magic again, it was like a part of me returned. Something I hadn't felt since... Tark died. It felt good. Like I could fight Kalus and maybe be a dragonmage again, at least a little part. And the whole time I was only helping him."

"He lied to you and tricked you," she said. "But the last laugh is on him. You tricked him right back. And in the end, you *did* help the dragonmages. And now we have you on our side, and we have the power to fight him."

Eliath looked into her eyes and smiled, and for the first time in a week, she felt that flutter inside her again. She pulled her hand back so he wouldn't feel her starting to sweat.

"So what do we do now?" he asked.

"Envoys from the different cities and powers are coming. There is a big meeting set for one week from today where the king and all the leaders will meet and discuss the plan. Then, I guess, we march."

Eliath pulled the amulet over his head and let it fall to his bare chest, which Elody tried hard not to look at. He started to pull the thin linen blanket back and then stopped.

"Uh... where are my clothes?" he asked.

Elody covered her mouth and chuckled before pointing to a chair on the other side of the bed where his clothes had been cleaned and laid out.

"I'll just turn around so you can get dressed," she said.

She turned her back to him and heard him shuffle out of bed. She tried hard not to peek and was mostly successful.

"Don't push yourself," she said. "Oryna said she'd come by to check on you in a bit."

She heard him sit back down, and she turned to see he'd found his pants.

"Can I get something to eat?" he asked. "It feels like I haven't eaten in days."

"Almost a week, actually," she said.

***

"Where is she?"

Elody heard shouting from the front of the tent and immediately recognized the loud voice. She stood to get a better look and couldn't suppress a smile when she saw him.

Berym saw her across the tent and walked swiftly toward her.

"Are you okay?" he said as he drew near. "Are you hurt? They told me you and Rinn were both in here."

"We're fine," she said. "I'm just here with Eliath."

"You're not hurt then?"

"We weren't even part of the battle," she said.

Over Berym's shoulder, Elody recognized Father Meral coming in the tent and over to their little corner.

"So many wounded," he said.

"There were many more," Elody said. "I have seen the priests and priestesses save so many lives the past few days that I cannot even count them all."

"And the word is we're going to do it all over again," Berym said.

"When did you arrive?" Elody asked.

"Only just now. The first thing I did was ask after you two, and someone pointed and said you were in the infirmary tent. I ran over as fast as my legs would carry me."

In her peripheral, Elody saw Oryna come out of the small tent in the back led by Rinn. She was walking much straighter, but she still held onto Rinn's hand for support. They shuffled over to them.

"I thought I heard someone loud and boorish," Rinn said. "And here you are."

"A knight is never boorish," Berym said. "I was only worried for a moment and let it get the best of me."

"It is good to see you, Berym," Rinn said.

The knight clapped Rinn on the shoulder and smiled.

"And you," he said. "Though I wish we could stop meeting like this. Always on the eve of battle. We've traded goblins for dragons, not a trade in our favor if you ask me, but here we are again."

Rinn reluctantly let go of Oryna's hand as she pulled away to examine Eliath. They all stopped and watched a moment before she stood back up.

"All healed up," she said. "You may feel a little stiff from being in bed for so long, but there should be no more pain from your injuries."

"Thank you," Eliath said. "Elody tells me you saved my life."

"There are many who saved your life," Oryna said. "A great many people considered you worth saving, it seems."

Elody saw Rinn look away and wanted to hit him.

"Mother," Father Meral said, stepping forward. "May I be of some help with the wounded?"

Oryna took his hands in hers and smiled at the older man.

"Of course, Father," she said. "You are Father Meral, yes? The head priest in Derne?"

Father Meral chuckled.

"The only priest in Derne," he said.

"I am Oryna," she said, "and I would welcome your

help."

Father Meral cocked his head and looked at her strangely for only a second.

"You are the Orphan Mother," he said. "I recognize your name if not your face."

"You may call me that if you wish," she said, "but I prefer just Oryna."

Father Meral bowed and then wandered off among the wounded to find someone to help. Everyone else was staring at Oryna.

"Who are you?" Rinn asked. "People just know you by name?"

"I am known in the church, that is all," she said. "I need to continue my rounds. Will you come with me, Rinn?"

Rinn nodded and took her hand.

"I must go as well," Berym said. "It is very bad protocol to arrive in the king's city and then run off to meet your friends before the king. But, I'm sure he will understand."

"Eryninn is the king's nephew," Elody said. "Did you know that?"

Berym laughed.

"I did not, but I always knew he was hiding something."

"A lot of somethings apparently," Elody said.

"Well, then, perhaps he can get some food brought out for my men."

"You brought people with you?" she asked.

"You don't think I'd go fight the Eldest all by myself did you? Not without a really good reason anyway."

He smiled.

"No," he said, "I brought two thousand strong

knights, and that is only half of our forces making their way here. The other half will arrive in a little less than a week, before the meeting the king's called. But I really must go and see the king."

"Go," Elody said. "We'll catch up later."

"Indeed we will," he said.

He gave her a hug and then hurried out, leaving her and Eliath alone again. Oryna made her rounds with Rinn's help, but she was more conservative with her healing, only helping the ones who were truly in pain. Rinn stayed by her side the whole time, but he kept glancing back at her and Eliath sitting in the corner.

"Just like old times," Eliath said.

***

Jalthrax tried his best to hide his boredom. Ilyaren had been going on for almost a half an hour about his plans once he was Eldest. Most of it centered around what he would do to bring peace among the dragons. It was an important topic, Jalthrax had no doubt, but all he wanted to do was fly. He felt his gaze drifting out over the trees more than once.

Would it be rude to start practicing his transformations? Ilyaren was almost always in his elven form, and Jalthrax was getting a little jealous. There were parts of Nirorn he simply wasn't allowed into in his true form. He had tried various forms while they were at sea for days, but he still couldn't get anything beyond his natural shape.

"There you are!"

Elody.

Jalthrax could hardly contain the smile on his face when she popped through the door at the top of the Dawn Tower. Ilyaren ceased talking immediately,

Jalthrax was thankful for that, and backed away as she hurried over to them. Wasting no time, she threw her arms around his neck and gave him a hug.

His growl of contentment was involuntary, and his smile grew bigger. She gave him one last squeeze and then stood up, but she continued to rub his neck. He always loved when she rubbed his neck. Jalthrax could feel the energy within him trying to get out, to leap from his body into Elody's waiting hands. Her every touch was charged and connected.

"I thought I might find you here," she said. "Though I assumed you would be out flying somewhere."

"The king has asked as many dragons to remain grounded as possible," Ilyaren said.

His tone was stiff. Gruff even. Jalthrax looked at Ilyaren and wondered why. Only a moment ago, he was talking quite fervently about his plans. Now he just glared. Elody noticed it too. She stopped petting his neck and stood up straight.

"What is going on?" she asked. "You've been hostile to me ever since we left the island. The whole trip back you said maybe three words."

Ilyaren glared back at her.

"You should *not* be Anarr's champion," he said.

Elody looked as shocked as Jalthrax felt. Though he'd been silent with Elody, Jalthrax and Ilyaren had talked the whole way home. About Anarr, about how amazing Ilyaren felt being in his presence. About all the duties he would have now as Eldest. Ilyaren had been uncharacteristically *chatty* since they left.

And now this?

"You are too young and know *far* too little to be called his champion," Ilyaren said. "You are a little girl with a little dragon. Anarr should have chosen someone stronger."

Jalthrax could feel Elody's emotions emanating from her. Only the slightest touch of them, but he could tell when her mood changed and what it had changed to. And right now he felt anger. Ilyaren was about to find out just how strong this *little girl* was.

"Who are *you* to judge me?" she said. "I don't remember Anarr granting *you* the power to name his champion."

"Do not speak to me as a child, *child*."

"Then stop acting like one," Elody said.

Jalthrax growled. Anarr had chosen *them* as his champions. Ilyaren was the only one who could understand him, but that was who needed to hear it anyway.

"Anarr was wrong," Ilyaren said. "You are both too young and not worthy of the title."

"Anarr seemed to think we were," Elody said. "You will be Eldest soon, the word of Anarr on Gondril. Why should it matter to you who Anarr calls his champion?"

Ilyaren raised himself up and stood over Elody, though not by much. Ilyaren's elven form was true to size, and Elody was tall for a human girl her age. Which put her eye to eye with the silver dragon in his current form.

"You will speak to me with respect, *girl*."

"*You* will do the same," she said. "I am the champion of Anarr, appointed by his own hand. You will be Eldest *if* Kalus dies."

Ilyaren fumed. Jalthrax could see his fists tighten and the veins in his arms pop out. Jalthrax took a step forward and raised his wings a little, though he wasn't even sure what he could do if Ilyaren did anything. He was the oldest dragon on Gondril. Probably the most powerful. Jalthrax could do nothing to harm him, but that didn't stop him.

With a shove that made Elody yelp, Ilyaren pushed past her and through the door. They could hear his hard footsteps echoing all the way down the tower.

Jalthrax felt Elody change instantly. She slumped, her shoulders and neck falling as she stumbled back. Jalthrax moved forward to catch her fall with his neck and let her lean against him. She put an arm around him for support.

"Thank you," she said.

He growled a response, but she couldn't understand him.

"Oh, I wish I could talk to you," she said. "The way he does. I'm so jealous he can just talk to you whenever he wants."

Jalthrax squawked, a pathetically simple response. Elody slid down and rested her back against him beneath his wing.

"Some champion we are," she said. "Even our own kind don't want us."

She was right. How would they convince dragons to listen to her. She had been charged with spreading Anarr's word to all dragons. That the bond between dragons and men had his blessing. But how could she do that when the dragon who was *standing* right beside her when she was anointed won't even listen?

And what if they couldn't stop Kalus? What would happen to all dragons if a true war broke out among them? Jalthrax already knew. Anarr knew it too. That was what made their role so important. No matter what, they had to deliver Anarr's message to his people.

But first, Kalus had to die.

CHAPTER THIRTY-NINE

GATHERING AN ARMY

GORTOGH WAITED IN silence, staring into the fire as he so often did. Kurgh would come for him any moment now, and he would face them. Touching the amulet for the dozenth time in the last hour, he felt a little surer of himself. Holding it in his hand filled him with comfort now.

His sword rested across his lap, glinting in the firelight. Gortogh wrapped his hand around the hilt and instantly felt the power within the blade. With the amulet in one hand, and his sword in the other, he felt truly powerful. The items were imbued with an immense power.

He only hoped it would be enough.

The sun peeked through the shaded opening of his cave as it crept across the ground. Kurgh was late. He should have been here by now. Gortogh was beginning to worry something had happened to him when he heard footsteps outside. Kurgh walked into the cave and nodded.

"They are ready," he said.

Gortogh took one last, deep breath and then stood.

Sheathing his sword, he followed Kurgh. They both climbed down the rocky path to the forest floor below. Gortogh could see Kurgh's buck standing patiently at the bottom. The deer had hardly left the shaman's side since they met.

"The strongest have arrived, so we can begin now," Kurgh said.

Gortogh nodded. Kurgh had already told him how this would work. A meeting of the tribal shamans was something that happened very rarely. It could just as likely lead to war as an agreement. It was not something called lightly. Gortogh had been against the idea when Kurgh proposed it, but it took little convincing for him to see it was the only way.

Kurgh had called upon his blood magic to cast a spell that only the most powerful of the shamans could cast. One that would send a call to all of Ogrosh's shaman and summon them to him. But it did not tell them why they were being summoned. They were simply expected to come.

Gortogh had one shot at this. If he failed, it was likely one of the shamans would simply kill him. Or worse, what remained of his tribe. But Kurgh had faith in him. Something he had never felt from anyone, even when others were enthralled by the amulet. They followed him blindly, not because they believed in him.

Kurgh had faith.

He had called the shamans because of that faith. And now Gortogh had to walk in there and imbue the rest of them with the same feeling. He had to make them see that his was the only way for them. If they did not follow him, Ogrosh would surely die. Maybe not right away, but it would happen. He knew it.

Through the trees up ahead, Gortogh could see the clearing the shamans waited in. It was midmorning, and there was no need for a fire, but still one burned. A tall bonfire stood in the center of the clearing, burning so hot Gortogh could already feel its warmth. But it wasn't the fire that gave him pause.

The bonfire was surrounded by hundreds of goblins. Each one a shaman ruler of his tribe or perhaps just a spiritual figure. But each one held great power granted to them by Ogrosh. Any one of them could have enough power to destroy him.

And they all wanted him dead.

"Stay close to me," Kurgh said.

Gortogh wasn't used to having someone else there to protect him. It made him uneasy. Being in a circle full of powerful goblins who want to kill you can do that to you. They took the last steps through the trees and into the edge of the clearing.

As they approached, the shamans parted to let them through. As they did, Gortogh could see a group of four shamans standing nearest to the fire, apart from the rest. Just like it had always been, there were five shamans who were considered the strongest and the most powerful. Only one of the five could call everyone here like this. Four of them stood glaring icily at him now.

Kurgh was the fifth.

Gortogh began his work long before it would be his turn to speak. His thoughts focused on the amulet, feeling it hum around his neck. The four shamans before them were focused on Kurgh. Gortogh ignored them. The rest were all looking at him. Some with hatred. Some curiosity. But all with great interest.

Gortogh thought of Ogrosh, of *being* Ogrosh. He

kept his gaze hard, the way a god would look upon his subjects. He met the eyes of every shaman who dared look at him and projected the power of the amulet on them. Some of the bitterness and hate left their faces in that moment. Others still would not be swayed so easily. He would need a display of power to show them the truth.

"Welcome, Kurgh," one of the four said.

He took a step forward, and Gortogh knew it must be Quorok. Kurgh had warned Gortogh about him most of all. He was considered by most to be the true leader of the shamans, and thus, leader of all the tribes. Though Kurgh insisted that the five were all equally as strong. Quorok pointed to the buck walking beside Kurgh.

"Did you bring us all a snack?" he asked.

He laughed, and the others joined him.

"That will hardly feed a few of us, let alone all of us," Quorok said.

Kurgh chuckled.

"He is not a meal, he is my friend."

Everyone laughed. Gortogh tensed, but Kurgh remained perfectly still and calm.

"Ogrosh sent him to me," he said.

"You made friends with your dinner?" Quorok asked.

More laughter. Kurgh with them. Then he stopped and glared at the four.

"You are all fools," he said.

He smiled, but the others didn't join him this time.

"You call us here to your pathetic tribe, and now you insult us?" Quorok said.

"I have learned so much since the last time we met," Kurgh said. "I called you all here to hear of my wisdom."

Quorok glared for a second before turning away. The

others began to join him, following him out of the circle. Guess they didn't want to hear what Kurgh had learned. Gortogh didn't blame them. If he had called some great meeting of warriors, they would have just killed him by now. Kurgh's little meeting was going much better than that so far.

"We have been to Ogrilon," Kurgh said.

That stopped them. The shamans all turned to look at him. Some with wonder in their eyes, others with skepticism or disbelief. The four looked at Kurgh as though he was crazy.

"What nonsense is this?" Quorok said.

Whether he truly thought it was nonsense or not, Gortogh didn't know. But the four of them had turned around and come back to where they first stood. Even from a few feet back, staying mostly hidden behind Kurgh, Gortogh could see the smile on his friend's face.

"You think Ogrilon is nonsense?" Kurgh asked.

"No, I think you are lying," Quorok said.

"Cast your spells of truth," Kurgh said. "All of you. See with Ogrosh's eyes that what I say is true."

Kurgh twisted in a circle, meeting the eyes of all the gathered shamans. Gortogh had warned him that this whole affair would be one great power struggle. Apparently, dedicating your life to Ogrosh didn't change the fact that they were all still goblins. They all still craved power, and they were all willing to kill one another to get the most.

Like all children of Ogrosh.

Gortogh saw many of the gathered goblins draw blood and whisper spells. There must have been more than a hundred present. Each from a different tribe. Goblin tribes only ever had one shaman if they had one at all. If each one here was from a different tribe, that meant there were more than a hundred goblin tribes. How could there be so many?

When the shamans had finished their spells, they all looked back at Kurgh who was patiently waiting. The four in front stood still, waiting for Kurgh to continue. None of them even moved to cast a spell.

"We found it," Kurgh said. "Gortogh and I found Ogrilon. And I have been to the great library and shared in its wisdom."

Gasps carried through the crowd. The ones who had cast a spell of truth knew now that Kurgh spoke it. They could see he wasn't lying. And their reaction was enough to paint doubt on the four shamans' faces.

"Tell us where it is," Quorok said.

"You believe me now?"

"Ogrosh would never lie. I believe you. Tell us where we can find the great city."

"Now is not the time," Kurgh said.

Murmurs flowed through the crowd. Quorok's face darkened.

"What treachery is this, Kurgh?"

"There are greater things at stake now," Kurgh said.

"You know where Ogrilon is, the city of legend. There is nothing greater than that."

"Ogrosh is in grave danger," Kurgh said.

He paused to let that sink in, but Quorok just laughed. The other laughed along as usual.

"How can a god be in danger?" he said. "Ogrosh is all powerful."

"The elves believed Ilothen all powerful as well. Now he is gone from our world, killed by his own brother."

"And who now threatens Ogrosh?" Quorok asked.

"The war between the dragons and humans, the war the new Eldest dragon has started, is growing out of control."

Quorok waved a hand.

"What do we care what the humans and dragons do? Let them kill each other for as long as they want I say. It can only make life better for us."

Gortogh could no longer stand behind Kurgh. He pushed his way in front and stood before the four.

"This is not just about men and dragons," he said. "This is about Anarr and Ogrosh and *all* the gods."

It was the first time he'd spoken, and he could feel the energy change in an instant. Hisses rose from the gathered. Quorok and the other three drew their knives and held them at the ready. Perhaps this was a bad idea after all. Quorok raised his knife to point at Gortogh.

"You have no voice here, betrayer," he said. "We all know the story now. You killed thousands of our kind for the glory of that elf. No doubt you would like nothing more than for your elven friends to kill all of us. Then where would Ogrosh be?"

Gortogh focused his mind on the amulet. Always there, humming softly on his chest. Pushing out with his thoughts, he tried to calm them. To make them see that he was a friend and only here to help. An almost imperceptible ripple went through the crowd. The tiniest change, but Gortogh could see some of the shamans soften toward him.

But that was only the start.

Now he would make them see the truth.

He *was* Ogrosh. He had to *be* Ogrosh. Had to feel it in every part of himself. Gortogh pulled himself up straight and rested his arms on his hips. He tried to appear strong, to look as he'd always imagined the powerful, beautiful Ogrosh when he was a child.

"*I* am Ogrosh's champion," he said.

There was no doubt in his mind, and no doubt in his voice.

"You are a murderer," Quorok said.

"No more than you or anyone else here," Gortogh said. "We all know the price for worship of Ogrosh. Blood. And death. It is our way. No matter the reason, those warriors followed me into battle and died a bloody death."

"You are proud of this?" Quorok said.

"No. I know the truth now. Ogrosh sent me to Molner to test me."

He looked around at all of them.

"And I failed," he said. "But Ogrosh failed all of us as well. I gave him another chance, and now he has given me one."

Shouts flowed from the back of the crowd as the anger built around his words. He knew that would insight them, which is what he wanted. Gortogh took a deep breath and channeled all of his strength, all of his will into one burst of power. Flexing his muscles until they strained, he roared as loudly as he could. At the same time he pushed with all his thoughts.

I am Ogrosh!

Some of the shamans in the outer circle fell to their knees, jabbering. Others looked at them with confusion, unsure of what to do. Were they really seeing Ogrosh made flesh before them? Was Gortogh really Ogrosh's one, true champion on Gondril? Some had already made up their minds, but the rest would take more.

And Gortogh knew just where it would come from.

Quorok drew his knife across his arm, cutting deep enough for the blood to gush. He grabbed it up and began chanting. Kurgh scurried back, but Gortogh stood strong. He could feel the amulet as a part of him now. Could feel the power that it gave him. It was more than just a bauble for tricking goblins into following him. It contained the blood of Ogrosh himself.

Never had Gortogh had much faith in Ogrosh. But standing there before the shamans, he was forced to believe. And it was working. The power of the amulet made him a believer as much as the rest of them. He knew the truth then.

He *was* Ogrosh's champion.

Quorok reached back and took flames from the bonfire behind him. In one quick motion, he threw them. They leapt from his hand and flew unwaveringly toward Gortogh. He closed his eyes. All he could do was stand and wait.

And pray.

He could feel the flames strike him. Could feel their heat around him, surrounding him. But he felt no pain. His fear faded in the moment it took to realize he was safe. Gortogh opened his eyes and folded his arms as the onslaught continued. The amulet pulsed against his chest, and the flames were thrown off like a discarded cloak. Quorok stopped and stood staring with his eyes wide.

That was all the display Gortogh needed. The rest of the shamans fell to their knees. Even Kurgh fell before him and bowed, burying his face in the dirt. It was a bit much, but it had the right effect. The other three high shamans sunk to their knees and bowed. Only Quorok remained standing.

Gortogh pushed out with his will once more. The

amulet thrummed and then pulsed, sending a wave of energy out in every direction. Quorok, the only one still standing, was thrown from his feet. He flew back and landed hard against the ground.

The shaman rolled to his knees and held his knife up. He went to stand, but as Gortogh stared into his eyes, his look changed. Quorok stayed like that for several seconds, never taking his eyes from Gortogh, until the knife fell from his hand. He bowed once and then looked up.

"Forgive me," he said. "My life and my tribe belong to Ogrosh."

All the others, Kurgh included, repeated the oath as Gortogh looked on.

Now he had an army.

CHAPTER FORTY

A MEETING OF MEN

THE KNIGHTS ARRIVED a little over a week later just as Berym had said they would. Everyone else to be at the meeting had arrived days ago. Now they all found themselves waiting for the last invitee.

Lord Dorn Kanden, High Commander of the Knights of Gondril, was the last to arrive. His squire announced him with more titles and fanfare than anyone Elody had seen so far, even King Tarathiel himself, who was almost five hundred years old. In her admittedly sheltered life, Elody had only met a few people who even had two names, much less one with so many titles.

Lord Kanden stalked into the room behind his squire, trailed by a retinue of knights to either side of him, like a shiny metal wake left by his boat.

"Lord Kanden," the king said, standing to greet him, "welcome to Nirorn. We have been anxiously awaiting your arrival."

The Lord Commander wasn't exactly late, but neither was he early. The rest of them had been there for several hours. Berym was there as representative of the knights until the High Command arrived, along with Father

Meral. Oryna alone had come to speak for the priests and priestesses of Threyl, but she spent much of her time talking with Father Meral.

The five dragons stood in their familiar elven form. Elody learned that after coming back for Eliath, Evranon was killed in battle. She had not met the new silver-haired elf who stood in his place.

And then there was Elody, Rinn, and Eliath.

They stood to one side of the room next to a stone pillar and tried to remain as inconspicuous as possible. So far, no one other than their friends had even acknowledged them. Elody kept worrying someone would come over at any minute and throw them all out.

The meeting took place in the same large banquet hall Eryninn's dinner was in. The king's council chamber was not large enough to accommodate this many people. To the left of the king stood his generals, looking quite perturbed. To his right was Eryninn, shifting nervously in his royal-looking clothes.

"The trip was long," Lord Kanden said.

His boots clacked sharply across the stone floor as he approached the king. Though the king bowed from the waist, the Lord Commander only nodded his head, a sign not lost on many in the room from where Elody was standing.

"The Knights of Gondril stand ready to defend her people once again," Kanden said.

"Then let us begin," the king said. "Rinn, please come here."

The king looked straight at them. Elody hadn't even been sure until that moment that anyone could see them. But now everyone was staring at them, waiting for Rinn. For his part, Rinn nodded and walked straight up to the king without hesitation.

"This man has been tasked by Anarr himself to kill the Eldest, Kalus," the king said. "And we will all see it done by any means necessary."

"Tell me," Lord Kanden said, "how will this be done?"

Rinn looked at the king who nodded. He reached under his tunic and produced the dragonbane crystal, letting it hang in the air a moment for everyone to see.

"This is a dragonbane crystal," Rinn said. "With it, I can kill the Eldest with a single thought. It is the same weapon the wizard Velanon used to kill the previous Eldest. Anarr has given it to me for this task."

Lord Kanden scoffed loud enough for everyone to hear.

"Are we to believe this boy spoke to a god? Did he invite you over for beer, boy?"

"I believe what he says," the king said. "And even so, it matters not where he got it. What he says about the crystal is true."

"Lord Kanden," Berym said.

He stepped before the Lord Commander.

"I will vouch for Rinn," Berym said. "He is as brave as any knight I have fought beside, sir."

Lord Kanden didn't look pleased at Berym's interruption, but he hid it well with a quick smile.

"My apologies for interrupting, your majesty," he said. "Please continue."

The king explained the plan to the Lord Commander while everyone else asked questions or just nodded along in agreement. The dragons remained silent on the matter, to Elody's surprise. Either they agreed with the plan the elven generals had laid out, or they were polite enough not to interrupt. Elody wasn't sure which.

The talk dragged on for hours. Rinn had rejoined them just as soon as he could get away, and the three of them sat bored in their little private corner of the room. The king had called for food to be brought in, and they had busied themselves with the table in front of them for a while, but now it was back to more talk.

Occasionally someone would raise their voice, and the three of them would bolt up and listen, but it was usually quieted quickly. Once everyone knew their part, the plan was mostly agreed upon by all the parties. Elody had already heard it, and there were few changes or new details. Just as she was beginning to nod off at the table, the door swung open with a loud bang.

An elven guard strode across the room to bow before the king.

"What is it?" the king asked.

"Highness, I'm sorry to interrupt, but there is a matter that requires your attention."

"Yes," he said, "speak."

"Sir, there are... two goblins outside the gate."

"Two goblins?" the king asked, annoyed. "You don't need my permission to shoot them."

"We tried, sir, but they're asking to come in and speak with you."

The king sat back in his chair and shook his head.

"And what do they want?"

"The one talking says that he is Gortogh the Mighty, Champion of Ogrosh, King of the Goblins."

Lord Kanden laughed out loud and was joined by some of the other knights. Some of the elves and dragons snickered as well, but in Elody's little corner of the room, no one was laughing. Elody remembered that name well. She would never forget it. She could see from how tense Eliath and Rinn were that they remembered him too.

Berym stepped before the king and bowed.

"Your highness," he said, "that is the goblin who attacked the city of Molner months ago. He was with the wizard when they killed Ferin, the Eldest."

"And now he is at my door?"

The king looked at the guard who could only shrug.

"That is who he claims to be," the guard said. "The other goblin made me repeat the title back so that I would deliver it to you correctly."

The laughing had stopped. The looks on everyone's faces had turned to confusion or surprise, some anger.

"Let him in," the king said.

"Your highness," Berym said, "you must not. We do not know what he is capable of."

"Sir Berym," the king said, "we are in a room full of knights, wizards, warriors, and dragons. Where else in all of Gondril could we meet someone under safer conditions? If this goblin wishes to speak with me and has somehow made it to my gate without dying, I would hear what he has to say."

Eryninn twitched next to the king and looked at Elody who could only shrug. The guard bowed and left, pulling the doors closed as he did. The room was silent except for a few private whispers as they all waited. When the doors finally opened, minutes later, there stood two goblins.

They looked like any goblin Elody had ever seen.

She wasn't sure what she was expecting, but it wasn't this. She wasn't even sure which one was claiming to be the king, though she thought it must be the taller one with the big sword on his back. The other one was cloaked in bones and feathers and looked like some sort of strange bird. Whoever they were, they had no fear walking into a room full of enemies.

"Your majesty," the tall one said. "I am Gortogh the Mighty, Champion of Ogrosh, king of the goblin people. I am honored you would see me."

"I must admit I am a bit surprised to receive you in my capital, Champion. I have never welcomed a goblin into my home before, so this is a first for me. What is it I can do for you?"

"You can stop everything you're planning," Gortogh said.

***

The room erupted into chaos. Lord Kanden yelled, Berym pleaded with the king to throw the goblins out, and the king tried futilely to bring order to it all. Elody just stared at the goblins in the middle of the room. They looked as calm as ever while the whole world seemed to burst around them.

When the king finally got everyone quiet, with a little help from the wizards, he stood before the self-proclaimed king of goblins and eyed him up and down.

"You know nothing of our plans," the king said, "yet you want us to abandon them?"

"Yes," Gortogh said.

"Why?"

"Your highness," Lord Kanden said, "this is ridiculous. We should not even be listening to this thug, much less asking him questions."

"I would hear what he has to say," the king said.

"This goblin is responsible for the death of knights under my command," Kanden said.

"And thousands of the people of Molner," Berym

said.

"I want him taken and strung up from your walls!" Kanden said.

The king looked hard at the Lord Commander and let his glare linger.

"You are in *my* kingdom, *Lord* Kanden," the king said. "Do not forget that."

Lord Kanden looked ready to reply but decided the better of it and took a step back. The king looked straight at Gortogh and nodded.

"I do not know your plans," Gortogh said. "I don't need to know them. Whatever they are, they will harm the people of Gondril."

The king had to raise his hand quickly before the outbursts even started, but it kept the room quieted down.

"And what does a goblin know of what is good for the people of Gondril? You *are* the one who led a goblin army in the Battle of Molner, are you not?"

"And the village of Jornath," Eryninn said.

The king looked at Rinn and Elody and then back to the goblins. Elody stared at them standing there, unable to move any part of herself. This goblin killed her father. Burned her village. Almost took away everything that she loved.

"All true," Gortogh said. "But none of that was my choosing."

The room erupted again, and the king was forced to employ a wizard's help to make his voice heard over the tumult. After everyone had stopped, the king stared down every man and woman in the room.

"If I have to shout again," the king said, "I will have a blanket of silence put over this entire chamber. Now, continue."

"The wizard Velanon," Gortogh said. "He forced me on threat of my life to attack Molner. I will not lie and say that my people were reluctant to do it, but I would never have willingly attacked a human settlement."

"Why should I believe you?" the king asked.

"Velanon manipulated me just as he manipulated so many. He didn't even care about Molner. He only wanted to draw the Eldest out so that he could kill her. All so that Kalus could become the new Eldest."

"But still you led the charge," the king said. "Do you think just because you were misled that you bear no blame?"

"Of course I am to blame," Gortogh said. "Why do you think I am here? I want to make it right."

"There is nothing you can do to make it right," Berym said.

Gortogh hung his head.

"You are all fools," the other goblin said.

Gortogh looked up and put his hand out, but the feather-coated goblin had already stepped in front.

"We attacked," he said, "we lost. Many thousands of goblins died. That is what happens in battle. We do not whine about it after. We have come to help you, but if you do not want our help, we will go and watch from the sides as you all dig your own graves."

"We don't need your help," Rinn said. "We have the power to stop Kalus. So you can just go."

Gortogh looked at them sitting there and shook his head.

"You have Velanon's magic crystal," Gortogh said. "The one that slays dragons."

Gortogh chuckled, but no one else was laughing.

"If you know what it is, then you know we need nothing from you," Rinn said.

"Where did you get that?" Gortogh asked. "No need to tell me, I know where you got it. From the hands of Anarr himself, no doubt."

Rinn looked down at Elody, and Gortogh stared at both of them. Rinn gripped her shoulder as Elody looked the goblin right in the eyes.

"We will stop Kalus," Rinn said.

"Don't you see?" Gortogh said. "This is what he wants! Anarr *wants* you to kill Kalus!"

"Why should that matter?" the king asked.

"Because it is Anarr's plan to rule over Gondril!" Gortogh said.

The dragons started to protest, but the king silenced them.

"And I suppose you spoke to Anarr as well?" he asked.

"I spoke to no gods," Gortogh said. "Just a wise old monk who showed me what I could not see. I thought that Velanon was just on some foolish crusade. To stop the dragons, he said. A thousand years ago, the dragons tried to wipe out the wizards to make dragonmagic the only source of real magic on Gondril. Tell me, what would it mean if that happened?"

The king looked to one of his wizards whose expression had changed to one of consternation.

"Velanon wasn't crazy," Gortogh said. "Kalus has put an end to dragonmages. He has begun a war with the other races of Gondril. And now Anarr orders his death."

"Because Anarr wants peace," Ilyaren said.

"Of course he wants peace," Gortogh said. "It's much harder to sneak up on someone who is waiting for an attack."

"But if Anarr wanted to rule the other races," Ilyaren said, "why not just let Kalus do the job he's already begun?"

"Because he cannot win," Gortogh said. "Not now. Look at yourselves. A room full of the most powerful people on Gondril, and you are planning Kalus's death. And you will win. Anarr knows that Kalus cannot win. Not now. He has been playing at this game for more than a thousand years, and he is patient enough to wait another thousand until the time is right."

"Enough," Lord Kanden said. "I have heard enough of this, and I hope that you have too, your majesty."

"Is that all you came to say?" the king asked.

"Whatever Anarr wants you to do," Gortogh said, "you cannot do it."

He paused and looked around the room. Elody could see on their faces what they were all thinking. This vile, stinking goblin is going to tell us right from wrong? Elody was thinking the same when the goblin turned at last to look into her eyes.

"The gods have cost the people of Gondril too many lives with their meddling," he said. "Only Threyl has never interfered with her people. She understood from the beginning. You cannot do what Anarr asks of you."

"See the goblins to the gate," the king said.

A guard moved to escort them out.

"When this is done," the king said, "perhaps we can speak again."

Gortogh bowed, but the other goblin only sneered. The guard led them from the chamber in silence.

"Well," the king said, "what do we do now?"

"You are not seriously considering what the goblin

said," Lord Kanden said.

"Only *I* know what I am considering, Lord Kanden, but neither do I know what everyone else thinks, and I would like to hear it."

"He is a murderer," Berym said. "That is all I need to know."

"Are we not all murderers in this room?" the king asked. "Anyone in this room who has never taken a life, step forward."

No one moved. Elody was still in shock from everything she heard. The goblin responsible for killing her father had just walked out of the room. No one stopped him. No one said a word. They just escorted him out.

"I do not kill without cause," Berym said.

"Goblins are evil," Eryninn said. "It is just how they are made."

The king shook his head.

"No one is willing to even consider what he had to say?"

"Perhaps he is right," Oryna said

She stepped away from the wall she'd been silently leaning against throughout the meeting.

"Forgive my impertinence, your majesty," she said, "but weren't the elven and dwarven people both nearly destroyed because of the meddling of their gods? Ilothen himself died fighting his brother because of their feud."

"You speak the truth," the king said. "But the gods affect our lives every day. Threyl answers your prayers, and those prayers change the world."

"But Threyl has never asked me to pray," Oryna said. "She has never asked me to pray for one person and not another. I have healed thieves and killers with her touch, and never once has she judged them unworthy. Threyl only gives me what I ask for."

The king seemed to think on that and then nodded.

"Then you believe we should heed the goblin's warning?" he asked.

"No, your majesty," she said, "only that we should consider what he said."

"We will consider it," the king said. "For now, we continue ahead as planned."

Elody didn't know what to believe.

As the talk went on, she had plenty of time to think on it. She tried to put who Gortogh was out of her head and instead listen to what he said. She had spoken to Anarr herself. Had stood in his presence. But did that mean she had to follow his wishes?

She didn't know.

What if this was all Anarr's plan from the beginning? Was Gortogh truly to blame for her father, or was he just following orders from the wizard? Would killing Kalus really bring about all the goblin had said?

She didn't know.

***

"I told you that talking to them would do no good," Kurgh said.

Gortogh smiled. The shaman was right, but that did little to dampen his mood this time. A contingent of a dozen elven guards escorted them to the eastern gate of the city and then stood watching as the big doors closed.

"What are you smiling at?" Kurgh asked.

"Just keep walking," Gortogh said.

He could feel the elves around him. The guards had stood perfectly still as they left and made no move to follow, but that meant nothing. The whole forest was crawling with the pointy-eared little devils. And they were always listening.

A little ways outside the city, they were met by Kurgh's buck who came walking up through the woods. Kurgh smiled and rested a hand on the creature's back as he had grown so fond of doing. Gortogh looked at him to say something but stopped as Kurgh drew his knife.

With a quick motion, Kurgh slashed into his arm. He was already chanting as blood poured down into his hand. They kept moving, Kurgh having no trouble chanting as they walked. When he finished, he reached out and touched Gortogh on the shoulder.

"Nosy little devils," Kurgh said.

"What?"

"The elves. I can sense them all around us. Several dozen at least. They must think we're quite the threat."

Gortogh chuckled.

"Whatever happened to goblins being sniveling and worthless?"

"I guess we've changed their minds," Kurgh said.

"We should keep quiet until we leave the forest."

"Oh, they'll follow us long after that I suspect. But don't worry. I've cast a spell that masks our speech. Anyone who catches the sound will only hear gibberish. It will make no sense to them."

Gortogh shook his head and smiled.

"You have quite a few tricks up your arm, Kurgh."

"*In* my arm you mean. Now tell me why you were smiling as we left. We learned nothing from all of that, and we've shown our entire hand. They know what we want now, and no one even bothered to listen to us."

"I never expected them to listen," Gortogh said.

"Then what was all of that for?"

"Because I know now who *needs* to listen."

Kurgh scoffed.

"I learned much from that meeting," Gortogh said. "I know who has the crystal, and I know how they got it."

"That girl and that man?"

"They are much more than that. The only way they could have the crystal is if Anarr gave it to them himself. They are the ones I have to talk to. They are the ones I must convince."

"What do you know of Anarr?"

"The monk told us the crystal was on the Isle of Dragons. The *home* of Anarr on Gondril. That is where they got it. Because Anarr wanted them to have it."

"And why should they listen to *you*?"

"I don't know that they will. But they are the ones I must seek. The elven and human kings will surely not listen, I knew that before we approached them. Though I am surprised they even heard us out. But they don't have the power to stop Kalus anyway. That man does."

Gortogh nodded to himself. He was sure this was how it had to be. How it was meant to be. He wasn't sure how he knew, but this was how it was supposed to happen. Anarr had his chosen, and Ogrosh had his.

All the pieces were in play.

CHAPTER FORTY-ONE

QUESTIONS

EXACTLY ONE WEEK after the meeting, the combined forces of the knights, priests, elves, and dragons marched once more toward Dragonhome and the Eldest who waited for them. And with those mighty forces, the likes of which Gondril had not seen for millennia, came Rinn, Elody, Jalthrax, and Eliath.

They all looked and felt painfully out of place.

The knights had given them a wagon, and the three of them rode together with Jalthrax flying above with the gold and silver dragons. Though some dragons died in the first battle against Kalus, many more still survived. Most of the wounds had healed now, but even wounded they would go. For the dragons of light, joining sides with the dark dragons was beyond what any of them could accept.

For this, Kalus had to die. Anarr had willed it, and now the dragons would carry out the orders of their god no matter the cost to their own. Even if something went wrong, they would not abandon the battlefield this time. For the dragons, the will of Anarr was all they needed.

Elody wasn't so sure anymore.

What Gortogh said had shaken her. She and Eliath had talked about it more after leaving the meeting, but even he said that Kalus should die. Elody didn't know whether that was because Kalus was the one who killed Tark or because that's what Eliath actually believed. Everyone had a different motive or a different reason it seemed. Who was she to believe?

On one of their stops, she found her answer.

"Hello," Oryna said.

"Hi," Elody said. "May I sit with you?"

She waved her hand at the spot on the ground next to her.

"It's not much, but I would gladly share it."

She smiled, and Elody sat down. She had only spoken with the priestess a few times since they met months ago before the Battle of Molner, but Elody had always felt a peace when talking to her. Like she listened to every word Elody had to say.

"Can I ask you something?" Elody said.

"Of course."

"Why do they call you Orphan Mother?"

"It is a nickname from when I was younger."

"You were an orphan?"

"For a time, yes. Though it was so long ago, I barely remember it."

"I doubt that," Elody said.

Oryna chuckled.

"You're right," she said. "It's just something I say to put people at ease. They want to hear that though things were tough there for a bit, everything is great now, and all of that doesn't matter."

"But it's not like that."

"No, it's not like that."

"Did someone take you in?"

"Threyl did."

"You mean the church?"

"No, I mean Threyl. She called to me. It was a terrible night, one of the worst of my life. There was nothing left for me to do but pray. So I did. And Threyl heard me. She called me to her and answered my prayer. From that moment, I became her devoted priestess."

"How old were you?"

"I was eight years old when she called me."

"Eight? You became a priest at eight years old? How is that possible? Didn't you have to train or something?"

"Do you know how to pray?"

"Of course I do."

"Did someone have to teach you how?"

"Well, my mom sometimes asked us to pray over a special dinner."

"But if you wanted to talk to Threyl, right now, would you need me to instruct you?"

"No."

"Then you already have all the training you need to be a priestess of Threyl. Congratulations. Now all you need to do is pray and be called to her service."

"So, she just called you at eight, and you could pray for power?"

"That is how it works, yes."

"I had to train every day for years and wait until I was fifteen to become a dragonmage."

"Well, most are not called at such a young age as I was."

"Was there ever anyone younger?"

Oryna smiled.

"No."

"Wait, I don't understand. Gortogh, the goblin, he said that Threyl didn't interfere with her people. And you said that she has never asked you to do anything for her. But she called you. She asked you to be one of her priests. Isn't that interfering?"

"The gods take pleasure in being mysterious," Oryna said. "Even Threyl. Perhaps especially Threyl. Of all the gods in the heavens, Threyl is the only one I know that has no home on Gondril. Each of the others has a place, somewhere in the mortal realm where they can meet and speak to their people. But not Threyl. She cannot speak to us, because she chooses not to."

"But just because she doesn't appear right in front of you doesn't mean she doesn't have a hand in all this."

"You are right. She does choose her priests, where many of the other gods let their priests come to them. They choose to become a cleric of their god, where Threyl chooses for herself."

"Then she does interfere."

Oryna chuckled.

"I suppose she does in a way. But once a priest, she asks nothing of us. She grants us power through prayer, but does not tell us where or how to use it. To my knowledge, I have never tried to use my powers for evil. But I have healed evil men. Men who, perhaps, went on to do evil things. Does that mean Threyl allowed the bad thing to happen?"

"I don't know."

"Nor do I, not for sure. But I do not think so. I believe Threyl would grant me my prayers even if I were to do something evil myself. The goddess does not define her priests as good or evil, though she does tend to call those who are good at heart. She chooses her priests, but they have their own will to decide what they will do with the power."

Elody sighed.

"I'm more confused now," she said.

"Gods," Oryna said and pointed to the sky. "Mysterious."

"So, Gortogh could be right. What we're doing right now could be evil."

"The same could be said of all actions."

"Now you're just *trying* to confuse me."

Oryna laughed.

"Tell me," she said. "If a goblin attacked your family, would you kill it?"

"Yes."

"And what if that goblin had a wife and small children who would die without him. Would you kill him then?"

Elody furrowed her brow.

"Yes," she said.

"I would as well," Oryna said. "But is it an act of evil? Those children will starve and die by your action. Some would say what you did was evil. But you did not mean for those children to die."

"But that's just it, you can do harm without meaning to."

"That is the consequence of any action. All you can do is what you think is right and hope that you are."

"So, is that what all this is? Hoping we're right?"

"I'm afraid so," Oryna said. "I wish that I could give you a more satisfactory answer, but I'm afraid I don't have one. But Threyl has taught me to follow my heart, and she has not led me astray yet."

"Then I guess I'll have to do the same."

Oryna smiled.

"That is all anyone can ask of us."

***

Rinn found Oryna resting against a tree, her eyes closed, deep in thought. He almost turned and left, not wanting to disturb her. She looked so beautiful and content sitting there. She had been through a lot with the wounded. And if something went wrong, things were about to get even worse. Rinn turned to tiptoe away.

"You're not leaving me are you?"

Rinn smiled. He should have known he couldn't sneak away from her. Rinn was a pretty sneaky guy, but she always had a way of knowing things she couldn't possibly know.

"I didn't want to disturb your meditation," he said.

"I was just lost in thought."

"About what?"

"Oh, something your sister said."

"Elody? What did she say?"

She took a breath and thought for a moment.

"Are we doing the right thing?" she asked.

"What do you mean?"

"I have been thinking… perhaps we shouldn't do this."

"Kill Kalus you mean?"

"Yes," she said. "Maybe the goblin king was right."

"About what? About Anarr wanting to take over Gondril?"

"It makes sense. What if we are playing right into his hands?"

Rinn scoffed.

"You do what Threyl wants you to do all the time."

She was on her feet in an instant.

"I do as I wish with the *help* of Threyl."

"It's the same thing," he said.

"I do nothing because she tells me to. I have never spoken to her. *No one* has ever spoken to her to my knowledge. So, no, I do *not* do as she tells me to do."

"So, because I actually *spoke* directly to a god, we're supposed to *not* listen to what he said? He's a god."

"The gods are mysterious, Rinn. I don't claim to know their ways or desires. I am only suggesting that maybe we should stop and think some more on this."

"Nothing? You want me to do nothing?"

"I want us *all* to stop and *think*."

"I have done nothing my whole damned life!"

He hadn't meant to yell, but his feelings were boiling over in a way he couldn't control. Why was he so angry? Why was he yelling at her?

"That is not true," she said.

"It must be so easy to be you," he said. "It must be so easy to have power and respect and a purpose. I'll bet you've never woken to a single morning where you asked yourself what you would do with the rest of your life."

"I never asked to be who I am."

"No, but it doesn't hurt now that you are. Things aren't so easy when you're nobody. Well, Anarr has made me somebody. He has given *me* the most important task on Gondril. It's my job to end this."

"This is not you," she said. "You are not this selfish person anymore, I know it. You don't need to impress anyone here, Rinn. You're important just as yourself."

"My whole life, I have never been important."

Oryna took a tentative step forward and reached out her hand.

"You're important to me," she said.

Rinn looked at her. Her face was soft and sad. What had come over him? Why had he gotten so angry at this woman who loved him? A woman he loved with all his heart. He looked down to where his hand was closed tightly over the crystal dangling from his neck.

Rinn hung his head.

"I'm sorry," he said. "I don't know what came over me."

She touched his arm and pulled him close.

"It's all right," she said. "I cannot imagine the stress you are under. All of this hinges on you now. It is an unfair position you've been put in. One, I believe, should not fall on your shoulders alone."

She picked up his chin and looked into his eyes.

"I believe in you," she said.

"I don't know if I'm strong enough," he said.

"I do. And if your strength falters, I will be right behind you to lend you mine."

Rinn wrapped his arms around her and crushed her to him. There were so many thoughts jumbling around in his head. He didn't know what to think anymore. Everything had seemed so simple when they left the island. He was given an important task, but a necessary one. One he was confident needed to be done. To end this all.

Now he wasn't so sure.

CHAPTER FORTY-TWO

DOUBTS

ELODY HOPPED DOWN from the wagon as a halt was called for the day. She stretched her back and wandered off in search of Eliath. She smiled when she rounded the tree and saw him there waiting for her.

As the marching army stopped each evening, they had been sneaking off for private lessons. Elody had been working on building up her own magic well so that she had *something* to fight against dragons with, and Eliath had been a huge help in her practice.

Also, she just wanted some alone time with him.

But she told herself it was for the training. Jalthrax spent his time split between her and the other dragons. He had even met some brothers and sisters, and although he'd never met them, family was family. She was happy he was getting along and now had someone to talk to, but it still made her sad he couldn't talk to her.

"Let's see it," Eliath said.

Elody smiled and took several steps back. Eliath arched an eyebrow, but she just closed her eyes. Reaching her thoughts deep inside her, she felt for her well of power. It was easy to find now. She'd gotten quite used to using it and had been practicing a lot. Drawing on her magic, she summoned enough to her hands to cast her spell.

Her hands made patterns in the air as her fingers weaved the blue threads of her magic. Elody pulled at the strands, feeling each one as though it were physically there in the air before her. The movements of this particular spell were fairly simple, but it required more power than she was used to drawing.

Without ever opening her eyes, Elody whispered something softly to herself. When she looked at last, Eliath was looking at her with the biggest smile.

"Did you hear it?" she asked.

"Of course I did! You can cast a spell of true sending without Jalthrax's power?"

"I told you I've been practicing," she said.

She curtsied and could hardly contain her smile. Seeing him look at her like that made her heart swell with pride.

"You really have come a long way," he said.

"I have to be strong if I'm going to be the champion of Anarr," she said.

His smile faded.

"What?" she said.

He stood quietly a moment before speaking.

"I just want all of this to be over," he said. "I hope that it can truly end once Kalus is dead."

Now it was Elody's turn to stand silent.

"Don't you want all of this to be over?" he asked.

"Of course," she said. "I'm just not so sure this is the way to end it."

"What do you mean? Kalus is the cause of all of this. And now we have a way to stop him. You and Rinn can put an end to *all* of this."

"But what if the result is something worse?"

"Can you think of anything worse than the deaths of thousands of dragons and dragonmages? Maybe the death of *all* dragonmages. Where would Gondril be then?"

"I don't know," she said.

"The knights and the dragonmages have kept a sort of peace ever since the kings fell. I have seen the parts of Gondril where there is no peace."

"But... what if the goblin was right?"

"You're going to listen to a *goblin* now?"

"No," she said. "I've spoken to others as well. I just don't know. I'm confused."

Eliath walked over and put both hands on her shoulders. He looked into her eyes and took a deep breath.

"You can do this," he said. "This is what we have to do. Gondril is being torn apart, and we have the chance to stop it right here and now."

Elody nodded. He pulled her in and hugged her tightly.

"I just don't want to see anything happen to you," he said.

But she wasn't thinking of Kalus or Gondril or the dragonmages just then.

All she could think about was Eliath.

***

Elody leaned against Jalthrax and rested quietly. It would only be another day or two before they reached Anarr's Teeth, and she was finding it harder and harder to sleep the closer they got. The slow, rhythmic breathing of Jalthrax beneath her comforted her. His scales were cool in the warm night. She laid her cheek against him.

"Bet that feels good," Rinn said. "It's hot out here tonight."

"There's room for one more," she said.

The two of them had barely spent any time together since their trip back from the isle. Rinn had spent most of his waking hours with Oryna. And with Rinn distracted, it was easier for Elody to spend more time with Eliath. But she did miss her brother.

She patted the ground next to her, and Rinn sat down. He laid his cheek against Jalthrax's side, putting them face to face. They sat together for several minutes, neither one needing to speak.

They could always do that, just be together without speaking. They had spent a lot of time together growing up. Rinn was her best playmate for all of her life. The one she did most everything with.

As much as she hated to admit it, he was the one who had always protected her. When there was danger, Rinn would put himself in front of her. When they got in trouble, Rinn always stepped forward and took the blame. And now he'd been tasked by a god to be her protector.

Someone was always trying to give him that responsibility it seemed.

"Long day," he said.

She nodded.

"This is nice," he said. "He really cools you down."

They both chuckled, followed by more silence.

"Oryna said you two talked earlier," Rinn said.

"I needed some advice."

"About... men?"

"Why would I ask a priestess for advice about men? I

probably know more than she does."

"I doubt that," Rinn said. "She... has her ways."

Elody slugged him in the arm.

"I'm not saying anything," he said. "Just that she's pretty smart when it comes to a lot of things."

"I like how she listens to me."

"She's good at that. I go on for hours sometimes, it seems, and she just smiles and nods through it all until I catch myself. She just laughs and tells me she likes listening."

"I guess you can get pretty smart if you listen to the world," she said.

"What did you two talk about?"

Elody hesitated. She and Rinn hadn't talked about what they were about to do. In fact, it seemed like Elody had talked to everyone *but* Rinn. She had been so concerned about her role in all of this, she hadn't even stopped to consider his.

Rinn was the one who would actually *kill* Kalus.

"Everything," Elody said. "I asked her if she thought we were doing the right thing."

"And what did she say?"

"I'm not sure."

Rinn laughed.

"She does that," he said.

"What do you think?" she asked.

He looked at her and sighed.

"I'm not sure," he said.

Elody rolled her eyes.

"I expected better of you," she said with a smile.

He seemed to think for a while before he spoke again.

"The elves have no god," he said at last. "The

Ilotharen I mean. They don't have a god, *really*, but they get on just fine. And Threyl. Oryna has taught me that Threyl doesn't interfere in the lives of her people. She gives of herself but asks nothing in return. Yet, all of her children also get along fine."

"So you think we are wrong?"

"I'm not saying that. Just that… well, so much of Gondril is a good and beautiful place without any help from the gods. And now, Anarr comes to us. Why? Why now? Why does he interfere when the others don't?"

"But what if we'd never met him?" she said. "What if we had gotten the crystal, and you had it now, and we had never met Anarr? You would use it to kill Kalus, wouldn't you?"

"In a heartbeat," Rinn said.

"If that is where your heart would lead you, why should it matter how you started down the path?"

"Because my killing Kalus would be to protect you, and I would do it without thought. But now, someone has made me think about it. I don't want to be the kind of man who rushes off and does the first thing he is told."

"But sometimes your instinct is your heart telling you what is right."

"But have we *really* thought about what we're doing? Have you?"

"A bit," she admitted.

"Then you must have the same doubts."

"Yes," she said. "I was hoping Oryna could tell me the answer."

Rinn chuckled.

"She doesn't really do that. If there's one thing she's taught me, it's that there is no clear right or wrong in any decision. You can only do what you think is right."

"And hope you are," she finished.

Rinn smiled.

"And hope you are," he said.

"Do you think this is right?" she asked.

Rinn looked down and thought a moment.

"I don't want to see more innocents die," he said. "If we don't stop Kalus, thousands of dragons will die, maybe as many mages. Thousands already have. Kalus is evil, I know that. And Dad taught us to fight against evil. He risked his life and went off to fight an evil king to make Gondril a better place for us. Shouldn't we be ready to do the same?"

Elody sunk down and laid her head on Rinn's leg.

"You're right," she said. "Dad would want us to do what is right."

Rinn put his arm around her.

"Then that's what we'll do," he said.

CHAPTER FORTY-THREE

THE NIGHT BEFORE

ELODY FOUND THE campfire Berym had arranged for them all easily enough. Jalthrax squawked behind her, and she reached back absentmindedly and stroked his head and neck.

"Come," Berym said, "sit."

He was stirring something in a pot over the fire while Eryninn watched on silently from his spot on the ground. Oryna was closest to her, so she sat down next to her. After their conversation on the road, she found herself feeling a little closer to the priestess.

"This is nice," Oryna said.

"Well," Berym said, "I know that you all have your own to sit with, but I thought we could eat together one last time before the world explodes."

There was that Berym grin. He always seemed to entertain himself more than anyone else.

Elody heard shuffling behind her and turned to find Rinn and Eliath. She wanted to ask Rinn to let Eliath sit next to her, but before she could think to say it, Rinn had already plopped down on the other side of Oryna. Eliath took the empty spot next to her, which made a part of her happy. But a little part missed her brother.

"I hope everyone's hungry," Berym said.

"If you are," Eryninn said, "there is plenty to be had at any of a hundred fires around you. I would avoid whatever is in *that* pot though."

"Quiet down," Berym said.

Berym handed everyone a bowl and then sat down next to Eryninn. The soup gave them all something to do and they ate in silence. Elody was thinking about tomorrow. Everyone else must've been too.

"Big day tomorrow," Berym said.

That was Berym. Always saying out loud what no one else wanted to talk about. Everyone nodded.

"We don't know what will happen tomorrow," he said. "No one knows what may happen on any given day. But tomorrow seems like one of those riskier ones."

"We have a plan," Rinn said. "One more day, and it will all be over."

"In more ways than you know," Berym said.

"What do you mean?" Elody asked.

"When Kalus is gone and the peace restored, I am leaving the knighthood. This will be my last command."

Eyebrows went up around the fire, but no one said anything.

"None of you look very surprised," Berym said.

"Happy," Elody said. "Not surprised, I'm happy for you."

"And the rest of you?"

"Happy and sad," Oryna said. "I guess this means I won't see you around Havnor much anymore."

"No," Berym said, "I plan to confine as much of my time as I can to Derne and… Narissa."

"And for that," Oryna said, "I am delighted."

"So," Eryninn said, "I'm just supposed to hunt goblins alone now?"

"I hope you don't have to hunt them at all," Berym said. "But if you do, you know where you can find me."

The knight smiled and clapped the half-elf on the shoulder. Elody could see now how close they'd become since they first met a year ago in Jornath. Eryninn was as quiet as ever, speaking only to interject the occasional opinion or dismissive comment. But with Berym, he seemed so much more at ease. The two sat together like old friends.

"What of the rest of you?" Berym asked.

"What do you mean?" Rinn asked.

"What will you do when this is all done?"

"You mean if we live?" Eliath asked.

Just for a moment, the fun stopped as everyone remembered what they were going to do tomorrow. They had gone over their roles a hundred times, but Elody knew from experience that meant very little.

"Back to Havnor, I guess," Rinn said. "If my aunt will still have me."

"I will stay with the elves for a while, I think," Oryna said. "Even with the best of outcomes, I will be needed to help the wounded for a few weeks at least. After that? I don't know. Perhaps it is time I went wandering again. The more I look around me, the more I see Gondril crying out for Threyl's love and compassion."

"More than ever, I would say," Berym said. "I thought long and hard about my decision to retire. Gondril needs the strong of heart more than ever it seems."

"Then why retire?" Rinn asked.

Berym sighed.

"Because I am tired," he said. "I have given my time

to Gondril and its people. Now, I think, I will take some time for myself."

He looked over at the four of them sitting together and smiled.

"I think Gondril is in capable hands," he said.

"I, myself, am not so sure of that," Eryninn said.

But Elody could see the grin on his stubbled face.

"Recruitment is up tenfold since the Battle of Molner," Berym said. "The knighthood will be stronger than ever in the coming years. Lord Kanden is a good man, if a little direct."

"He certainly is… something," Elody said.

"I know he can be rough, but he is just what the knighthood needs now. It was his vision after the Kingdom Wars that formed the knights for good to defend Gondril. He will make sure that another Molner never happens again."

Eryninn scoffed.

"I don't even think *he* is arrogant enough to make that claim."

"The knights are growing stronger," Berym said. "Soon they will be able to defend Gondril against any threat. That is a good time for me to let someone else have all the glory. And all the scars that go with it."

"What will you do with yourself?" Eryninn asked. "Just hang your sword over the fireplace mantle and stand your armor on a wooden dummy in the corner?"

"I was thinking of just putting it all in a chest," Berym said. "Her will be done, I won't need them anymore."

Eryninn squeezed his friend's shoulder.

"I hope that is true," he said. "I really do."

CHAPTER FORTY-FOUR

THE FINAL BATTLE

THE ROAR OF dragons and men filled the air, deafening everything in sight.

Elody clutched Jalthrax's neck for support. It had started so suddenly that it shocked her out of her thoughts, and she nearly leapt out of her robes. It's all for show, she reminded herself. The elven soldiers, the knights, the dragons, they were all shouting and roaring at the swarm of dragons circling Dragonhome.

Beside her, Rinn kept touching his chest, feeling for the crystal hidden beneath his tunic. Not that his tunic would hide it from Kalus, but he didn't seem to care. He just kept touching it to reassure himself that it was still there. The plan remained the same.

Oryna's chanting behind her was low and soft, and it gave Elody some small measure of comfort having her there. Most of the Threylian priests were ready behind the lines to heal any wounded, but Oryna had insisted on joining their small group as protection. Threyl could grant her spells that might hold back dragon magic for a short time. Any time they could get would help.

"Where is he?" Eliath asked.

He was almost shouting over the din of the army at their backs. The five of them were hidden at the edge of a grove of trees across the open expanse of ground that lay before Dragonhome. That ground had seem many battles and so much blood. Elody only hoped it would see very little today.

"This isn't how it was last time," Eliath said. "Kalus came right out and met with the king without fear."

"He knows we've been to the island," Elody said. "He's being cautious. Maybe trying to sniff us out to see what he can find."

"My spells will hide his prying for as long as I can keep it up," Oryna said. "It is up to the soldiers and dragons to draw him out."

"I can sense him," Rinn said. "I can feel all of them, thousands of them."

His fingers closed over the crystal beneath his tunic.

"I can feel Kalus. I know it's him. I don't know how, but I know exactly where he is and how to reach him. I could kill him right now with a thought."

"No," Eliath said. "Not now. The plan is to let him come to us. If you were to simply assassinate him as he hides somewhere in his hole, the other dragons would attack in revenge."

"You don't know that," Rinn said.

"If Berym fell dead right this minute," Eliath said, "would you pack up and go home, or would you shout and scream and charge for all that you're worth?"

Elody looked into his eyes and knew he saw the truth of it, but he never removed his fingers from the crystal.

"I can feel him," Rinn said. "And he's not moving."

***

"Where in the nine hells is he?" Lord Kanden shouted.

Berym bristled next to him. The elven king stood at his right with Eryninn beside him as they waited for Kalus to appear. The elven wizards chanted softly behind them, encasing them all in an unseen dome of magical protection should some dragon get brave.

"Thalaras," the king said, "order the rest of your dragons into the air. We need to put on a real show of it if this is to be believable."

The gold dragon, still in elven form, bowed and then left.

"They just circle," the king said softly. "Are they waiting for Kalus as we are?"

"No doubt Kalus is waiting on us to make the first move," Berym said. "If I had fought and soundly defeated a foe, and two weeks later they arrived on my doorstep for another fight, I would want to know what weapon they have behind their back."

"But we have superior forces," the king said. "With the knights and the priests, we are stronger now."

"Perhaps that is why he waits," Eryninn said. "Maybe he is not so confident this time."

Lord Kanden shouted orders to his runners, and they bolted off with messages.

"Perhaps we should start firing," Lord Kanden said. "That should provoke a fight."

"We do not want to provoke a fight," the king said. "We want to draw Kalus out *without* starting a fight."

"Might not be so bad if we took a few dragons with us," Lord Kanden said.

Berym had to swallow his pride and hold his tongue. He had spoken truly when he said the High Commander was a good man, but what he had not said was that Berym had always hated him. Too rich, too arrogant, too much. He had come from a wealthy family before the Kingdom Wars, and had used his influence after to bring the knights together.

For that Berym could respect the man, but he never liked being in his presence. In fact, he avoided it as much as he possibly could. He looked forward to telling him of his retirement at the conclusion of the day's events. Which he secretly hoped would start soon.

"He knows," Eryninn said. "He must know. Someone else has been feeding him information that we didn't know about."

"He cannot know," the king said. "Only my most trusted advisers and the ones standing here know that we have the dragonbane crystal."

"Somehow," Eryninn said, "he knows."

"If that is true," Berym said, "then our little staged battle will become a real one. We are prepared for that if it must be."

"Yes!" Lord Kanden said. "Draw the lizard out of his damn hole with a *proper* battle! He'll be forced to show."

Berym tensed his whole body and forced his ire down.

"That was not the plan," Berym said. "For now, we stick with the plan."

"Your plan was doomed to fail from the start," Lord Kanden said. "Draw the dragon out, murder him, and give a fancy speech about how wrong they've all been. Do you think they will just roll over and accept that?"

"You gave your objections at the meeting," the king said.

"Well, I may get it my way yet," Lord Kanden said. "If Kalus doesn't show, we will have to go in and drag him out."

"Let us be patient," the king said. "We are not in a hurry."

Lord Kanden scoffed and then stepped a few feet away to talk with his commanders. Above, a dragon screeched and then circled over their little group as it descended toward the ground. The dragon landed just behind them, and an elf slid from the saddle on its back and ran toward them.

"Your highness," the elf said. "Another army approaches."

"What?" Lord Kanden said.

He strode over to rejoin them.

"What other army?" the king asked.

"A goblin army, your highness," the elf said. "Ten thousand strong at least. They approach from the west."

"That is not possible," the king said. "We would have seen a force so big."

"They just appeared, my lord," the elf said. "One moment they were hidden by the trees, and the next they were there."

They all looked at each other in stunned silence, no one sure who should speak first. Of course, it was Kanden.

"The damn lizard set a trap for us!" he said. "The damn goblins must have found out our plans and then joined up with Kalus!"

"That's why Kalus was waiting," Eryninn said. "He was holding until the goblins arrived."

Lord Kanden spun around to one of his messengers.

"Tell Lord Hugo to take his brigade left and cut those goblins off!"

He was practically spitting the words, his face turning red.

470

"We've been tricked, gentlemen," he said. "And we must figure out what to do about it quickly."

"Call a parley with the goblins," Berym said. "Gortogh seemed reasonable enough. Talk with him. Perhaps we can stop this before it starts."

"With what?" the king asked. "When he came to us, we laughed and threw him out. I might have joined the other side myself."

"He will speak with you, your majesty," Berym said.

The king turned back to the elven scout.

"Find the goblin champion and tell him I wish to talk," he said.

The elf bowed and climbed back into the saddle of his silver dragon. With a whoosh of air, he was speeding to the west and the army of goblins that approached.

"Let us hope he will listen to us more than we listened to him," the king said.

***

Elody saw the dragons break off and fly west.

"Something is wrong," she said.

Everyone followed the dragons, but they saw nothing. Within minutes, the truth became clear.

"The goblins," Eliath said. "An army of them. Bigger than the one that attacked Molner even."

"What are they doing?" Elody asked.

"Marching toward us," Eliath said.

Everyone looked around with eyes wide. They were tucked away, just behind the trees in the little forest, but they were also right in the path of the approaching army. They would be spotted for sure.

"Why are they here?" Elody asked.

The panic in her voice rose. Their whole plan relied on them staying hidden until Kalus showed himself. Only then would they reveal themselves and deliver Anarr's message.

"They've stopped," Eliath said.

He was right. The goblin army had stopped just beyond the forest. The ones in back formed up behind the front lines and then just stood there waiting.

Elody watched as a smaller silver dragon glided down in front of the goblins to land before them. A small group of goblins came forward and met with the elf who dismounted from the dragon.

"The king must have called to speak with them," Rinn said.

"The question is," Oryna said, "whose side are they on?"

"You have to ask?" Eliath said.

"I would say the answer is not entirely clear," she said.

"He said over and over that we can't kill the Eldest because of something Anarr wants. So now he's here to stop us by fighting *for* Kalus."

"Eliath is right," Rinn said. "He was ranting about not killing Kalus."

They watched the elf talk to the two goblins who had broken rank with the rest of the army. They spoke for only half a minute before the elf mounted his dragon and then took to the skies once more. Some of the dragons from the other side had flown closer.

As they approached, Elody could see the goblins bring forward large war machines. Catapults, ballista, things she had never seen before, all pointed to the skies.

"What are they doing?" she asked.

"It looks like they came ready to fight," Eliath said.

To Elody's surprise, a group of goblins at the head of the army began to dance. She could hear them chanting, their voices rising as the dragons flew nearer. As one, they threw their hands to the sky, and she heard a loud thunderclap.

Then the heavens opened and rained blood.

The droplets fell from clear, cloudless skies, pouring over the field in front of the goblin army. As the blood hit the ground, it began to sizzle and smoke, some striking the approaching dragons. Their screams echoed across the field. The dragons suddenly thought the better of their approach and circled back to Dragonhome.

"They attacked the dragons," Oryna said.

"Maybe not all the dragons know the plan," Eliath said. "I wouldn't trust the dark dragons either."

The two goblins at the head of the army looked straight in their direction. Elody ducked behind a tree and waved her hand at the others to do the same.

"They can see us!" she said.

"They can feel us," Oryna said. "The shamans of Ogrosh are very powerful with their blood magic. They can sense the presence of life almost anywhere."

Eliath stiffened and drew his hands up.

"They're coming this way," he said.

Elody shot out from behind her tree and looked. He was right. The two goblins were coming straight for them.

"What do we do?" she yelled.

"We see what they want," Oryna said. "If it's a fight, we will give them one. Though I do not think that is what they want."

The two goblins knew exactly where they were hiding and walked swiftly and with purpose toward them. In a moment, everyone knew exactly who the two goblins were.

"Greetings," Gortogh said.

The other goblin Elody recognized from the meeting as well. The feathery one with all the clacking bones. Though she didn't know his name.

"You've just told the enemy exactly where to find us," Eliath said.

"They can see us no more than they can see you," the other goblin said.

"Kurgh protects us with the blessing of Ogrosh," Gortogh said. "Just as Threyl protects you."

"What do you want?" Rinn asked.

"To talk with you," Gortogh said. "You are the ones I must reason with. You must be made to see the truth."

"You already made your case," Eliath said.

"You do not understand," Gortogh said. "I am no king. I was not made to meet with kings and commanders. I am just a warrior who was tricked into doing something I didn't want to do. I don't ask for forgiveness, and I expect to receive none. I just need you to listen."

"This is madness!" Eliath said. "Because of you, people are dead."

He jerked a finger at Elody.

"Her father is dead! Tark is dead! Because of what you did!"

"*I* am listening," Oryna said. "Let him speak."

"You are all about to make a grave mistake," Gortogh said. "Just as I made when I did all those things you accuse me of. You are about to do the same right now. You are being tricked into doing just what someone stronger wants. Only they need you to do the hard work while they sit back and reap the rewards."

The goblin turned and looked right at Elody. He took

a step toward her but stopped when she inched back.

"I know that I am responsible for your father's death," he said. "I am not asking your forgiveness for that. I am only trying to make Gondril a better place for us all."

"Why shouldn't Kalus die?" Elody said, finding her voice. "Look at all that he has done. All the suffering he has caused."

"Perhaps he *should* die," Gortogh said. "But not at the hands of a god. None of us should meet such a fate. We are not things to be played with, yet that is what they do."

"When Kalus shows himself," Rinn said, "I will kill him. It is as simple as that."

Gortogh held up an amulet hanging from his neck.

"This amulet contains the blood of Ogrosh himself. Through its power, I was able to bend the will of thousands of goblins. I used them to kill thousands of people because I did what I was told. Men like your father. This is what Anarr is doing now. Bending the will of his people to destroy others."

"Yet you use it now to control your people," Elody said.

She pointed to the goblin army behind them all. Gortogh looked at her and nodded.

"But now I use my own judgement. I know which side is right, and I am on that side. And when this is done, I will find a way to destroy this amulet so that my own people can be free of Ogrosh, just as he wants. We must free the dragons of Anarr."

"We cannot merely ask him to leave," Oryna said. "What did you want us to do?"

"Are you actually listening to him?" Eliath yelled.

"I am willing to hear him out, yes," Oryna said.

She looked at Rinn who had pulled the crystal from his tunic and was twisting it between his fingers now.

"Rinn?" she said.

He looked at her, and his eyes softened just a little.

"I'm listening," he said.

"What would you have us do?" Oryna said, turning back to the goblin. "If we do not kill Kalus, he will continue killing more dragons and more mages. We cannot allow that."

"It is not Kalus we most stop," Gortogh said. "It's Anarr. Kalus is actually in the way of Anarr's plans, which is why the god wants him dead."

"But we have to stop him," Rinn said. "Whether it's what Anarr wants or not, it's what must be done."

"Then stop Anarr," Kurgh said plainly. "Think for yourselves. Don't do what Anarr has told you to do *merely* because he told you to do it. Do not follow orders blindly as Gortogh once did. As *I* once did. It will lead to ruin."

The shaman was watching Rinn with interest now, staring at his chest as he spun the crystal. Kurgh pointed to it.

"*That* is Anarr's influence," he said. "That crystal is the blood of Anarr."

"That crystal," Eliath said, "can destroy any dragon on Gondril, even the Eldest. Why would Anarr make such a thing?"

"To end a war that would cost him his children," Kurgh said. "He had no choice but to give up a piece of himself to stop Ogrosh from destroying him."

Somewhere nearby, drums started rhythmically beating.

"Is that our side?" Elody asked.

"I don't know," Eliath said.

"This crystal is our only hope," Rinn said. "Without it, we have very little chance of stopping Kalus."

"That crystal," Kurgh said, "is the last of its kind. The last of Anarr's soul on Gondril."

"Then it *truly* is our last hope," Rinn said.

"You must destroy it," Gortogh said. "And with it, Anarr's bond with the world."

"You're insane!" Eliath said. "If I hadn't thought you were crazy before, I *know* it now."

"We cannot simply give up our only real weapon," Oryna said. "It is our only chance to end this without more loss of life."

"Destroying it is the only way to end this for good," Kurgh said.

"Say that you are right," Oryna said. "What will happen if we destroy it?"

"I don't know," Gortogh said. "Anarr and Ogrosh will recede from the world, I think. At least that is what I understand."

"And you would let that happen?" Elody asked. "Let your own god lose his power? Maybe his life?"

"Ogrosh has learned from his mistakes," Gortogh said. "Just as I have. I believe he knows what we are doing and what will happen when we do. He has guided me here to see it through."

Gortogh's hand closed over a bronze amulet on his chest.

"I see that now," he said.

Oryna looked at Kurgh.

"You would do this?" she asked.

"It is the will of Ogrosh," Kurgh said calmly. "I would do anything for him. Even destroy him if that is his wish.

But I do so now with my eyes open."

They were willing to give up their own connection to their god to see this done. Elody didn't know why, but she believed them. Her doubts became real then, and she understood.

"The crystal is evil," Gortogh said. "It was not made to be so, but Anarr and Ogrosh both tried to poison it against one another. In doing so, they made it a weapon instead of the symbol of peace and cooperation it was meant to be."

"You have to destroy it," Kurgh said. "It is the only way to stop the gods from meddling with us all. It is what Ogrosh wants."

"Well, let's just do that then," Eliath said. "Because doing what Ogrosh wants instead of Anarr sounds like a fine idea!"

"Ogrosh only wants to make right what he made wrong," Kurgh said. "He is banishing himself from the world so that we can all choose our own path. That is the sacrifice he makes for us."

The roar of a thousand dragons split the sky.

Elody's ears felt like they would burst, and she held her hands over them to stop the ringing. She saw the dragons circling Dragonhome break off and fly straight for the invading army. The gold and silver dragons went to answer them.

The fighting had begun.

"We have to destroy it!" Gortogh said.

The sky exploded.

Fire, acid, lightning, and ice rained down through the trees above as the dragons crashed into one another. All of it bounced off of a barrier above them thanks to Oryna and the crystal, but Elody ducked out of instinct.

Jalthrax pulled at Elody's hand, but she jerked him back and gave him a hard glare. The screeching of clawing, biting, dying dragons drew them all up to the fighting.

Elody grabbed Rinn by the shoulder and spun him around.

"We have to do something!" she said.

"What do you want me to do?" he shouted.

"What if he's right?" she said. "What if we have to destroy it?"

"Then we're all dead," Rinn said. "If we destroy this, we have nothing to fight with. It will be our army against theirs."

"And ours," Gortogh said. "My men are ready to fight if we must."

Rinn looked at her, and she could see that he didn't know either.

"I know this is what must be done," Gortogh said. "I don't know how I know, but I know."

Rinn took the crystal from around his neck and looked at her. She nodded. She didn't know why, but she nodded.

"Don't," Eliath said. "We can't do this. They're counting on us to end this."

"Then we will end it," Rinn said.

***

"We need more support from your wizards!" Lord Kanden shouted.

Berym saw the king nod, but he gave no other orders. He knew they were already doing as much as they could. Kalus's dragons had attacked without warning or provocation, but they were ready for it.

The skies were filled with swirling, clawing, biting dragons. Fire and ice met to make large clouds of steam.

Sprays of acid rained down over their soldiers. Things were going well, but they had only just started.

On the ground, the elven wizards were pummeling the dark dragons with powerful magic. Many younger dragons fell after only a few blasts. Berym had never seen wizards fight. They were quite adept at hunting dragons. But it was the elven soldiers and knights that drew Berym's attention the most.

A thousand crossbow bolts filled the air as they were released in volleys from the knights, followed by the thump-crack sound of catapults lobbing boulders into the air. A blue dragon roared and then was hit in the head with a boulder, dropping it like a stone.

"The goblins said they were on our side," the king said. "Why aren't they attacking?"

Berym had almost forgotten about them. The king was right. The goblins just stood ready to fight, but none of them moved or responded. Even from here he could see the siege weapons and machines they had brought for fighting dragons, but they had yet to fire a single shot.

"And where is Kalus?" the king asked. "We can hold long enough, but the idea was to lose as few lives as possible."

That was already looking like a lost plan. The battlefield was littered with the bodies of dragons. Some dark, some light, almost all dead. A group of knights was running to Kalus's dragons as they fell and stabbing them down with long spears designed for just such a purpose. There was blood everywhere.

And then he appeared.

Kalus stepped from his cave and spread his wings, stretching them to the sun so that they caught the brilliance of his golden scales. He roared a challenge to them and then leapt into the air.

"Let us hope Rinn ends it quickly," the king said.

Let us hope.

***

Gortogh swung his sword down with all his strength. Elody could see his muscles ready to burst through his skin as he tensed for the blow. The sword struck true, hitting the small crystal right in its center, and she flinched expecting some kind of explosion.

Nothing happened.

The crystal was pushed into the dirt a bit, but otherwise, it looked the same. Not even a scratch where the sword had hit it. Not deterred, Gortogh took several steps back and moved everyone out of the way. He pointed the tip of his sword at the crystal, and Elody watched, amazed, as a bolt of blue lightning coursed down the blade and leapt from the tip.

It struck the crystal with a loud bang. The ground exploded, sending clumps of dirt and grass high into the air. But when the smoke and dust had cleared, the crystal was still there. In a large hole now, but still unmarked.

Eliath chuckled.

"You cannot just destroy something made by gods," Eliath said.

"There were once five of these," Gortogh said, "only this one remains. Someone figured out a way."

"This is foolish," Eliath said. "We should be using that crystal to end this. Can you not hear the suffering of the dragons in battle? Don't you hear the screams of the dying? We have the power to stop this!"

Elody saw, for the hundredth time, the doubt in Rinn's eyes. She put her hand on his arm.

"What else can we try?" she said.

Jalthrax took a step forward and blasted the crystal with his breath. Elody saw the frost collect on its surface and thought, for just a second, that maybe he could do it. But when he stopped, nothing had changed.

"Wait," Kurgh said. "The crystal was made to bond goblins and dragons together. Ogrosh and Anarr made it to bond their peoples together in blood. The high shamans were the first true dragonmages."

"So?" Elody said.

"So perhaps it requires the same bond to break it," Kurgh said. "Perhaps you two need to destroy the crystal together."

Elody looked at Rinn who only shrugged.

"Thrax?" she said.

The dragon looked at her and nodded. She reached her mind out toward him and felt the dragon's power flow into her fingertips. They curled with power, the magic crying to get out. She began casting her spell, weaving the blue threads of energy between her hands. Beside her, Jalthrax sucked in his breath.

She released her spell at the same moment he released his breath. They both hit the crystal with a wave of freezing ice. Elody couldn't see through the fog of frost, so she just blasted it with everything she had until the magic was all used up. When all was done, the crystal remained intact.

"He's coming!" someone shouted.

They all looked up to where an elf riding a silver dragon circled overhead.

"Kalus is coming this way!" he yelled.

They all looked at each other in a panic.

Kalus was coming.

CHAPTER FORTY-FIVE

THE UNBREAKABLE BOND

"PICK IT UP!" Eliath said. "We have to stop him."

"No," Gortogh yelled. "We have to stop *all* of it."

Elody didn't know what to do. When she looked at Rinn, she could see he didn't know either.

"What should I do?" he asked.

"I don't know," she said.

"If we can't destroy it, are we supposed to use it?"

"Yes!" Eliath said. "Pick it up and use it. End this *now*."

They all felt the ground shake as Kalus, the Eldest, landed before them. He was obscured by some of the trees they had been hiding behind, but he obviously had no trouble finding them. Had he sensed the crystal, or had he merely followed everyone to them?

Before anyone could move, Eliath ran into the hole that held the crystal and picked it up.

"No!" Elody screamed.

She saw his body jerk and spasm and almost ran in after him, but Rinn grabbed her arm and pulled her back.

"Rinn, let me go!" she yelled.

But he held her fast. She pinched him, and he let her go with a yelp, but by the time she got loose, Eliath had stopped. Without looking back, he held the crystal up for Kalus to see. From the look on the dragon's face, he didn't know they had it.

Kalus roared, shaking the ground.

He inhaled and blasted them. The breath of a thousand-year-old dragon is as intense as any power on Gondril, but they felt none of it. The flames licked and lapped at them, but they flowed to the sides, blocked by an invisible barrier.

"Did you do that?" Elody asked Eliath.

He shrugged.

"It was me," Oryna said, panting. "But I can't take much more. We have to do something."

Eliath turned to face Kalus and closed his eyes.

"No!" Gortogh shouted.

Kurgh raised his arm, and Elody saw a white knife in his hand.

"No!" she screamed.

Elody didn't expect the shaman to cut *himself*. It confused her for a second. He gathered blood as it poured from his wound and began chanting, praying to Ogrosh. And he was looking straight at Eliath.

Elody ran, taking three bounding steps, and crashed into Kurgh. The blood in his hand dribbled out before he could finish his spell.

"Stop this!" Gortogh yelled.

The shaman shoved her off and stood ready with his knife. The wound on his arm had begun to close over, but he sliced it again and drew more blood. She tried to get close to him, but he waved the knife at her, and she stumbled back.

Jalthrax was at her side, and she heard him draw a breath.

"Stop it!" Oryna yelled. "You'll kill us all!"

But Elody wasn't sure who she was talking to. Jalthrax drew his breath, but Kurgh finished his spell before he could attack. A blade made of blood flew from the shaman's fingers, aimed straight at Eliath. He wasn't even looking. He was so lost in trying to control the crystal that he never saw it coming.

But Rinn did.

He leapt in front of the blade's path. It hit him in the stomach, slicing through armor, clothing, and skin. His face contorted. Blood gushed from the wound, and Rinn collapsed.

Elody screamed and ran for him.

Kalus drew in another breath and blasted them all again.

"Oryna, help!" Elody cried.

"I can't!" she screamed. "We'll *all* die if I drop this barrier!"

Elody cried out and fell over her brother.

***

Gortogh watched as everything fell apart. The blade hit the man, Rinn, in the stomach and cut him wide open. Kurgh took a glancing blow from the breath of the silver dragon but managed to get out of the way of most of it. The other man, Eliath, was trying to use the crystal to kill Kalus.

Elody screamed and ran to Rinn.

"Come out of there!" Kalus roared.

He began ripping what was left of the trees apart to get at them. He breathed deeply and blasted them all with another breath. Gortogh ducked, but the flames spread around them once more, never nearing them.

"Oryna!" Elody yelled. "Help him!"

"I can't!" Oryna said. "If I drop this barrier, we'll all die!"

The girl was crying, wailing. Kurgh ran to her and grabbed her shoulder.

"Get off!" she said.

"I'm trying to help him!" Kurgh yelled.

They fought. Gortogh didn't know what else to do, so he ran for Eliath to stop him. He tackled the man, and they wrestled on the ground.

"You'll kill us all!" Eliath yelled.

Gortogh didn't have his sword in his hand, but he still had some of the residual strength. He fought the man off easily enough and wrapped his hand around Eliath's clenched fingers.

"Let go of me!" Eliath said.

Gortogh pried his fingers open and grabbed the crystal with his other hand. He wasn't prepared for what happened next. The instant his hand closed over the crystal, he felt like he'd been hit by a boulder. His head jerked back, and his body spasmed.

He could feel the crystal reaching for his mind. Its power was seeking him out, trying to overwhelm him. And it was winning. Gortogh was smart for a goblin, but he had no true power. He had no training with magic.

The crystal grabbed at his mind, and he felt something hot against his chest. He looked down and saw the amulet of Ogrosh glowing red. The amulet and the crystal fought for his body and soul. Try as he might, he couldn't open his hand to drop the crystal. Nor could he pry the amulet from his neck.

With a loud blast, Gortogh was flung back against a

tree. He slumped to the ground and shook his head. Only his magical strength saved him from breaking his spine. His vision blurred for a moment. When he could finally see, his hand was empty. The crystal was gone. He crawled to his knees and searched for it. For a moment, he thought maybe it had been destroyed.

He saw it.

Lying where he had stood only a moment earlier, the crystal rested on the ground waiting for someone, anyone, to pick it up. Waiting for someone else to control and seduce with its poison.

Elody shouted something, and Gortogh looked up to see Kurgh cut his arm and draw the blood out. Before Gortogh could stop him, Kurgh pressed the blood into the man named Rinn's wounds and chanted. The gash across his stomach closed over, and the blood stopped.

"Rinn!" she said.

The man opened his eyes and bolted upright. Elody threw her arms around him, and he hugged her back. Her tears came even harder now, and the man cried too.

It was such a strange thing to see. Gortogh had never known goblins to have such a bond. Such a fear of losing one another. Brotherhood was not something goblins knew of anymore.

In that moment, Gortogh knew the answer.

He knew how to destroy the crystal.

"The two of you," he said.

Gortogh rushed over to grab them both by the arm.

"The two of you have to destroy it!" he said.

Rinn was trying to stand, but Elody had to help him up. Gortogh grabbed Rinn's arm and helped him.

"Don't you see?" Gortogh said. "The crystals were formed in blood. The unbreakable bond between brothers. That is what it takes to unmake the crystal. The two of you must destroy it together!"

They looked at each other and then looked back at him, confused. Gortogh pointed at the crystal.

"Do it," he said.

"How?" Elody asked.

"Hit it," Gortogh said.

"With what?" Rinn said.

Gortogh looked around for his sword, a rock, anything. He felt the heat of the amulet against his chest and had a better idea. He pulled the amulet from his neck and held it out.

"With this," he said. "Smash it with this."

He took Rinn's hand and slapped the amulet into it.

"Smash it!" he said. "The two of you, together."

He pointed to where the crystal lay on the ground. They took two steps toward it and then looked down.

"Go on!" Gortogh said.

Brother and sister knelt down. They looked at each other, and took a last, deep breath. And then smashed the amulet down onto the dragonbond crystal as hard as they could.

Gortogh heard a loud bang and felt his feet leave the ground just before everything went dark.

***

Elody heard a roar of laughter through the darkness. She tried to clear her head, but all she heard was ringing in her ears. It stung to open her eyes, and she was nearly blind. Slowly, she began to see again.

The trees around them were gone. Leveled flat. She looked down and saw the broken amulet sitting on the ground. When she picked it up, the pink, shattered remains of the crystal lay beneath it.

They had done it.

"Fools!" Kalus roared.

Elody looked up to where the dragon was standing before them, laughing. Her eyes could only just focus, but she could see enough to see his shape in front of her. Around him, dragons lay everywhere. It was then that Elody noticed the skies were a bright blue. They weren't dark and clouded with flying beasts.

Every dragon had been knocked from the sky by the blast.

Rinn stirred, and she grabbed his arm to help him sit up. Eliath was already on his feet and holding his hands out feebly.

Elody managed to get to her feet, but she wobbled when she tried to stand. She felt Jalthrax push against her, and she reached out for his magic, even though she knew her spells would not harm Kalus. Just being near Jalthrax gave her strength. She leaned on him for support.

"Anarr wants this to end," she yelled.

Kalus only laughed harder.

"You speak for Anarr now, little girl?" he said. "Of course you do, you're hearing his word as I speak. *I* am Anarr's word on Gondril, little mage."

"You are wrong," she said. "Anarr wants you dead for all that you've done. I am his champion!"

"You are nothing!" Kalus said. "Whatever blessing of Anarr you had, you have lost it. Look for yourself."

Elody looked down to where he nodded at Jalthrax and saw that something was different. Her eyes stung from the bright light, but she looked and saw that Jalthrax no longer glowed a silver sheen. His scales were now nothing but white. They still reflected the sunlight, but they no longer had their brilliance.

"Anarr has taken his blessing from your dragon, little girl," Kalus said. "You do not speak for Anarr. He has forsaken you. And now you have no power to stop me."

"Take a look at yourself, Kalus," Gortogh said.

Elody didn't know where he'd come from, but he looked about as steady as she felt. Everyone was on their feet now, but few looked like they could hold it for long.

"The little goblin king," Kalus said. "How nice of you to put yourselves all in one tight little spot for me to dispose of at once."

"It is you who have lost Anarr's blessing," Gortogh said. "It is *you* he has forsaken. *You* have lost his brilliance."

Kalus snorted but pulled his claw forward and stared at it. Even with her eyes too blurry to see, she could see Kalus's color. He was no longer gold. His claw was red. His face was red. His whole body was red.

"What?" Kalus screamed.

"Look around you," Kurgh said.

Kalus's head spun in every direction, and the rest looked with him. All around there were no dragons of light to be seen. The ground began to stir as the dragons woke from where they fell, but Elody could hear from every direction that they had all discovered the same thing.

There were no more dragons of light. No more of Anarr's brilliance.

No golds, no silvers… nothing.

"What have you done to me?" Kalus roared.

"It is not what we've done," Kurgh said. "It is what Anarr can no longer do. He cannot help you anymore, Kalus."

The dragons were stirring now, and Elody saw a shadow from behind as two larger dragons stood over them. They were white and red, but she didn't know if they were friend or foe. They didn't move to attack, but she could only hope they were friends.

Kalus took a deep breath, and Elody flinched. But when he went to breathe out, nothing happened. Kalus gagged and sputtered. He tried again, but again he could not breathe his fire. Kalus thrashed like mad, clawing at the ground and roaring.

"What have you done?" he screamed. "Attack! Kill them all! They have killed Anarr!"

No one moved.

The dragons lay in disarray, none of them knowing what to do or even who to follow. Even Jalthrax could only stare at his own scales in disbelief. Kalus looked around for someone, anyone, who was an ally. He found a blue dragon nearest him and must have recognized him.

"Vaylin!" he yelled. "Kill these humans! Order the attack on the gold and silver dragons!"

"There *are* no more gold and silver dragons," the blue dragon said.

"I want these people dead!" Kalus screamed. "I order you! I am the Eldest!"

Vaylin sneered.

"The decree says that I follow the eldest *gold* dragon," he said. "I see no gold dragons here."

Kalus roared and turned on the blue dragon and the others behind him.

"You!" he said to a huge red. "Destroy these puny people!"

The red dragon behind Vaylin looked around at all

the other dragons on the ground. They were starting to get up now. Some had even taken to the sky and flown away. Some were circling above, not sure what to do next.

"Do as I say," Kalus said, "or our arrangement is off! You will lose everything I promised! You will be nothing once again!"

The red dragon chuckled.

"You said if we helped you, you would see to it we were treated as equals," he said.

He looked left and then right and shrugged.

"I'd say we're equal," he said. "Thanks, *Eldest*."

The big red laughed, and others around him joined in.

"Come on," the red said.

And with that, he leapt into the air and flew off toward the mountains. And once one or two left, they all began to leave. Elody wasn't sure which ones were dark dragons and which were formerly dragons of light, but it didn't seem to matter. They were all leaving now.

Kalus roared and flapped his wings, taking to the sky. He drew in another breath and looked down at them. Elody yelped and crouched down, and Rinn threw himself over her. But another roar from behind made her look up in time to see the large white and red flying straight for Kalus. They were joined by two other red dragons as a battle ensued.

Kalus roared and bit and snapped at every dragon in sight, friend or foe. Though Elody doubted he had many friends left. Fire, ice, and steam filled the sky as they fought, but in the end, Kalus roared and flew away. The red dragons gave chase for only a few seconds before turning back.

All around, the dragons were looking at themselves

and others. No one could tell the dragons of light from the dark dragons. None were more brilliant than another. Did that mean they were all dark now? Elody knew better.

"We did it," Rinn said. "We stopped Kalus."

"And rid the world of Anarr's influence at the same time," Gortogh said.

Elody put her hand on Jalthrax and knelt down.

"Are you okay?" she asked.

Jalthrax looked at his scales again and nodded.

"You're not hurt?"

He shook his head, and she threw her arms around his neck. She felt Rinn beside her as he put his arms around her.

It was over.

They had done it.

CHAPTER FORTY-SIX

GOING HOME

ERYNINN STOOD ON top of a hill watching the knights break camp. The elves were doing the same, and most of the dragons had already flown. The ones who would never fly home were still left to deal with, but that was for another day.

He heard Berym tromping up the hill behind him, as loud as ever. They stood, watching, for several minutes before someone spoke.

"You're really doing this?" Eryninn asked.

"I really am," Berym said. "I've already told Kanden."

It would be another day before all the camps were broken and the soldiers on the march. The grassy plains between Molner and Dragonhome were littered with the remains of battle, the blood-soaked earth looking parched. What little grass had been was burned or blasted during the battle.

The plains were a wasteland for the dead now.

"Gondril is marked with so many scars like this one," Berym said.

"As is her history," Eryninn said.

Berym nodded, followed by more silence.

"Did we do something good here?" Beryl finally asked.

"Who decides what is good?"

"Do *you* feel good about it?"

Eryninn looked around and shrugged.

"I don't know what to think," he said. "Anarr has lost much of his power, and from where I stand, the less we see of gods, the better off we all are."

"But what if Anarr was one of the good ones? What if, now, we are left with something worse?"

"You mean Ogrosh?" Eryninn asked.

"I mean any of the dozens who would seek to replace him in power."

"You mean Ogrosh."

Berym looked west where the goblin army was still camped, and Eryninn saw him shiver. It was a frightening sight. Not something most humans on Gondril could ever see and live to tell about.

"I do not think so," Berym said. "This Gortogh... I don't believe that's what he wants."

"This is not about what he wants," Eryninn said, "this is about what Ogrosh might want."

"If what I hear is to be believed, Ogrosh wants a peace between our peoples."

Eryninn shook his head.

"I find that very hard to accept."

"As do I," Berym said. "But shouldn't we try?"

Eryninn smiled.

"I will miss our talks, old man," Eryninn said.

"Old?" Berym said. "You are more than ten years my senior."

"Yes, but you will always *look* older than I do."

The two men grasped arms and held them like that

for a long while.

"What am I going to do without you to hunt with?" Eryninn asked.

"I think you'll do fine with your new friends."

"They don't have your subtlety," Eryninn said.

The knight laughed long and hard.

"No," he said, "I suppose they don't."

"Will you come and visit?" Eryninn asked.

"If you tell your friends not to shoot me on sight, I will."

"Oh, I think you will always have a place in Ilothar."

"Is that where you'll stay?" Berym asked.

"My uncle has asked me to stay with him, yes."

"He's not a bad guy, your uncle. You should have met him sooner."

Eryninn grinned, and Berym pulled him into a hug. Hugs always made Eryninn uncomfortable, and this one was no exception. But he found, this time, that it had more to do with the knight's armor than his arms.

He gave Berym a clang on the back.

"Go home," Eryninn said.

"You too," Berym said.

***

Elody found Eliath sitting among the scorched earth and flattened trees where they had been during the battle. While the rest of the forces were packing up, he had remained here, sitting silently. She walked over and sat down next to him.

They remained like that for several minutes. Just sitting and watching.

"I'm sorry," he said.

"There's nothing to be sorry for," she said.

"I could have gotten us all killed."

"Any one of us could have gotten us all killed. It's just one of those things that can happen in a battle."

Eliath nodded.

"Where's Jalthrax?" he asked.

"Flying around somewhere," she said. "Still getting used to being a white dragon, I think."

"I still can't believe that."

"I guess the dragons of light received Anarr's blessing while he was around, but now that he's gone, they look just like all the others."

"Tark would have been *so* tickled to see it. Everyone the same now, no light or dark."

Elody laughed at the thought of the big red taking pleasure in all this. He most certainly would have.

"The dragons of light have always been bigger and lived longer than dark dragons," Eliath said. "I wonder if that will change now."

"I don't know. Might take a few hundred years to see, and we'll both be dead by then."

Eliath forced a chuckle.

"Do you really think Anarr is just gone?" he asked.

She waved her hand at the remaining dragons, all of whom were now colored red, white, black, green, or blue.

"Something big happened," she said.

"What did you think would happen when you broke the crystal?"

"I didn't think we could break it. I just hit it, but I expected nothing to happen. If I could have used it myself, I probably would have picked it up and killed Kalus before he burned us all up."

"That's all I was trying to do," Eliath said.

"I know that. I would have done the same if you were in danger."

He looked into her eyes, and even with all the death and destruction surrounding them, she still felt a flutter in her chest.

"I don't know what I'd do if something happened to you," he said.

He was staring at her, looking deep into her eyes.

"I don't—"

He kissed her.

Before she could get the words out, he leaned in fast and again pressed his lips against hers, cutting her off. It wasn't her first kiss ever, but it felt like her first *real* kiss. He let it linger just a moment longer and then pulled away, and she couldn't help following him just a few inches, trying to meet his lips again.

Not sure what to do next, Elody turned away so he wouldn't see the giant smile on her face.

"I've wanted to do that for a long time," Eliath said.

"Me too," she said.

It sounded stupid, but that's what she thought to say.

"Well," he said, "what do we do now?"

Elody cleared her throat and tried to recover.

"I guess I'll go back to Havnor," she said.

"That's where I was thinking of going," he said.

Her smile widened until she thought it would break her cheeks.

"What will you do there?" she asked.

"Find a job, I guess. I need to figure out where I'm going with my life."

"I can talk to my aunt. I have a feeling she'll need a new apprentice soon."

Before she knew it, Eliath had his arm around her and pulled her close. He kissed her again, only this time he didn't pull away so quickly.

She wanted to stay like that forever.

***

Rinn brushed Oryna's hair off of her forehead and wiped a cool rag over her face as she shifted beside him. He blew lightly, drying her skin, and her eyes opened just a crack.

"Hey," he said.

She opened them wider and looked around.

"You're awake," he said.

She groaned and tried to sit up.

"Slow down. You collapsed after Kalus fled, and we were unable to wake you. I had the knights move you here where I could look after you."

They were in one of the few tents that had yet to be packed up. Some of the more seriously wounded were there being tended by the priests, but Rinn had taken one of the beds for her. He knew she wouldn't like it, but she didn't get a say in the matter.

"What happened?" she asked.

Her voice was hoarse. Rinn tipped a cup of water to her lips, and she took a few sips.

"You blacked out after holding Kalus's fire back," he said. "You saved our lives."

"No," she said, "what happened after."

"Kalus fled along with most of the dragons. It's sort of chaos out there for dragons right now. Anarr has fled as well, or been banished, or something. The king and his wizards are still working to figure that one out."

"Then the fighting is done?"

"Yes. It was over the minute we destroyed the crystal."

Oryna sighed and laid back down.

"Wounded?" she said.

Rinn looked around and then back to her.

"Father Meral has kept things well in hand," he said.

She tried to sit up again.

"I should help," she said.

"No, you should rest. You're in no shape to help anyone."

He gave her a gentle push, and she had no strength to stop him.

"You could have died," he said.

"The Goddess would not let that happen."

"That's not what it felt like. I... I was so worried about you. You didn't move. Your eyes were open, and you just stared into space for hours before finally slipping into sleep."

She reached out and took his hand.

"I'm sorry I scared you," she said. "I have only pushed myself that hard twice before in my life. I've been fortunate enough to always have someone near me who could care for me after."

"Well, try not to do it again. What if I'm not there to protect you next time?"

She smiled.

"Are you my protector now?"

"If you're not going to do the job, someone has to."

She chuckled and then groaned.

"Don't laugh," he said. "You're just going to hurt yourself."

"Then you stop being so cute," she said.

He squeezed her hand and then saw her breathing become deeper. He was about to let go and wipe her face again when she took a sharp breath and opened her eyes.

"Ow," she said.

"Where does it hurt?"

"My whole body is just weary. It aches to move."

"Well, everyone else is breaking camp, but the king has ordered the tent to stay until all the wounded can be moved. I guess that includes you."

"I will go back to Nirorn with the wounded when I can."

"I was thinking I would go with you," he said.

"With me?"

"I've spoken to Eryninn, and he is going back with the elves as well. He's invited me to come if I want, and I knew that's where you would be going."

"Don't you have to get back to your aunt?"

Rinn leaned down and kissed her gently.

"She'll understand," he said.

***

"It is time," Kurgh said.

Gortogh looked up at him from where he knelt on the ground. The shaman held his hand down, and Gortogh hesitated in taking it.

"Come," Kurgh said.

Gortogh nodded and took his hand. Kurgh yanked him to his feet and waited. Gortogh took a deep breath and then nodded for Kurgh to lead on.

"Make way!" Kurgh shouted.

The goblins gathered as Gortogh walked through their ranks. He had remained at the front of the goblin line after they returned, not wanting to leave his men. They asked him again and again to tell the story of how he and Kurgh had stopped the Eldest, Kalus. The story may have been a bit embellished, but it wasn't entirely untrue.

They loved the story, and they were good men. He ate with him. Laughed with them. No one tried to kill him, which was a change. For maybe the first time in his life,

Gortogh truly felt like a goblin warrior. One of his people. The amulet was gone, and they still looked to him as a leader. And somehow, even without it around his neck, he felt the presence of Ogrosh.

He knew Kurgh had seen him praying. He tried to hide it, but the shaman always had a way of knowing.

"You feel him now," Kurgh said.

"Yes," Gortogh said.

He tried to walk ahead, to avoid the question, but Kurgh was there beside him. Always beside him. Gortogh sighed and shook his head.

"What about you?" Gortogh said. "Do you feel less of him? The amulet and the crystal were Ogrosh's last ties to Gondril. I have heard some say that Anarr is gone now. Yet, I still feel Ogrosh as if he were beside me."

Kurgh started to speak, but Gortogh had to stop and slap soldiers on the back. It was something he still wasn't used to. They no longer kneeled and held him at a distance. Nor did they draw swords and try to gut him. To them, he was a warrior now. A leader among them.

"Ogrosh feels... distant," Kurgh said as they resumed walking. "And yet, my power is stronger than ever somehow. I believe this is how he meant for it to be. We can feel him and pray to him. He is always with us. But I think we will never see him again on Gondril."

"Does that sadden you?" Gortogh asked.

"How could it not? I would give my life's blood to be in his great presence. I only wish I could have met him just once. To look upon him and talk with him. But I know in my blood that he is gone."

Gortogh nodded. They hadn't talked about it since everything happened, but Gortogh thought the same. This was what Ogrosh had wanted. What he had tried to do for thousands of years. To leave his people to make their own way. And now they could.

But there was one task left to do.

Kurgh took Gortogh by the arm as the rest of the soldiers fell away to the circle of shamans. The four high shamans stood before him in the center, ringed by hundreds of others. Beyond them, the chieftains and strongest warriors of the tribes had gathered.

The last thing to do to make the tribes whole. Gortogh would have to answer for his crimes. He knew this would happen. This was how it had to be.

When he gave Elody the amulet to smash the crystal, Gortogh had given away his last bargaining chip. The only thing that would have saved him from his own people. Now, the amulet was no more. The goblins were no longer held in his thrall.

"Gortogh of the southern tribes," Quorok said. "Come forward."

Gortogh looked at Kurgh, and the shaman nodded. Kurgh had told him to expect this. The shamans would want his blood to pay for his sins. This would be his end.

He was ready.

This was how it should be. He and Kurgh had discussed what would happen when he was gone. Kurgh would spread the new word of Ogrosh to all the shamans. To the people themselves if the high shamans would not hear him. He would tell them of Ogrosh's plan to see them all united as one.

The shamans would gather and crown a king. Someone wise and strong who could rule all the tribes as one and lead them to Ogrilon. From there, they would all learn from the monk and the library. They would restore Ogrilon and all its glory.

The children of Ogrosh would be great again.

Gortogh stepped forward, his head held high. As he did, he slowly unclasped the buckle across his chest and dropped the scabbarded longsword. He heard Kurgh kneel and pick it up behind him. Three more steps brought him before Quorok and the other three high shamans.

"Kneel," Quorok said.

They were to sacrifice him to Ogrosh, Kurgh had said. Open his throat and let Gortogh's lifeblood spill in Ogrosh's name. The last of such ceremonies in the new goblin society, he hoped. Ogrosh wanted no one's blood. Kurgh will show them the way.

"Are you ready?" Quorok asked.

Gortogh nodded.

He was ready.

He felt someone behind him. Feathers tickled at his back. So, it was to be Kurgh doing the deed. It seemed appropriate. Kurgh had probably even asked to do it. He'll make it quick and painless.

Kurgh leaned over him. Something touched his head.

"Rise," Quorok said.

Gortogh looked up, his face betraying confusion. Kurgh's hands were on his shoulders then, lifting him up. Gortogh stood and looked at the shamans in front of him. Kurgh tried to grab his arms, but the shaman wasn't fast enough. Gortogh lifted the thing from his head and brought it down to see it.

A crown. Made of gold and gems.

"All hail Gortogh the Mighty!" Kurgh shouted. "Champion of Ogrosh! *King* of his people!"

King?

A cheer went up among the goblins, spreading wide

and far through the ranks until they were all hooting and howling.

"It has been decided," Kurgh whispered in his ear.

Gortogh spun to look at him.

"But why?" Gortogh asked.

"Because you are his champion."

"That was all just a lie. The amulet made them believe that."

"There is no amulet now," Kurgh said. "And still they believe it. If you'd like to address them and try to convince them otherwise, you are welcome to. You are the king after all, you can say whatever you like. But the chieftains will only laugh."

Gortogh turned in a slow circle where the shamans were all howling and cheering. The chieftains and warriors beyond them were as loud as could be. Not a face of dissent could be seen among them.

"Like it or not," Kurgh said, "you are our king. Now all you have to do is lead them all."

Lead them all.

King Gortogh.

***

Berym wasn't entirely comfortable walking through the goblin army, but he tried hard not to seem it. The loud cheers and shouts that had rippled through their ranks a few hours ago had calmed, but they were all still in high spirits. And getting drunker by the minute it seemed.

The guard leading him through the army had told Berym of the news. The goblins had made Gortogh their true king. Berym didn't even know he wasn't king all along. The guard led him through the smaller campfires on the grassy plain as Berym followed behind. Soon enough, they found who he was looking for.

"King Gortogh," Berym said.

The goblin was sitting on the ground at a burnt out fire with no one around him except the shaman who always seemed to be near. They had found a quiet place in the sea of goblins to rest. Gortogh chuckled softly.

"That is not a title I will ever get used to," he said. "What can we do for you good knight?"

"May I sit?" Berym said.

The goblin looked him up and down, staring at his thick plate armor.

"Can you rise again once you do?"

Berym genuinely laughed.

"We'll see!" he said.

He took a seat next to the goblin.

"The knighthood has sent me to speak with you," he said. "To find out your intentions. Call it my last assignment."

"Why you?" Kurgh asked.

"Honestly? No one else would come."

"Are you here to tell us to go home?" Gortogh asked.

"Why would I do that?"

"I have seen the looks of the elves and your knights. We make them uncomfortable."

"Perhaps. But the elves make the knights uncomfortable. No one can tell one dragon from the next, and that makes *everyone* uncomfortable. It is an uneasy alliance we have formed here."

"It has always been the same," Kurgh said. "It *will* always be the same."

"That I cannot say," Berym said. "The gods created each of us alike in so many ways, and then turned us all against each other."

"Not Ogrosh," Kurgh said. "The Blood God sought

peace and brotherhood from his brothers and sister. It was Anarr who brought the war against the children of Ogrosh. And he has paid a heavy price."

"A shame," Gortogh said. "Perhaps without gods we could have all lived in peace together."

"You speak of things as though they are already set in stone," Berym said.

"It was you who hated us most of all in the elven king's chamber," Gortogh said. "And with good reason."

"I did," Berym said. "But you came and showed me that I was wrong. I am strong enough to admit that. I have changed my mind about you, King Gortogh. Is there no room for us all to change?"

Kurgh laughed.

"You want change, Sir Knight?" he said. "Start with your own people. I see the looks on their faces."

"They have no reason to trust us," Gortogh said. "Not after what we've... what I've done. I do not expect forgiveness, nor do I give it to myself. All I can do now is try to help my own people. I have a lot to make up for."

"I know a thing or two about redemption," Berym said. "You may spend your entire life trying to repent for your sins."

"Shouldn't I?" Gortogh asked.

"For a time, yes," Berym said. "Just don't take too long. You may find that you've wasted much of your life looking for something only *you* had the power to grant."

Gortogh shook his head.

"I do not know where to even begin," he said.

"Change," Berym said. "Your people have found a leader in you. They have placed with you the power to change. Use it for good."

"That may redeem me to my own people, but how can

I make up for what I have done to others?"

"You may find that in doing one," Berym said, "you achieve the other as well. Just don't spend the rest of your life feeling like you owe anyone."

Gortogh nodded, and they sat in silence for a moment.

"So, what do you intend to do?" Berym asked. "I have to tell them something."

Gortogh thought a moment and then smiled.

"I think it is time for us to go home," he said.

Berym smiled and stood with ease, dusting off his arms.

"More spry than I look, eh?" he said.

Gortogh chuckled.

"What about you, Sir Knight?" he asked.

"My name is Berym. I never liked being called Sir, and I am no longer a knight anyhow."

"Did they throw you out for talking to us?" Kurgh asked.

Berym laughed.

"No, I am retired."

"But you are young yet," Gortogh said.

"I am, yes, and thank you," Berym said. "I plan to enjoy it while I still have it. I owe one last debt to someone. Someone who has waited a long time for me to repay it."

Berym saluted the goblin king and the shaman. His duties done and his goodbyes said, he turned and marched for home.

***

Elody peeked through the tent flap and saw Rinn sitting in the back corner next to a bed. She shuffled quietly through the rows of wounded and stood over him. He was so attentive washing Oryna's sleeping face that it took a minute for him to notice her there.

"Hey," he said.

"How is she?" she asked.

"Good. She's just tired. The magic took everything she had."

"I know the feeling."

She pulled a nearby chair and sat down next to him.

"I'm going with Oryna back to Nirorn," Rinn said.

"I know."

"Tell Aunt Jelena I'm sorry?"

"Sure."

Rinn stroked Oryna's face and sighed.

"What now?" she asked.

"What do you mean?"

She smiled and nudged him, nodding to Oryna. He grinned.

"That's not entirely up to me, I guess, but I have some thoughts."

Elody put her arm around him and rested her head on his shoulder.

"What about you?" he asked.

"Eliath kissed me," she said.

Rinn chuckled.

"I was beginning to think the boy was just plain stupid."

"You're not mad?"

"No. He's a good man. He just needs a little direction."

"Sounds like someone else I once knew," she said.

"Yeah. Sounds like it."

Elody sighed and dropped her arm to Rinn's waist to hug him, and he put his arm right back around her. They stayed like that for a while, neither one needing to speak. Neither really knowing what to say.

"Where's Jalthrax?" Rinn finally said.

"He's waiting outside. Some of the knights are riding back to Havnor in a bit, and they offered Eliath and I a ride."

"How's the new color look on him?"

"He's fine with it. It'll take a little getting used to for me."

"So… I guess we did it. Stopped the evil wizard, saved the world."

"Well, Kalus stopped the wizard, but we stopped Kalus, so I guess we deserve some of the praise."

"Had a little help too," Rinn said.

"A lot of help," she said.

"Everyone's going in a different direction it seems."

"It looks that way. But isn't that how life is?"

"I don't know. I don't remember much before we moved to Jornath, but I always thought that you and I would just grow up and have families and live there in the village together. Well, not together, but nearby."

"I thought that for a long time too," she said. "Things sometimes have a way of changing for you whether you ask for it or not."

"We could still go back you know. Rebuild the farm, the village."

"I don't think we can go back," she said.

"Why not? It's just mud and wood and land. It can all be rebuilt."

"It's time for us to build new things."

He nodded and pulled her closer.

"I'll miss you," he said.

"I'll miss you too," she said.

"Oryna and I will be back in Havnor after a month or so," he said. "Once the wounded are taken care of."

"I don't think I'll be there," she said.

"I thought you said that's where you were going."

"I am, but I'm not staying. Just going to say goodbye to Aunt Jelena."

"When did you decide that?"

"Just now."

"While we've been talking?"

"Yup."

"Was it something I said?"

"Maybe," she said. "Maybe I just see now that I have to move forward."

"Where will you go?"

"I don't know," she said. "Eliath has been everywhere. Maybe I'll let him decide."

"He's going with you?"

"I haven't asked him yet, but yes."

"I'm a little jealous," Rinn said. "You're going to go off and have some wild adventure, and I won't be there to…"

She knew he stopped before saying *to protect her*.

"I won't be there," he said.

"Maybe it's time we had our own adventures," she said.

She looked down at Oryna who was still sleeping soundly and smiled.

"I'm a little jealous too," she said.

With one last embrace, she stood and brushed her robes.

"Turn around," Rinn said. "You've got some dirt on the back."

She spun around, and he brushed the back of her robes down. When she turned back, he stood and pulled her close.

"Bye, El," he said. "Send me a message some time and let me know you're safe."

She hugged him and sniffled into his shoulder, not bothering to wipe away the tears. He pushed her back and held her at arm's length just the way her father always had. She never realized how much Rinn looked like him. It felt like so long since she'd really looked at him that now she almost didn't recognize the man standing in front of her.

"I love you," she said.

"I love you too," he said.

She turned and left before she could start crying again.

Jalthrax was waiting for her outside in all of his new, white brilliance. The sun shown brightly on his perfect white scales and reflected in every direction, nearly blinding her.

"White is a good look for you," she said. "You shine almost as much as you did when you were silver."

The dragon squawked at her, and she bent down to rub his neck.

"I guess we're off to new adventures, Thrax," she said. "Are you ready to go?"

Jalthrax nodded.

"Ready," he growled.

Note from the Author

Wow. I can't believe it's finished. I'm thrilled to finally finish the story and put it out into the world. The story I envisioned when I started went in a very different direction by its end. The notes I have from before I started Book 1 are laughable. Seriously, I laughed reading them. It's funny where things take you sometimes.

If you've made it this far, I truly thank you. I started writing Dragon Bond for me, but I absolutely finished writing it for you. It has been wonderful telling the story of Rinn, Elody, Jalthrax, and Gortogh, and I am proud to put it out into the world for you.

And now, I'm off to write in new worlds about new people. But this isn't the last story of Gondril. Maybe not even the last story about these heroes. There's still a lot left to tell, and I hope to check back in some day soon and see where everyone's life has taken them. In unexpected directions, no doubt.

If you liked the books, send me a message and let me know. I'd love to hear from you. Thank you for sticking with me through this journey. I hope you enjoyed it as much as I did.

Damon J Courtney
damon@damonjcourtney.com
http://damonjcourtney.com/

October 20th, 2014